Return to Peyton Place

Return to
Peyton Place

Grace Metalious

WITH AN INTRODUCTION BY

ARDIS CAMERON

Northeastern University Press
BOSTON

PUBLISHED BY UNIVERSITY PRESS OF NEW ENGLAND
HANOVER AND LONDON

Northeastern University Press
Published by University Press of New England,
One Court Street, Lebanon, NH 03766
www.upne.com
© Copyright 1959 by Grace Metalious
Introduction © 2007 by Ardis Cameron
Printed in the United States of America
5 4 3 2 1

First published in 1959 by Julian Messner, Inc. Reprinted in 2007 by Northeastern
University Press/University Press of New England by agreement with Marsha
Metalious Duprey, Cynthia Metalious Geary, and Christopher Metalious.

Library of Congress Cataloging-in-Publication Data

Metalious, Grace.
Return to Peyton Place / Grace Metalious ; with an introduction by
Ardis Cameron.
    p.   cm. — (Hardscrabble Books : fiction of New England)
ISBN-13: 978-1-55553-669-5 (pbk. : alk. paper)
ISBN-10: 1-55553-669-7 (pbk. : alk. paper)
  1. City and town life—Fiction. 2. New England—Fiction.
3. Domestic fiction. I. Cameron, Ardis. II. Title.
PS3525.E77R48 2007
813'.54—dc22   2007007182

For Jacques Chambrun who tulked me into this book in the first place.

Never Enough

Peyton Place and the Making of a Literary Sequel

Dear Grace Metalious
Just one thing I noticed. When Rodney
Harrington and Betty Anderson had their little
episode at Silver Lake, it was a very humid
evening in summer. Rodney Junior was born
the last of October in New York. How was
this figured?
With appreciation,

A. Farnsworth Wood
January 26, 1960

IN THE FALL OF 1956, Mrs. Thomas H. Leary sat down to read the season's hottest new book, a controversial novel about a fictional New England town called *Peyton Place*. But her reading was fraught with difficulties. Her son, a student at Dartmouth College, "was disgusted," she wrote in a letter to Grace Metalious, "and my husband wasn't much better pleased." Distracted and frustrated by the men in her family, she could not give the story her complete attention. A few years later, however, the Seattle housewife had occasion to try again. "After recently reading *Return to Peyton Place*," she explained, "I simply had to go back again to 'Peyton Place' and review the story." Alone at last, Mrs. Leary raced through the two novels, confirming her first impressions: "To *me* the story was completely fascinating . . . please keep writing—your talent is too good to hide."[1]

Mrs. Leary was not the only person who read *Peyton Place* on the sly. Neither was she alone in imploring the young author to continue writing, "no matter," as one letter writer put it, "what they say!" From around the country, readers expressed keen interest in the young author's work, often petitioning Grace Metalious to write more

"Peyton Place" stories. "Congratulations on your book, Return to Peyon Place," a "bookworm" from Charlotte, North Carolina, wrote. "I liked it better than Peyton Place. By next year this time I hope there will be a new Peyton Place book out."[2] After reading *Return*— "true to life, imaginative, really good reading"—a fan from the Bronx explained that he had followed the characters for five years, and they now seemed like part of his life. "I hope that you are contemplating in writing more about Allison, Joey, Selena, Constance, Mike, etc. . . . I am sure the American public shares my same feeling."[3] Millions it seems did. Three weeks after hitting the book shelves, *Return to Peyton Place* sold almost three million paperback copies, which, according to Dell publications, "made it the fastest selling paperback since *Peyton Place*."[4] "Please," implored a *Return* fan from Brookline, Massachusetts, "give us another book soon."[5]

Like Mrs. Leary, a number of letter writers found themselves returning to *Peyton Place* after reading *Return*. "Dear Grace," a fan from Oregon enthused, "I have just finished reading 'Return to Peyton Place.' After I had read it, I picked up the copy of your first 'Peyton Place' to renew my acquaintance with these characters you have so beautifully created. Then I returned to your last novel and read it again through to the last word." Like many others, this reader came to think of the characters as "totally real"; a community of fictive friends. "It is a rare gift indeed," wrote another, "to have the ability to make every character alive and filled with such intensity that they will walk and breathe and live to the extent that when the reader puts aside the book, he feels he has known each of them personally."[6] One woman confessed that she dreamt nightly about the residents of *Peyton Place*, "and always in 'technocolor!'"

To the relief of many fans, the story of Peyton Place continued for more than a decade after its original publication. Both *Peyton Place* and *Return* became popular films, and in 1964 a television serial starring Dorothy Malone—and introducing Mia Farrow and Ryan O'Neal—was broadcast to over sixty million nighttime viewers. Its stunning success forced ABC to add an additional evening slot, making it available to prime-time audiences an historic three nights a week. Soon after, an avalanche of *Peyton Place* books rolled onto the literary marketplace, beginning with the imaginatively titled *Again Peyton Place*, followed in quick succession by *Carnival in Peyton*

Place, The Evils of Peyton Place, Hero in Peyton Place, Nice Girl from Peyton Place, Pleasures of Peyton Place, Secrets of Peyton Place, Temptations of Peyton Place, and finally—just in case anyone missed the point of the series—*Thrills of Peyton Place.* But it was not Grace Metalious who would author these works. While Twentieth Century Fox patronized the famous writer, it gave Grace Metalious no role in writing the scripts for either film. Producers at ABC even went out of their way to publicly denounce the original novel, calling its author "negativistic" and "hateful." And the paperback series, supposedly written by Roger Fuller, was actually the product of unknown writer(s) working under a corporate pseudonym invented by Pocket Books. "Perhaps," the respected magazine writer Otto Friedrich quipped, "Roger Fuller is a former police reporter for the *Brooklyn Eagle,* a schoolteacher with a mortgage payment overdue, a Barnard girl with a feverish imagination, and so on."[7] Even *Return* was partially ghostwritten, the idea for a sequel dreamed up by Dell publications and Hollywood producers who didn't have to read Grace's fan mail to know audiences wanted more of Allison, Joey, Selena, Constance, and Mike.[8]

It was not what Grace Metalious imagined for herself as a writer. Already hard at work on a second novel entitled *The Tight White Collar,* she sought to prove that *Peyton Place* was more than a "flash in the pan." *Return,* she told reporters, was just "so much sludge. It was written for the gentlemen of Hollywood who will do anything to make a quick buck. I wish that I had never let it happen."[9] And resist she did. She stormed around the house. She hung up the phone. She said, "No, no, no, no, no."[10] But her writerly ambition—her intense desire to insert herself into the realm of the "serious" writer—competed almost daily with less transparent needs: a bottomless hunger for love and validation, and a restless, unending search for financial security. People she loved pressed hard. Hollywood called again and again. Enormous sums were held out. Her agent pleaded. Piqued, Grace Metalious slammed the door to her study, hunkered down at her typewriter, and reluctantly returned to the New England town so many of her characters had longed to escape.

But like her heroine, the promising young writer Allison MacKenzie, Grace returned to Peyton Place with attitude. If she was going to have to write this stuff, she was going to have some fun. In a matter of months, she spit out a story that cynically echoed her own traumatic experiences as a young writer who found herself cheated by crooked agents, misrepresented by reporters, vilified by critics, and bullied by editors, publishers, and greedy Hollywood producers. No longer the starry-eyed ingénue of *Peyton Place* days, Allison gains fame and fortune in *Return*, not because her writing is regarded as good, but rather because her book is declared indecent, even pornographic. Allison becomes a celebrity by becoming a "hack"; a female writer of popular, "sexy" books. Dramatizing her own experiences, Metalious takes a potshot at the backstage operations of book publishing, where publicity agents and editors take control of Allison's novel long before she decamps at Penn Station. "She did not know that in New York certain wheels had been set in motion and that the novel was no longer altogether hers, or that its fate was not to be left to chance" (71–72). When she objects to the misrepresentations and distortions, her agent smugly asks, "You want your book to sell, don't you?" (86). Like her creator, Allison is upset and disillusioned. "What a dirty business this is," Allison realizes. "How meaningless . . . how goddamned silly this all is" (88, 92).

Sludge? Maybe. But as with so many "bad" novels, *Return to Peyton Place* has some good stories to tell.

In the spring of 1955, Grace Metalious was thirty-one years old, the mother of three children, and the wife of a New Hampshire schoolteacher. In their small "Hansel and Gretel" cottage called "It'll Do," the Metaliouses made do. But by summer, nothing seemed to work. Drought turned their dirt road into a swirling dust bowl. In July, the dug well dried up, along with the Metaliouses' credit line. "Frozen French-fried potatoes are a bit beyond your budget," Grace remarked years later. "But you buy them because they do not have to be washed before they can be cooked and eaten." The humidity made everyone grouchy. The marriage soured. More and more, "It'll Do" worked less and less. Then, as her best friend and neighbor Laurie Wilkins put it, "all hell broke loose." That August, Grace sold her "fourth baby," a longish novel about a small New England town called Peyton Place, to a New York publisher. Before the summer was over, Grace Metalious found herself sipping a daiquiri at "the fanciest saloon in NY." "I was an author," she later wrote, "with a contract which said so. I had a French agent and a lady publisher. I was in 'Club 21.' I had arrived."[11]

Peyton Place was an instant success, a publishing phenomenon even by today's standards. Three months after publication, it topped the *New York Times* bestsellers list, where it stayed for more than fifty-nine weeks. "I was living in the Midwest during the fifties," recalled Grace Metalious's biographer Emily Toth, "and I can tell you it was boring. Elvis Presley and *Peyton Place* were the only two things in that decade that gave you hope there was something going on out there." By year's end, one in twenty-nine Americans had purchased the novel, and by 1958, *Peyton Place* cracked twelve million copies sold, making it the best-selling novel up to that time (only *The Godfather* would sell more copies in the twentieth century). "This book business," Grace wrote a friend, "is some evil form of insanity."[12]

Hitting the ground with unexpected fury, *Peyton Place* was soon to become the silent generation's perfect storm. Decried by conservative critics as "wicked," "sordid," "cheap," "moral filth," and a "tabloid version of life," the novel was declared indecent in Canada, France, and Italy. It was banned in Providence, Rhode Island, Ft. Wayne, Indiana, and Omaha, Nebraska, where politicians blamed the book for corrupting American teenagers. "I don't know why you want to read it," one perplexed bookseller announced, "but we are willing to sell it at $3.95." Wealthy communities that measured their refinement by the kinds of books they kept in the town library took pride in banishing *Peyton Place*. In upscale Beverly Farms, Massachusetts, a sign was posted on the front lawn of the town library: "This Library does not carry *Peyton Place*. If you want it, go to Salem," a working-class town to the south. Among conservatives, the enormous popularity of the novel signaled the moral dangers of postwar liberalism. "This sad situation," thundered the influential conservative William Loeb, editor of the *Manchester Union Leader*, "reveals a complete debasement of taste and a fascination with the filthy, rotten side of life that are the earmarks of the collapse of civilization." Across the country, hundreds of men, women, and teenagers competed with disapproving officials, parents, and, at times, husbands and sons, to secure a copy. In some states, town officials simply cut of library funding when librarians failed to comply. "I am so sorry that I can not say that I read your book," a reader from Mesquite,

Texas, explained to Grace. "I cannot afford to buy it and I have no access to a library. My state is still in the hands of thieves and for that reason it is very backward."[13]

More judicious reviewers, however, found much to like in *Peyton Place*, at times comparing it to the small-town rebellions of Sherwood Anderson, Sinclair Lewis, and John O'Hara. Carlos Baker, a professor of literature at Princeton University, praised the novel, singling out Grace Metalious as representative of the new "emancipated modern authoress" unafraid to ferret out the nation's "bourgeois pretensions." The writer Merle Miller made tribute to the "great narrative skill" of the author: "she may outrage you, but she never bores you," he wrote in *Ladies Home Journal*.[14] In December of 1957, the women editors of Associated Press newspapers voted Grace Metalious the most outstanding woman writer of the year. In tandem with her "sexsational" novel, the author became a household name, "one of the most talked about women in America," *Life Magazine* announced. More famous than *Anthony Adverse*, *Peyton Place* outsold *God's Little Acre, Gone with the Wind*, and every other work of fiction published up to that time.[15] Publishers scratched their heads; dozens of them had rejected the novel.

The main story of *Peyton Place* follows the lives of three women who, in different ways and for different reasons, come to terms with their identity as women and as sexual persons in the represssive atmosphere of small-town America. Allison MacKenzie, very much like Grace, is a young girl growing up in a fatherless household. She dreams of becoming a writer to escape a cloistered life of repressed emotions, conventionality, and dependence. Her working mother, Constance, whom Allison believes to be widowed, lives a lonely and sexually-frustrated life, haunted by the fear that her long-ago adulterous relationship with a married man will be revealed and ruin both her life and and that of her daughter, the offspring of her passionate relationship with him. But the dramatic center was most clearly located in the story of Selena Cross, the dark-complexioned girl who lived across the tracks but whose beauty, intelligence, and sensuality captivate the town and frighten Constance. More than any other character, Selena represented the darkest side of American sexuality in the 1950s. A holder of youth's secrets, Selena is haunted and trapped by the sexual appetites of her stepfather, Lucas, who has been sexually abusing her for years. Seizing a moment offered to her on a snowy night just before Christmas, she and her younger brother smash in his head and bury his body in the sheep pen behind their shack.

What polite conversation hushed up, *Peyton Place* opened up to readerly fantasy, invention, and guarded conversation. Typically unused to candid portrayals of incest, abortion, oral sex, female lust, and female sexual pleasure outside of sleazy magazines and pulp books, readers dog-eared pages, exchanged scenes with friends, and memorized lines. In the imaginary topography of *Peyton Place,* readers—some of whom had never picked up a book before—readjusted both the parameters of the "normal" and their own relationship to it. So, too, did they find a depth and authenticity lacking in much of popular culture. "The first requisite these days of a best seller," a woman from Springfield, Oregon, wrote to Grace Metalious, "is that it be liberally sprinkled with sex. However . . . you have taken the reader into the intimate world of this so vital part of life. I found a depth in the book that I have not found in any other so called 'best seller.'" She was not alone: thousands of women and men, young and old, mostly working class and white, wrote of how the book opened up to them "real life" in ways that seemed "true to life," "honest," "really good writing." If for some it was a sex manual, for many others it was a way to remap the insistent contours of sexual and gender normativity.

It is often difficult for readers today to imagine the social landscape that confronted the "silent generation," but in 1956 many sexual acts betweeen consenting adults, including sodomy, oral sex, and sexual intercourse with a partner not legally one's one, were prohibited by law in most states. Abortion was illegal and understood to be an unfit topic for conversation. Rape was a word seldom printed and always uttered in a whisper. Birth control was unreliable and hard to get. Divorce was a source of shame, even a sign of mental instability. In several states it was illegal for a physician to even discuss contraception with an unmarried patient. Female sexual agency was itself highly suspect: a concern among policy makers and, at times, a cause for medical and psychiatric intervention. Forced sterilization remained a viable option with which to treat delinquent girls. Homosexuality was punishable by fines and incarceration. Books that printed such things were confined to railroad stations, newsstands, and drugstore racks, where gaudy covers and titillating images signaled their trashy place on the margins of respectable literature.

Yet even as sexual frankness in popular culture gained traction in the mid-fifties, especially after the famous *Kinsey Reports,* talk about sex in the private sphere remained difficult. "They coped," the writer Annie Dillard recalled of her mother's friends. "They sighed, they permitted themselves a remark or two; they lived essentially alone." Sexual knowledge was difficult to locate in an era when communication between parents and children, and even among friends, was often circumspect and limited. In her fictionalized account of growing up in the 1950s, *That Night,* Alice McDermott recounted how her mother struggled to tell her daughter that their neighbor Sheryl, an unmarried teenager, was pregnant. "After a botched, embarrassed and only sporadically explicit attempt to explain what Sheryl had done, she told me, 'Let's say the stork missed our house and landed on hers.'" For some, *Peyton Place* was all they had, and because it was published by a respectable, hardback firm, readers could purchase it openly in department stores, five-and-dimes, and in quality bookstores. "I learned a few things from your book that I will not soon forget," a fan wrote to Grace. And like many books, *Peyton Place* circulated as gossip, outrageous tale, and hot commodity in ways that brought the hidden but suspect into everyday conversation. "I heard my mother and her best friend whispering in the kitchen," one reader recalled. "As soon as I entered they whipped a book into a bag, but they were too slow. I had caught my mother reading Peyton Place, a book banned by our own town library." Peyton Place was not just a written text, it was also a "spoken text," a story whose meanings and influence increased as readers discussed it, exchanged passages, and used it to interpret, measure, and reimagine their own lives.[16] "Please keep on writing," fans implored the controversial author.

Grace Metalious had every intention to do just that. Before starting *Peyton Place* during that "winter of horrors," she had completed another novel while her husband, George, attended the University of New Hampshire under the G. I. Bill. Entitled "The Quiet Place," the story was based on a professor who had lost his position at the university due to his homosexuality. In the wake of *Peyton Place,* Grace planned to rework the manuscript she now called *Tight White Collar.*

But the reception of *Peyton Place* as a "dirty" book—"a bad book without redemption"—stunned and wounded her, putting her on the defensive well before she had time to cultivate confidence as a writer. Not unlike the nineteenth-century literary domestics illuminated by historian Mary Kelley, Grace Metalious was a housewife who struggled to write, primarily as a way to earn money.[17] When she heard that her agent had sold *Peyton Place* to a small but well-regarded publishing firm called Julian Messner, she thought that "If I made $10,000 . . . I could pay off all the money we owed and have enough left over to see me through the winter."[18] It was, after all, her first publication. But as the "hullabaloo" unfolded, the newly published author found herself at the center of intense controversy: an "ordinary" housewife and mother whose "filthy" book called into question her fitness as both. "I don't know what all the screaming is about," she told Patricia Carbine of *Look* magazine. "To me *Peyton Place* isn't sexy at all. Sex is something everybody lives with—why make such a big deal about it?"[19]

The controversy catapulted sales overnight, but her fame vastly outpaced her confidence. A few months after her publishing debut, the young author was invited to appear on television's hottest new talk show, *Night Beat*. The brainchild of Ted Yates and Mike Wallace—whose irreverent and and confrontational interviewing style quickly earned him the nickname "Mike Malice"—*Night Beat* pioneered late-night programming, pulling into television's orbit millions of viewers eager to watch Mike take on the rich and famous.[20] Grace arrived by limousine, her new boyfriend, local New Hampshire disc jockey T. J. Martin, in tow. Nervous and uneasy in the public eye, Grace felt especially vulnerable under the *Night Beat* gaze, not only because of its hard-hitting reputation, but because the show was recorded live, an unedited hour that pioneered tight camera close-ups, black backgrounds, and one-on-one exchanges. The arrangement was designed to make guests sweat, and Grace obliged. Already uncomfortable in the requisite panty-girdle and skirt that replaced her comfortable dungarees and flannel shirt, she visibly wilted under the hostile gaze of Mr. Malice. "I thought your book was basic and carnal," Wallace thundered. "You did, huh?" Grace squeaked. "What gives you the right to pry and hold your neighbors up to ridicule?" Grace's eyes moistened.

Poised offstage in her Schiffli-embroidered dress, fashion commentator Jackie Susann watched in fascination and horror as Wallace hammered away at America's most successful authoress. As Barbara Seaman tells the story, Susann prayed for divine intervention. "Don't let this woman cry in front of millions of people," Jackie pleaded. "Get her through this show, God, and I won't smoke another cigarette tonight."[21] Grace played with her ponytail, twitched, pulled at her skirt, but she didn't cry. Then, suddenly, she altered course, rattling Wallace by calling him by his hated birth name, "Myron," and asking him to tell the audience how many times he had been married (three), a subject still taboo on television and especially sensitive to the reporter.[22] But to watch Grace Metalious on old television interview shows is to see a person much in conflict with herself: a vast insecurity and emotional vulnerability cohabitating with a keen intelligence and driven ambition. Wallace remembered liking her, "he found her 'ample, not unattractive'" he told Toth. Others recalled her plainness: a drab ordinariness made more pronounced, perhaps, by her earthy use of language and her sharp wit. When Carbine, later a founder of *Ms* magazine, asked Grace if there was anything about sex that offended her, the young author quipped, "Far worse to me than any sex act is unattractive food, and I'm no gourmet."[23] To read Grace Metalious was to expect sartorial fireworks, confident poses, and ebony cigarette holders. Al Ramrus, a writer for *Night Beat*, imagined the author of *Peyton Place* as "a very flamboyant, outspoken, colorful woman," but he found instead an overweight wife and mother who "could just as easily have been sitting behind a drugstore counter."[24] Susann, with her "spiky false lashes, chain smoker's gravelly voice, and glittery dresses," was equally stunned by Metalious's plainness.[25] But it was the popular writer's complete lack of promotional skills that made the future author of *Valley of the Dolls* rethink her own career plans. "How could this woman, 'chunky, depressed, and colorless,' Jackie wondered, write such a popular book "almost in spite of the author's publicity efforts?"

Grace, too, was amazed by her success. It dazzled and at times frightened her. Unlike Susann, who could bring all the elements of Hollywood hucksterism into the promotion of her books—pioneering bookstore signings, personal appearances, and celebrity tie-ins—Grace knew little about publishing and even less about promotion. She imagined book publishing to be a noble endeavor, a business run by professor-types in corduroy jackets with patches on their elbows and pipes always at hand. She found an agent by going to the Laconia, New Hampshire, library and picking out the first French name on the list. Handsome, charming, and debonair, he would eventually cheat her of hundreds of thousands of dollars. If Jackie Susann brought to publishing "show-business vulgarity," Grace brought images of art and culture, erudition and refinement. Press agents, producers, and promoters shocked, then irritated and bruised her. Publicity of all kinds rekindled a constant sense of inadequacy—not pretty enough, never able to fit in, unloved and ultimately unlovable. When reporters flocked to Gilmanton to interview her, she hid in Laurie's farmhouse. "She was a very scared girl," Gilmanton neighbor Ken Crain remembered. "After the book came out, nobody let her be, and she was even more scared."[26] Even New York City—which once excited and thrilled Grace—grew increasingly traumatic, its tinsel tarnished by the pressures to produce another best-seller. Twenty months after her literary arrival at "Club 21," Grace Metalious distanced herself from the city, settling into her beloved Granite State retreat, the Cape-styled house she had purchased with her fifteen-hundred-dollar advance for *Peyton Place*. Whenever she got back from New York, "she'd sort of embrace the fireplace," her former friend and lawyer recalled, "as if it were the Rock of Gibraltar."[27] Even after neighbors shunned her and friends bled her dry, Grace never stopped calling Gilmanton, New Hampshire, "home." "Here I was safe," she told a reporter. "I drank, I wept."[28]

Twenty months after the publication of *Peyton Place*, Grace hugged the fireplace, embraced the April mud season, and looked forward to "my return to normalcy." In February she had married Thomas James (T. J.) Martin, the man she publicly and scandalously admitted was her lover. "My life," Grace told reporters, "has resumed a pattern now. The only thing that is over is the storm. At last I have found my way safely home."[29] When reports circulated that Grace Metalious was planning to write another *Peyton Place* book, she fumed, "That's a damn lie. . . . I'm not going to write about Peyton Place again, that's for sure." And she meant it.

Not long before their marriage, Grace and T. J. had taken an extensive road trip out West. There they met with Jerry Wald, a sharp-eyed, up-and-coming producer who was fast turning Grace's "fourth baby" into a major motion picture for Twentieth Century Fox. But it soon became clear to everyone that Grace was not to have any part in the making of the film. Her "consulting job," she quickly realized, was a joke. Hollywood was a "wasteland," a "junk heap," the treatment of women "dreadful," with actresses sorted and branded like "cattle." What Wald wanted was simply the publicity generated by Grace's presence in Hollywood. Grace Metalious left in a fury, but not before giving Wald a searing tongue-lashing and the scriptwriter John Michael Hayes a Bloody Mary in the face.[30] "The whole trouble with Hollywood and me," she would generously write a year later, "was that we did not know each other's language."[31] But if Hollywood and Grace had a communication problem, Wald had no intention of providing a translator. Like the colonists who bought Manhattan for mere trinkets, Wald profited by the tangled languages that separated writers from their stories and authors from their titles. *Peyton Place* might have been Grace's "fourth baby," but Twentieth Century Fox was its legal guardian. The studio owned movie and television rights to *Peyton Place* but also, and most unusually, owned the name. There would be no residual rights. *Peyton Place* was now a brand name, a simple commodity uncoupled from individual authorship. It could return or not, depending on the commercial needs and plans of Twentieth Century Fox.

In the wake of *Peyton Place*'s success as a film, Jerry Wald became convinced that lightning could strike twice, and legally nothing prevented him from creating a script for a new *Peyton Place* film. Indeed, the idea of hiring anonymous writers to produce stories from outlines created by corporations was central to the emergence of the cheap-book business and the expansion of a mass audience. Early in the twentieth century, literary syndicates such as the famous Stratemeyer group operated by developing ideas for books, pitching them to publishers, and then outlining them for ghostwriters hired to develop the story, usually into a "series" published under pseudonyms like Carolyn Keene, the invented author of girl detective Nancy Drew.[32] Even before the syndicates, however, entrepreneurs of dime novels and story papers had depended on "unauthored discourse," pulling into the production process anonymous writers who could meet tight deadlines and write according to formulas designed by others.[33] "In authorship, as in more tangible things," noted the historian Mary Noel in 1954, "demand expressed in dollars and cents created a supply. With capital came the 'hack,' who was as much a product of the Industrial Revolution as was the Hoe printing press."[34] Wald adapted the concept to suit the needs of studios, using "tie-ins" that increasingly bound authors and their hardback firms to paperback publishers and Hollywood studios. When Wald telephoned Gilmanton in the spring of 1958, all he wanted was a ten-page script. Grace's return to normalcy was over.

It took Grace thirty days to write *Return to Peyton Place*. What began as a ten-, and then twenty-page "original screenplay" for twenty-five thousand dollars huffed and puffed into a ninety-eight page "novelization," which Dell agreed to publish if Wald came through with a movie version. Wald had smartly reversed the "tie-in" process whereby hardback publishers contracted for a book only if a paperback firm guaranteed it by purchasing reprint rights or Hollywood showed interest by buying movie rights. *Return to Peyton Place* became the first published book that originated as a movie "treatment," a practice Wald made famous and that in turn made him one of Hollywood's most successful producers. It made Grace angry and sick.

Grace Metalious gambled that readers would understand the book for what it was: "a Hollywood treatment. It was never intended as anything else."[35] To her, the short-page novella was an expensive bone tossed to a greedy Jerry Wald. She may also have been thinking of her many fans who so often requested a sequel. And certainly the beginnings of the novel must have given her a sense of satisfaction: payback time. Here she used her considerable narrative skills to illuminate the cupidity she experienced as a young writer thrown, as she saw it, to the literary wolves. The main story of *Return* follows Allison MacKenzie and her family after she finds success by selling her novel *Samuel's Castle* to a small publishing house in New York City. More parody than satire, the novel strolls down Grace Metalious's own rise to fame like a bitter vogueing act. As with her own novel, *Peyton Place,* the publication of *Samuel's Castle* raises the indignation of townspeople, causing her stepfather, the Greek schoolmaster Mike Rossi, to lose his job and the neighbors to shun her and her family. And like her own bewilderment at having to rewrite *Peyton Place* to meet the demands of editors and publishers, Allison is forced to make alterations to *Samuel's Castle* that she fears will ruin her book and turn her into a hack. When she meets her new publisher, Lewis Jackman, we can feel Grace's own anger at Kathryn Messner, who forced Grace to change the incestuous relationship between Selena Cross and Lucas Cross into a nonfamilial rape by making Lucas the stepfather of Selena rather than the father. "No one," Messner and her editor pointed out, "would believe the story otherwise. Incest simply didn't exist, at least that's what people believed at the time."[36] "There are places, Miss MacKenzie, where your manuscript is a little too much," the suave Mr. Jackman tells Allison in *Return*. "He fingered pages of her manuscript and Allison wanted to slap him. She felt as if she had had a child and that Lewis Jackman was now fondling that child in a depraved, obscene fashion" (56). If readers wouldn't believe in child sexual abuse, Grace would show them publishers, agents, and Hollywood producers who raped writers and prostituted themselves every day. Grace always believed that by turning Lucas Cross into Selena's stepfather, her editors had turned "tragedy into trash." In *Return*, Grace slapped back.

But *Return* also provides readers a small window into Grace Metalious's vulnerability and intense insecurity. Known for her generosity of spirit and purse, the celebrated author often lent people, even strangers, large sums of money. She took unusual amounts of time to write back to her fans; she never turned away strangers who came knocking at her door; and she didn't ignore fans who asked for her autograph, even while dining out. But, like Allison, it all seemed to Grace an unearned celebrity. "I feel like such a fraud," Allison tells Lewis. "I know it's only me, little Allison MacKenzie. Why doesn't everyone else see that?" (93). Grace Metalious knew what it meant to feel inadequate; to live as an outsider hungry for acceptance, validation, and love. Running throughout *Peyton Place* is a pervasive sense of Otherness, of people who are not quite "right" and who feel the weight of being different. In *Return*, readers could marvel at Allison's success, make that dream their own, and recognize in themselves the writer's longing for acceptance and validation as well as for material things. But it was Allison's undercurrents of unease in the public world of success and fame that performed in the sequel some of the emotional and psychic services rendered by the original.

"Walking through the lobby of the Plaza, Allison looked at the expensively groomed, beautifully dressed women who sat chatting or strolling about. They were at their ease, in their element; places like this were a customary part of their daily lives. For them there was nothing dreamlike or exotic about stopping at the Plaza for cocktails. Will it ever be like that for me? Allison wondered" (60). Readers wondered, too.

But writing *Return* gave Grace the literary shakes. Concerned that she had sold out on some level, she also worried that *Peyton Place* might be remembered as a one-shot wonder. She began to drink heavily. But she also fought back. In both novels, Grace Metalious floats the unfashionable notion that popular stories and mass-circulated books are not mindless "ooze," as literary critics so famously asserted throughout the fifties. Acutely aware that women writers were especially vilified for their popularity and high sales figures, Grace positioned Allison in opposition to the "boy geniuses" so admired by Norman Page and represented by David Noyes, who wrote what Allison referred to as "Novels of Social Significance." "David was twenty-five and had been hailed as a brilliant new talent," we learn in *Peyton Place*. "He wanted to reform the world and he had a difficult time understanding people like Allison who wanted to write for either fame or money" (PP, 356). In *Return*, Allison's book sells in the millions, not because it is good, David suggests, but because of its "sexy" parts and fraudulent publicity. David belittles her for her radio and television appearances, until Allison finally yells, "Maybe you don't care what happens to your books, but I care what happens to mine. What's the good of writing anything if nobody reads what you write?" (89). Like Grace, Allison wanted to write quality books, but she also took pleasure in knowing that millions of readers—many of whom had never picked up a novel before—had found her story to be meaningful and compelling. Nor would she concede to David the right to define the boundaries of quality. "She had made up her own mind: if there was a price to be paid for all this, then she would pay it. But she would not take David's way, would not sneak out the back door. She was young, but not so young that she still believed that art could be found only in a cold-water flat" (92). The cult of the solitary genius struggling alone in his garret fit the American literary imaginary, but Allison "had outgrown" it. Like her creator, she never confused poverty with literary merit, or popularity with bad taste.

Whatever Jerry Wald thought of the effort is unclear. Scriptwriters would rewrite the story anyway, so it had little effect on him. But no one else involved with the project was pleased. "We used her name," Helen Meyer of Dell Publishing recalled. "But we hired somebody else to do the writing."[37] Too short, it was also at times incomprehensible. Grace refused to look at it again. In her place, Dell hired Warren Miller, a reputable writer of fiction whose novels had sold well. He took on the job, Emily Toth explains, as a "hoot" and earned a flat fee for the effort of several thousand dollars.[38] Miller continued the saga of Allison's return to her small New England town as a celebrity authoress. Selena Cross, Betty Anderson, Constance MacKenzie, and Mike Rossi return to their lives, each haunted in some way by the shadows cast in *Peyton Place*. Miller obviously enjoyed hacking out the melodramatic sequel, but where his fun begins and Grace's ends remains uncertain. Just how the autumn birth of Rodney Junior "got figured" is also unclear. Grace never met Miller, and if she had? "Another Bloody Mary down the shirt," T. J. offered.[39]

Given Grace's distaste for Wald's treatment idea, we can read *Return* as a mélange of cynicism, irony, self-parody, and spoof. And Grace Metalious's fingerprints are all over it. Consider the weird tale of Roberta Carter and her panting daughter-in-law, Jennifer. In *Peyton Place,* Ted Carter is the handsome boyfriend of Selena Cross, but his ambition to become a famous lawyer trumps his love, and he drops Selena when she is put on trial for the murder of her father. In *Return* disloyal Teddy gets his. Ted marries Jennifer, the daughter of a well-known and prosperous Boston lawyer. Unlike the loving and loyal Selena, Jennifer is manipulative, selfish, and wanton. Together the young couple visit Peyton Place often to see Ted's overly involved mother, Roberta Carter, and her husband, Harmon, both of whom had teamed up long ago to murder Roberta's first husband, the naive, but wealthy, Dr. Quimby. It is classic Grace Metalious melodrama/camp. Roberta is out of fifties central casting: a whining, clinging mother who is jealous of her daughter-in-law's relationship with her son. She spies on their lovemaking. She thrills in their violent sexual encounters in Ted's childhood room. What is to be done? In true pulp fashion, Roberta plots to kill off the lustful Jen. And how, readers might wonder, does an ordinary woman in small-town America manage that? "Roberta Carter began to read murder mysteries . . . During the day . . . she wrote down the plot of each novel and listed the clues that had finally landed each murderer in the nets of the police. In this way, she discarded murder by shooting, stabbing, strangling, and poison" (200). What was left? Keep turning the page, the author answers. A lover of Nancy Drew, Grace Metalious knew how to use suspense, but she also understood that fiction was where many readers turned when seeking knowledge about life and sex, so why not murder?

Return was a publishing success, but the reviews tortured Grace. "Whatever the inspiration that sent a flat-wheeled caboose clattering after Author Metalious' steam powered first novel, Peyton Place," Time magazine announced, "the sequel bears all the marks of a book whacked together on a long weekend."[40] Critic Elizabeth Bayard, an admirer of Peyton Place, was irked. "It takes more than spying on the eating, drinking, and love-making habits of Mr. Mrs. and Miss America to make a memorable novel," she scolded. Grace had hoped the book would pass "unnoticed" or at least that reviewers would understand that it was a script written for Hollywood. "People are all saying I couldn't write a second novel. It's a Hollywood treatment . . . It was a foul, rotten trick. They made a hell of a lot of money on Peyton Place and they wanted to ride the gravy train . . . I've been played for a sucker all around."[41] Her emotional swings grew more intense and frequent. She drank more. Fights with T. J. escalated. Money rolled in and then flew out. "The bottle is empty," Grace told a friend, "and I can see myself at the bottom."[42] There were still many highs after Return: Grace would complete two more novels, both of them well received by critics and audiences alike. Her oldest daughter, Marsha, would provide her with a grandchild, and Grace would remarry her first husband, George. But Return had taken a toll. "Return to Peyton Place should never have been written," George Metalious later wrote. "It was another event in a series that helped in undermining Grace's confidence and contributed to her feelings of inadequacy."[43] But Grace also began to recognize the logic of Jerry Wald's universe. Peyton Place had become a cash cow. If the author had lost her "baby," she nevertheless maintained cultural capital as the authorized voice of Peyton Place, whatever its commodified form. But it was a Faustian bargain Grace made reluctantly with herself. When money needs pressed, taxes came due, and business ventures turned sour, Grace returned with new ideas of how to milk the Peyton Place cow.

"I think Hollywood would like another P.P. script," Grace wrote to her agent in the summer of 1961. "In spite of the fact that I've screamed No, No to this idea I might consider it now because of a project in which George and I are interested here in New Hampshire. It would not interfere with the new book because any day that I can't turn out a silly script for those silly bastards at 20th century I'll turn in my typewriter and get a job in an insurance office or something."[44] She was responding to a letter earlier that year from Jerry Wald, who had just previewed the rough cuts to *Return to Peyton Place*. "I can certainly say that lightning does strike twice in the same place." The film featured the music of Franz Waxman, whose score for *Peyton Place* won an Oscar. Eleanor Parker played Allison's mother Constance, and Carol Lynley replaced the elusive Diane Varsi as Allison. Unlike the *Peyton Place* movie, which premiered in Camden, Maine, without Grace, Wald agreed to Grace's request that the first showing of *Return* be held in Laconia, New Hampshire, the closest town to Gilmanton that had a movie theater.

The success of the book and the early cuts of the film convinced Wald that there was money still to be made with Peyton Place. "One of the future projects I have in mind," he wrote, "is a story dealing with the conflicts between the townspeople and the constantly changing influx of students and teachers into a small New England town which has a college which offers a rather special situation, which should provide possibilities for interesting dramatic conflicts." The new sequel, he suggested, might be called "Spring Riot in Peyton Place."[45] Grace thought the idea "nuts," then went on to develop a storyline of her own.

Only the outline remains. At the age of thirty-nine, Grace Metalious died suddenly, if not surprisingly, of "chronic liver disease." Known as the writer's disease, cirrhosis built up dangerously in her liver before many in her family even knew that she was sick. A few months before her death, the motel that she and her husband George owned—"one of the future projects"—failed, and Grace wrote a panicked letter to her agent. "I could write another book, but as at December 12th, 1963, I feel that a contract and all the worry that that involves would be impossible for me. Is there a magazine market which could be met from Gilmanton, is there a newspaper market for Gilmanton gossip?"[46] Can writing kill? "Disenchantment," Grace once wrote, "is a slow, painful, agonizing process. Sometimes it is a long road, and in the beginning you don't even know you're on it, then when it is too late you can't even fight or find a way back." *Return* was not a book Grace was proud to have written. But it is an enduring monument to an agency embodied in writing's social life. To reread *Return* is to enter into the complex relationships between authorship, book production, hierarchies of taste, readerly desire, and the labor of writing in an age of commodity production. It is also to grasp the thin hopes and fears of a young woman born on the social and cultural margins of America: an outsider even to those who knew her best. "I'm glad you came," Allison tells a friend at the end of *Return*. "You've helped me a lot . . . by reminding me that the world isn't full of mobsters waiting to cut me down. And by showing me that work will exorcise all the ghosts that haunt me" (238). Grace may not have written this ending, but it was the kind of "happily ever after" finale she dreamed a literary life could ultimately provide. To the delight of her fans, Grace Metalious kept on writing, but in the end, words failed her. They were never enough; the demons always returned. Grace Metalious died in Boston, Massachusetts, and returned for the last time to Gilmanton, New Hampshire, where she was buried in the spring of 1964.

This essay is part of a work-in-progress entitled "Tales of Peyton Place: The Biography of a Big Book." I would like to thank the National Endowment for the Humanities, the John Simon Guggenheim Memorial Foundation, and the University of Southern Maine for their generous support in funding this project. I am especially grateful as well to the Metalious family, to whom this work is dedicated. My debt to Marsha Metalious Duprey is deep and unending; my deepest regret is that I could not write her mother into a better ending.

Stonington, Maine   ARDIS CAMERON
January 2007

Notes

1. Letter, Mrs. Thomas H. Leary to Grace Metalious, March 8, 1960. Courtesy of Marsha Metalious Duprey.

2. Letter, M. B. "bookworm" to Mrs. Metalious, March 20, 1960. Courtesy of Marsha Metalious Duprey.

3. Letter, Harvey Tauman to Grace Metalious, February 16, 1960. Courtesy of Marsha Metalious Duprey.

4. Otto Friedrich, "Farewell to *Peyton Place*," *Esquire* (December 1971): 310. See also, William H. Lyles, *Putting Dell on the Map: A History of Dell Paperbacks* (Westport, Conn: Greenwood Press, 1983), especially pp. 35, 45.

5. Letter, Ralph E. Hoyt to Grace Metalious, February 28, 1960. Courtesy of Marsha Metalious Duprey.

6. Letter to Grace Metalious, February 17, 1960. Courtesy of Marsha Metalious Duprey.

7. Otto Friedrich, "Farewell to *Peyton Place*," *Esquire* (December 1971): 160.

8. On the question of who wrote *Return to Peyton Place*, see "Reminiscences of Helen Honig Meyer," Interview by Mary Belle Starr, February–June 1979, Oral History Research Office, Columbia University, 2003; Emily Toth, *Inside Peyton Place: The Life of Grace Metalious* (Jackson: University of Mississippi, 2000); William H. Lyles, *Putting Dell on the Map* (Westport, Conn.: Greenwood Press, 1983), 35.

9. Grace Metalious, quoted in John Rees, "Grace Metalious' Battle with the World," *Cosmopolitan* (Sept. 1964): 54.

10. For a detailed account of her resistance based on interviews with T. J. Martin, Grace Metalious's second husband, see Toth, *Inside Peyton Place*, 217–224.

11. See "All About Me," *The American Weekly* (May 18, 1958): 8ff.

12. Ardis Cameron, "Open Secrets: Rereading Peyton Place," in Grace Metalious, *Peyton Place* (Boston: Northeastern University Press, 1999), i–xxx.

13. Letter from Treiva Jean Reed to Grace Metalious, February 1, 1961.

14. For a more detailed account of the reception of *Peyton Place*, see Cameron, "Open Secrets," xx–xxiv.

15. Dorothy Roe, "Queen Elizabeth—Woman of the Year," *The San Francisco Flash*, December 26, 1957. My thanks to David Richards for this citation.

16. Mary Ellen Brown, "Motley Moments: Soap Operas, Carnival, Gossip, and the Power of Utterance," in Mary Ellen Brown, ed., *Televison and Women's Culture: The Politics of the Popular* (London, Sage Publications, 1990), 183–198.

17. Mary Kelley, *Private Women, Public Stage: Literary Domesticity in Nineteenth-Century America* (Oxford: Oxford University Press, 1984).

18. Grace Metalious, "Me and 'Peyton Place,'" *American Weekly* May 18 (ff., 1958): 13, vertical file, Gale Public Library, Laconia, New Hampshire.

19. Patricia Carbine, "Peyton Place," *Look* (March 18, 1958): 108.

20. Mike Wallace, with Gary Paul Gates, *Betwen You and Me: A Memoir* (New York: Hyperion, 2005) 1–4.

21. Barbara Seaman, *Lovely Me: The Life of Jacqueline Susann* (New York: William Morrow and Company, 1987), 239–242.

22. For a full account of the scene see Toth, *Inside Peyton Place*, 164.

23. Carbine, "Peyton Place," 108.

24. Quoted in Toth, *Inside Peyton Place*, 163.

25. The description is from Michael Korda, "Wasn't She Great?" *New Yorker* (August 14, 1995): 66–72.

26. Ken Crain, quoted in Merle Miller, "The Tragedy of Grace Metalious and Peyton Place," *Ladies Home Journal* (June 1965): 112.

27. Miller, "Tragedy of 'Peyton Place,'" 112.

28. Friedrich, "Farewell," 310.

29. Metalious, "Me and 'Peyton Place,'" 21.

30. Toth, *Inside Peyton Place*, 173.

31. Friedrich, "Farewell," 310.

32. See especially Deidre Johnson, "From Paragraphs to Pages: The Writing and Development of the Stratemeyer Syndicate Series," in Carolyn Stewart Dyer and Nancy Romalov, *Discovering Nancy Drew* (Iowa City: University of Iowa Press, 1995), 29–40.

33. The term is from Michael Denning, *Mechanic Accents: Dime Novels and Working Class Culture in America* (London: Verso, 1987) 24.

34. Mary Noel, quoted in Janice Radway, *A Feeling for Books: The Book-of-the-Month Club: Literary Taste, and Middle-Class Desire* (Chapel Hill: University of North Carolina Press, 1997), 132.

35. Grace Metalious, quoted in "Farewell to Payton Place," 310.

36. Leona Nevler, interviews with author, January 2001, September 2002.

37. "Reminiscences of Helen Honig Meyer," 80. Oral History Research Office, Columbia University, 2003. Interviewed by Mary Belle Starr, Spring 1979.

38. For a detailed account of Miller's role in ghosting *Return*, see Toth, *Inside Peyton Place*, 219.

39. T. J. Martin, quoted in Toth, *Inside Peyton Place*.

40. "Son of P.P. ," *Time*, November 30, 1959.

41. Friedrich, "Farewell," 310.

42. Miller, "The Tragedy of Peyton Place," 112.

43. George Metalious, in *Girl From Peyton Place,* 125–126.

44. Grace Metalious to Oliver Swan, June 22, 1961, Paul Reynolds Collection, Columbia University Rare Book and Manuscript Library, New York.

45. Jerry Wald to Grace Metalious, Feb. 9, 1961, Paul Reynolds Collection, Columbia University Rare Book and Manuscript Library, New York.

46. Grace Metalious to Oliver Swan, Dec. 12, 1963, Paul Reynolds Collection, Columbia University Rare Book and Manuscript Library, New York.

Return to Peyton Place

PART ONE

1

SOMETIMES, WINTER COMES gradually to northern New England so that there is an element of order and sequence to time and season. When the first snow comes it is not surprising because it has been expected for quite a while. When winter comes that way, it usually begins to snow big, fat flakes at mid-morning and by noon there is a thick edge of white on everything. The skies clear after lunch and the sun comes out and by the time school is out in the afternoon all the eaves on all the houses in town are dripping melted snow.

Then the old-timers say, "'Twon't stay. Not this time. Not yet."

And everyone who is still young enough is disappointed and a little apprehensive because maybe it's really true that old-fashioned winters have left northern New England forever.

Old-fashioned winters usually happen after hot, dry summers. Then the fall rains begin right after Labor Day and they are cold, wind-driven rains that are gray and destructive, and after those rains there is no beautiful autumn, no glory of red and gold leaves. The trees turn quickly from green to withered brown and the rain cuts the leaves from the branches in fast, vicious swipes. After the rains, the ground freezes hard and quickly and one day is like the next, cold and gray and waiting for the snow.

Then it begins. A fine powder that sifts down from the dark sky in a seemingly unending screen and does not accumulate on streets and roads until after the wind has had enough of blowing, and cold, dry piles of white have gathered around the base of every fence post and tree. By suppertime the wind dies down and still it snows, so fine and thin that children are afraid it will take forever for enough of it to fall to cover the palms of their mittened hands.

But those who are older remember other old-fashioned winters. They are the ones who check the gallon gauges on oil-burner fuel tanks, who have long since made sure that their car radiators are full of anti-freeze, and who know that with the coming of tomorrow's dawn, the wind, too, will return.

Fireplaces do not exist in the houses of northern New England purely for their friendly, hospitable hearths. They are there because every once in a while there is an old-fashioned winter and power lines break like dry straws in the face of the wind and snow. Those who remember have small, wood-burning stoves in their cellars to keep water pipes from freezing; every wood box is filled and over-flowing with logs and kindling, and the young sit in front of blazing fires and wax their skis and wonder what the accumulation will be at Franconia by morning.

That was the way winter came the second year after Allison MacKenzie returned to Peyton Place. It was four o'clock on a No-vember afternoon, and Allison was standing in front of the window in her bedroom when she saw the first flake of snow.

Perhaps it will be tomorrow, she thought. Maybe tomorrow Brad will call and say, I've sold it, Allison, I've sold it; your novel has been accepted and will be published in the spring.

2

TUTTLE'S GROCERY STORE was located on Elm Street, Peyton Place's main thoroughfare, at a point halfway between the Citizens' National Bank and Prescott's Pharmacy which stood on the corner of Maple Street. From the front window of Tuttle's, the old men who hung around the store in the winter could look out and see the courthouse and the benches where they loitered when the weather was warm and fair. During the summer, Tuttle's was something of a tourist attraction, for it was one of the few remaining stores in northern New England where you could buy Cheddar cheese by the slice or by the pound from Ephraim Tuttle's enormous cheese wheel. Tuttle's still sold rock candy and licorice drops by the penny-worth, and a nickel would buy a fat pickle, sour enough to set your teeth on edge, from a huge barrel that stood in a dark corner at the back of the store.

Right after Memorial Day, every year, Ephraim Tuttle made his yearly concession to what he called the "summer trade." At that time he brought brightly colored bolts of gingham and calico up from his cellar and lined them all in a neat row on the front counter as had his father and grandfather before him in the days before ready-made clothing. Once in a while, someone bought a few yards of material to make curtains for a summer camp, but otherwise the bolts of fabric stood on the counter until after Labor Day, when Ephraim sent them off to Ginny Stearns to be washed and ironed and then rewound to be stored in plastic coverings in Tuttle's cellar for another winter.

"Waste of space," said Clayton Frazier, "settin' all that cloth right up there on the front counter that way. Nobody ever buys nothin' to speak of."

"Lends the place a tone," said Ephraim. "Summer folks like tone. What they call *atmosphere*."

But with the coming of fall, Tuttle's reverted to what it had always been—a rather dusty, very old sort of general store where you could buy almost anything, if you were able to find it. This jungle of merchandise included magazines and cough drops and ear plugs and old sunglasses; tomatoes in a cellophane package and fish by the pound on Fridays only, eggs that you took from a carton yourself and put by the dozen into a paper bag; deerskin work gloves and pipe tobacco, Alka-Seltzer and lollipops and the Sunday papers. In the fall, Ephraim shut off the two circular ceiling fans that had whirred around slowly all summer and set up his potbellied wood and coal stove, but it was not until he took down and put away the awning, which shielded his front window all summer long, and began saving wooden packing crates suitable for sitting purposes, that the old men who occupied the benches in front of the courthouse knew it was time to move across the street to wait for winter.

3

"Gonna snow," said Clayton Frazier. "Gonna snow sure'n hell."

"'Bout time," said one of the old men who sat with his feet up on the base of the stove. "November. And we all knew it was gonna come early this year."

"Foolishness," said Clayton, and sat down on the one wooden chair that was reserved for him. "I've seen it cold as this many a time and it never snowed 'til clear into January. But it's gonna snow today. Sure'n hell."

"Don't snow in hell, Clayton," said another man, and waited for a chuckle from his friends.

"How'd'you know, John?" asked Clayton Frazier. "Been there lately?"

And then the men around the stove did laugh, and Clayton leaned back happily and lit his pipe.

The front door of the store opened suddenly, letting in a sweep of cold air that immediately stifled all conversation around the stove. Clayton Frazier looked up at the stranger who had entered, and the only way that anyone could have known that Clayton was upset was that he kept his pipe out of his mouth when everyone around the stove could tell that he hadn't drawn on his pipe anywhere near long enough to be satisfied with its glow.

"Ephraim!" said the stranger.

Ephraim Tuttle looked up slowly.

"Ayeh," he said. "What can I do for you?"

"Ephraim," said the stranger and laughed. "For God's sake, don't you remember me?"

Everyone around the stove knew who the stranger was, but not a man moved to make an acknowledging gesture.

"I'm Gerry Gage," said the stranger, still laughing and now clapping Ephraim Tuttle on the shoulder. "S. S. Pierce Co., out of Boston. Don't you remember? It was me that remembered about bringing that Navy fellow back to town, the fellow that was murdered by his own daughter. Remember me now?"

"Stepdaughter," said Clayton Frazier, and put the pipe into his mouth.

"Well, whatever she was," said Gerry Gage. "Anyway, it was me that remembered."

"Ayeh," said Clayton.

4

There was a silence, and the stranger rubbed one of his gloved hands over the edge of his briefcase.

"Well," he said at last. "What do you need, Ephraim? I've got your usual list here, and I could go by that."

"The usual," said Ephraim.

Gerry Gage was suddenly angry. "Listen here," he said, "I only did what I thought was right. I never meant to do anything in the first place. I just happened to mention something about a fellow I let off here in Peyton Place. A hitchhiker. How did I know I was talking to the sheriff? It was him that started everything. All I did was what I thought was right. That's all."

Sheriff Buck McCracken glanced at Gerry Gage. "Whyn't you do the business you come for," he said, and he did not ask it as a question.

Gerry began to make check marks next to the items listed on a slip of paper in his hand.

"No need for any of you guys to hold a grudge against me," he said. "A man doing what he thought was right."

"Ain't nobody in Peyton Place holdin' a grudge against you that I know of, Mr. Gage," said Clayton Frazier. "It's just that some people talk a God-awful lot, and that does get tirin'."

"Believe me," said Gerry Gage, "I know exactly what you mean. Believe me, in my business I meet a lot of talkers. But then, it takes all kinds to make a world," he added, as if he were the first man ever to have noticed this.

"Ayeh," said Clayton.

"By the way," said Gerry. "After all that murder business and all, I asked to be transferred off this route. And I was, too. The company understood. I mean, about all the notoriety and all. I haven't been back this way since the cops dragged me back to answer a lot of questions about Lucas Cross."

Nobody said a word, and, as the seconds passed, Gerry Gage became more and more uncomfortable.

"Well, anyway," he said, finally. "What's new in Peyton Place? I haven't heard much about this neck of the woods since all that stuff about the murder quieted down in the papers."

"Nothin'," said Clayton Frazier.

"What?" asked Gerry.

"Nothin'," repeated Clayton. "There's nothin' new in Peyton Place. Seldom is. Nothin's different at all."

And to the uneducated eye of a stranger it would have appeared that Clayton Frazier's words were true. Peyton Place looked as it had always looked—pretty, quiet and untouched by turmoil. In the late winter afternoon the lighted windows of the shops and houses presented friendly, innocent faces to each other and to the rest of the world.

The war was over and the Harrington Mills no longer throbbed in twenty-four-hour shifts straining to fill the demands of Army contracts, but that was true of factories nearly everywhere. Leslie Harrington still lived alone in his big house on Chestnut Street, and while time and the loss of his only son, Rodney, had aged and gentled him a little, he was still Leslie Harrington, a fact of which everyone in town was still very much aware.

Down the street from Leslie, Dr. Matthew Swain still practiced medicine and his friend, Seth Buswell, still wrote editorials for the Peyton Place *Times*. The house of Charles Partridge was as empty as it had ever been, for neither time, nor acquisitions, nor the lawyer's wife, Marion, had been able to fill it with any degree of warmth or love. None of the old families had moved away, and no new people had moved into town, leastways, as Seth Buswell put it, not enough of them to shake things up or to amount to anything.

No, nothing much had changed in Peyton Place. At least, nothing that anyone was willing to pour into the ears of a stranger. And if there had been changes in private situations and in individuals, surely these changes were the concern of those to whom they had happened and, again, nothing for the ears of a stranger.

Nope, thought Gerry Gage, as he left Tuttle's Grocery Store and climbed into his car, nothing new in Peyton Place. Hell, that girl killing her old man was probably the only big thing that ever did or ever will happen here.

Gerry Gage drove his car down Elm Street toward the highway that led to White River and was, as he put it, damned glad to be heading for a town where there was a hotel with a bar, where other salesmen gathered and there was something to talk about, drinks to be bought, and jokes to be told.

In the Thrifty Corner Apparel Shoppe on Elm Street, Selena Cross finished covering a counter top full of blouses that were on sale.

Then, looking up, she saw a flake of snow flatten itself and spread against the windowpane. She left the counter and walked toward the front window of the shop to make sure that what she had seen was really a snowflake, and as she looked she noticed a car with Massachusetts license plates heading toward the highway to White River. She wondered briefly, as people will in a town like Peyton Place, just who from out of state was visiting whom, but then Gerry Gage's car was out of sight and Selena thought no more about it.

It really is snowing, she thought. I'll have to hurry home to Joey.

She glanced up again as another snowflake fell against the window and saw two hurrying figures cross her line of vision. For just a second, her heart thumped hard and then she turned quickly away from the window.

Outside, the two figures turned quickly into Maple Street and were out of sight.

"Hurry, darling," said Ted Carter to the girl whose arm he held. "I don't want my wife to freeze to death during her very first winter in Peyton Place."

The girl laughed up at him. "Remind me to buy a pair of flat-heeled shoes tomorrow. I can't keep up with those long legs of yours when I'm wearing high heels. I saw a shop back there—Thrifty something—I'll go there tomorrow."

Ted Carter did not laugh with his wife and his steps grew even more hurried.

"They don't sell shoes at the Thrifty Corner," he said, and, holding tightly onto his wife's arm, he tried desperately not to think of Selena.

3

SELENA CROSS HAD JUST STARTED to turn off the lights in the store when the front door banged open and Michael Rossi came in.

"Hi, Selena," he called. "In the words of us natives, 'It's gonna snow, sure'n hell.'" He brushed at the shoulders of his overcoat where the snow had already left a fine, white dust and he stood there and grinned at her.

"Hi, Mike," said Selena. "How's Connie?"

"Fine," he answered, "and I have strict orders to bring you home with me. Connie always makes hot buttered rum for everyone on the day of the first snow. Come on, get your coat. The car's right outside."

Selena turned her eyes away from his. "I can't," she said. "I've got to get home to Joey. It's snowing."

"Selena," said Mike, and his voice was very gentle as he put his hand on her arm, "come with me. It'll be all right. When I saw that it was going to snow, I told Joey to go right to our house from school. He's there now, with Connie and Allison. Come on, Selena. It'll be all right."

She looked up at him, her eyes darker than ever, dark with re-membered fear and horror and pain.

Mike Rossi picked up her coat and helped her into it. There was in his way of doing this something of the bullying gentleness of a nurse with a convalescent patient.

"Come on," he said. "You're staying for dinner, too. I'll drive you home, afterward, if you want to go."

Selena's hands fumbled blindly with the buttons on her coat, and as they left the shop she tried the front door carefully before she fol-lowed Mike to the car.

Time had been good to Michael Rossi. His shoulders were still broad and straight under the dark cloth of his coat, and, if there was a slight thickening at his waistline, it was only his wife who knew of it and laughed at him in the privacy of their bedroom.

"Is my Greek God getting a little old and paunchy?" Constance teased, and smiled at him in a way she knew he found challenging.

He took her hands and pressed them against him. "Paunchy, eh?" he said, laughing. He smiled into her eyes, returning her challenge.

"Show-off," she said. "Always strutting around like a bantam rooster."

Constance broke loose from him and made a dash for the bath-room, but she was not fast enough. He grabbed her again and held her tightly while she struggled, laughing, against him.

"I don't strut," he said. "Take it back or you'll rue the day."

"Never, never, never," cried Constance, and squealed and kicked when he began to tickle her, his hands moving all over her body.

Her struggles loosened the belt of her robe, and he stripped the garment from her.

"Stop it!" Constance yelled. "Stop it at once!" She tried to sound severe but did not succeed.

As Mike kissed her his fingers began to unbutton her pajama coat; then he slowly pushed the coat off her shoulders and she let it slide down her arms and fall to the floor. His hand found the tie of her pajama bottoms, he eased them over her hips until they slithered down around her ankles. Then he lifted her up and out of the crushed circle of pink silk and carried her to the bed.

"You are nothing but a big corny Greek, Mike," she said, and was surprised to hear how her voice shook. I sound like a frightened bride, she thought.

His lips brushed against her nipples, his mouth caressed her. "And you," he whispered, "are nothing but a pure and innocent Peyton Place housewife."

"What are you going to do about it, Mike, an old man like you?" she said, her voice slow and teasing.

"I shall corrupt you," he said, and when he bent toward her again her body twisted and she flung her arms over her head.

"Ask me for it," he demanded, his voice harsh.

"Go to hell. I'll never ask you!"

"Yes, you will," he said, "oh yes, you will."

"Make me," she cried. "Make me, darling, make me." And then, quickly, "Now, darling. Now."

"Say it, damn you. Say it to me now!"

Constance arched her body and twisted it in the effort to get even closer to him. Her hands clutched him and she threw her head back.

"Say it," he repeated, his voice low and savage.

The words tore from her throat, anguished, as if they were the last words she would ever utter.

When it was over he held her in the curve of his arm, and she felt protected from the whole world and safe against all its dangers.

"You're never the one to go to sleep first," she murmured drowsily against his shoulder.

"It's ungentlemanly," he replied. He stroked her hair and smiled in the dark. "Besides, only old men go to sleep on their women."

Constance sighed, and just before falling asleep she said, "Everybody knows Greek gods never grow old."

9

Mike kissed her gently and thought, There is nothing in life that's better than this, lying beside the woman you love, in your own bed, in your own house.

The house was still the same white, green-shuttered house that it had always been, and, in spite of Mike's marriage to Constance, the townspeople still referred to it as "the MacKenzie Place."

"Don't let that bother you, darling," Constance had told Mike. "Long after everyone thought I'd become a MacKenzie, they still called this house 'the Standish place.' Don't worry. It'll happen. One day, everybody'll say 'Rossi house.'"

"I should live so long," said Mike ruefully.

Mike had gone to Leslie Harrington, who knew more about real estate than anyone in Peyton Place.

"Listen, Leslie," he had asked, "what do you think Connie's house is worth?"

"Connie's house?" asked Harrington. "What the hell are you talking about, Mike. You and Connie and Allison aren't going to leave town, are you?"

"You ought to learn to mind your own business, Leslie," said Mike. "But if it's any satisfaction to you—no, we aren't about to leave town. Now, how much is Connie's house worth?"

"Well," Leslie hedged, "real estate values went up with the war and all. But Connie's house, well taken care of as that's always been—let's see. Hm-m, well, I'd say, off-hand, that I'd go eighteen five on it."

"Jumping Jesus!" roared Mike. "Eighteen thousand five hundred dollars! Where the hell do you think you are? Downtown Dallas?"

Leslie Harrington leaned back and smiled. "Nope," he said, "but if I was Connie, I'd never take a nickel less."

Mike had gone back to Constance and said, "Darling, will you please sell me your house for, God help us all, eighteen thousand five hundred dollars?"

"What ever in the world for?" she asked, puzzled.

"Never mind why," he told her. "Just will you?"

"Yes," she said.

Mike took every cent he had managed to save and made a down payment on Constance's house. Then he borrowed the rest and finished paying for it. And when everything was done, he held the new deed, with his name on it, in his hand.

"Leslie," he asked. "Is it my house now?"

Leslie Harrington leaned back and smiled. "Yes, Mike, it is. And Connie got a good price, too, even if I do say it myself."

"Well, if it's really mine, I want to give it away as a gift," said Mike.

The chair in which Leslie Harrington had been leaning back fell forward with a thump.

"What the hell are you talking about?" he asked.

"It's my house," said Mike, "and I want to give it to Connie for her birthday."

"Well, of all the goddamned foolishness I've ever heard of," roared Leslie, "this beats it all. You didn't have to buy the goddamned thing. We could have changed the deed to read so that your name was on it. You didn't have to go through all this nonsense."

"It wouldn't be the same," said Mike.

So it was done, and Mike brought the new deed home to his wife and it read: KNOW ALL MEN BY THESE PRESENTS, That I, Michael Rossi of Peyton Place, State of New Hampshire, for the sum of one dollar and other good and valuable considerations to me in hand paid by Constance Standish MacKenzie Rossi of Peyton Place, State of New Hampshire, do hereby give, grant and convey to her, her heirs, successors and assigns forever, in fee simple, absolute, all that certain tract of land, with the buildings and improvements thereon, situate in Peyton Place, State of New Hampshire.

Constance burst into tears. "You nut," she wept. "You didn't have to go through all that nonsense."

But her tears were tears of pride and happiness, and she held her husband very tightly.

"Thank you, darling. Thank you."

"Well," said Mike and grinned down at her, "it's nothing to cry about. Listen, do you think people will start calling this the Rossi Place now?"

Constance went to the sideboard and fixed a drink for her husband.

"Nope," she said cheerfully, "they won't. Not for a while."

She took a sip from his glass before she handed it to him.

"But I'll know, darling," she said. "I'll call it the Rossi Place for the rest of my life."

And now Mike's car drew up to the house he had bought from his wife and given to his wife. He looked at it with proprietary eyes. It had never seemed to him his own until he had given it to Constance. What made it his was that he had earned the right to give it away.

"Here we are," Mike said, and Selena's head jerked around, her eyes frightened and startled. His voice had brought her back to the reality of Peyton Place. In her thoughts she had been worlds away. Only daydreams now could protect her from the horrors of memory.

She walked up the path in front of the MacKenzie Place and the front door opened quickly, revealing Allison's delighted smile.

"Selena!" cried Allison MacKenzie. "For Heaven's sake, we've been waiting and waiting for you to get here. Hi, Mike." Allison put up her cheek to be kissed. "Did you bring the milk?"

"Yes, my darling daughter," said Mike and slapped Allison on the behind. "Now everybody inside. It's cold and it's gonna snow, sure'n hell."

"Hello, darling," said Constance, and came to put her arms around her husband and then Selena. "Come on in. Shut the door. Listen, I've got the most divine brew brewing. If you have just one cup of it, you can't possibly catch cold. It's my own secret potion, handed down to me from my great-great-grandmother, who was a witch. Guaranteed protection against head colds and malignant spirits." She put her hand on Selena's arm.

Selena Cross looked across the room to where her brother, Joey, sat waiting for her. The living room was bright and warm. The blaze from the fireplace cast warm dancing shadows on everything.

"Come and sit down, Selena," said Constance.

Selena stood in the doorway of the living room, and Joey stood up.

"Hi, Joey," she said.

"Hi, S'lena," said Joey. "It's snowing."

"Yes, Joey," said Selena. "It's snowing."

There was a little pause, and neither Mike, Constance nor Allison then could find anything to say. Selena's presence had, for a moment, brought the darkness of unhappiness into that light, gay room. They shared her pain, they stood around her like bodyguards fearful of assassins. They could think of nothing to say that would release Selena from the strain of memory and the pain of loss. Finally, Mike broke the tension.

"Good weather for a hot buttered rum," he said. "And, as for you, Joey, I've got a dozen Cokes with your name written all over them."

Selena held Allison's hand, and finally she sat heavily and gratefully on a chair by the fire.

Thank you, she cried inside herself. Thank you. Thank you. Thank you. Thank you for still loving me. You are the only people who care.

It was not the kind of love she wanted most, but it was better than nothing.

4

IT WAS A LITTLE after eleven o'clock that same night when Mike Rossi stopped his car in front of the Cross house, and Selena and Joey got out.

"I'll come in with you, Selena," said Mike. "I'll help Joey to get a fire going."

Selena stopped him with a gesture of her hand. "No, thanks, Mike," she said. "We'll manage. Thanks anyway."

Mike did not insist. "All right, then."

"Run up ahead and turn on some lights, Joey," said Selena, and when her brother had gone she turned back to Mike. "Good night," she said. "And thank Connie for me again. It was kind of her to have us. Tell her it'll be my turn next time."

"Anytime, Selena," said Mike. "You know that. Good night."

Selena waited until he had turned his car around and headed for his own house before she walked up the path to her front door.

"I started a fire," said Joey.

"We'll have some hot chocolate," said Selena.

"And a game of checkers, Selena."

"It's too late, Joey. School tomorrow."

"Not if the snow keeps up all night."

"All right," Selena said, relenting, and went toward the kitchen. "I'll be right with you."

Would it be better if we talked about it? Selena wondered as she heated milk. But what words did one say to alleviate a horror-filled memory?

The first time it had snowed after Lucas Cross's death, Selena had not realized, at first, what was happening to her. It had been late afternoon, she remembered, when it started. It had begun as it did today, with the first snowflake flattening itself against the front window of the store. Selena had watched it and suddenly she had been filled with an unreasoning, all-consuming panic. She had run to the telephone and called Constance Rossi.

"I'm closing the store early," she told Constance, unable to keep her voice from trembling.

"Selena! What is it? Are you ill? I'll be right there."

"No. No, please, Mrs. MacKenzie," cried Selena. "It's just that it's snowing and I have to get home to Joey."

"Quick, Mike," Constance said to her husband. "Get the car. We've got to go to Selena."

"What's happened?" asked Mike.

"I don't know," said Constance. "But Selena sounded hysterical, and she called me Mrs. MacKenzie. She said she had to hurry home to Joey because it's snowing."

But when Constance and Mike Rossi arrived at the Thrifty Corner, the shop was in darkness.

"Oh, darling," cried Constance. "Please hurry."

The car skidded on the new-fallen snow as Mike wrenched the wheel and headed for Selena Cross's house.

They saw her running down the dirt road that led to the Cross house, her feet flying from under her as she ran, her unbuttoned coat flying behind her.

"Wait!" shouted Mike. "Wait, Selena!"

But she did not hear him. They saw her fall and pick herself up, and she was already through the front door of her house before Mike and Constance could jump out of the car and follow her.

Joey Cross was on his knees on the hearth, building a fire as he did every evening during the winter so that his sister would always find the living room bright and cheerful when she came in out of the cold. But now his thin body was rigid and his eyes were glazed. Selena flung herself at her brother so that both of them were kneeling on the hearth. They held onto one another as if they were drowning, and Joey cried, "S'lena, S'lena, S'lena," over and over.

14

Her trembling fingers tried to cover his lips and she sobbed, "Oh, Joey. Oh, Joey."

"He'll come back," Joey whispered, his voice faint with fear. "He'll come back, Selena."

"No, Joey. No, Joey. He can't come back ever again."

But her whole body shook and she glanced fearfully over her shoulder. Constance had come forward into the room, but Mike had gone back to close the door so that all Selena saw was the dark outline of his body against the light and she began to scream. She pushed Joey away from her and in one motion she was on her feet, her fingers tight around the top of the fire tongs.

"Selena!" shouted Mike and came toward her. "Stop it!"

He grabbed her wrist and twisted, and the fire tongs fell to the floor and still Selena screamed.

"Let go of me, Lucas! Let go!"

Mike Rossi slapped her hard across the face, and his arms were waiting to catch her as she fell forward in a faint.

Joey Cross stood up, still dazed. "Go home," he said to Mike. "I can take care of my sister."

"You sit down and shut up," said Mike and carried Selena to the couch. "Constance, get a blanket. They're coming home with us."

Always, after that, when it began to snow and the wind swept and shrieked behind it late in a winter afternoon, Mike Rossi always went to where Selena and Joey Cross were and brought them home with him. But Selena and Joey Cross would not spend the night with Mike and Constance and Allison. When it was late, and the wind had died down, Selena always stood up and said, "Come on, Joey. It's time to go home."

Selena carried the cups of hot chocolate into the living room.

"I'll beat the pants off you," she said, as she sat down at the checker board opposite Joey.

"Go ahead and try, big stuff," said her brother.

The wind was a whisper around the corners of the house, and Selena and Joey pretended not to hear when a board creaked or a log snapped.

"I saw Ted Carter today," said Selena.

"Him," replied Joey.

15

"He had his wife with him."

"They make a good pair," said Joey. "Why don't they go back to Boston where they belong?"

"Ted doesn't belong in Boston," said Selena. "He belongs in Peyton Place. At least, that's what he always said."

"Ted Carter always said a lot of things he didn't mean," said Joey.

"Never mind," said Selena. "I don't like to hear you talk like that, Joey."

"He's a rat," said Joey. "A two-faced rat."

"Stop it at once."

"How can you stick up for that guy after the way he treated you?" demanded Joey.

"Ted did what he thought was right and that's the end of it," said Selena.

The end of it, thought Selena; life has so many endings. Maybe Ted did what he thought was right, but it stung all the same.

Selena mechanically moved a checker toward the center of the board, remembering the last time she had talked to Ted. It had been just after the war had ended and Ted had been at the Harvard Law School less than six months. In Peyton Place to see his parents, he had telephoned Selena and asked to see her.

"Sure, Ted," Selena said. "Come over about eight o'clock."

"Ted Carter wants to talk to me," she told Joey. She had no secrets from Joey. They had shared too much ever to keep anything from each other. "How'd you like to go to the movies or something?"

"Him?" Joey said, too contemptuous even to mention his name. "You're going to let him come to the house after the way he acted when you were—"

"When I was waiting to go on trial?" finished Selena. "Joey, you don't have to be afraid to mention that. It's not good to think about something a lot and never talk about it."

"What if he wants you to go back with him?" asked Joey angrily. "What're you going to say?"

Selena turned away and fussed with a bowl of flowers on an end table.

"I don't know," she said. "But I think I'll say yes."

"You're nuts," said Joey disgustedly. "You're worth a dozen Ted Carters."

16

Selena rubbed her knuckles gently over his head. "You're prejudiced." She smiled.

Joey went off to the movies, as joylessly as to a chore. And Selena waited for Ted, hardly able to breathe at the thought of seeing him again. She knew it was a terrible mistake, but she permitted herself to hope. More than anything in the world, she wanted to be with Ted again. Terrified by life, she had in desperation come to think that only with Ted could she ever be safe.

"It's been a long time, Selena," he said. He stood with his back to the door, nervously turning his hat in his hand.

Selena motioned him to a chair, and thought, How reluctantly he has entered my house. It was obvious to her at a glance that he had come not out of love, or even desire, but only because his New England conscience had nagged him into it.

"I didn't know that you and I had to bother with social niceties," Selena said, a tight smile on her face. "But if that's the way you want it, all right." Then, in a false "social" voice, like a little girl playing grownup, she said, "Yes, Ted, it has been a long time. Would you care for a drink?"

"I don't drink," said Ted. "And I shouldn't think you would, either."

His tone was almost sanctimonious, and it annoyed Selena.

"Why?" she demanded. "Because Lucas was a drunkard? Is that what you meant?"

"Selena, for Heaven's sake, I didn't mean anything of the kind."

"Then what did you mean?"

"I don't know," said Ted uncomfortably. Selena's tight control made him nervous. He wanted to get on his knees, declare his guilt, beg forgiveness, but, instead, he only said, "This cocktail business has always seemed sort of citified to me."

"I wasn't going to offer you a cocktail, Ted. It's eight o'clock in the evening and I thought you might like a brandy to settle the excellent dinner your mother must have fed you before she let you out."

"No, thank you," said Ted, rather stiffly. He sat in an armchair, his hands on his knees; he leaned toward her yet was remote, isolated by his feelings of guilt and the anguish that seeing Selena caused him.

Selena poured brandy into a large snifter. "Well, Happy Days," she toasted, hoping the irony of it would not be lost on him. "I don't suppose you smoke, either?"

"No."

"Well, I do," she said defiantly, and lit a cigarette. "What did you want to talk to me about?" she asked.

Ted stood up and walked to one of the front windows. He put his hands in his pockets and tipped his head back as if to ease tightened muscles in his neck.

"I'm thinking of getting married," he said. "To a girl I met in Boston."

Selena did not make a sound. She put her glass down silently and put her cigarette into an ashtray.

"I see," she said at last, and her voice had not changed.

Ted turned around slowly and extended his hands as if asking for help.

"I haven't told anyone else yet," he said. "I wanted to tell you first."

"Why did you bother?" Selena asked, and this time the bitterness showed. "Why?"

"Peyton Place is a small town. People are going to talk, and I just didn't want you to hear it from someone else."

"That was damned white of you, Ted," she said.

"Selena, for God's sake, don't make it any harder than it is."

"Oh, is it hard, Ted?" she asked. "Why should it be? I knew back before the trial that the great Ted Carter wasn't going to be able to afford a murderess for a wife. So why should it be so hard for you to tell me about your new girl?"

"You know damned well how I feel about you, Selena," said Ted in a tight voice. "That's never going to change. We had a lot together, you and I, but we wouldn't have a thing together in the future."

"Don't you dare come in here and tell me how much you think of me," shouted Selena, jumping to her feet, her fists clenched. "Everyone in town knows how you feel about me, so don't stand there and make pretty speeches. You're a little late."

"Selena, will you sit down for a minute and hear me out? I want to try to explain this to you as best I can."

"There's nothing to explain, Ted," she said wearily. "Why don't you just leave?"

He put his hands on her elbows. "Please," he said. "Sit down."

Selena shrugged and sat down and swirled brandy around in her glass.

"Selena, you know that I've always wanted to be a lawyer," began Ted. "Not just an ordinary lawyer like old Charlie Partridge, but a first-class lawyer."

"There was a time when you didn't think Charlie was so bad," interrupted Selena. "Of course, that was back when you didn't know whether or not you'd ever get to Harvard and Charlie was still in a position to help you."

Ted ignored her barbed remark because there was no answer for it. It was true. He knew better than anyone else how true it was.

"Harvard alone isn't going to make me into a big success," he continued. "Being a successful lawyer takes backing. You've got to have someone big behind you to give you a push."

"I begin to see the light," said Selena, pouring herself more brandy. "This girl in Boston, could her father perhaps be a big-time lawyer?"

Ted looked at the floor. All the reasons that had made so much sense to him as he had walked toward Selena's house now seemed utterly shameful. Face to face with the reality of Selena, the machinations of making a career were both sordid and childish. But he had already committed himself to it; there was no turning back. In his heart he knew that salvation for him lay with Selena, but it could not be. It could not be. He soothed himself with this thought. It could not be! It was Fate at fault, not Ted Carter. It is by such means that weak men salvage their pride.

"Her name is Jennifer Burbank. Her father is John Burbank of Burbank, Burrell and Archibald, one of the biggest law firms in Boston."

Selena threw back her head and began to laugh. "No, stop," she gasped. "Honestly, it's too much! Jennifer Burbank! The biggest law firm in Boston!" She tried to stop laughing but was almost afraid to, for if she did not laugh she knew she would cry.

"Selena, please," begged Ted.

And Selena stopped laughing. She twitched her head, and her long, dark hair flew away from her shoulder and rested on her back. Now there was no possibility of tears. Her purple eyes were almost black, and the soft red mouth that Ted had kissed so often was set in a tight little smile.

Dear God, thought Ted, looking at her, I can see now how she must have looked when she murdered Lucas. I never thought she could look like that.

"Tell me about her, Ted," Selena was saying in a soft voice. "What does she look like? Small, blond, with a pink and white skin and breasts like lemons?"

"Selena!"

"Oh, but be careful of that kind, Ted," Selena continued, her voice too controlled, too soft. "Some of those rich-bitch Boston families are terribly inbred, you know. She's bound to be a delicate type. Peyton Place would kill her. That thin blue blood can't stand up to our winters."

"We won't be living in Peyton Place," said Ted quietly. "When I finish at Harvard, her father is going to take me into his firm."

"And tell me, Attorney Carter, do the too-blue Burbanks know about us? You and me, I mean, and about Lucas? Or did they stop reading newspapers when Henry Adams died?"

"They know that you and I were at school together."

"My, my," said Selena, in mock surprise. "Listen to little Ted Carter. 'At school.' Did you ever notice that it's only people with a private school education who talk about having been 'at school'? Have you noticed that, Ted? The rest of us poor slobs who went to public schools always say 'in school.' I'm so happy to see you're learning the language of your new family, Ted. I'd hate it if your inlaws had to think of you as a *meatball*."

"Selena, will you please not talk this way? Can't we talk to each other like old friends? This isn't *you* talking, Selena."

"Maybe it isn't the old Selena, Ted. Maybe you're right, maybe it isn't *me*. But it's *going* to be me, Ted. I don't want to be good old sweet little innocent Selena, everybody's friend. And most of all, Ted, I don't want to be *your* friend." Her voice was no longer soft; it tore from her throat, tortured and coarsened.

"Get your coat and get out of here," she cried.

Ted stood up and watched Selena pour herself another drink. He put on his coat and stood helplessly in front of her.

"Will you kiss me good-by?" he asked.

"Get out of here!" Selena screamed. "I never want to see you again. You make me sick, do you understand? I'd as soon kiss dirt as kiss you. Now get out!"

When he had gone, she sat for a long time, holding the brandy snifter in both hands. Then she stood up slowly and walked into the kitchen and poured the drink down the sink, as if Ted's presence had tainted it.

She was sitting in an armchair, knitting, when Joey came in.

"What happened?" he asked at once.

"He's going to be married," answered Selena calmly. "To a girl named Jennifer Burbank from Boston, Massachusetts."

Joey looked at his sister and began to unbutton his coat

"Does it hurt, Selena?" he asked at last.

She rolled up her knitting and put it away in a box.

"Yes," she said, and went into the kitchen to make coffee.

Joey's black king went click-click-click across the checkerboard and he removed three of Selena's red men.

"That's eight games for me," he said. "Who was going to beat the pants off who?"

"Whom," corrected Selena.

The clock on the mantelpiece struck twice. "It's two o'clock in the morning," said Selena. "To bed."

Joey stood up and stretched. "I think I'll just get a blanket and curl up here on the sofa," he said casually. "I want to watch the fire."

"All right, Joey," said Selena. She kissed his cheek. "Good night."

The wind had died down to almost nothing now, but, beyond the black squares of the front windows, Joey could see the endless flakes that would fall all night. He tried the lock on the front door again and put another log on the fire.

Selena lay facing the window, watching for first light, praying for day and an end to night's menace. I wish I were a child, she thought. I wish I still believed that ghosts were real and houses truly haunted; it's my own memories that haunt this house. She cried noiselessly into her pillow. She thought of Ted, but it was not for him she cried. He was merely the symbol of all she had lost. All I have now, she said to herself, all I have now is loneliness. That's the prize I've won from life.

It was daylight and the wind had started up again before Selena and Joey slept.

5

MAYBE IT WILL HAPPEN today, thought Allison MacKenzie as she awoke. It had been her waking thought every morning for two months.

She jumped up and ran to close her bedroom window against the early morning cold and stood shivering with her hands against the sash, breathless at the beauty she saw outside. For a moment, she pressed her forehead against the cold windowpane, as if to shock herself awake and scatter the night dreams, to make way for those of the day. So much of her days were spent in reverie, dreaming of the phone call from her agent, Brad Holmes, that never came: dreaming of her novel, printed, bound, published, and of the fame and success that would follow.

It was still snowing and the wind picked up huge handfuls of it and hurled them everywhere in gigantic plumes. Everything Allison saw was white and clean and soft looking, so that it appeared the whole world was new and pure and it was as if nothing bad or evil could ever have happened there.

Allison went softly, on bare feet, to open her bedroom door and, as soon as she had done so, she felt the little tendrils of warmth from downstairs creep around her ankles. She jumped back into her bed and snuggled down under the blankets to wait for the room to warm up.

The whole world is still asleep, she thought, remembering a childhood fancy, and I am the only one awake.

At once, she felt warm and safe and sure of herself, much as she had felt when she had been a little girl and had gone to her secret place in the woods at Road's End. Except that it was better now, for she had learned not to be afraid when it was time to go back to the world of reality. Living in New York, she thought, has at least done that much for me. Her experience with Brad, that brief, intense interlude, made her feel old and wise. She knew she was neither of those things, but she wanted very much to think so. When you've

22

given so much of yourself, she thought, it's necessary to salvage something from the ruins, no matter how small it is. Even a lie.

It's going to snow all day, she thought. And I shall get up and eat an enormous breakfast and help my mother with the housework after my father has gone off to school. I'm not a famous author, I'm just my mother's daughter.

She never called Michael Rossi "father." Sometimes, jokingly, she said "Daddy-O," and hoped he understood that she meant more than she could yet bring herself to say; but most often she called him Mike. It was just to herself that she said, "My father." At first, she had done so as an experiment, to see if she would be overcome with guilt at her disloyalty to Allison MacKenzie, her own father who was dead, but she had felt nothing. It was as if Allison MacKenzie had never really been her father at all, but just a man with whom her mother had had a rather unfortunate love affair a long, long time ago.

"I've never been sorry," her mother had said. "I loved him and he was good to me. And I got you. That's a lot more than most women ever have."

At first, when Allison's bitterness against her mother had been at its peak, she had repeated the ugly word over and over to herself.

Bastard.

And she had thought that she would die of shame and horror. She guarded her secret as well as her mother had ever done. She hugged it tightly to her, carried it with her, waking and sleeping. *Illegitimate, out of wedlock*—words like these leaped off the pages of the books she read; they seemed to be printed in a heavier type. More than that, at her most sensitive period she had the feeling they had been used only to wound and hurt and insult her.

She had never told anyone the facts of her birth, not even Stephanie Wallace, who had been her roommate in New York, nor Bradley Holmes, who had been her lover.

During the weeks and months of self-pity and self-laceration that had followed when Allison first returned to Peyton Place, she had wondered often and bitterly about Bradley Holmes. She did not even know how to place him, how to identify him in the scheme of her life. Could he be called her lover, she wondered. But that implied love, and on his side there had been none. No, he was simply her first man, the one who had introduced her to sex, who had taken something from her. And given her something, too. For this reason he was important to her. A man she would never forget. For all the sophistication of her writing, Allison could not yet rid herself of the belief that you had to marry the man with whom you had made love.

She had wasted a lot of time hating Brad, but in the end it was due to him that she had begun to understand her mother and to love her again. Knowing herself now to be human and capable of weakness, she no longer expected others to be supermen, not even her mother.

Allison heard a stirring downstairs, and in a few minutes her mother's laugh drifted up the stairwell to Allison's room. Her mother and Mike never got up separately, just as they never did anything apart from one from the other. If she had ever needed anything to convince her that what she and Brad had was not love, she had only to look at Mike and Constance. Allison had heard them giggling together like school children more than once as they made coffee.

"It's indecent," Allison had laughed, for her mother always bathed while Mike was shaving.

"I can't help it," Mike said. "Your mother always has aroused the most shocking feelings in me. And, I suspect, she always will."

"Shocking my arse," said Constance inelegantly. "The day that you're shocked by anything will be occasion for the declaration of a national holiday. School children will celebrate it with fireworks, parades, and essays."

When Allison went downstairs it was to the smell of coffee and bacon, and the first thing she saw was her mother, in a pale blue robe, her golden head outlined against a snow-covered windowpane. Allison's eyes stung with tears as they always did when she saw something beautiful.

"Good morning, darling," said Constance, and kissed Allison's cheek. "Isn't this a morning!"

"This morning I am masquerading as a short-order cook," said Mike, as Allison put her cheek up. "One egg or two?"

"Two!" cried Allison, suddenly overwhelmed with love and a wonderful certainty that today was going to be a marvelous day.

"It's going to happen today!" she cried, and almost danced over to the stove to pour herself a cup of coffee.

"Oh, darling, I hope so," said Constance. "Did you dream that it would?"

"No, but I know it just the same," said Allison, and sat down at the kitchen table. "Today Bradley Holmes is going to call me from New York. 'Hello, Allison,' he will say. And I'll say, 'Hello, Brad.' And then he'll say, 'I have wonderful news for you. I've sold your book.' Then if I don't faint I'll start to cry, and he'll tell me to whom he's sold it and you, Mother, will have to call Mike because I'll never be able to do it, and when Mike comes home he'll break down and get two bottles of that champagne he's been saving and we'll all celebrate."

Mike assumed a pose with his coffee cup raised and said, "And I'll stand like this and say, 'Here's to Allison MacKenzie and her best seller *Samuel's Castle*.' And then, ladies, we shall all proceed to tie one on."

"And then," said Constance, "I'll have to get busy and call up everyone we know and say, 'Please come over to our house because we are having a party for the celebrated authoress Allison MacKenzie,' and then Mike will have to start serving beer because we don't have that much champagne in the cellar."

"Damn it," cried Mike, "now the eggs are burning!" And all three of them laughed.

Allison sighed. "Brought back to earth by burning eggs. How prosaic." But she preferred the dream, and said, "Wouldn't it be wonderful if Brad *did* sell it?"

"Yes, it would, darling," said Constance. "It would make us all so happy, and you especially. You deserve it, darling. Not just because you have a wonderful talent, but because you've worked so hard."

"It'll happen," said Mike. "One day soon, mark my words. Now come on, let's eat. I'll be late for school."

Worked so hard, Allison thought. It was an accurate description, yet it did not begin to express all that she had put into her novel. The years of writing and the drudgery of rewriting. What made it so hard was not, after all, the book itself, but *doubt*. Doubt haunted her, plucked at her nerves, kept her from sleep and rest. Would it be any good? Would it find a publisher? She could never trust her own judgment. The chapter that read so well at midnight would appear in the light of day as fit only for the wastebasket. It was a book she had cried over—as much, she sometimes thought, as any mother ever cried over an ungrateful child.

Samuel's Castle was the culmination of over two years of work for Allison. When she had first returned home at the time of Selena

Cross's trial, she had come in defeat as a writer; for, although she had managed to support herself with what she earned as a short story writer for the magazines, her novel had been a failure. Bradley Holmes had told her flatly that he could not sell her book, and that, even if he could, he would not do so. The publication of an inferior work would do her more harm than good in the long run, he had told her.

"Try the novel again," Brad said. "Wait until you're older, more experienced."

Well, Allison had thought ruefully when she got home, she was certainly more experienced if not much older.

David Noyes, whom she had met in New York, was the only person to whom she had ever told the whole story of her brief affair with Bradley Holmes, and it was David who came to Peyton Place to help and comfort her.

"I won't say it didn't hurt like hell, Allison," David had said to her. "No man likes to hear from the woman he loves about her sex experiences with another man. Women think we do, but we don't. The single standard is something that women have accepted much more readily than men. I think they invented it." He laughed, was silent for a moment, then said, "It's ended, Allison—you and Brad, that's all over and done with. And now is going to be the roughest time of all for you because you have to pick up the pieces of your life and try to assemble them into a pattern."

"Oh, David. How? It's always easy to give advice like that, high-sounding and vague. I want you to help me. Be specific. I don't want advice. I guess what I want is a prescription."

"Get to work," David had told her. "It may sound trite but it's true. Work your damned head off. Work. To work at one's chosen task is one of the truly great satisfactions that life offers. It's a better healer than time."

In the end, Allison had said that she would try.

"And about us, Allison?" he asked then, his eyes sad and imploring.

"Nothing about us, David. Not now. Not yet. Maybe not ever. Perhaps when you think about it, you won't be so sure that you want secondhand goods." She turned her head away from him; her lips tight, trying to hold back the tears. She did not know whether it was the memory of Brad or David's question that had caused something in her breast to break.

"Shut up," said David harshly. "I've never been a hold-out for virginity."

"I'll write to you, David. Maybe when I've gone back to work it'll be different. Maybe it's true. Perhaps time and work will accomplish what I haven't been able to."

So David Noyes had gone back to New York, and Allison had unpacked her manuscript and gone to work.

Samuel's Castle was the story of Samuel Peyton, a rich Negro, who had married a white girl and had escaped from the ostracism of the world by building himself a castle on the hills outside of Peyton Place. This was the background, the counterpoint to the story of a town very much like Peyton Place and of the people who lived there. When Allison had finally finished writing the sixth draft and had sent it off to Brad, he called her the day after he had received it. It was not usual for an agent to give all his attention, and so quickly, to the work of a new, young, virtually unknown writer, Allison knew.

"Allison, it's great!" Brad had said joyfully. "I'll sell it! I'm certain of that."

"At last," said Allison laconically, too tired and sick of the manuscript now to care what happened to it. She had done her best for it; now it was in the hands of others. It did not seem to belong to her any more.

"Listen, is Peyton Place at all like the town in the book?"

"Yes. Why?"

"Oh, nothing. Except that it must be one hell of a snake pit."

"Peyton Place is no different from any other small town, Brad, and neither is the town in the book. They're all alike."

"Keep your fingers crossed, baby," said Brad. "You'll be hearing from me!"

And every day since, Allison had awakened with the same first thought: *Maybe it will happen today.*

"I've got to get at that living room today," said Constance when she and Allison had finished the breakfast dishes. "It looks like a pigpen."

The living room did not look like a pigpen, but Constance was a meticulous housekeeper and the least sign of dust was enough to send her scurrying for the vacuum cleaner.

"You just went over that room with a fine-toothed comb the day before yesterday," said Allison.

"Nevertheless," said Constance, "I can't go around giving champagne parties for authoresses in dirty rooms."

"I'm going out to shovel the front walk," said Allison, "and get the cobwebs off my brain. It must be cobwebs that make me have such impossible ideas the first thing in the morning."

She bent to the task. Holding the shovel with its familiar, worn handle in her mittened hands, she hoped that work as mechanical as removing snow would deaden her too active mind, would stop the endless brooding on the novel and its fate. Allison had finally to admit to herself that the novel was more than a book, more than a job of work—her whole life depended on it. She could imagine herself only as the author of *Samuel's Castle*. If she was not that, she was not anything.

It was eleven-thirty in the morning when Allison came in from outside. She was stamping snow from her boots when she heard the phone ring, and picked up the extension in the kitchen.

"Hello, Allison?" It was Bradley Holmes.

It can't be. It can't be, Allison said over and over in her head. Wishes don't come true just like this. "Yes, Brad," she said into the receiver, trying not to reveal her intense excitement.

"Sit down, darling," he said. "I've got wonderful news for you!"

It can't be. It can't be. Please, God, let it be.

"Allison? Allison, can you hear me?"

"Yes, Brad, I can hear you. Don't shout."

"I've sold your book!" he shouted.

Constance was making Allison's bed when she heard her daughter shout.

"Mother! Come quick!"

Dear God, thought Constance, and ran for the stairs. She's hurt herself.

Allison was crying into the telephone. "Yes," she was sobbing. "I can hear you, Brad. I can hear you."

"It can't be," cried Constance, and grabbed for the phone.

"This is Constance Rossi," she said. "What happened?"

"I sold Allison's book to Jackman," said Brad. "She'll have to come to New York on Monday."

"Jackman," repeated Constance stupidly. "Monday."

"Tell her to call me and let me know what train or plane she's coming on. I'll meet her. And tell her I'll make reservations for her at

28

the Plaza. Jackman, I think, is going to put everything behind this book. I have the feeling Allison will soon be able to afford the best hotels and she ought to start getting used to them."

"Yes, Mr. Holmes. Good-by, Mr. Holmes," said Constance.

6

CHESTNUT STREET WAS a wide, tree-shaded avenue which ran parallel to Elm Street, one block south of the main thoroughfare. Chestnut Street had always been, and still was, considered to be the "best" street in Peyton Place. Every town has its Chestnut Street. On the hottest summer day, the Chestnut Streets are cooler than all the others. The houses that line these streets always indicate, unmistakably, that they were built at a time when servants were cheap and plentiful, and that the owners could afford them. To the people who live on the other streets, those houses are always mysterious. One thinks of secret rooms and hidden staircases.

There had never been any danger that anyone undesirable would find his way to Chestnut Street, for each great house was surrounded on all sides by the land of the individual owner. The land was "Old Land," acres of ground that had belonged to the families who had come to live in the shadow of Samuel Peyton's castle when the castle was new.

The men who lived on Chestnut Street were the life's blood of Peyton Place. They were the men with money and position and, therefore, the men who were in control.

"Takes more than money to run a town," said Dr. Matthew Swain to his friend Seth Buswell. "Folks'll take just so much of cottoning down to money and then they say to hell with it."

"Then the ungrateful bastards unionize," said Leslie Harrington before Seth could answer. "I can't open."

The men of Chestnut Street were gathered at the home of Matthew Swain for one of their Friday night poker games. These games had become legend in Peyton Place.

"Age cannot wither him, nor custom stay his lousy, two-edged tongue," said Seth, looking at Harrington.

29

"I can open," said Charles Partridge. "And I will."

Charles Partridge still jumped into a conversation, as he had always done, when words between people threatened to become unfriendly; but he needn't have bothered to play the role of pacifist between Leslie and Seth, for those two hurled insults at each other only from habit now. The animosity that had motivated them in earlier years had been forgotten at last.

After the death of Rodney Harrington, Leslie's only son, his friends on Chestnut Street had been worried about the wealthy millowner. Overnight, Leslie Harrington had changed from the hard, pushing businessman he had always been to a blurred imitation of himself. Even those who had always hated Leslie began to feel sorry for him.

"He got his comeuppance at last," said a great many people in Peyton Place. Some said it with complacent pride, as if Leslie Harrington's comeuppance had been the result of their efforts.

"Yep. But it don't seem's though he should have got it so hard, all at once like that," said others.

If Leslie Harrington could have heard the voices, he would have felt that fate was words, that his life was nothing except as it was described by others. Gossip brought back to Peyton Place the dead and the missing. Rodney's and Betty's names were spoken more often now than when they had lived in Peyton Place. The rusty voices of old men and women were like a litany.

"Mebbe. But I'll wager there's some that ain't as sorry as others that Leslie Harrington got his at last."

"Oh, yeah? Like who?"

"Like John and Berit Anderson over on Ash Street."

"Yep. Run that girl of theirs right out of town, Leslie did. Can't blame the Andersons if they ain't sorry for Leslie now."

"Wonder what happened to Betty Anderson. John never says a word about her. Like she was dead."

"Well, I guess when she went and got herself knocked up by Rodney Harrington it was the same to John as if she *was* dead."

"Yep. Them Swedes got their pride just like anybody else."

"Mebbe she's livin' over to Rutland. Didn't she have an aunt over there?"

"Nah. Jared Clarke's been over to Rutland a million times, and you can trust Jared to know if Betty was living there and to tell everyone here about it."

There had been plenty of speculation in Peyton Place about what had happened to Betty Anderson, just as there always was about a girl who left town the way Betty had. But what no one in town knew, not even the men on Chestnut Street who usually knew everything that happened in Peyton Place, was that Leslie Harrington had made a quiet search of his own for the girl he had tried to destroy. He had not gone to Buck McCracken because Peyton Place's sheriff was a notoriously slow mover and, besides, he had a big mouth. If he contacted a nearby branch of the Missing Persons Bureau they would send people to town to ask questions, and this, above all, Leslie did not want. There were no private detectives in Peyton Place, nor in the whole state, for that matter, and they would have been impossible anyway. They, too, asked questions.

And so it appeared that Leslie Harrington had failed, but failure was a luxury that Leslie had never permitted himself and he did not intend to start now. He'd find a way, he was sure. It might take time, but he'd find a way.

"I raised, Leslie," said Matthew Swain. "Are you playing cards or daydreaming about chorus girls?"

"I'll see you, Matt," said Leslie, and shoved coins into the middle of the table. "Straight as a string with a black queen high, Matt. Beat me."

"Can't," said Matthew Swain disgustedly. "You always did have the goddamnedest luck, Leslie."

Not always, thought Leslie. Not quite always.

"Saw Ted Carter today," said Charles Partridge. "Had his wife with him. Nice-looking girl."

"Humph," said the doctor.

"Now hold on, Matt," said Leslie. "You can't hold it against Carter forever just because he didn't stick by Selena Cross. After all."

"After all, my ass," said Dr. Swain. "None of my business anyhow. Come on, deal."

"A young feller like that, trying to make something of himself and get ahead in the world. You can't blame him," continued Leslie, as if

Matt had not spoken. "It'd be all right if he was going to stay right here in Peyton Place, but it wouldn't do for him to have a wife like that anywhere else. People got long memories, most of 'em."

"Yes, they do," said Seth Buswell. "And not only about murder. There's other things folks remember."

"What the hell are you trying to say, Seth?" demanded Leslie. "Come on, spit it out. Better to say it than sit there thinking it all evening."

Seth threw his cards down on the table. "About Betty Anderson and her kid, for one thing," he said angrily.

Leslie looked as if Seth had slapped him across the mouth.

"Now, now," said Charles Partridge. "All that's over and done with. Water over the dam. Doesn't do any good at all to keep bringing it up. Let's play cards."

"Who brought anything up?" demanded Seth. "Did I start anything? It just seems to me that before Leslie starts in talking about anybody else in town, he ought to look after his own fences."

Leslie put his cards down very quietly and looked Seth straight in the eye.

"I've been trying to find that girl for two years," he said quietly.

His three friends stared at him in disbelief, but there was no mistaking the truth etched in the suddenly obvious lines in Leslie's face.

"Why?" asked Matthew Swain gently.

"Goddamn it," cried Leslie, "because of my grandson. That's why. He's the last of the Harringtons, and I don't know where he is."

"Why didn't you let us help you, Leslie?" asked Charles. "We didn't know."

"Well, I'd never lift a goddamned finger to help you, Leslie," said Seth angrily. "What're you trying to pull anyway? You want to find the girl so that you can get her baby away from her, is that it?"

"Seth," said Matt Swain. "Be quiet a minute."

"I never said I wanted to take the boy away from his mother," said Leslie defensively. "If I found them, naturally I'd take them both in. If she wanted to come, I mean."

"Yeah, and you'd make damn sure she didn't want to, wouldn't you?" said Seth bitterly. "Christ, but you are a son-of-a-bitch, Harrington. You always were, but I was dumb enough to think you'd changed with age."

"Seth!" shouted Dr. Swain. "Shut up!" He turned back to Leslie Harrington.

"Would you, Leslie?" he asked. "Take them both in, I mean?"

Leslie looked at his hands. "Yes," he said at last. "I would. I want to. But I've done everything I know how, and I still can't find her."

"What have you tried, Leslie?" asked Charles.

"Christ, I even went to that goddamned family of hers. If they knew anything, they weren't telling, and, as for the girl, she never did have an aunt over to Rutland."

"Anything else?" asked Seth, still not convinced of Leslie's motives.

"Well, what the hell else could I do?" demanded Leslie. "Listen, Seth, I know how it sounds. But, Jesus, I couldn't go to Buck McCracken. And as for that Missing Persons outfit, they'd have had cops all over town asking questions. I even thought of hiring a private detective, but they'd have been the same way. I tell you, I was afraid."

It was a word that Seth had never thought he'd hear from Leslie Harrington. Afraid. And he began to understand, a little, the emptiness that filled Leslie's life.

"We could help you," said Seth finally.

"How? What can we do?" asked Leslie.

"We can put advertisements in the personal columns of the newspapers," said Seth.

"Ah-h," said Leslie disgustedly. "That was one of the first things I tried. I had ads in every paper in towns from the Canadian border clear down to Boston."

Seth leaned back in his chair. "Leslie," he said, "go into any house on Ash Street, or into the home of any of your mill hands, for that matter, and look at the newspapers they read. They don't buy the Boston *Herald* or the Concord *Monitor*. They buy tabloids. Either the Boston *Record* or the New York *Daily News* or other newspapers like them. Those are the papers with all the stories about knife killings in Harlem and rapes in the Back Bay, the gossip columns about people in New York and Hollywood. I'll bet anything that wherever Betty Anderson is, if she buys a newspaper at all, she buys one of those."

"What if she doesn't read the personal columns?" said Dr. Swain. "I imagine that there are a lot of folks who don't."

"Maybe not," said Seth. "But she reads Winchell, I'm sure of it. Leslie, you could buy an inch of space on the same page as Winchell's column in every newspaper in the country that publishes him."

"That'll cost you something, Leslie," said Charles Partridge, who, some said, took better care of other people's money than he did of his own.

"Can you fix it up, Seth?" asked Leslie.

"Yes," said Seth. "Not from here. I've got to go down to Manchester, day after tomorrow. I'll do it from there."

"Now we'll see," said Leslie, and smiled at his friends. "Now we'll see."

When Leslie and Charles had left, Matthew Swain helped himself to another drink and then extended the bottle to Seth.

"What do you think about Leslie, Seth?" he asked. "Do you think he means what he says?"

Seth gazed at his friend. "Well, for Christ's sake, Matt, it was you telling me to shut up in the beginning when I didn't believe him. Now that he's got me convinced, you turn around and ask if I think he means what he says."

Dr. Swain smiled. "I guess what I really was wondering was whether I believe him."

"What is it, Matt?"

Matt made a gesture of self annoyance with his hand. "Oh, hell," he said. "I guess I've known Leslie Harrington for too many years and I'm cursed with one of those long memories I'm always yapping at other people about. Don't pay any attention to me, Seth."

"No, you don't," cried Seth. "Don't pull that on me, you old bastard. Now what the hell are you driving at?"

Matt Swain looked down into his drink. "I keep remembering," he said. "I keep remembering how Leslie never could stand to be beaten at anything. Not even when he was a kid."

"But he did get beaten," Seth said. "The worst beating a man could take, just about. He lost his son, Matt. His only son. It changed him, you know that. He's never been the same."

"Like I said, Seth. Don't pay any attention to me. It's been a big day and I'm tired to the point of imagining things."

But when Matthew Swain went to bed, he was wondering. Does the leopard change his spots, or does he merely camouflage himself

34

by hiding behind something? Behind something that would fool even the most observant eye. Matt groaned aloud. Like Leslie, he was alone. Whether he groaned or roared with laughter, no one would be disturbed. Matt was haunted by nothing but loneliness, and he had decided he was too old to take the cure.

7

ROBERTA CARTER SAT up in her bed so silently that the top sheet barely rustled against her nightgown. She looked across the narrow aisle that separated her bed from Harmon's and saw that he was well covered and sleeping soundly. In the dark, she stood up and fixed her pillows under her blankets so that if Harmon awoke and looked across to her bed it would appear that she was there, asleep. She left her slippers on the rug, just as they had been when she had taken them off, and she was very careful not to disturb the folds of her robe at the foot of the bed. Then she tiptoed across the room and out the door. The rest of her plans had been carefully made earlier in the evening and she had smiled to herself as she carried them out right under the very noses of the people concerned.

It had been a very good dinner that evening, she congratulated herself. Heavy enough to make Harmon feel full and rather logy afterward, but not heavy enough to make Ted and Jennifer feel anything but contented and well fed. Then there had been the sedative in Harmon's coffee, not enough to hurt him, of course, but just enough to make him say that he couldn't keep his eyes open a minute longer by nine o'clock.

"Well, now, dear," Roberta had told him. "You just sit still one more minute and I'll go up and turn down the beds."

"Oh, please let me help you, Mother," said Jennifer, jumping up.

Roberta put a restraining hand on her shoulder. "Now, you just sit down and finish your coffee, dear," she said. "I won't be a minute."

"But I'd like to help you," protested Jennifer.

Roberta was hard put to keep annoyance from showing on her face and in her voice. That was just one more thing about Jennifer, she thought. Always arguing over the simplest things. Ted had never been like that. The only time her boy had ever been pigheaded about anything was when he was younger and had a crush on Selena Cross. But he'd got over that and he'd never dug his heels in about anything since. Now it appeared that Jennifer, who had seemed so sweet and tractable when Ted had been courting her, had a little stubborn streak that could prove to be very annoying if it weren't curbed. But right now was not the time to be annoyed.

"All right, then." Roberta smiled. "Why don't you and Ted go into the kitchen and make a pot of coffee? I'd love a fresh cup when I come down."

Roberta went upstairs, humming to herself, and turned down the beds in her room. Then she went down the long hall to the room that had always been Ted's and which he now shared with Jennifer whenever the two of them came to Peyton Place for the weekend. That had been another of Jennifer's ideas. Roberta had wanted "the children," as she called Ted and Jennifer, to use the large guest room next to her room, but Jennifer had turned stubborn again.

"But, dear," Roberta had said, "that old room of Ted's is way down at the end of the hall, and the bathroom is at this end. It just won't do, dear. You'll be much more comfortable right here next to me."

"That's sweet of you, Mother," said Jennifer, "but really, we'd rather use Ted's old room. Wouldn't we, Ted?"

"Doesn't matter to me," said Ted.

He did not see the sudden glare that his wife gave him, but Roberta did.

"Well, it matters to me," said Jennifer with a pretty pout. "I like your old room. It has so much of you in it, and I like to think of you as a little boy, sleeping there."

Ted put his arm around her. "Anything you say, darling." He smiled.

Roberta had made up the bed in Ted's old room, but right then she had begun to wonder just what it was that Jennifer had to hide that she wanted to be stuck off in a corner somewhere in a house with her own inlaws.

She's talking about me! The thought had come to Roberta in a flash, like a divine sign from Heaven. She's talking about me! Trying to turn my boy against me!

Well, as Roberta put it to herself, she'd never been one to let herself be undermined without fighting back. But she couldn't begin to fight until she knew what she was up against. And it did not take her long to find a way.

Roberta smiled to herself as she turned back the blankets on the big double bed in Ted's old room. She spread an extra quilt across the foot of the bed, and then she went very quietly to the room next door. It was a small room, containing a bed, dresser and one chair, and had originally been used as a maid's room when old Dr. Quimby, Roberta's first husband, had been alive. In later years, Roberta had used it as a place to store extra blankets and dishes and other odds and ends which a family accumulates over the years.

Harmon Carter and Ted would have been surprised indeed to see the narrow bed freshly made up and to find the hot-air grate open. It was a good-sized grate, fully twelve inches square, and Roberta had examined it carefully from both rooms. When it was dark in the storage room, no one could possibly tell, without getting down on all fours under Ted's bed, that the lever had been moved and that the squares in the grate were now open. Roberta had occupied the bed in the storage room every time Jennifer and Ted came to Peyton Place to visit. In six months she had heard many things. She knew that Ted had nothing to say about the apartment that he and Jennifer rented in Cambridge. It was a lovely apartment, large and sunny. Roberta had seen it herself, but Ted was not comfortable there because Jennifer's father paid the rent.

"Damn it, it makes me feel kept," said Ted.

"What would you have us do?" demanded Jennifer. "Would you move me into some furnished room and support me on what you could earn as a part-time soda jerk or gas station attendant?"

"Lots of guys work their way through," said Ted. "A little work never killed anybody. I've always worked."

"What if you fell down on your grades?" asked Jennifer. "Daddy's firm doesn't take in people who got bad grades at law school. Not that they object to a nice, gentlemanly 'C' once in a while, but they don't like men who make a habit of getting marks like that. Oh, darling," she said, her voice dreamy and gentle now, "someday it's going to be Burbank, Burrell, Archibald and Carter. Won't that be wonderful? Won't it make a little pride swallowing now worth while?"

"Burbank, Burrell, Archibald and Carter," said Ted. "Yes, darling. It'll make everything worth while."

Roberta was pleased when she heard that from her side of the grate. Her Ted had never been a small thinker and he wasn't going to become one now. And it wasn't as if the Burbanks did everything for the children. She and Harmon sent them a nice check every week. There had been a few bad moments, too, during Roberta's eavesdropping. Once, Jennifer had questioned Ted about Selena Cross.

"Were you in love with her?" asked Jennifer.

Roberta held her breath as Ted hesitated. "No," he said at last, and Roberta let out a silent sigh. "We went around together a few times, but that's all."

"Is she pretty?"

"She's all right."

"Is she prettier than I?"

"Sweetheart, no one in the world is prettier than you."

Roberta had listened shamelessly as her son made love to his wife and once she had almost felt sorry for him. Jennifer seemed to be awfully wishy-washy about sex, and sometimes she had sounded frightened and it had taken Ted hours to calm her and then arouse her gently so that she let him take her. It hadn't been that way with Harmon and her, Roberta remembered, smiling in the dark. But then, too much sex wasn't good for a man who had to keep his mind on his books. Luckily, Harmon had never been a student. In six months Roberta had heard the children making love only three times, and after each time, Ted had been pale and shaky the next day. Yes, thought Roberta, it was a good thing that Jennifer was a little frigid.

Never once, in all the time that Roberta Carter had spied on her son and his wife, did she feel shame or remorse. Ted was her son, her only son, and she had a right to see that everything went well for him. If he was disturbed about anything, she wanted to know. And if his wife should try to turn him away from his mother, she had a right to know that, too. It did not matter to Roberta that in six months' time she had never heard Jennifer make a single derogatory remark about her. The girl might, in the future. Just because she hadn't until now was no reason to suppose that she never would.

"My!" exclaimed Roberta, coming into the living room and giving an exaggerated shiver, "it's going to be another cold night. Still snowing, too. Our windows won't be open much tonight, I can tell you that."

"Ours will," said Jennifer and laughed. "I'm married to the biggest fresh-air enthusiast in captivity."

Harmon yawned. "Warm or cold," he said, "bed's going to feel good to me."

Roberta put up her cheek to be kissed. "I'll be up shortly, dear," she said.

When she did go upstairs it was ten o'clock and Ted and Jennifer were playing backgammon in front of the fire, and at ten-thirty, when she crept down the hall toward the storage room, she could hear their voices coming faintly up the stairwell. Roberta Carter locked the storage room door behind her and got silently under the warm blankets in the narrow bed. It was quarter to twelve when she heard Ted snap on the lights in the room next door.

Jennifer Burbank Carter was twenty-two years old and never once, in the six months of her marriage, had she undressed in front of her husband.

"It's not nice," she had told him with finality.

Jennifer had always lived in an environment where everything was Nice. There had been Burbanks in Boston for almost as long as there had been Cabots and Lowells, and the standards of behavior in Jennifer's family had not changed in over two hundred years. A lady did not make an exhibition of herself, ever.

Once, when Jennifer was twelve, she had gone shopping with her mother and in one of the stores they had seen a girl with bright, blond hair and a swollen-looking, red mouth. The girl was chewing gum and looking at costume jewelry and she had a pair of enormous, hard-looking breasts under a very tight sweater. Jennifer had stopped and stared at the girl until her mother noticed. Mrs. Burbank's face got very red and she almost shook Jennifer when she took her arm.

"I've never seen such a display of vulgarity in my life!" said Mrs. Burbank. "Remember, Jennifer. Women who have to use their bodies to create an impression are vulgarians of the cheapest, crudest sort."

"But, Mother—"

"Don't argue, Jennifer. You know I'm right. As you grow older, you'll realize it even more."

39

For a long time after that, Jennifer thought of her body only as something to be kept clean, covered and hidden. As she grew older she was measured by her mother's dressmaker and in due time she found a dozen satin and lace brassières in a box on the foot of her bed. Later, there had been wispy panty girdles to be worn on dress-up occasions, but there had never been any discussion of any sort on the subject of underwear between Jennifer and her mother.

When Jennifer was sixteen years old and in her last year at a very fine girls' school just outside of Boston, she roomed with a girl named Anne Harvey. Anne was a year older than Jennifer, and her father was head of the largest brokerage house in the state of Massachusetts. Anne was a big, muscular girl but so full of good humor that the other girls at school never teased her about her looks. They admired her and made her captain of the volley-ball team and president of the student council, and every one of them wanted to be "Anne's best friend." But Anne chose Jennifer Burbank.

The two of them were inseparable. They went everywhere together and were thought of as a team, but Jennifer never could manage to feel secure in her relationship with Anne. There was too much competition, she thought, and was very, very careful never to offend Anne because Anne had a hundred little ways of letting her know that the school was full of girls who'd give their eye teeth to be in Jennifer's place.

One spring afternoon, Jennifer was alone in the room she shared with Anne. She was changing her clothes, getting ready for a trip into town, when Anne came in quietly. Jennifer whirled around quickly and grabbed for her robe.

"I didn't expect you," she said, almost stammering with embarrassment.

"Don't let me bother you," said Anne. "I just came up for a book."

"If I'd known you were coming, I'd have used the bathroom but I—"

"For Heaven's sake, Jennifer," said Anne in good-natured exasperation, "it's not the end of the world. We're both girls, you know."

Jennifer turned away in confusion and as she did so she tripped over the edge of her robe, almost falling, and dropping the robe altogether.

"Be careful!" cried Anne, running to her. Anne's hands were on Jennifer's waist. "Did you hurt yourself?"

Jennifer could not move. "No," she said. "I'm all right."

Anne did not take her hands away. "You scared me," she said softly.

Still Jennifer did not move, but kept her back turned as Anne's hands caressed her soft skin.

"Such beautiful, lovely skin," whispered Anne into Jennifer's ear. Suddenly her hands tightened hard enough to make Jennifer gasp.

"Stop it," said Jennifer. "You mustn't."

Anne's hands were gentle again, the fingers trailing softly. She heard Anne's breathing go ragged and felt Anne begin to tremble. But Jennifer stood as still as stone and without knowing how she knew, she knew that Anne was making a terrible, terrible effort to keep her hands light and soft.

"You're so beautiful," said Anne, and began to sob. "So lithe and perfectly made and beautiful."

And then Jennifer turned around. She moved away slowly from Anne's hands and went to lie down on her bed.

Anne went on her knees next to the bed, her face wet with tears.

"Oh, yes, my darling," she said. "Yes, you are."

She kissed Jennifer on the mouth, a long kiss, and when she raised her head, Jennifer was looking straight into her eyes.

"For Heaven's sake, Anne," she said coldly. "Don't be so sloppy."

Anne rocked away from her as if she had been struck and Jennifer stood up slowly. She walked over and picked up her robe, but she did not put it on. She stood in front of Anne, nude.

"Now, I'll have to bathe again," she said and walked into the bathroom, her robe trailing from her hand.

All the while she was in the tub, she could hear Anne crying. She walked back into the room, still drying herself, and watched Anne looking at her. She dressed slowly and carefully.

"I'll be gone for a while," she said when she was clothed. "Wait right here. Don't go down to dinner without me."

Anne waited. Not only that day, but every day after that whenever Jennifer felt like telling her to wait. She waited for the rare occasions when Jennifer allowed herself to be touched and she let her wretchedness show whenever Jennifer sat naked in front of the dressing table and said, "Brush my hair, will you, Anne?" She lavished gifts on Jennifer and dropped all her other friends, and whenever Jennifer

41

snapped her fingers, there was Anne, waiting to do as she was told. Once in a great while, Anne rebelled.

"I don't need you!" she shouted. "There are plenty of others who'd love to be in your place."

"Really?" asked Jennifer, raising her eyebrows. "Others? Right here at school?"

"Right here at school," said Anne.

"Hm-m. I wonder if Miss Fenwick knows about that. Do you imagine so, Anne?"

"Don't threaten me," said Anne angrily. "You wouldn't dare go to her with anything like that."

"Maybe," said Jennifer. "Maybe I would and maybe I wouldn't. I'm not like you and you know it. Go ahead and get yourself someone else. Boston is full of young men who, I'm sure, will find me just as attractive as you ever did."

Anne snorted. "I know your kind," she said. "You'd never have anything to do with a man now. You put too high a value on your virginity to give it away for less than a wedding band."

"Darling, don't be naïve," said Jennifer with a little laugh. "I've been doing a lot of reading since I found out about you. All kinds of reading. A man is the easiest creature in the world to fool. I'm not worried about my virginity or the lack of it."

"What do you mean, 'lack of it'?" demanded Anne furiously. "Have you already been with a man?" She grabbed Jennifer's shoulder and shook her. "Have you?"

"Take your hands off me, Anne," said Jennifer coldly. "You have no need to be concerned about my affairs. You said yourself that you could find plenty of others to take my place. Well, go ahead."

"Oh, God," cried Anne, "I didn't mean it, darling. Please forgive me. I didn't mean it. Tell me it isn't true about your being with men."

Jennifer pushed Anne's arms away.

"Not yet, it isn't true. Not yet. But don't annoy me, Anne, or I might just have to go out to discover if I've been missing anything."

Anne Harvey and Jennifer Burbank were "best friends" all the rest of the school year and during the next summer. Jennifer dated frequently, but she had answers for every one of Anne's miserable questions.

"I have to," she told Anne. "What would my parents think if I never went out with men?"

"I can't stand it!"

"Oh, don't be so sloppy," said Jennifer impatiently. "You bore me when you go all weepy like this. I go out with men because I have to. I'm afraid you'll just have to take my word for it, Anne."

When Jennifer denied intimate knowledge of men, Anne found it easy to believe. Not only because she wanted to, but because Jennifer's very appearance lent truth to her words. Anyone would have believed her. There was nothing of the voluptuary in Jennifer's appearance, none of those obvious points that men look for. She did not have the big breasts, the swinging hips, or the rich mouth that most men think adds up to a "good piece."

Like most frigid women, Jennifer needed men. It was not, on her part, lust but hatred that motivated her actions. To her, the sex act was not an act of shared communion; she shared nothing and only used men. When they were finished, she pushed them off with disgust. Not disgust with herself, but with them. She had her first man the summer she was seventeen. He was a Portuguese fisherman nearly forty years old with hard hands and a dark, sharp face. She met him on the beach every night for a week.

After that there was a long series of college boys in the back seats of cars or at a motel. She never went with the same one twice, and after she had had a man she never spoke to him again. He ceased to exist.

Even the college boys who had stroked her breasts and thighs, even they sometimes doubted, seeing her, that they had really succeeded. It was not that her manner was shy and virginal, she had too much style for that; it was that she looked unapproachable, like a girl one would hesitate even to kiss. She held her head high, her features were fine and revealed not a hint of coarseness; she had small breasts and hips. The boys who had known her in the back seats of their cars had a difficult time believing this was the same girl. This was Jennifer Burbank. The other was a brazen, shameless, coarse creature. The young men could see no connection between these two people, so utterly different one from the other.

It was Jennifer's father who introduced her to Ted Carter. He had singled Ted out at the law school, he spotted him as one of the promising young men. Ted came to tea and Jennifer watched him, clinically observant. She saw how respectful he was to her parents, but she saw even more than that. Watching him, she became aware that Ted was the kind of man who would grovel and toady to gain the success he wanted. Jennifer smiled behind her teacup and said to herself, Well, Ted-boy, if that's what you want, that's what you are going to get. The thought of how much Ted would have to pay for his success gave her infinitely more satisfaction than any man ever had or ever would.

Their wedding was announced a few weeks later. And on the first night of their honeymoon she tried out on Ted all the sadistic tricks she had used on Anne. She teased, she withheld herself from him, and only after she had exhausted him and reduced him to begging did she yield; and then it was as if she were conferring on him a priceless gift. Ted never doubted that she was a virgin. Nor did he suspect that within a few days after the return from a honeymoon in the West Indies she began to be unfaithful to him. It was impossible for Ted to be suspicious of the daughter of Mr. Burbank. Jennifer had correctly judged him; he had married a law firm, she was only a means. He would take anything, would permit nothing to stop him short of his goal.

"Let me get into bed before you open the windows, darling," said Jennifer. "These Peyton Place winters are colder than anyone would ever believe."

"I'm not going to open them yet," said Ted Carter. "I don't want you to catch cold."

"But it's late, darling. And you said you wanted to go skiing tomorrow."

Ted got into bed next to her. "Tomorrow I want to go skiing. Not tonight," he said.

"Sometimes I think that you're insatiable," said Jennifer, laughing at him.

"Open your mouth a little," he said.

"No."

"I'll make you."

"I don't like to be kissed wet."

"You'll learn."

"You'll have to teach me."

Every time Ted made love to his wife, he had to seduce her first, and while this excited him at times beyond endurance so that he climaxed before he could enter her, he often wondered, the next

44

day, if Jennifer would ever welcome him freely so that he could feel as if she wanted his body as badly as he wanted hers. Sometimes, when he was not with Jennifer, he remembered the way Selena Cross had opened her arms to him and the way her mouth had been as eager as his.

But when he was with Jennifer, he could think of no one but her. A few times, he had taken her by force, tearing her clothes off, slapping her until she lay still on the bed, naked and helpless under his eyes and hands. Afterward, he was overcome with shame and wept as he begged her forgiveness. But in some dark corner of his mind, he realized that the times when Jennifer goaded him into violence were the times she enjoyed the most. It was a silent, unspoken contest between them, with Ted determined to win her with gentleness and Jennifer equally as determined to turn him into a savage animal. She never hated him so much as when he begged forgiveness.

She came to his bed in nightgowns that covered her completely, and it took his most gentle efforts before she let him undress her. She seemed to be terrified of showing herself and sometimes her body quivered like a frightened bird when he uncovered her breasts to caress her.

"No!" she cried, as he opened the buttons on her gown. "Oh, no, don't. Turn off the light, darling. Don't."

"Yes, I will," he said against her throat.

"Teach me," said Jennifer. "Make me open my mouth, if you can. Maybe I won't let you."

"Come here."

She moved away from him and began to redo the buttons on her nightgown.

"No," she said. "I'm not going to let you."

He pulled her to him roughly.

"Be sweet," he pleaded. "Please, be sweet."

She laughed up into his face and taunted him. "Listen to my big brave man begging for favors. Sit up, Fido, Mamma give you liver."

Ted jumped out of bed and yanked the blankets off her.

"You little bitch," he said harshly, his hands trembling. "You little bitch."

He grabbed her nightgown at the neckline and tore it from her body and his hands left angry, red marks against her white skin.

45

"You love it," he said into her mouth, bruising her lips as he bit into them. "You love it and you know it."

And then it was Jennifer who was insatiable. Her body heaved and her eyes glittered.

"Hit me," she cried. "Hit me."

"You're goddamned right I'll hit you," said Ted. "I'd like to kill you."

He used his belt on her until her back and buttocks and thighs were covered with welts and when he finally took her, her lips were red with blood from his shoulder and she fainted.

"Dear God, what have I done," cried Ted.

He began to weep. "I'll never do it again, darling. Never. My God, I'm no better than an animal. I'll never do it again. Please. Please forgive me."

Ted slept at last, the sleep of exhaustion, and for a long time Jennifer lay awake in the dark, smiling. She touched the welts on her thighs, running her fingers over them hard so that the pain burned all through her and her teeth gleamed white in the dark room. She moved so that her back scraped against the sheet, hurting her, and her nipples grew rigid and she felt the tightening of excitement between her legs.

"Again," she whispered into Ted's ear. "Again."

But Ted did not awaken. He stirred in his sleep and his hand found her breast and covered it gently. And finally, Jennifer, too, slept.

In the narrow bed in the storage room, Roberta bit her lips to try to stop her trembling. She was stiff with horror and with the effort she was making to keep herself silent.

I knew it, she thought. I knew something was wrong with that girl. She's crazy, that's what she is, making Ted do a thing like that. Ted was never that kind of boy. He was good and clean. Oh, dear God, what am I to do?

She waited another half hour and then she let herself out of the storage room and crept back to her own bed, but it did not comfort her. She could not stop trembling.

She's crazy. Jennifer is crazy. She's making Ted crazy. Oh, dear God, help me. I've got to do something.

But when the sun rose on another gray, threatening day, she had had no answer to her prayer.

8

I'M GOING TO REMEMBER every single thing that happens, thought Allison MacKenzie, as the train pulled away from the Peyton Place railroad station. Everything has to stay very sharp and clear this time, so that when I'm old I'll be able to remember every little detail. Too many things happen, and when they do people always say, "I'll never forget," but they do, and then the image blurs with time and finally they don't remember very much about anything. I suppose that's why some people keep journals and diaries. They do it so they can never forget what happened to them. But I'll remember everything without writing it down. When I'm very old, I'll remember how it was the day I left Peyton Place to go to New York to sign a contract for my first book.

Allison had gone to bed late the night before her trip, and even then she had been unable to sleep, and she had awakened early. When she had gone to her bedroom window the tops of the snow-covered trees outside were just turning pink.

In the east, the sky was the color of a pale, pale winter rose. She breathed deep the cold snow smell, almost sweet; she thought she could taste it on the back of her tongue.

Allison wet her fingers and then brushed them across the thick slab of snow on the outside window ledge. The snow stuck to her hand and she put her fingers quickly into her mouth.

It's going to be sunny but cold, she thought, and nothing will melt away or change while I'm gone. It will all be the same when I come back.

She ran downstairs to the kitchen to start the coffee and she paused as she was setting the pot on the stove.

Except me, she thought suddenly. I'll be changed. I won't be the same.

Suddenly, it was terribly important that she look at everything, and that she remember everything she saw. She sat down abruptly at the kitchen table. Her mother almost always kept a yellow cloth on that table, and a low copper bowl filled with yellow flowers.

She does it so that even on cloudy days we eat breakfast at a table full of sunshine, thought Allison in amazement. I never realized that

47

before. And in the living room the colors are subdued and relaxed so that you want to lean back and put your feet up, but in the bedrooms they are very soft so that when you lie down nothing glares on your eye. And all the curtains are really picture frames. I've got to remember everything just the way it looks this morning.

The gas burner on the stove made a hissing sound as the coffee boiled over.

"Damn it!" cried Allison, jumping up.

"And what cloud were you on?" said Constance, coming into the kitchen. "I could smell coffee all over the house."

"I was thinking that I'd better hurry and get dressed," said Allison.

"Sit down and have some coffee," said Constance, laughing. "It's more than two hours until your train leaves."

"Good morning, Famous Author," said Mike Rossi, coming into the kitchen. "Good morning, Famous Author's mother."

Constance kissed him. "Good morning, Maker of Bad Jokes Early in the Morning and of Which There Is No More Revolting Creature."

"That talkative so early?" asked Mike. "This *is* going to be a day!"

"Yes, it is," said Allison, "and I've got to dress."

"You've got to eat something first," said Constance.

"I can't," objected Allison. "I'll throw up on the train if I do. Hurry up, Mother. You have to dress, too."

Mike and Constance drove her to the station, and all of them went inside while Mike bought Allison's ticket.

"Clear through to New York, eh?" asked Mr. Rhodes. "Round trip?"

"Nope," said Mike. "One way."

"Save money, buyin' the round trip," said Mr. Rhodes. "How long she gonna be gone?"

"Who?" asked Mike.

"Why, Allison, of course," said Mr. Rhodes. "She's the one goin', ain't she?"

"Yep."

"Goin' down to get that book of hers sold, ain't she?"

"Yep."

"Well, it don't take forever to sell somethin' like that. Saves to buy the round trip."

"But she may decide to fly back, or drive, or walk, for that matter."

"Don't make no difference. She can cash in the ticket, if she don't use it."

"All right," said Mike, resignedly. "One round-trip ticket for New York."

"That man had me running around in circles when I first came here," said Mike when they were outside, "and I've never managed to get the best of him yet. And how the hell does he know why Allison is going to New York?"

"Everybody in town knows," said Constance. "Does that surprise you?"

"No," Mike admitted. "But I've never been able to figure out how it happens. If somebody farts on Chestnut Street, the guy in the stockroom at the Mills knows about it in a matter of seconds."

"You're vulgar," said Constance.

"I know it," said Mike.

Allison stood still and from far away she heard the whistle of the train.

It's coming across the river, she thought. And the arch of the trestle is black and sharp against the sky. By now a passenger must have looked out the window to see Samuel's Castle far above him.

"What's that big place up there?" the passenger asked.

"Why, that's the Peyton Place," replied the conductor. "Got a whole town named for the feller built that castle, just down the line."

Allison stood very still in the cold, watching and listening, and at last the faraway sounds were a roar and the train rounded a curve in the track and came straight toward her through the towering banks of snow.

A conductor was on the platform between two cars, leaning out, one gloved hand clinging to a rail on the side of the car, and one foot a step lower than the other. His high-crowned cap had a brass plate on the front that read "Boston and Maine R.R."

"Peyton Place," called the conductor, "Peyton Place."

His voice seemed to echo down the long tunnel of snow and to rise over and around Allison so that the sound came back to her filled with an ineffable sadness, and she felt the old, familiar sting behind her eyelids.

"Good-by, darling," said Constance. "Be careful now, and call me as soon as you get there."

49

Allison turned to her almost with a start.

"Good-by, Mother," she said, and put her arms around Constance. "Yes, I'll call you." She turned to Mike.

"'By, Poppa."

Mike bent and kissed her. "So long, Gertie. Good luck."

Her bags were already on the platform and the conductor was holding her elbow to help her up the steps.

"Don't forget to go to Saks for my shirts," Constance called. "I wrote down the size and colors for you."

"—'BO'O-AARD!"

Go back! Allison thought in sudden panic. Go back to what you have and hold onto it tight! Nothing is going to be the same when you get back. Run! She was on the platform and the train was moving. Her mother was waving, the winter sun on her golden hair. Jump, Allison! Run! Mike had one arm raised, waving, the other around Constance's shoulder. Get off, Allison!

"Seats in the forward car, Miss," said the conductor, and held the door open for her.

And then it was too late. Allison found a seat next to a window and turned her head quickly to wave to Mike and her mother.

"Don't forget to call me," Constance was shouting. "Good-by, darling."

But Allison could not hear the words. She only saw that her mother's lips were moving and that her hand was still raised; then she was gone and the train was moving very fast.

Not enough sleep and too much coffee, thought Allison as she tried to relax. But it was not until the train had stopped at Boston and she had transferred to the New York train at South Station that her stomach stopped quivering. Of all the ridiculous things! she scolded herself. Anybody would think I was going to be away from home for ten years instead of five days. Even the snow won't be any different when I get back, let alone anything else. Of all the foolishness!

She ate lunch in the dining car and returned to her seat; the train moved with a soothing motion, lulling her anxieties and fears.

I'm going to New York! she thought. I'm an author. Not just a writer for the magazines, but An Author! I made it!

Her nervousness was gone now; she relaxed and watched the frozen landscape slide past her window, and recalled her meeting with Norman Page the day before.

They had bumped into each other outside Seth Buswell's office.

"I'm supposed to be back at work," said Norman, "but this calls for a celebration. Come on over to Hyde's and I'll buy you a cup of coffee. It's wonderful news about your book being published, Allison. Wonderful. I'm so very glad for you."

Behind the plate-glass window of his office, Seth Buswell looked at his watch and made a threatening come-in-here gesture at Norman, but Allison stuck her tongue out at him and Seth laughed, and Allison and Norman crossed the street to the diner.

Norman Page no longer used his crutches when he walked, and Peyton Place marveled at his recovery.

"Got guts, that boy," they said.

"Yep. Nobody'd ever think he'd been hit during the war at all."

"It certainly was a terrible thing, his getting all shot up like that."

"Ayeh. But he come through it good. Walks just like everybody else now."

When Peyton Place discussed Norman Page, Matthew Swain and Seth Buswell did not take part in the conversation, nor did they look at one another lest a glance betray the terrible secret they shared with Norman and his mother, Evelyn.

"Except nobody has to worry about Evelyn giving anything away," said Seth Buswell. "She's told herself that lie so long and so often that now she really believes that Norman was wounded in the war."

"Less said about the whole thing the better," said Matt Swain gruffly.

Norman Page had not received a leg wound in battle. He had been discharged as a psychoneurotic, and Evelyn had made the trip, alone, to bring her son home. She had taken him directly from the Army hospital to a large, midtown hotel in New York City and there she had begun to school him in the things he must say and do at home. Norman had been wounded in battle. His right leg had been practically shot out from under him. He must practice with the crutches she had bought for him and never, never let anyone know that he had been discharged from the Army for any other reason than his leg. When Norman had protested she had screamed at him.

"Do you want everyone in Peyton Place to think you're crazy? Think of me, Norman. At least, spare me this!"

And Norman, weaker than he had ever been, sick and tired and beaten, had come home to a hero's welcome.

It was Matthew Swain who realized almost at once that there was nothing the matter with Norman's leg. He had confided in Seth, and the two of them had contacted an old friend of Matt's who was a doctor in the Army. They had learned the truth, then, and had done all they could to protect Norman. No photographs of Peyton Place's hero appeared in Seth's newspaper, lest some other paper pick up the story and reprint it for its human interest.

"If that happens, someone who was in the service with him might recognize him," said Matthew Swain.

So the legend that Norman Page was a war hero persisted in Peyton Place. Eventually, Norman discarded his crutches for a cane and at last he used nothing at all for support and walked upright by himself. But Evelyn Page had so thoroughly convinced herself of the truth of her own lies that often, when it was cloudy and looked like rain, she would ask her son, "How does your leg feel?" Norman always said, "Fine."

"Tell me all about it, Allison," said Norman, as Corey Hyde put coffee cups down in front of them.

"There's nothing much to tell, really," said Allison. "I started reworking a book I had written in New York right after I came home, and now my agent has managed to sell it. It sounds so simple when I say it that way."

"Who?" asked Norman. "I mean, who bought it?"

"A house called Lewis Jackman and Company. In New York."

"I never heard of them," said Norman. "But then, that doesn't mean anything. About the only publishers I ever heard of are Lippincott in Philadelphia and Little, Brown, in Boston."

"Jackman is a very small house," said Allison. "Brad—that's my agent, Bradley Holmes—says I'll be much better off with a small house because they'll have more time to spend on my book."

"What's your book about?"

"It's always hard to describe what a book is about. It's just about a town and the people in it and what they do and think and feel. Just an ordinary small town in northern New England."

"Like Peyton Place?" asked Norman.

"If you want to think of it that way," said Allison defensively. "But as far as I'm concerned, the town in *Samuel's Castle* is just like any small town anywhere."

"How do you know so much about small towns anywhere?" demanded Norman. "The only one you ever lived in is Peyton Place."

"Don't be silly, Norman," said Allison crossly. "Small towns are small towns everywhere."

Suddenly, it was as if they were very young again, the way they had been in high school, when they had sat on the banks of the Connecticut River and had argued about books and people and words.

"Remember, Norman?" asked Allison, her voice gentle. "Remember how I took you to my secret place once, up behind Road's End?"

Norman's voice was low. "Yes," he said, "I remember."

"You kissed me," said Allison.

"Yes."

"It seems so long ago."

"Yes."

Allison made herself brighten and gave a little laugh. "Well, what are we so down in the mouth about?" she asked. "It *was* a long time ago."

"You wore your hair in a pony tail and the buttercups made little, yellow shadows on your skin," said Norman, as if she had not spoken.

"I've got to go," said Allison. "I'm leaving for New York tomorrow, and I've a million things to do."

"Yes," said Norman. "Of course." His eyes glistened with unshed tears. "Good luck, Allison. Don't forget to come back to us."

Allison leaned across the table and touched the back of his hand.

"I won't forget, Norman," she said gently. "I'll be back."

Walking home from Corey Hyde's diner, she wondered if success had already begun to change her. Road's End, buttercups, the day she kissed Norman—all that seemed so remote now. It was another world; and she was a wholly different person, not young Allison grown up but, simply, Allison. Allison sometimes felt that she had created herself, just as surely as she had created the characters in *Samuel's Castle*.

The train lurched and Allison's forehead bumped hard against the windowpane.

"NEW HAVEN!" called the conductor. "NEW HAVEN, NEW HAVEN."

Oh dear, thought Allison, sitting up and rubbing her forehead. There's still such a long way to go. Does Providence come after New Haven? No, it can't possibly. Damn it, I never can remember.

She smoothed her skirt and lit a cigarette to try to get the train-sleep taste out of her mouth.

I hate the snow when it looks stepped on and has black specks all over it, she thought crossly as the train picked up speed. Damn it, my head aches.

She went to the ladies' room and swallowed two aspirin and some water, and when she got back to her seat she flipped disinterestedly through the pages of a magazine. There was one of her stories. "Marianne Said Maybe." Complete with four-color illustration. She read it through, and then flung the magazine down on the seat.

What inexcusable tripe! she thought viciously. But then her eyes cleared. No more. Not now. Now I'm an author of books. It'll be different now. Now when anyone in Peyton Place wonders what I do for a living and I say that I write, they'll know what I'm talking about.

The news of the sale of Allison's novel had traveled quickly through Peyton Place, and as she leaned her head against the back of the train seat, she smiled a little and imagined the comments and conversations she had evoked all over town.

"Allison MacKenzie went and wrote a book."

"Some feller down to New York sold it for her, I heard."

"Who's he? The New York feller, I mean?"

"Dunno. Some feller down there makes his livin' sellin' books."

"What's it about?"

"Dunno. Calls it *Samuel's Castle,* so I reckon it's somethin' to do with the castle up on the hill."

"It'd seem that way."

"Don't see how anybody could set and write a whole book about some nigger marryin' up with a white girl."

"Don't seem as though anybody could."

"Well, Allison MacKenzie was always one for makin' things up in her head."

"Ayeh. Well, there's some calls it makin' up and there's others call it lyin'. Take your pick."

"When you put it in a book and get paid for it, it ain't lyin'. It's makin' up."

"Same thing, if you ask me."

"Nope, it ain't. Writin' is one of them what'cha call creative arts."

"Well, listen to him! Where'd you get fancy words like that?"

"Elsie Thornton, the schoolteacher, told 'em to me. Says writin' is like paintin' pitchers and all like that."

"Lyin'! Allison MacKenzie was always a little liar."

"Don't seem to me," said Clayton Frazier, putting an end to the conversation, "that any of us got any business discussin' books. Ain't one of us read one in thirty years."

"Well, I'm sure gonna read Allison's."

"Me, too."

"Talk, talk, talk," said Clayton.

Allison was smiling to herself and a young man in the seat across the aisle from her leaned forward and smiled back.

"Cigarette?" he asked.

Allison shook herself. "Oh," she said. "No. No thank you."

"GRAND CENTRAL STATION, NEXT!" shouted the conductor. "GRAND CENTRAL."

Allison jumped up and adjusted the jacket of her suit and straightened her hat. When the train came to a halt, she was one of the first ones off and she carried her two bags herself rather than stop one of the hurrying redcaps who passed her as if she were invisible. Her arms were aching as she came into the main lobby of the station, and she stopped still as she saw Bradley Holmes coming toward her.

I thought I'd forgotten what he looked like, she thought in sudden panic. I hadn't forgotten at all. I have to get away. He mustn't see me.

She turned, her eyes seeking the stairs that would take her to the street. But she was too late. Brad had seen her.

"My dear," he cried, and put his arms around her. "I thought you'd never get here!"

"Hello, Brad," said Allison, and her throat began to ache. "Here I am."

9

LEWIS JACKMAN WAS a tall thin man of forty-five years; he had a cavernous, carved-looking face and smooth, dark hair. His voice was very deep and soft. Allison thought he looked like young Abe Lincoln. There was something dark and brooding, almost melancholic, in his face.

He looked at her with dark, searching eyes. "You know, Miss MacKenzie, after twenty years of reading manuscripts and meeting authors I have come to be pretty good at guessing what a writer will look like from reading what he's written." He smiled, but his smile did not relieve the brooding sadness of his eyes. "I must confess that this time I was completely at a loss. I didn't know what to expect. There's youthful energy and curiosity in your novel, but there is also a long lifetime of lived experience. Now that I see you, all I can say is that I'm amazed. And, of course, very proud to be the publisher of your remarkable novel."

"Thank you, Mr. Jackman," she said.

"I want to go over it with you," he said, "page by page. I'd like it to be as nearly perfect as we can make it." He began to turn the pages of the manuscript, those familiar typed pages that she had given her life to. "There are a few changes—minor ones—that I think will help to give the novel greater unity and more impact."

"Changes?" Allison turned to Brad. "You didn't tell me there had to be changes," she said.

"It's not unusual for a publisher to request changes, Allison," said Brad. "Mr. Jackman has had a great deal of experience with books."

"What changes?" demanded Allison, turning back to Jackman.

He fingered pages of her manuscript and Allison wanted to slap him. She felt as if she had had a child and that Lewis Jackman was now fondling that child in a depraved, obscene fashion.

"There are places, Miss MacKenzie, where your manuscript is a little too much, if you get my meaning."

"No, I don't, Mr. Jackman," said Allison. "I don't get your meaning at all."

Jackman put on a pair of heavy, dark-rimmed glasses. "For instance, here," he said. "In chapter fourteen you have a poor, demented woman committing suicide by hanging. Now, that's all very well, but I think that we could all do with fewer gory details. I don't believe that it is necessary to describe the body swinging on the end of the rope, for one thing, nor to go to such great lengths in the description of the bulging tongue and eyes and the color of the face. In the first place, it's been done many, many times before; and in the second place, it's not very good taste."

Allison jumped to her feet. "I don't give a damn if it's been done in every book that's ever been published and I also don't give a damn about what you consider good taste. What I've written happens to be true, good taste or not."

"Miss MacKenzie," said Jackman, "believe me, I know how you feel. All authors of all first novels feel the same way. You have the feeling that I am defiling a child of yours, isn't that right?"

Allison sat down. "How did you know?" she asked.

"I've published a great many first novels," said Jackman, smiling. "Now listen to me, Allison. May I call you Allison?" She nodded. "Allison, I am not going to ask you, as I have never asked any author, to make changes with which you are not in agreement. However, I do think that if we talk a few things over we can wind up with not only a good book, but a fine book. Shall we try?"

Allison nodded, ashamed of her outburst. "All right," she said, "let's try."

They spent the rest of the afternoon in discussion. On a great many points Allison refused to budge, and Jackman gave in to her. A few times Allison yielded to Jackman, and once or twice Bradley Holmes had his say. Once Allison strode to the window and whirled on both men, crying, "Whose book is it, anyway? If you can both do so much better, why don't you write your own book?" Except for that single outburst the afternoon went pretty well. She and Jackman signed the contract at four-forty-five, and as soon as she and Brad were out of the office he said, "I need a drink."

"I'll treat," said Allison.

"No, you won't," said Brad and took her arm. "Don't let that fifteen-hundred-dollar advance go to your head. It'll be a long time before there's more where that came from."

"Why?" asked Allison, as they stepped out into New York's exciting twilight. "How long do you think it'll be before they publish?"

"Late spring, probably. That'll give you the rest of the winter to make the changes we agreed to make. Perhaps in April."

"So long?" asked Allison. "I thought it would be sooner than that. It won't take me long to make the changes. It involves just patching, really. There won't be any major rewriting."

"Count on April," said Brad. "Then you'll be surprised and happy if it's sooner."

"Where are we going?"

"To the Oak Bar at the Plaza," said Brad. "It's right over there. Allison, I'll never understand why you didn't want to stay at the hotel. You can't spend the rest of your life staying with people in grubby little flats in the Village."

"To me, Brad, it is not a grubby little flat," said Allison. "I was very happy there once. And I like Steve Wallace."

"Steve," said Brad. "What a ridiculous name for a girl. Really, you'd be much better off here at the Plaza."

"It's short for Stephanie," said Allison and laughed at him. "Besides, I don't like to stay in hotels by myself."

They sat side by side on a leather-covered seat in the dark, paneled room. When their cocktails came Brad raised his glass to her.

"To your success, darling," he said. "I wish everything wonderful for you."

"Thank you," said Allison and drank. She put down her glass and looked around. "This is a nice room."

"Yes," said Brad. "We should be drinking champagne, but I'm saving that for later, at dinner. I'll take you to '21.'"

Allison did not answer.

He has no nerves at all, that man, she thought. He acts as if I were merely an old friend, as if there had never been anything more than that between us. She could feel her cheeks begin to redden as she remembered the way they had been together. Her hand trembled when she picked up the glass.

Brad telling her she kissed like a child and teaching her to kiss like a woman. Brad undressing her, looking at her, making her want him to look at her. Brad with the words of seduction so ready on his lips and the technique of lovemaking so practiced and perfected as to be almost a perversion at his fingertips. And her shamelessness after the first time of pain and fear, wanting him again and again, thrusting herself at him, caressing him with her hands, as he had taught her to do, until he was erect and stimulated and ready to take her once more. And the words of love that had poured from her until Brad put a stop to them and brought to an end all her dreams.

"But I'm married," he had said. "Didn't you know?"

Allison's glass was empty, and Brad signaled the waiter.

"You will dine with me, won't you?" he asked.

"No," she said quickly. "I can't. I have another engagement. In fact, I'm late now."

"I've ordered another drink for you, so you'll have to stay a minute anyway," said Brad. "With whom are you dining?"

She was suddenly angry at this cold, nerveless man. "With David Noyes," she said.

"Ah, yes, David," said Brad and smiled. "You know, after you left New York the last time, David came to call on me. He seemed highly disturbed that you had left and wanted to know if I knew the reason for it."

"And what did you tell him?" asked Allison, her eyes dangerously hot.

"David Noyes," said Brad, as if she had not spoken. "A fine talent, that boy. Pity his stuff doesn't sell better. But he gets marvelous reviews and one can't have everything."

"What did you tell him?" asked Allison again.

"Tell him?" asked Brad. "What should I have to tell David? I told him that you'd decided you'd had enough of New York and wanted to go home for a while."

Allison was furious. "Thank you very much, Brad," she said. "But you needn't have been so careful of my honor, you know. I told David all about us. I wrote him a letter and told him everything."

"Oh?" said Brad, sipping his drink. "And what did our Angry Young Man have to say about that?"

"How can you act like this?" she demanded, her voice low and trembling. "As if nothing at all had happened."

"And what did happen? What happened, Allison, so dreadful that you sound like this now? That your face flushes and you tremble with anger?" asked Brad, and he was not suave and smiling now. He was almost as angry as she. "I'll tell you what happened. You lost your virginity and became an adult. You lost your pretty illusions about sex and became a writer. You stopped thinking of love twenty-four hours a day and began to dwell on reality. What the hell are you complaining about? I think you gained far more than you lost."

"I hate you," said Allison in a harsh whisper. "I hate you."

"No, you don't," said Brad and put his hand on her arm to prevent her from leaving. "You're insulted because I haven't regarded your maidenhead as a pearl beyond price, but you don't hate me. You don't hate me at all, Allison. You're still a little bit in love with me, and I with you, and that's the way it will always be between us. We each have our own reasons for feeling as we do, but the feeling is there and we are stuck with it."

"I have to go," gasped Allison. "I have to leave right now. Don't get up. I'll find a taxi."

"Of course I'll get up," said Brad, and did so. "I never permit a lady to whistle for her own cab."

Walking through the lobby of the Plaza, Allison looked at the expensively groomed, beautifully dressed women who sat chatting or strolling about. They were at their ease, in their element; places like this were a customary part of their daily lives. For them, there was nothing dreamlike or exotic about stopping at the Plaza for cocktails. Will it ever be like that for me? Allison wondered.

As they walked down the steps to the sidewalk, a doorman opened the door of a Rolls. A woman stepped out, a gloved hand holding her fur coat close. She was the most beautiful woman Allison had ever seen. She walked past Allison with unseeing eyes. If Allison had not smelled the odor of her scent, she might have believed the woman to be a ghost.

Brad touched Allison's arm. "Rita Moore," he whispered. "The actress." He smiled, watching Allison turn to catch a last glimpse of the famous actress. "It won't be long now, Allison. I have the feeling that within a few months you'll be getting very friendly with people like Rita. And a few months after that you'll be saying that celebrities bore you."

No chance of that, Allison thought, getting into the taxi. The Rita Moores are too many worlds away from me. I am snowbound in my obscurity.

10

LATER THAT SAME EVENING, Allison sat with David Noyes in a dark corner of a little restaurant in Greenwich Village. She was wearing slacks and a pullover sweater and David had on an open-necked sport shirt. They had come to this place because Allison had been much too tired to dress and face the chic of an uptown restaurant after her afternoon with Bradley Holmes and Lewis Jackman.

"Let's see it," David had said, as soon as she stepped through the front door of Steve Wallace's apartment, holding out his hand for the manila envelope that Allison carried.

Allison tossed it to him. The manila envelope contained her copy of the contract she had signed that afternoon.

"Sweetie!" exclaimed Steve. "You're beat. Come on, I'll run a hot tub for you. Let this monster stew in his own juices. Contracts, indeed."

Allison had sunk gratefully into the hot, pine-scented water, and felt the tight nerves at the base of her neck begin to loosen. She thought about Lewis Jackman's dark, unhappy face; and Brad's harsh, wounding words. Could life really be reduced to Brad's simple equation? She thought not. One plus one makes two—at least, it ought to make two. By Brad's reckoning it added up to one and one, each as separate as before.

"Allison!" shouted David from the other side of the bathroom door. "This is marvelous! Say what you will about Brad Holmes, there's no one like him when it comes to getting a contract for one of his authors. Come on out of there, I want to talk to you."

"Well, I don't want to talk to you," said Allison. "I want to go somewhere for dinner, somewhere small and French where I don't have to get all dressed up, and I want to drink a whole bottle of wine. Then, maybe I'll talk to you. Can Steve join us?"

"No," said David. "She's entertaining one of her buyer friends from out of town."

"You go to hell," yelled Steve, and threw a magazine at David.

Allison came out of the bathroom, wrapped in Steve's terrycloth robe, a towel around her head.

"Can't you come with us?" she asked Steve.

"No, sweetie. I've got a date. And not with a buyer, either," said Steve. "This one tells me he's going to make me the biggest star in television. Naturally, I don't believe a word of it, but he has a charge account at El Morocco, so who am I to say no?"

Allison finished picking at the last shred of chicken on her plate and then leaned back against the leather seat. The candle on the table flickered smokily; the muted voices of the other diners swirled around her. Nothing can touch me now, she thought. Her joy in her success was so intense that she felt isolated and unreachable.

"I didn't realize I was so hungry," she said, smiling at David.

David poured wine into her glass. "It's wonderful, isn't it?" he said. "There's no other feeling like it, except for holding your first printed book in your hand. But signing a contract is something you never get used to." He smiled and picked up his glass. "I've done it four times, and it still makes me feel special."

"It made me feel neat," said Allison, trying to find the perfect word, the word that would describe it most exactly. "It was as if all the loose ends of my life were nicely tied up in a bundle and then I didn't even have to worry about the bundle."

"What about changes?"

"Nothing that really amounts to anything. Brad says he thinks Jackman will publish in the spring."

"Rewriting is the lousiest job of all," said David. "It makes you feel as if you're being forced to travel back through a place you never wanted to visit to begin with, where everything is shabby and frayed at the edges and the ground is littered with torn newspapers."

"Not I," said Allison, laughing. "It makes you feel like that because you're a genius. I'm not. I'm a hack and very pleased with myself."

"Stop belittling yourself," said David. "You're no hack, and if you were, you'd never have to say it yourself. The critics would say it."

Allison put down her glass and stared at the candle's wavering orange flame. The high elation had begun to leave her, but she had known it could not last. As her happiness dissipated itself—it was as if it were seeping out of her pores, she thought—doubts began to enter.

"Sometimes I get scared, David."

"We all do."

"What if nobody buys my book? What if nobody likes it if they do buy it?"

"Then there is nothing to do but try again." He poured more wine. "Come on. Drink up and stop worrying. This is supposed to be a celebration. Do you want to go to a movie or something?"

"No," said Allison. "Let's just sit here and talk."

"I'm an obliging soul. What do you want to talk about?"

"I don't care," said Allison. "Anything. Everything."

"Are you over Bradley Holmes?" asked David.

Allison picked up a cigarette. "I guess there was never really anything to get over," she said. "I didn't love him to begin with." But she could tell by the way her heart raced that she wasn't over him yet. The memory of herself and Brad still had the power to move her.

"Is that what *he* told you?"

"No. He said that I did love him, a little, and that he loved me a little, too."

"Crap," said David. "That guy may be good at contracts but he's the biggest crap artist in New York."

"Because he said what he did about love?"

"Love, my can," said David. "Maybe he wants to sleep with you again, but that's the extent of his love."

"Stop it," said Allison, snapping the cigarette between her fingers. "I don't want to talk about it."

"Why?" demanded David. "Does it still scare you? Shame you? Make you want to run?"

"No," cried Allison. "Now, stop it, David."

"I can't stop it," said David with quiet desperation. "I have to know about *me*, you see." He moved the ashtray and then stared into it, as if he might find the answer there. "I've been waiting a long time, Allison. I have to know."

"Not now, David. Let's go." I'm not ready yet, Allison thought. Brad's like a poison in my system. I have to get rid of him completely, before I can be good for anyone else.

"No," said David. "Let's get it over with."

"Get what over with?"

"Us. You and me."

"David, for Heaven's sake, can't we leave things the way they are? Can't we be friends without this everlasting talk of turning it into something else?"

"I told you before, Allison. I told you two years ago and it's still true. I don't want to be your goddamned friend. I want you, and I want you any way I can get you. I'd like to marry you, but if you don't want that, I want to be your lover. I want to live with you if I can, but if I can't, I want you anyway."

"Oh, David," she sighed. "I'm so tired I can't think now. Let's go home."

They sat close together on the sofa in Steve's apartment. Allison's head rested on David's shoulder and he stroked her hair.

"David?"

"Yes?"

"Kiss me."

He turned her face toward his and kissed her gently, as if he were afraid to hurt or startle her, and Allison put her arms around him. He began to seek her tongue with his and his hand rested gently on the underslope of her breast, and very quickly Allison began to kiss him harder. Her mouth opened and she moved against him and he pressed her back gently, so that she was lying down. His hand touched the skin under her sweater and he stroked her.

"But not here, darling," he said against her cheek. "And not today. Not until you're sure."

"I'm sure," Allison lied. She wanted him to take her; she wanted David to drive Brad out and claim her for himself.

"You're sorry for me," David said. "I don't want that."

She sat up and tugged at the bottom of her sweater.

"Damn it," she cried. "Don't always be telling me what I am and what I'm not!"

"I'm playing for big stakes, Allison," said David. "I want all of you, or I don't want you at all. I want you whole and unafraid and I don't want you haunted by the ghost of Bradley Holmes."

Allison burst into tears. "Please, David," she sobbed. "Please wait. Just a little longer."

"I'll wait," said David. "It's a habit I seem to have acquired." He put his arms around her. "Come on, darling. Stop crying. Everything's going to be all right. I'm here."

Allison fell asleep with her head in his lap. Steve Wallace found him holding her when she came home at one o'clock in the morning.

11

THE WINTER PASSED with agonizing slowness. It seemed to Allison as if not only every stream and inch of ground, but time itself was frozen by winter's iron, unyielding grip.

Allison MacKenzie had finished the revisions on her manuscript before Christmas and had mailed them to Lewis Jackman. She had worked with a craftsman's skill, with the coolness of a surgeon. She got a two-word telegram in return.

"Well done."

In January, Bradley Holmes telephoned and told her that Jackman was ready to publish and that he planned to release the book on April tenth.

"Did you have a good Christmas?" asked Brad.

"Very nice," said Allison. "Steve Wallace and David Noyes came up for the holidays."

"David again?" asked Brad. "Every time I see or talk to you, I seem to trip over David Noyes."

"Does that annoy you, Brad?" asked Allison stiffly.

"Not particularly."

"Well, it doesn't annoy me, either. I enjoy having David around."

"Why not get a French poodle?" asked Brad. "At least you wouldn't have to listen to him chatter."

Allison slammed down the receiver.

David's and Stephanie's visit had been a joyful interlude for Allison, breaking the monotonous ritual of her days. She took long walks with David and talked to him about her work. They held hands as they walked, they drew closer together; but it was, Allison felt, the closeness of friendship, nothing more.

She invited Seth Buswell and Matt Swain to come on Christmas Day. Allison wanted these old friends to meet the two people who meant so much to her now. It was her attempt to tie together her old life and the new. It bothered her that there should be such a high wall separating the two parts of her life. She wanted it not to be so, she wanted to be able to move easily from Peyton Place to New York City without being assailed by a sense of strangeness.

The old friends and the new took to each other well. Seth talked literature to David for hours, talked as if he might never have the chance again. To Allison's amazed delight, Matt Swain sat on the sofa beside Stephanie and listened for hours to her stories of life among the TV actors. He never took his eyes from Stephanie's bright young face.

When they had gone back to New York, Allison met Matt Swain on Elm Street coming out of the pharmacy.

"Allison," he said, "I liked those friends of yours."

"Especially Stephanie," said Allison, smiling at him.

Doc Swain looked over Allison's head to the bleak, wintry hills that ringed the town. "There's something about her face, Allison—I don't know what it is—there's something about her face that breaks my heart. When I look at her I feel young again—and, at the same time, I feel very old. I guess she makes me remember my youth, and that gives me a greater awareness of my age." He smiled at Allison, almost apologetically.

"You're not old, Doc."

"I wish I thought so," he said. "Dear God, how I wish I thought so."

Now, having just hung up on Brad, Allison pushed the phone away from her and turned unseeing eyes toward the window. She knew without really looking that gray, gaunt winter stood just outside the window.

By now, everyone was tired of the winter; it had lost the charm of newness. But everyone continued to talk about the weather, because there was very little else to talk about that winter in Peyton Place.

"Got us a real, old-fashioned winter this time."

"Ayeh. Ain't been this much snow in fifty years."

"That's what everybody says every winter," said Clayton Frazier. "Every damned year it's the most snow in fifty years."

"Well, it's true this year. Them fellers up to Mount Washington got it all figured out. When the thaw comes there's gonna be two hundred and sixty inches of snow that's gotta melt. Gonna be floods all over the place."

"There won't be no flood," said Clayton.

"The hell there won't. With all that snow meltin', the river'll go over its banks sure."

"The Connecticut ain't a floodin' river," said Clayton Frazier. "And that's the end of it."

"You'll see, you pigheaded old bastard. You'll see."

But Clayton Frazier was right. There was no flood. An early thaw set in at the end of January, and the snow began to melt gradually. In February nearly all the snow was gone, and by the end of the month the ice in the river had begun to loosen around the edges. When March was half gone, people began to look around and think that spring would come again after all. But this time it would come gently, like a well-mannered maiden, and not like a roaring, screaming harlot barging her way into northern New England.

On the twenty-fifth of March, Allison received the six advance copies of her novel, and immediately burst into tears.

Now she knew what David had meant when he spoke of the thrill that came with holding one's first book. She stroked the paper jacket and studied the photograph of herself on the back. Then she removed the jacket and looked at the smooth, black binding.

Samuel's Castle she read, and under the title on the spine, *MacKenzie.* She gazed at it with eyes that slowly filled with tears. Here was the end result of years of work, this compact thing she could hold in her hands.

"It's the most beautiful thing I've ever seen," said Constance, and she, too, began to cry.

"Here we go again," said Mike. "This is costing me a fortune in handkerchiefs."

"But it is," wept Constance. "I never saw a more beautiful book in my life."

"Neither have I," agreed Mike, putting his arm around her.

"And it's mine," cried Allison. "*Mine.* There's no one between these two covers but me. Nobody did it for me, nobody told me what to say. I did it myself."

"If this keeps up," said Mike, "we're going to go broke buying champagne."

Allison did not pay much attention to the note Lewis Jackman had sent her along with the books.

"I have taken the liberty," he wrote, "of sending individual copies of *Samuel's Castle* to various people in Peyton Place. I think their reactions to the novel may be of some publicity value to us in our advertising."

Who cares about advertising? thought Allison. Let Lewis Jackman sell books. All I ever want to do is write them.

She began to inscribe the six copies she had received. For David, with all my love, Allison. For my Mother and Mike, with love and gratitude. For Selena Cross, with love, Allison. For Dr. Matthew Swain, who remembers poems about Eternity, with love from Allison. For Seth Buswell, who paid me the first money I ever earned for writing, with best wishes, Allison MacKenzie. And the sixth copy she kept for herself. She propped it up on her dresser so that she could see it when she first awoke in the morning.

At eleven o'clock that night, Seth Buswell called Matthew Swain.

"Have you read it?" he demanded, his voice harsh with excitement.

"Read what, for God's sake?" asked Matt.

"Allison's book!"

"No, I haven't," said Matt patiently. "I work for a living, remember? I've got more to do than sit around reading books all day."

"Matt, all hell is going to break loose."

"What are you talking about?"

"She's got everybody in town in it!"

"What the hell do you mean?"

"I mean thinly disguised portraits of every single person in Peyton Place," said Seth.

"Oh, stop it," said Matt. "Allison wouldn't do a thing like that."

"I don't say it was intentional," said Seth, "but by God, Matt, people are going to take it that way. She's got rape, incest, murder, suicide, and a dozen different kinds of screwing around in that book!"

"So? Sin isn't at home only in Peyton Place, you know. It dwells in other places, too."

"Matt, don't argue. Sit down and read it. That's all I can tell you. Oh, yes. Marion Partridge got a copy from the publishers. They want her to sit down and list her reactions to the book and let them know. She called me an hour ago, sore as a boil, and she wants Allison MacKenzie run out of town on a rail."

"Marion's always been a troublemaker," said Matthew Swain. "Born that way, Marion was. Well, I'll get busy and start reading right now."

"Matt?"

"What?"

"Call me back when you finish. No matter what time it is. I want to hear what you have to say."

Matthew Swain built a fire in the fireplace of his living room. He made himself a tall drink, and when he had changed to his robe and slippers, he sat down and began to read.

"There is a little town in northern New England," he read, "and all year long the hills that roll gently away from it are green, for they are topped with pine. On the highest hill of all, like a jewel in the center of a crown, sits Samuel's castle."

Matthew Swain read until three-fifteen in the morning, and when he had finished Allison's novel, he picked up the telephone and called Seth Buswell.

"I still say it could have happened anywhere," he said. "It doesn't have to be here."

"Matt, you've lived in this part of the country all your life. Do you know of any other New England town with a castle right in its own back yard?"

"Well, no," said Matt. "But it could happen. There's no law says that castles are limited to Peyton Place."

"Tell that to Marion Partridge and every other woman in town like her," said Seth. "Wait and see, Matt. Just wait and see."

"I know," said Matthew Swain. "I know. I guess I was just trying to convince myself that nothing is going to come of this."

"Stargazer," said Seth.

"I'm afraid so, Seth," said the doctor. "I'm afraid so. There's no doubt of it, Seth. All hell's going to break loose here when that book is published."

69

PART TWO

1

ALLISON WAITED. Now that her novel was scheduled for publication, there was nothing to do but wait. She could not work. She had planned on beginning her second novel, but soon gave up all thought of it. She found it impossible to plunge into something new before knowing how the critics and public would accept her first effort. She did not worry, but waited with a quiet resignation that only occasionally broke down. At those times, impatience and a terrible sense of urgency assailed her and she wanted to strike the walls of her room with her fists, as if the walls themselves were a barrier to immediate publication.

While she was writing her novel, it had seemed an endless task; she could not imagine that a day would come when the pile of manuscript on her desk would be gone. She felt like a convalescent, at ease with herself, quietly grateful that she had come through. She sat at the window and gazed out at Peyton Place, the part of the world she knew best. She felt that for two years she had, in a sense, been cut off from life; she had not participated in it actively, with her whole being, but only as an observer, clinically detached. Sometimes she was afraid that this had become too much a way of life for her, and she wondered if her rejection of David had not been motivated by a fear of entering passionately into life again.

Every day she picked up her copy of *Samuel's Castle* and wondered what its fate was to be. Obscurity, she thought. That was the fate of most first novels. She did not know that in New York certain wheels had been set in motion and that the novel was no longer altogether hers, or that its fate was not to be left to chance. Fate had an accomplice, a man she had never heard of, named Paul Morris.

Paul Morris was a small, compact man with a crew haircut, soft brown eyes and a smile which, people said, would charm the pants off a nun. He was thirty years old and for the last ten of those years had worked in New York at the nebulous trade known as public relations.

At the age of eighteen, Paul had managed to get himself hired by a small advertising agency by tacking five years on his age and claiming that he was a graduate of Columbia University. As he said later, the closest he had ever come to Columbia was riding down Morningside Drive on a bus, for his formal education had ended after two years at a high school in the Bronx.

By the time he was twenty, Paul felt that he had learned everything about the advertising business that could be useful to him later and he went, with excellent references, to a job in the publicity department of one of the largest radio stations in New York. It was there, he said later, that he really found himself. He rose quickly in his chosen field. Within three years he was head of his department, married a girl singer who gave up her budding career for him and moved into an apartment at a good address in the East Sixties.

Two years later he opened an office of his own, and many of the big names with whom he had worked in radio and who were to become the pioneer stars of television followed him. The printing on his door read, "Paul Morris, Publicity and Public Relations," and, as Paul said, he could always tell a square the minute he spoke to one, because the square always asked, "Just what is it that you do, Mr. Morris?"

For his clients, Paul Morris did everything, and he did it better than anyone else. One of the most important clients was a man named Jerry Baldwin who had a coast-to-coast television program called "Fun with Uncle Jerry." Baldwin was an alcoholic who could enjoy sex only with girls under fifteen. It was Paul Morris' job to see to it that none of Baldwin's escapades became open scandal. Paul had often arrived on the scene of a barroom brawl, minutes ahead of the police, to drag Baldwin, fighting and screaming obscenities, into a waiting automobile, and he had been called upon frequently to soothe, with cash, the outraged parents of teen-age girls.

"You'd better knock it off, Jer," he told Baldwin. "You're going broke. Pay-offs aren't deductible, you know."

Another of Paul's prize customers was an ex-gangster named Manny Kubelsky, who had turned respectable in his old age and wanted the whole world to know it. Paul saw to it that Manny made the gossip columns every time the ex-hood gave to charity or opened another store in his chain of sporting goods shops. Paul found a teacher who erased the lower East Side from Manny's speech, and a good tailor who succeeded in making the little mobster look like a Madison Avenue executive. Paul traded Manny's long, black Cadillac for a medium-sized, gray Buick and he had Manny's apartment redecorated to look like the home of a moderately successful businessman.

"You can't afford ostentation, Manny," said Paul.

"Ostentation, my ass!" cried Manny, sulking over the loss of his velvet drapes and white fur rugs. "I don't want to live like no bum, neither."

"*Any* bum," corrected Paul patiently.

Very often, a man grows to hate a person who knows his innermost secrets and hidden vices, but this was not the case with Paul Morris and his clients. He was everything to them from nurse to father confessor and they worshiped him. He procured jobs for them, got their names and photographs into newspapers and magazines, bought them front-row seats for opening nights and patched up lovers' quarrels.

"Just what do I do?" Paul Morris often said. "Why, everything or nothing, depending on your point of view. But if you want me to do it for you, it'll cost you, and cost you plenty."

When Lewis Jackman began to realize that in Allison MacKenzie's novel he had a book which, with good advertising and clever publicity, could be turned into a runaway best seller, he sent at once for Paul Morris. The realization of what he had had not been long in coming to Jackman. As soon as the comment cards which he had sent out with each advance copy of the book began coming back to him, Jackman knew.

"Makes Caldwell sound like a choirboy," read one card.

"Tobacco Road with a Yankee accent."

"Earthy. Real. Truthful."

"Wowie!"

These were the remarks of the booksellers. From the people to whom Jackman had sent books in Peyton Place, there was an ominous silence.

Paul Morris read all the comments and studied a photograph of Allison MacKenzie.

"She's just a kid," he said to Lewis Jackman.

"Exactly," replied Jackman.

"But I've read the book. No kid ever wrote that!"

"She did, though. Makes rather a nice gimmick, doesn't it?"

"I'll say," said Paul. "The face of a schoolgirl and the mind and vocabulary of a longshoreman. We just might have something here."

"That's what I think, Paul. Do you think you can do anything with what we have?"

Paul Morris sat quietly and tapped a pencil against his front teeth.

"Can you get her to come down here?" he asked at last.

"Yes, I'm sure of it. The thing that may make it easier all around is that she wants this book to be a big seller almost as badly as I do."

"Call her up right now," said Paul. "I'll wait. Tell her you need her the day after tomorrow for four or five days."

Jackman picked up the telephone and called Allison MacKenzie. After a few minutes of conversation, he winked at Paul Morris and formed the words "She'll come" silently with his lips. He spoke into the telephone a moment longer, and when he hung up he was grinning.

"Not only is she coming," he said, "but she's very excited about the whole thing."

"Good," said Paul. "I'll start setting up appointments as soon as I get back to my office."

"Just a hint for what it's worth, Paul," said Jackman. "Allison is sweet, tractable and co-operative, for the most part, but when she turns stubborn she's pure, shell-backed Yankee and next to impossible to deal with."

Paul laughed. "You're paying me to cope with little problems like that," he said. "Don't worry about a thing."

"I won't worry," said Jackman, and although he smiled there was a little edge of warning to his voice. "I know you won't botch this one, Paul."

You're damned right, I won't, thought Paul as he left Jackman's office, for although he had plenty of clients as it was, the job he was going to do for Jackman now was the first one he had attempted for a book publisher. Jackman had opened a whole new untapped field for him, and he was determined to do the best job of his career on Allison MacKenzie and *Samuel's Castle*.

"Hundreds of books are published every year," Paul told his wife. "If I do a spectacular job this time, there'll be other jobs. It's a potential gold mine."

Allison had taken Lewis Jackman's telephone call in the kitchen, where she, Mike and Constance had been drinking coffee. Watching her on the phone, Constance realized how lacking in animation Allison had been these past weeks. Just talking to someone in New York, Constance thought, brings her back to life again. With a pang, she wondered whether Allison would ever be content with Peyton Place again.

"Mr. Jackman wants me to go down to New York," Allison said, when she had hung up the phone. "I'm going to be interviewed by some newspaper and television people. He says that they are all very interested in the book and want to talk to me."

"Why, that's wonderful!" said Constance. "When do you have to go?"

"The day after tomorrow."

"Good Heavens!" Constance exclaimed. "What are we doing just standing here! We've got to find you something to wear."

Michael Rossi did not say anything, but his eyes narrowed a little as Allison and Constance left the room. He could hear them upstairs, laughing and chattering, as they looked over Allison's wardrobe.

I don't like this, he thought. I don't like it at all.

He felt there was a reckless fervor in Allison's manner, an eagerness to throw herself into life. He did not want her to be hurt. He had read her novel and, unlike Constance, he had not been blinded by a mother's love; he knew its publication would not pass quietly in a town like Peyton Place, that those who were offended by it would strike back. Sometimes he found himself hoping that the book would not be a success; he was afraid that Allison was all too ignorant of what success can do, how destructive it can be.

But he said nothing to Allison and Constance, for he would have had no answers for the questions they would have asked. He didn't know precisely why he felt as he did, he only knew that he had a feeling of apprehension and that he wished that Allison were not going to New York. Later, he was to wish desperately that he had voiced an opinion, no matter how vague, for his anxiety had been more well founded than he knew.

2

WHEN SHE GOT OFF the train at Grand Central, Allison spotted Lewis Jackman immediately. His height would have made him recognizable even if she had forgotten his face. She had seen him only once before, but he had a darkly handsome face that was hard to forget. Jackman was so touched by her youth that he held her hand a moment longer than was necessary. Allison saw revealed in his eyes a naked longing that caused her heart to lurch.

"I've reserved a room for you at the Algonquin," he said. "At our expense, of course. It's close to everything and still has a certain literary flair about it that I think you'll enjoy." His voice was warm, resonant, but his words impersonal; he acted like a man determined to let nothing interfere with business.

"I've read about the Algonquin," said Allison. "Do famous people still gather there to insult the world and each other?"

"Not any more," laughed Jackman. "But their ghosts survive. The place is full of them. I asked the manager to be sure to give you one of the haunted rooms."

They were sitting on one of the sofas in the hotel lobby having a cocktail when Paul Morris joined them.

"Hello, Allison," said Paul and smiled his famous smile. "I read your book and I think it's terrific. I enjoyed it tremendously."

"Thank you very much," said Allison, thrilling to the words of praise she knew she would never tire of hearing.

How nice he is, she thought. Not at all what I expected. Well, what *did* I expect? she asked herself, and smiled inwardly at her own answer.

She had only just heard of him from Jackman and had expected a caricature of a motion picture publicity man. Someone with dark-rimmed glasses and hair that was a shade too long and who smelled of constant hurry and tension.

Paul Morris began to talk about New England, the towns he had visited and the summer camps he had attended as a child, and within fifteen minutes Allison felt as if he were an old friend she had known all her life. This was the measure of one of Paul's greatest talents because, in reality, the only time he had ever set foot in New England had been to cart one of his clients, an actress with a penchant for the bottle, to a theater in Boston. He had been forced to spend the weekend there, stuck in a small hotel room near the North Station, and when he had finally been able to leave he had sworn to God that it would be a long, cold day in hell before he ever left New York again.

"We're having lunch with Jim Brody tomorrow," said Paul. "Ever hear of him?"

"I think so," said Allison. "Doesn't he write some sort of newspaper column?"

"I'll say he does," said Paul. "A column that's syndicated in over six hundred papers all over the country. He wants to interview you."

Allison's hands began to tremble. "I'll never be able to think of anything to say."

"Yes, you will," said Paul. "All you have to do is be yourself. Now, listen. This is going to be a very important interview. Not only because Brody is big, but because it's your first time out. What are you going to wear?"

"I have some new dresses," she said, "and my mother let me borrow her mink stole."

"No," said Paul, "I don't want you to look dressed up. I want you to look very young, innocent and little girlish. Come on. Let's go upstairs and take a look."

The three of them went up to Allison's room, and Paul examined every garment in her clothes closet. Allison felt that she should be embarrassed and she knew that with anyone else in the world but Paul she would have been. But he handled her clothes so impersonally that she could not mind. Besides, she was beginning to have the feeling that none of this had anything to do with her. Finally he selected a gray wool with a round, white collar.

"This one," he said.

"But that's not new," Allison argued. "I've had it two years and the only reason I brought it along on this trip was to wear it home on the train because it doesn't wrinkle easily."

"This one," said Paul again, more definitely. "And no fur stole. The coat you had on downstairs is fine."

Before Allison knew what was happening, he had picked up her hairbrush and was working on her hair.

"No fancy hair-do, either," he said. "Get a rubber band and tie it all up in a pony tail."

"But I haven't worn my hair like that since I was fourteen," she objected.

"Exactly," said Paul with a smile. "And no make-up except for a tiny bit of lipstick. Do you have a pink one?"

"No."

"I'll bring one when I come to pick you up," said Paul. "I'll be here at twelve-thirty."

"But I don't want to go dressed like a child," Allison almost wailed. "I want to look nice."

Paul put a friendly arm around her shoulder. "Sweetie," he said, "you'll be a smash. The United States has glamorous lady authors, and old lady authors, and housewifely lady authors and school-teacherish lady authors. We do not have a scrubbed, clean-looking, young girl author, and you are going to fill this big gap. Trust me, will you?"

Allison looked into the soft, dark eyes that smiled into hers.

"All right," she said at last. "I'll be ready at twelve-thirty."

"And go to bed early tonight," said Paul as he went out the door. "I want you to look as if you'd had twelve hours' sleep tomorrow."

When he had gone, Allison turned to Lewis Jackman.

"Do you think I'll be all right?" she asked nervously.

"My dear," said Jackman, "don't give it another thought. Just leave everything to Paul."

But now that Paul Morris was gone, all of Allison's doubts began to return.

"Is all this necessary?" she asked Jackman. "I mean, this masquerading as something I'm not in order to impress someone?"

"Publicity is a delicate business, Allison. We are paying Paul Morris quite a lot of money to handle it well for us. He is an expert in his field, and the best thing for both of us to do is to put ourselves entirely in his hands. You do want to sell books, don't you?"

"Of course I do," said Allison.

"Then just do as Paul says," said Jackman. "I repeat, he's an expert."

Allison walked to the window of her room and looked down on New York spread out and waiting. As if it wants to be conquered, she thought. She sat down on the edge of the bed and lit a cigarette, then piled the pillows against the headboard and, for the first time since she had arrived, relaxed and began to feel herself. Until this moment, she thought, I've been playing a role, the role of the young novelist coming to New York to see her publisher. It was too unreal.

"I never expected it to be like this," she said to Jackman.

He smiled and pulled a chair over to the bedside and sat down. Like a doctor, she thought, and smiled at him.

"It never is," he said. "Authors always have a hard time learning the facts of literary life today. It's not that it's so complex, but rather that writers don't want to accept the facts."

"Try me," Allison said.

"It's quite simple, Allison. Publishing is a business—like any other. The motive is profit. Books are something we sell. The only difference between a so-called good publisher and a so-called bad one is that the good ones like to think a profit can be made from publishing good books."

"Which kind are you?" Allison wanted to call him Lewis but could not yet bring herself to do so.

"I have always imagined I am a good one," he said, smiling. "You know, publishers are very much like authors in a way. After I got into this business it took me quite a few years to accept the reality of it. I suppose that in my youthful fervor I believed that a publishing house was something like a charitable institution for the talented young men and women who submitted their manuscripts. I had to make up my mind to one of the primary facts of business life, which is that the first duty of a business is to stay in business. If my company had gone under, I wouldn't be much good to you now."

"You have a way," Allison said, "of making the most unreasonable things sound like sweet reason herself."

Jackman laughed. Allison looked up at him, startled, not knowing why. Then she realized what it was. "That's the first time I ever heard you laugh, Lewis," she said.

"I suppose I am a little out of the habit of it." He touched her hand with his fingertips. "You must come to New York more often, and stay longer. Apparently you are good for me."

They were both silent then, looking into each other's eyes. Jackman was the first to turn away. "You touch something in me, Allison. But I have no right to talk like this. I am married. I have a son who is almost as old as you."

Allison turned her hand over; their palms touched. He bent down and kissed her, a kiss that for all its gentleness shook her with its intimation of suppressed passion. "Even your lips are young," he said, his voice soft, hardly more than a whisper. "Even your kisses taste young." He moved toward her again. And Allison thought, I don't care, I don't care, I want this. She opened her arms to him. He was on the bed with her and they were lying side by side.

They spoke not another word to each other, as if both realized that there would be time for speech later. Now they wanted only each other, and with a terrible hunger. He undressed her with hands that trembled like a boy's and, noticing this, she permitted herself to feel a moment of selfish triumph. When their naked bodies touched she gasped; it took her breath away, it was like the shock of diving into a mountain pool.

She was ready for him in an instant and, when he began to stroke her breasts, she cried out and opened herself to him. He took her with a harsh intensity that left her spent and breathless and dazed. She felt Lewis' lips kissing her eyelids. She felt release flowing through her, she cried soundlessly. Lewis held her close and said, "Oh, my dear, my dear," over and over again, and caressed her gently and with love.

Later he took her to dinner and gazed at her across the table. He made Allison feel she was the rarest being in the world.

"You are so beautiful," he said, so softly that the words barely reached her ears, as if he had spoken across vast distances.

"Only moonstruck boys have ever told me that, Lewis," she said.

"Then I am a moonstruck boy, my darling." His face became sad again, the word "boy" had reminded him of his age and of the great difference between his age and Allison's. Allison was aware of what he must be thinking and reached out and took his hand.

"You are young, Lewis," she said. "You are young when you are with me because you have love to give. A man is old only when he's exhausted his store of love."

"I wish that were true, Allison. How I wish that was true! It would make us contemporaries. I've spent as little love in my nearly fifty years of life as you have in half that time. I want to tell you about this, Allison, not only because you have a right to know but because I *want* to tell you."

He told Allison of his loveless marriage to a neurotic wife. "I married young," he said, "young and full of hope. Because I loved her I hoped she would change. But she never has. We should have got a divorce twenty years ago, but then my son was born and for a long time that was enough for me." Lewis was so unused to revealing himself that it embarrassed him; he paused often and shifted the silverware beside his plate. "I gave up all thought of personal happiness. We drifted along. My son's at college now. And my wife . . . she is very much an inhabitant of her own world. A world she has created out of her own neuroses. Madness, I should say, but it's not a fashionable word any more, is it? *Nice* women, women of good family, don't go mad; they have neuroses. Only peasants are susceptible to madness these days." He looked down at Allison's hand in his. "You will have gathered by now that I stay with her out of pity. But don't let me give you the impression that it is a noble thing to do," he said, sarcastic at his own expense. "It's not an act of courage or sacrifice, Allison. Believe me. It's an act of weakness, I'm afraid. The courageous thing would be for me to leave her. But I haven't yet had the strength to do that. Instead, like a weakling, I sit and wait for her to commit suicide or get run over by a car. I have the absurd dream that one day I will be free of her without doing anything myself."

"It may happen yet, darling," Allison said, reassuring him.

"Oh, Allison, don't let me draw you into my silly dreams. Nothing happens but what we make happen."

"I don't care, Lewis. I don't care about any of that. Just love me and everything will be all right."

He smiled his love to her, but behind the sadness of his eyes he thought, Oh God, how young she is. How young she is.

That night Allison slept in his arms and felt safe, protected from a menacing world.

3

SHORTLY BEFORE ONE O'CLOCK the following afternoon, Allison sat next to Paul Morris at the bar of a Third Avenue restaurant called Kelly's. It had a floor made of small hexagonal tiles, and the old gas chandeliers, converted to electricity, were still in use.

"Brody's been coming here for twenty years," Paul told Allison. "He made the place fashionable."

"I lived in New York for over a year," said Allison, "and never heard of it. It must be very, very fashionable indeed."

Paul picked up his drink and was silent for a moment. Then he said, "Look, doll, I'm not trying to put words in your mouth or keep them out, for that matter, but don't mention the fact that you once lived in New York to Brody."

"But what if he asks me?" demanded Allison.

"Then hedge," said Paul, and put up a hand to stop the words that came to her lips. "Look, you're a clever kid. You've written a novel that has not only been published but is going to be a best seller. You're smart enough with words when you want to be, and I want you to be extra, super smart with Brody. Don't tell him about living in New York. And another thing. During the war Brody got the Pulitzer for news coverage in Italy. You might remember to mention that. It's his pride and joy and not many people remember it."

"How did you happen to remember?" asked Allison.

"Trade secret," smiled Paul, "but I'll tell you. Ever since I set this interview up, I've been reading stories by and about Jim Brody. I've studied everything about him so carefully that I bet I could tell you what color pajamas he wears to bed."

Jim Brody was a big, hearty-looking man who looked as if he enjoyed food and good jokes. When he walked into Kelly's, practically everybody there waved and called out a greeting to him. A waiter removed a "Reserved" sign from a back table and another waiter put down a huge glass of beer before Brody had even had time to take his coat off.

"Here we go, honey," whispered Paul Morris. "Smile."

"I can't," Allison whispered back. "I'm too scared."

"Yes, you can and no, you're not," said Paul and led her to Jim Brody's table.

"Hi," said Brody, barely glancing at Allison as Paul introduced her. "Sit down."

Allison sat next to Paul Morris. He fools you, she thought, looking at Brody. He's so big and friendly looking, like a Saint Bernard, except for his eyes. His eyes are cold and they see everything.

"Want a beer?" Brody asked.

"I'll have one," said Paul. "Miss MacKenzie doesn't drink."

How can he lie like that and still smile? wondered Allison, shocked, as she remembered the dry martini she had just had at the bar.

"How old are you?" asked Brody.

Before Allison could answer, Paul took a slip of paper from an inside pocket of his suit coat.

"I wrote down all the biographical stuff, Jim," he said. "Thought it might save time."

Brody took the paper and studied it. "Nineteen, hm-m?" he asked, glancing up at Allison.

For a moment she was speechless. She was twenty-three years old and was just opening her mouth to say so when Brody spoke again.

"You look even younger than that," he said. "Been writing long?"

"Ever since high school," she said.

"Ever sell anything?"

"Just short stories. To the magazines."

"What kind of stories?"

"Oh, you know. Just silly, frothy things for a lot of empty-headed women."

Brody smiled. "Be careful how you talk about American women," he said. "A helluva lot of them read my column."

"Not the same ones who read my stories," said Allison. "You write about real things and real people."

"And your stories weren't real?"

"I suppose they were, to the people who read them, but they never were to me. In my stories, all the heroines were blond and beautiful with green eyes and fabulous figures, and all the men were tall, dark and handsome with square, cleft chins and tweed jackets."

Brody threw back his head and laughed, and under the table Paul Morris gave Allison's hand a gentle squeeze of congratulations.

"Well, you certainly don't have characters like that in your novel," Brody said. "I read it last night. Where'd a kid your age learn so much about smut?"

Allison was suddenly and thoroughly angry. "I'm very sorry that you think my book is smutty, Mr. Brody," she said. "I never intended it to be. All I tried to do was to be truthful and to give an accurate picture of small towns as I know them to be. The things that happen in *Samuel's Castle* happen everywhere, and I should think a man who's smart enough to get the Pulitzer would know that."

"Oh," said Brody, with a smile. "You know about the Pulitzer."

"Yes," Allison lied, praying that she was right. "I remember when you got it. Your picture was in all the papers."

Why, it isn't hard at all, she thought in surprise. I can lie every bit as well as Paul when I put my mind to it.

"You've a good memory," said Brody. "Most people remember the column I wrote yesterday and that's as far back as they go." A waiter put another glass of beer in front of him and Brody picked it up. "Tell me, Miss MacKenzie," he said, wiping a tiny mustache of foam from his top lip, "what are people in your home town going to say about your book?"

"They have already said it," said Allison. "Mr. Jackman, my publisher, sent advance copies to a few people in town and the word circulated very quickly."

"And what have they said?" asked Brody.

Allison's fists clenched and her eyes burned with remembered rage.

"They say that I should be run out of town," she said and her voice quivered. "They say that my mother should sell her house and that my father should lose his job and that we should all leave Peyton Place forever."

84

"And will you?" Brody asked. "Leave town, I mean."

"Never!" cried Allison. "I was born in Peyton Place and I'm going to live there just as long as it suits me."

Brody looked at her. "I was born in a small town in Indiana," he said. "When people in small towns get riled up they can make things pretty unpleasant for whoever got them mad."

"I know it," said Allison.

Brody drained his glass and another was waiting. "Well, to get back to my first question. I used the wrong word, so I'll rephrase. Where did a girl your age learn so much about sex and sneakiness and perversion?"

"If you come from a small town you don't have to ask me that, Mr. Brody," said Allison. "There are no secrets in a small town."

"Then what you're saying is that Peyton Place taught you everything you know."

"That most certainly is not what I said, Mr. Brody. I merely reminded you what small towns are like."

Brody smiled. "Cagey, aren't you?"

"Not unless you want to think of me that way," said Allison. "I was trying to be truthful."

They ordered lunch then, and Brody asked her casual questions about Peyton Place and the people who lived there.

"Must be quite a town," he said as he stood up to leave. "I'll have to go up there for a visit one of these days."

When he had gone, Paul Morris took Allison's hand and squeezed it hard.

"You did it, sweetheart!" he said.

Allison was tired and angry. "What was the idea of telling him that I'm nineteen years old?" she demanded. "I'm twenty-three, and you know it."

"Honey, that's publicity," said Paul Morris, "and nine-tenths of all publicity is nothing but pretty stories someone made up sitting in an office just like mine. Look. Do you really believe all the crap you read in movie magazines about the stars? Do you really think that our sexy sirens are in their early twenties, that they attend P.T.A. meetings and get up every morning to make breakfast for their kiddies?"

"I never thought much about it one way or the other," said Allison irritably.

85

"Well, start thinking, sweetheart," said Paul. "Publicity is used to create an illusion about a place, a thing or a person. An illusion that people will believe because they want to believe it. Publicity is a means of selling merchandise and the merchandise can be a hotel room in Miami, a box of soap powder, or a human being. We're going to sell you, Allison, because if we do it well enough we will, in turn, sell copies of your book."

Allison looked at him in horror. "I'm not something on a bargain counter!" she cried. "I'm a person. Me!"

Paul put a hand on her arm. "Honey, I know that and you know that, and everybody in the world knows that everybody else is a person. But what we are going to do with you is to make you into a very special person. One that millions of people will recognize. They'll know your name, your face and your book. In short, we are going to try to make you into a celebrity."

Allison said, "Now that I'm of age again, I'd like a drink, please."

"You can't have one right now. After today, people here are going to remember that you sat with Jim Brody and that you didn't drink with him. In fact, he'll probably put the fact that you don't drink in his column, so you can't turn around now and do anything to disturb the illusion."

"This is ridiculous," said Allison.

"Is it?" asked Paul. "Listen. We're going to sell you as a genius type. A sweet, untouched, young girl from the country who lived for years with a situation until she could not stand the sham and hypocrisy of it any longer and exploded into print with the truth. Now the public already has the idea that sweet, untouched girl geniuses don't drink, so whenever you are in a place where people might remember, you don't drink. It's as simple as that."

"The whole thing is nothing but outrageous lies!" said Allison.

"Not really," said Paul. "Don't things happen in Peyton Place the way they happen in your novel?"

"Of course they do," said Allison. "But I certainly never meant to imply—"

"Look, doll. You want your book to sell, don't you?"

"Yes, but I still don't see—"

Again he cut her off. "Leave it to me," he said. "And talk to everyone I introduce you to just the way you talked to Brody. Do what I tell you and together we'll make *Samuel's Castle* into the biggest thing that ever hit the book business." He glanced at his watch. "Come on," he said. "We're due over at C.B.S. in twenty minutes. You're going to be interviewed by Jane Dodge. Her show is on in the morning but she tapes all her interviews."

"I've heard her," said Allison. "She has the loveliest, deep voice."

"That's right," said Paul. "The voice of an angel and the soul of a true bitch. Come on. I hope we can get a cab."

"With Jane," said Paul, before they went into the studio, "don't belittle women's magazines, women's organizations or women's anything. She's a professional Woman and has made a big, profitable business out of it."

Jane Dodge wore a large hat, long black gloves and used an ebony cigarette holder. She was so sleek and had been made up with such precision that she looked to Allison like a manufactured article.

"For Christ's sake, Jake," Jane was yelling, as Paul led Allison over to her, "are you going to screw around all afternoon or do we get a show taped?"

"Almost ready, Jane," said the man named Jake.

She turned to meet Allison. "Oh, hello, sweetie," she said. "We'll be able to get going if that dumb bastard ever gets things organized."

Her sharp, quick eyes behind green, harlequin-glasses scanned the sheet of notes Paul Morris had handed her and she mumbled under her breath.

"Nineteen. Peyton Place. Only child. First book."

Allison stood watching her, her heart thumping.

"Ready, Jane."

Jane Dodge watched the nervous man named Jake and at a signal from him she began to speak in the deep, soft voice that Allison remembered.

"And now, ladies," she said into a microphone, "it gives me great pleasure to introduce all of you to a little girl I met several years ago in New England. Her name is Allison MacKenzie and she's only nineteen, but my little friend has managed to fool quite a few of us. She is the author of the sensational new best seller, *Samuel's Castle* and, girls, if you haven't had an opportunity to read this marvelous book yet, let the dishes go and run to your bookstore. Well. Good morning, Allison. How are you, dear?"

When it was over, Allison's knees were trembling and all she wanted to do was to get out of the hot, stuffy studio and into the fresh air.

"Paul, sweetie," Jane Dodge said. "Leave a copy of that book for me, will you?"

Paul took a copy of *Samuel's Castle* from his briefcase and put it on Jane's desk.

"Thanks a lot, Jane," he said. "It was a great interview."

Allison could not take her eyes off the book Paul had put down.

"Haven't you read it?" she asked Jane.

Jane looked at her in astonishment and then she began to laugh.

"Sweetie," she said, "with the rat race the way it is these days, I don't even have time to read Lenny Lyons any more."

When Allison and Paul were outside, she turned to him.

"I know men who work in the woods who don't have the vocabulary of that woman," she said. "And as for two-faced hypocrisy, Jane Dodge would make the women of Peyton Place look like children."

"Could be," said Paul cheerfully, "but thousands of women listen to her every morning. And when they listen tomorrow morning they'll hear you. And then they'll run out and buy *Samuel's Castle* because Jane told them to. Because anyone who's a friend of dear old Janie's is a friend of theirs."

What a dirty business this is, Allison thought wearily. And I am part of it now. I have given in to it without a struggle. I want my book to be read. I want it to be a best seller. And so I do these awful things. How easy it is to become a liar and a fraud when you are able to tell yourself you're doing it with the best intentions.

Paul hailed a taxi, but Allison said she wanted to walk. Paul's last words as he drove off were, "Allison, we are going to sell one hell of a lot of books."

Walking crosstown to meet David she felt a moment of fierce hatred for Paul. But it's not Paul, she told herself, he's only doing the job he was hired to do. And he's doing it damn well. It's me. I've become a huckster. I'm not doing the job I trained myself to do. I should be home with Mike and Constance writing my new novel.

But now it was not only the excitement of publication that kept her mind from her work, now there was also Lewis Jackman. For the first time since she met Paul at Kelly's did she think of Lewis, so caught up had she been in the hectic business of publicity. Now, walking the busy street in the bright spring weather, she remembered his voice and the touch of his hands. This is the thing that matters, she told herself, not a few lies to people who make a living out of lying. What's growing between Lewis and me, that is what matters.

As she walked toward the café where David waited for her she thought of him with a pang of guilt. But we don't choose an object for our love, she told herself. Love chooses us. Lovers can always find an excuse for the hurt they do to others, she thought. And the excuse is always love itself.

She met David at an Italian coffeehouse in the West Fifties, a dark place with guttering candles on marble-topped tables. The walls were covered with a dark red cloth that absorbed what little light there was. There were mirrors, speckled and yellowed with age, in which she saw her face, wavering and dark, as if seen through smoke. At the back, the only bright object in the place, stood a great, ornate, silver coffee machine. When the operator depressed one of its long handles, steam hissed through tightly locked coffee grounds and a delicious elixir, the very essence of coffee, dripped drop by drop from a silver faucet into a small cup.

David watched Allison as she entered and looked for him and walked toward his table. He thought she moved with a new assurance. He smiled to himself. Our little Allison is growing up, he thought. Allison dropped wearily into the chair across from David, and the waiter brought coffee and Allison recounted her day. She told David about Paul Morris, Brody and Jane Dodge.

David listened quietly, not interrupting once. Allison was too full of herself to notice how angry David had become and was startled when she finished speaking and heard David's voice tremble with anger as he said, "You're not in this business to sell books! You're supposed to be a writer, not some clown on a radio or television program. Not some idiot running off at the mouth to some fifth-rate lush of a reporter."

"You just shut up, David!" cried Allison, doubly angry because his words echoed her own thoughts. "Maybe you don't care what happens to your books, but I care what happens to mine. What's the good of writing anything if nobody reads what you write?"

"People discover good books for themselves," replied David. "And *Samuel's Castle* is a good book. People would have realized that in time without every paper in the country touting it as a work of pornography."

"It isn't pornography," cried Allison.

"*I* know it isn't," said David. "*You* know it. But what about people who read Jim Brody's column? They're not going to see any of the beautiful things in your work. They're going to buy and read it for your graphic sex descriptions."

"Mind your own damned business," said Allison.

David stood up. He took a newspaper clipping from his pocket and threw it on the table. "Get the news while it's still hot, Allison. Your interview with Brody is in the late afternoon edition. He lost no time. And neither have you. You've got what you wanted, Allison—success with a capital S. It will be interesting to see what you do with it, or what *it* does to you." He smiled bitterly. "We don't seem to have much to say to each other any more, do we?" Then he walked out. Allison sat for a moment without moving; then, she read Brody's column.

"If you want your young girl to learn the facts of life the hard way," Brody had written, "make sure that she's brought up in a town like Peyton Place. That's what happened to the young authoress of a sensational new best seller called *Samuel's Castle*. Here is a book that pulls no punches." The column ended with, "And what of Allison MacKenzie, the youngster who kicked over the rock of New England respectability to expose the rot underneath? She says, quite cheerfully, that business at her mother's dress shop has fallen off by 50 percent and that her father, the principal of the Peyton Place High School, will probably lose his job. But we don't think that Miss MacKenzie has much to worry about. *Samuel's Castle* should make her rich and famous."

For a moment she felt sick and angry, infuriated by Brody's betrayal. Then she slowly crumbled the newspaper clipping and pressed it into a small hard ball. If that's the way the game is played, she thought, then that's the way I'll play it.

4

In the first five days of Allison's stay in New York she gave nine interviews to members of the press and to people in radio. She was interviewed twice on television. Before it was over she had become a polished performer, had learned to parry and thrust with the best of them, to think twice before she spoke and to phrase her answers with such care that even the most unethical reporter had a hard time misinterpreting her statements.

On what turned out to be her last night in New York, she dined with Lewis Jackman at a fabulous new restaurant that was then all the rage. It was one of the postwar "expense account" restaurants; real money was never spent there, only company money. The menu was so long that only people of leisure had the time to read it all, and only professional gourmets understood what they read. Waiters stood by to translate as well as to serve.

The headwaiter led Allison and Lewis to one of the "good" tables reserved for celebrities. These tables surrounded a white marble fountain where sprays of water bloomed like an exotic tree.

The headwaiter bowed to Allison as he drew out her chair. "We are very happy to have you here, Miss MacKenzie," he said, and Allison gave him the gracious, noncommittal smile that success had taught her to use.

"I'm very proud of you, Allison," Lewis said. "Only a few weeks ago you were a writer, and today you're an author." His loving smile took the sting out of the words, but Allison understood what he meant and smiled ruefully.

Was it only five days ago? she thought, with wonder. She remembered her outraged innocence at discovering that Jane Dodge had not read her novel. Of all those who had interviewed her since, only one reporter claimed to have read it; and there was one who said he had "perused" it. But they all, each and every one, wrote knowledgeably about it.

Her thoughts were interrupted by the presence at the table of a burly businessman who stood beside Allison's chair and asked for her autograph on the menu. He offered her his small gold pencil. "It's for my wife," he said. Men who asked for her autograph always smiled apologetically and said it was for their wives. Allison wrote her name across the wide margin of the menu and returned it to the man with a smile.

How meaningless, she thought, how goddamned silly this all is. And yet, it had a strong appeal. Only a saint or a psychopath, she thought, would willingly withdraw from the world of the celebrated to an ivory tower. It was something Allison had wanted for a long time, had dreamed of since she was a girl and had traded Hollywood fan magazines with Selena. She had made up her mind: if there was a price to be paid for all this then she would pay it. But she would not take David's way, would not sneak out the back door. She was young, but not so young that she still believed that art could be found only in a cold-water flat.

"Shall I order for you, Allison?" Lewis asked.

"Please," she said.

And while the waiter hovered with pencil poised above the order pad, and the steward came and consulted with Lewis over the wine list, Allison recalled that day when she walked crosstown and met David at the coffeehouse. She had thought about it often. Success, the knowledge that almost everywhere she was stared at, made her suspicious of herself and her every action. Am I doing this because I *want* to? she often asked herself these days, or am I doing it because Success demands it?

She wondered if she had not provoked the argument with David, whether she had not entered the coffeehouse unconsciously wishing to end their relationship. David was a reminder of her old life, of the days before she became an author and was merely a writer, struggling to achieve something. She had outgrown him.

Allison sometimes found herself thinking—in those rare moments when her new life left her any time for thinking—that Success brought with it a fantastically hastened maturation. It reminded her of those flowers whose bloom had been forced to meet the demand of the market. The maturity may have been artificially induced, but it seemed to her, nevertheless, real. It brought with it a heightened sensitivity, a deeper and sharper perception.

This new insight sometimes revealed to her things she would rather not have seen. About David, for example. His anger in the coffeehouse, she realized now, was motivated in part by envy. He was envious of her success, what must have seemed to him an easy success. He had been working for years, had published four novels, and it had brought him none of the material rewards that he now saw pouring into Allison's lap. It had made him bitter and nasty at the moment she must needed his understanding.

To Allison, it was another lesson in the complexity of life. David's sudden realization of his lack of success, a realization forced on him by knowing Allison, had changed him, just as surely as winning success had changed Allison.

There ought to be some way of ordering success, Allison thought as the waiter served her hot cherry consommé from a silver bowl. In just the right amount. In the perfect quantity for each of us, not too much and not too little. But she knew it could not be ordered that way. Life would not be controlled, it could not be molded into the shapes we wanted it to be.

After the third autograph hunter had interrupted her dinner, Allison said to Lewis, "I feel like such a fraud. I know it's only me, little Allison MacKenzie. Why doesn't everyone else see that?"

"They are blinded to that simple fact, darling, by another simple fact: they do not know you. When they look at you they see the public woman, the figure created by Paul Morris and columnists and interviewers."

He took her hand. He did not do it often; in public he was usually circumspect, he kept up the pretense of the publisher-author relationship. "Nothing very bad can happen to you, Allison, as long as *you* don't forget who you really are."

"I'll never forget," Allison answered.

"No, I don't think you will. I think your practical New England common sense will protect you. I'm not worried about you, Allison. And you mustn't be either. Please try to enjoy this while it lasts. You know, one of the facts you haven't faced up to is that it may not last forever."

"While it lasts." She repeated the phrase. It had the sound of tumbrils in it. It chastened her. "I love you for many reasons, Lewis," she said, "and not least of all for your wonderful talent for throwing a bucket of cold water on me at just the right moment."

"And I love you. And this wine and"—pointing at Allison—"that face makes me want to leave this place. I want to be alone with you."

Allison picked up her purse. "Tell the driver to hurry," she said, smiling at Lewis and not taking her eyes off him.

In a few minutes they were in a taxi and Lewis was saying to the driver, "Hurry, man. We're on our way to visit a sick friend."

"There's a lot of it around, Mac," the driver said. "Spring is the most dangerous time of year. You gotta watch yourself."

Allison had a hard time suppressing her laughter. She buried her face in Lewis' shoulder. He kissed the top of her head and gently stroked her face and throat.

And when they got to Allison's room, though they had been together every night, they faced each other with passionate longing, with a hungry intensity, and only half undressed they began to seek each other.

Afterward, they smoked in the darkness and talked until dawn. Allison told him that she was going to take an apartment in New York. "I want to be near you, Lewis. I want to be there when you need me. Marriage isn't important to me."

Not now it isn't, Lewis thought, but it will be, it will be. He knew the terrible odds against them, but loving her, desiring her, he fell in with her plans and said nothing of his misgivings. It's just that I've lived so long and seen so much more than she has, he told himself.

And Allison lay in the curve of his protecting arm and asked herself, Have I chosen this because marriage now would interfere with my plans? Is it possible that I don't want to share what I've achieved with anyone? And when finally she fell asleep she groaned in anguish, tormented by her dreams.

When she woke at noon Lewis was gone. He had left a note on the desk. *Darling. Only you beside me when I woke this morning could have convinced me that all this was not the most beautiful dream of my life.*

Allison smiled and folded the note. She ordered breakfast sent up to her room and had the operator put in a call to Peyton Place. She wanted to tell Mike and Constance that she was going to stay in New York.

She was sipping her orange juice when the phone rang. It was Constance. Allison's voice was jubilant when she said, "Isn't it wonderful,

Mother? *Samuel's Castle* has been out just twelve days and it's already on the best-seller list in the *Times* and *Tribune!*"

"I'm so glad for you, darling," Constance said.

"Mother? What is it? There's something wrong, Mother, I can tell by your voice."

"Oh, darling," Constance's voice broke down. "Oh, darling. Mike's contract hasn't been renewed."

"*What?*"

"That's right. Everybody else at the school got a contract for the coming year except Mike. He's through here."

"But why?" demanded Allison. "Did they give him a reason?"

"They just said they thought it would be better all the way around if he got a job some place else."

"Well, of all the filthy, rotten tricks!" said Allison.

"Never mind, dear," said Constance. "Just come home as soon as you can. We've got to think about moving."

Allison packed her things hurriedly and before she left the hotel she called Paul Morris.

"Do you know what's happened with all your rotten publicity?" she demanded. "My father's lost his job!"

"What?" shouted Paul.

"He's been fired. Canned. Let go. Is that clear enough?"

"Allison, stay right where you are. I'll be right there."

"Don't bother. I'm leaving here this minute to go home."

"Allison, for God's sake, tell me what happened?"

"There's nothing to tell," said Allison and began to cry. "He's just through in Peyton Place, that's all. We'll have to move and my mother will have to sell her house."

"Allison, I'm truly sorry," said Paul. "I guess you'd better go home. I'll call you in a few days."

Then she phoned Lewis at his office, but he was out and she could only leave an impersonal message for him with his secretary.

As Paul Morris said later, Rossi being fired couldn't have happened at a better time. The papers were hard up for news that night and welcomed his story. Before Allison reached home the front pages of the Boston papers were covered with black headlines about her and her family.

PEYTON PLACE HEAD OUSTED the papers shouted, and under the headlines was the story. According to the press, Michael Rossi had been fired because his stepdaughter, Allison MacKenzie, had written a shocking book about a small New England town. Paul Morris had seen to it that the title of the book was prominently displayed. Allison held the newspapers crushed in her lap as the train swayed toward Peyton Place.

Dear God, what have I done, she wept silently.

5

NOW IT WAS MAY, and the process of turning northern New England into a vast summer boardinghouse had begun. Along the "Rocky Coast" of Maine, in the "Heart of the Lakes Region" and "High in the White Mountains" of New Hampshire and "Among the Rolling Hills" of Vermont, summer cottages were given thin coats of paint that would begin to peel and blister by the end of July. Hotel owners unnailed boards from windows and wondered if the front-porch chairs could stand one more season of almost uninterrupted rocking.

Every town that boasted an attraction of any sort was flooded with signs that read, "Rooms. Day. Week. Season," while the more exclusive hotels placed discreet advertisements in the New York *Times* that said "Reservations Suggested." Golf courses were rolled and mowed, tennis courts repaved, swimming pools cleaned and filled and cretonne slip covers returned to the seats of wicker furniture.

Highway departments hired extra men to pick up the discarded waxed paper and beer bottles of summer picnickers, and merchandise in native-owned stores was marked up 20 per cent. Northern New England was preparing itself to work at the only big industry it had left—the tourist.

In Peyton Place, Ephraim Tuttle made sure that the circular ceiling fans in his store were in working order and he put up the awning that shielded his front window. To the accompaniment of derisive remarks from Clayton Frazier and the other old men who had occupied the packing-crate seats around his stove all winter long, Ephraim removed his bolts of gingham and calico from their plastic coverings and lined them up in a row on the front counter.

"Gives the place a tone," he said defensively as he did every spring. "Summer folks like tone."

"Goddamned foolishness," said Clayton Frazier.

"Ayeh," said Ephraim in agreement.

But, nevertheless, he began to dismantle his wood and coal burning stove that same afternoon, and the old men moved to the benches in front of the courthouse across the street. The "Season" had officially begun in Peyton Place.

Peyton Place was not a tourist town in the true sense of the word, for it had no lake, ocean front or mountain of its own. But summer people driving west to Vermont, east to the White Mountains or north to Canada usually detoured to Peyton Place in what they called a "side trip." The more morbid of the visitors nudged one another and remembered that "this is the town where that girl murdered her father." They drove with maddening slowness past the Cross house and said, "Her stepfather, and she buried him in a sheep pen right there behind that house." But this year they came to stand and stare at Samuel Peyton's castle.

"That's the place that girl wrote the book about," they all said.

"Have you read it?"

"Of course. I loved it. So true to life."

"I hear that the natives in Peyton Place are in an uproar over the book."

"I know it. The poor girl's father lost his job over it. Well, it just goes to prove what I've always said. New England is a fine place to visit but I wouldn't want to live here."

"The narrowness is something fantastic, isn't it?"

"If I were Allison MacKenzie, I'd be worried for my life. No kidding. Some of the faces on the natives have an absolute look of stone."

"And she seems to be such a darling. I saw her on television and she's so sweet looking."

"I put a copy of *Samuel's Castle* in the glove compartment when I knew we were coming up this way. I'll bet if we found her house and went there that she'd autograph it for us."

"Let's ask somebody."

"One of those old men sitting over there."

The pale blue convertible drew to a stop at the curb in front of the courthouse and, without seeming to do so, the old men on the benches stared intently at the two women who got out of the car and approached them. The women wore identical white shorts and striped jersey shirts and their toenails were painted with red, chipping polish. Their shoes were sandals made entirely of thin straps with heels that clacked against the pavement and their noses were red with yesterday's sunburn. They wore harlequin-shaped sunglasses in red frames and carried oversized handbags. They stopped in front of Clarence Mitchell, who occupied the end seat on the bench nearest to them.

Through half-closed eyes, Clarence had watched the car with the out-of-state plates draw to a halt. As soon as it had, he had taken a pocket knife and a piece of wood from a trouser pocket and begun to whittle.

"There's a pair of beauties for ya," he said to his neighbor.

"Fifty if they're a day and got themselves rigged up to look sixteen."

"Reckon they're wearin' iron brazeers under them shirts?" asked Clarence speculatively.

"Must be. Their tits'd hang down to their belly button if they didn't."

"Pardon me," said the first woman to Clarence, "my name is Mrs. James Delafield and this is Mrs. William Cameron." She paused, but when Clarence kept right on with his whittling she went on. "We want to find the house where Allison MacKenzie lives. Could you please direct us?"

Clarence glanced up. "Who?" he asked.

"Allison MacKenzie," repeated Mrs. James Delafield.

Clarence assumed a puzzled air. "Never heard of no MacKenzies around here," he said. "You, John?"

John Barton pushed his hat up over his eyes and looked at the woman.

"Nope," he said. "Nobody around here named that, that I know of."

"But you *must* know her," protested Mrs. William Cameron. "She's very famous. She wrote a best seller."

"Best-selling what?" asked Clarence.

"Why, a *book*," said Mrs. James Delafield. "A best-selling book. Everybody's talking about it. *Samuel's Castle.*"

"Don't get much time for readin', myself," said Clarence and went back to his whittling.

The women stood by indecisively for another moment, and then Clayton Frazier, who had remained silent until now, spoke up.

98

"Why don't you try the telephone book," he said. "Seems as though if there's anybody named MacKenzie livin' here they'd be in the telephone book."

The faces of the two women cleared. "Why, yes!" said Mrs. James Delafield. "Now why didn't we think of that, Elaine?"

Mrs. William Cameron smiled at Clayton Frazier. "Why, of course," she said. "Thank you. Thank you very much."

An almost inaudible chuckle traveled the length of the benches as the two women went into the courthouse and then back to the car. There was no MacKenzie listed in the Peyton Place telephone directory. Disappointed, the two women drove away.

"Well, at least they wasn't from the newspapers," said Clarence. "Always askin' questions and wantin' to take your picture. That's somethin' in their favor."

"Yep. Twice in one lifetime is twice too many for anybody. Or any town, for that matter."

"Yep. They was worse this last time, though, than they was about Lucas Cross."

"Yep. But this time it didn't last so long."

"You got no call to say anythin', Clayton. The way you was so friendly with that newspaper feller from Boston the first time."

"Friendly with him this time, too," said Clayton. "Nice feller, Tom Delaney. Always was."

"You'd fit in good down to New Yawk or some place like that, Clayton. Always gettin' your picture in the paper."

"That," said Clayton smugly, as he put his hat back down over his eyes, "is because I am a quaint but typical New England type with a face hewn of the granite of my native land. Said so, right in the *Daily Record*."

The men laughed again and settled back to rest in the sun and watch the traffic on Elm Street.

The tumult and the shouting engendered by the publication of *Samuel's Castle* and the careful fostering of publicity by Paul Morris was short-lived but decisive. Within seven weeks of publication, Allison's novel had reached the number-one spot on best-seller lists all over the country, and at the end of the second week in June, Bradley Holmes telephoned the biggest news of all.

"Allison?"

99

"Yes, Brad."

"I've sold it to Hollywood!"

Allison sat down abruptly. "Hollywood?" she cried. "But, Brad, that's marvelous! I can't see how they'll ever make a movie from it, but it's still marvelous."

"Aren't you going to ask me what I got for it?" asked Brad.

"Oh," said Allison, with a quick laugh, "I forgot!"

"Two hundred thousand dollars," said Brad with the same reverence he would have used for "In the name of the Father, the Son and the Holy Ghost."

Allison gasped. "Brad, for Heaven's sake. I can't believe it!"

"It's true, though Jackman gets 10 per cent and I get 10 per cent. That leaves you with one hundred and sixty thousand dollars."

"It's unbelievable. It's almost indecent."

"Never mind, darling," said Brad. "After taxes the only thing that will seem indecent is the government. Can you come down to New York on Friday to sign the movie contract?"

"I suppose so, if I must."

"How are things in Peyton Place?"

"The same. People still aren't speaking to me, for the most part and Mike hasn't a job."

"Is your family planning to move?"

"No. They feel the same about things as I. Mike is trying to get a job in one of the towns around here but, so far, nobody'll have him."

"Don't be sad, Allison," said Brad. "We *are* selling books."

"I know," said Allison, and knew before she had hung up that if she had asked Brad, At what price? he would have given her the practical answer.

"At three ninety-five a copy," he would have said.

Allison sat down wearily at her desk where a stack of mail waited. In the beginning it had been exciting to receive fan letters. Where one word of praise for *Samuel's Castle* was enough to make her happy, Allison now opened letter after letter containing nothing but admiration for her work. From all over the United States people wrote to praise her talent and the courage she had shown in exposing ingrown small towns for what they are.

But there were unfavorable letters, too, many of them anonymous, telling Allison that her work was trash and filth not even fit for burning. Men wrote her notes filled with obscenities while others proposed marriage and a few offered to come to Peyton Place to "take her away from all that." Allison and Constance separated the letters into what they called "good" and "bad" stacks, and in the evening Mike read all the bad ones aloud, acting out the part of the writer with such hamminess that Allison and Constance were reduced to helpless laughter.

But although Allison laughed, the unfavorable letters were like the cavity in a tooth to which her mind, like a probing tongue, returned again and again. At times, she was depressed to the point of tears and overwhelmed with the idea that the world was made up entirely of women who had read *Samuel's Castle* and hated her. Constance's rage was like that of a tigress whose young was threatened.

"Of all the goddamned nerve!" Constance shouted. "Some rotten-minded bitch whose husband is probably sleeping with the village whore has the nerve to write like this to Allison!"

"Allison," said Mike calmly, "women who write letters like this are sick. Sick with envy and greed and jealousy. Don't cry. It may sound trite, but try to be a little sorry for her."

"But why does she hate me?" wailed Allison, sounding for all the world like a grade-school child who hasn't been invited to a party. "What did I ever do to her?"

"You wrote a good book and got paid for it and became famous," said Mike flatly. "And this is the way the world turns."

Allison had been back in Peyton Place for over a month, sharing with Mike and Constance their involuntary exile. She spent restless nights prowling about the house, unable to sleep, unable to read. Invariably, dawn found her at the kitchen table writing long letters to Lewis. Her body ached for him; in loneliness, her love for him grew. She lived for his letters, and they came nearly every day, full of a gentle, enveloping love.

Both Mike and Constance told her to leave, assured her there was no reason for her to stay. But she could not leave them. She had brought this trouble upon them and she knew that her staying with them was an act of devotion they needed so badly now.

She had not told them about Lewis. That was a secret she shared with no one. She held it close to herself with a superstitious fear, as if she were afraid that spoken aloud it would disappear into thin air.

6

PEYTON PLACE HAD BECOME a solidly divided camp. People were either for or against Allison MacKenzie, and there was no middle ground. The majority was almost frighteningly against her. People who had done things far worse than those described in *Samuel's Castle* were the first ones to stand up and attack Allison.

"How does she know about all them dirty things in the book unless she done them herself?"

"She never saw or heard anything like that in Peyton Place!"

"I always thought that Rossi feller was too good lookin' and slick for his own good."

"You wouldn't think Constance would stand for such goings on."

"Always was uppity, Allison was. And a liar."

"The whole kit and kaboodle of them oughta be made to leave town."

"Well, Rossi won't be teaching here any more, I'll guarantee you that," said Roberta Carter. "Marion Partridge and I took care of him."

And that much was true. Charles Partridge had been elected to the school board when Leslie Harrington had decided not to run again, but when it came to the question of Rossi and his contract to teach for the coming year, old Charlie had been no match for his wife and Roberta.

"He's not going to teach here, Charles," said Marion, "and that's the end of it. Roberta and I are voting against him and there is nothing you can do."

"This has always been a decent town," said Roberta, "with a decent high school. Allison MacKenzie did not learn filthy language at the Peyton Place High School, nor did she gain her knowledge of filth and perversion in this town. Young people learn things like that in the home."

Except Ted, thought Roberta with the sickening coldness in her stomach that was always there whenever she thought of Ted and his wife, Jennifer. He was always a good, decent boy until he married. He never learned anything else but decency and goodness in his home. It was Jennifer that had taught him all those bad things.

"You're absolutely right, Roberta," agreed Marion. "Believe me, I know people and I'm not often wrong. I always told Charles that Constance MacKenzie was no better than she should be. I'll never set foot in that store of hers again, I can tell you. It was bad enough when she hired Selena Cross, a confessed murderess, to work for her, but when she led her own flesh and blood into the paths of wickedness that was the bitter end."

"Oh, for Christ's sake," said Charles Partridge in disgust.

"Charles," said Marion icily, "there is no need to curse. You sound like a character out of that filthy book."

"I've been saying 'Oh, for Christ's sake' ever since I learned to talk," said Charles.

"Well," said Roberta, "I'd certainly never stand for that kind of talk from Harmon."

"I'll bet," said Charles in a rare burst of spirit. "You probably had all that kind of talk you could take from old Doc Quimby."

"Charles!" said Marion in a cold voice, "that's enough!"

"Don't feel badly, Marion," said Roberta. "Charles knows that it's wicked to speak badly of the dead."

"Oh, for Christ's sake," said Charles.

It as at that moment that Doc Swain entered the school board office and said, "As soon as the prayer meeting's over, I'd like to say a few words about the reappointment of Mike Rossi."

"You're too late," said Roberta.

"It's already been put to the vote," Marion told him. "The school board is now on record, as of this date, against the renewal of the contract of Mike Rossi."

Charles Partridge shrugged his shoulders, indicating to Matt that he had tried and failed.

"Now that I'm here," Matt said, "I think I'll say my piece anyway."

"If you have anything to say, you can say it at town meeting, Matt," Roberta told him.

Matt ignored her. "Mr. Chairman," he said, and Charles quickly said, "The chair recognizes Dr. Matt Swain."

Matt stood at the long board table, across from Roberta and Marion. "It seems we aren't content with pillorying Allison MacKenzie because she had the courage to hold up a mirror and make us look at ourselves, we have to attack her through her stepfather and punish an innocent man because *he* has the courage to stand by his child."

Doc Swain put his hands in his pockets, bent his body forward and looked down at the table. "It's a sad day for all of us," he said in a low voice. "We've come a long way from our early days in this land when our grandparents, those misguided fools, thought that courage was a virtue." He raised his voice. "I ask you this, ladies. I ask you this. Will we now reward cowardice? Since courage has become a punishable offense in your eyes, I propose we set up statues to the men who beat their wives and abandon their children."

Roberta stirred restlessly in her chair, her mouth drawn to a tight line. It was as if she thought that by keeping her mouth closed tight she would not be able to hear Matt's words.

"Years ago," Matt continued, "years ago I was afraid that Peyton Place was too much isolated from the world. Now I have the opposite fear. I'm afraid we have come all too close to the foolishness—and worse than foolishness—that's raging through our land today. Radio and television is a mixed blessing. It looks to me like we're trying to get into the act—and in the worst possible way."

Roberta cleared her throat, and Marion tried to catch Charles Partridge's eye, but Doc Swain would not wait for them.

"We've joined the rest of the country with a vengeance. We're setting back the clocks and imitating the witch hunters who are a shame on the pages of our history. We who prided ourselves above all else on our individualism are now demanding that everyone conform. Be like us, think like us—or into exile you go."

He turned to Charles and in a tired voice said, "I think that's about it, Charlie. The only hope I have left is that one day—and I trust it will be sooner rather than later—we'll look back on what we have done and have the decency to feel ashamed of ourselves. I thank you, ladies, for your kind indulgence."

And he turned and walked out of the room, leaving Roberta and Marion speechless.

"Do I hear a motion for adjournment?" Charles asked.

Marion and Roberta were not the only women in Peyton Place who stopped shopping at Constance's Thrifty Corner Apparel Shoppe. Dozens of women who had bought exclusively from her now made shopping expeditions to Concord and Manchester and they saw to it that their daughters did the same. Occasionally a husband, with all the furtiveness of an amateur about to hold up a bank, sneaked into the store to buy a pair of socks, but for the most part the men too kept away.

"It'll blow over," said Constance, determined to keep her shop open. "In a little while they'll have something else to stew about and they'll be back. To give me the newest gossip if nothing else."

Matthew Swain roared his outrage to anyone who would listen to him. Those who would not listen voluntarily had an arm gripped in the doctor's firm grasp and were forced to stand still while Matthew talked, and he pulled no punches in his words.

"What the hell are you looking so outraged for?" he demanded of several of his patients. "Maybe you can fool the town, but you can't fool me."

And then the doctor was liable to drag up some bit of scandal or gossip about the patient himself, and when the patient left Matt's office he was apt to keep his mouth shut about *Samuel's Castle* in the future.

Seth Buswell, as had always been his policy in the Peyton Place *Times,* took neither side. But he reprinted only favorable reviews of *Samuel's Castle* and only the favorable letters which came to him for doing so. He kept it up in the face of diminishing advertising and canceled subscriptions, and Allison would never have known of this if Norman Page had not told her.

"Fifteen people canceled yesterday," he told Allison. "I don't know how much longer he'll be able to keep going."

Allison went at once to Seth. "I appreciate everything you've done, Seth," she said, "but please don't hurt yourself like this any more. Print the bad reviews. Heaven knows there are plenty of them. And as for unfavorable letters, I can bring them down to you by the bushel basket."

Seth smiled at her. "Remember, Allison," he said, "what you said to me once, a long time ago, about men standing up to be counted?"

"Yes," she said, "I remember."

"Well, I'm standing up. Count me." He picked up his jacket. "Now that's enough of the long faces and the noble talk. Come on over to Hyde's. I'll buy you a cup of coffee."

"Thank you, Seth," said Allison very humbly.

"Chin up, Allison. Summer's coming. There'll be plenty of things happening then, and plenty for people to talk about."

"I hope so," said Allison, and took Seth's arm as they crossed Elm Street.

And as the weeks went by, flowing as gently as melting butter from spring into summer, Seth's words of prophecy began to turn into words of truth.

7

ON SUNDAY AFTERNOON, when he was six years old, Timothy Randlett did an impersonation of Al Jolson singing "Mammy." This one performance had been enough to convince not only his mother, Peg Randlett, but also the assorted aunts, uncles and cousins who were relaxing in the Randlett living room, passively digesting a heavy dinner, that Timothy was born to be an actor.

"I always knew he was different," said Peg Randlett to her husband Sam. "He was born with a gift."

Sam Randlett was one of six brothers and four sisters and he was the first one of his family to "Make Good." Sam was a foreman in a brewery in Newark, New Jersey, and he made what was described, in the idiom of his family, as a Good Week's Pay. But when Peg began to spend money in a fashion referred to by her sisters and brothers-in-law as Hand Over Fist for dancing and elocution lessons for Timothy, Sam rebelled.

"Money don't come that easy, Peg," he said. "I work plenty hard for my week's pay. Too hard for you to be throwing it away on foolishness."

"Sam, I should think you'd be ashamed of yourself. A man in your position denying his son the advantages."

"Suffering God! Is it an advantage to spend money so that you can dress the boy up in a velvet suit and make him show off in front of the family every Sunday? I don't mind telling you my sister Helene thinks there's something the matter with Tim. The way he's always off in a dream world some place and won't play with his cousins like all the other kids."

"Helene has no soul," said Peg. "She's got those three stupid children of hers and a husband that'll never amount to anything and she's just jealous of you and Tim."

"Peg, that's enough!" roared Sam. "She's my sister and she's a good woman."

"Then tell her to keep her nose out of our business," retorted Peg. "If she's so good, she'll do that much."

"I won't stand for any more," said Sam. "You're turning the boy into a sissy and a pantywaist."

"Timmy is going to be a great actor when he grows up," said Peg, "and neither you nor any of your brothers and sisters are going to stand in his way. You wait and see, Sam Randlett. Someday you'll be sorry."

By the time Tim was nine years old, Peg Randlett's plans had been a long time made. One day, after Sam had left for the brewery, she hauled her suitcases and her son into a waiting taxicab, made a stop at the bank where she withdrew all the money from a joint savings account she had shared with Sam, and she and Tim boarded a train for Hollywood, California.

Timmy Randlett had a mop of blue-black curly hair, enormous blue-green eyes and the pallor and mien of a choirboy. Although he was of only average intelligence, he had a remarkable amount of poise for a child his age and he had learned early in life to take orders and direction. Besides, as one Hollywood producer put it, Timmy could cry good. One of the major Hollywood studios cast him in a picture as a woebegone orphan who is taken in, befriended, taught and loved by an aging, crusty sea captain, only to have the welfare society step in and attempt to remove the child from this unconventional, unsanitary environment. But the social worker that the welfare society sends to investigate is young and pretty, and the sailor who helps the old sea captain around the lighthouse is young and handsome, and together the two of them unearth the fact that the sea captain is, in reality, the father of the orphan child's mother who ran away from home at the age of sixteen to marry a carnival barker. The smash ending of the film showed the orphan child sitting in the lap of the man he now knew to be his Grampy, with his little, thin arms encircling the social worker and the sailor, tears of gratitude running down his pale cheeks. The picture was called *The Littlest Sea Captain* and it made Timmy Randlett a star who shone brightly in the Hollywood firmament until he was fifteen years old. Then he was a has-been, with stringy legs, a hollow chest and pimples.

Peg returned to the East with her son. She took an apartment in New York and saw to it that Timmy finished his education. But it wasn't easy. Twenty-room mansions with swimming pools and fifteen servants are expensive in Hollywood, to say nothing of chauffeured limousines and furs and jewelry and handmade suits. By the time Timmy, who was now called Tim, was sixteen years old there was very little money left. Producers and directors who had wooed Peg Randlett with money and attention and offers during Tim's short career now refused even to speak to her on the telephone, and people nagged her about things like the rent, the gas bill and the unpaid balances on her checking accounts. She died when Tim was nineteen, hating her son for giving her everything and then, when she had just begun to get used to it, snatching it all away with his awkwardness and his acne. Peg Randlett should have clung to life with a little more determination for by the time he was twenty, Tim Randlett had begun the long, laborious trip known as the comeback.

During the next fifteen years, Tim Randlett worked hard at every acting job he could get. He acted in soap operas and played VooDoo the Magician in a radio serial. He took small parts in Broadway productions and slightly larger ones with road companies. With the advent of television he found himself almost constantly employed, but he left New York every summer just the same to act with various stock companies. In barns, tents and old theaters made of broken clapboards, in small-town auditoriums and small-city music halls, Tim Randlett was a star.

He was thirty-six years old the summer he signed with the Barrows Company to play stock at the Barn Theater at Silver Lake, eight miles north of Peyton Place. He had been at the lake only three days when Seth Buswell drove up and asked to interview him.

"I'm with the Peyton Place *Times*," Seth said. "We're not much of a paper, by big-city standards, but we get around. It'll be free advertising for your play, if nothing else."

Tim had just finished with a late afternoon swim and was standing on the beach, drying himself with a white towel. He was a shade over six feet tall with a slender, wedge-shaped body that appealed to women and was the envy of older, paunchier men. His blue-black hair was dusted with white at the sides of his head, but his deeply tanned face was youthful and unlined. Seth Buswell patted his wide belly and sighed.

"Sure," Tim was saying. "And I have heard of Peyton Place. I guess everyone has since *Samuel's Castle* came out. Do you know the girl who wrote it?"

"Known her since she was a baby," said Seth.

"Wonderful!" said Tim. "I'd love to meet her. Think you could fix it?"

"Might," said Seth. "Want to take a ride over to Peyton Place? We can talk on the way."

"Give me ten minutes to dress," said Tim.

Seth sat down on a tree stump and watched the actor run swiftly away from him, toward a building at the other end of the beach. Seth glanced at his watch and sighed again.

"Nothing like a man like that to make a man like me feel old, fat and foolish," he thought woefully.

Later, on the same afternoon, Selena Cross locked the front door of the Thrifty Corner behind her and crossed the street to Hyde's Diner for a solitary dinner. On this particular evening, Joey was attending a class party and would not return home until nine-thirty. Selena did not like to eat alone in the Cross house.

"Evenin', Selena," said Corey Hyde, as she sat down in a booth. "Joey out gallivantin'?"

"His class is having a clambake down at Meadow Pond," said Selena.

"Oh. Things pretty slow over at the Thrifty Corner, ain't they?"

"We're getting along," said Selena, a little edge of annoyance to her voice.

It had been a long, hot day, and in almost nine hours Selena had sold only one blouse, two pairs of socks and one pony-tail clip.

"Rotten shame, I say," said Corey. "All that fuss over one little book. Mess of foolishness, I call it."

"What's good for dinner, Mr. Hyde?" said Selena. "I'm starved."

"Pot roast," said Corey, a little put out at Selena's lack of sociability. "Is that all?"

"Nope. Got some pork chops, if you want, but they're no good. Mostly fat. Summer folks'll eat 'em, though. Got some fish chowder, too, but that's canned."

Selena sighed and lifted her heavy, dark hair away from her neck.

"Can you make me a salad?" she asked. "Something cold, with a lot of cucumbers in it."

"Sure," said Corey. "Put some crabmeat in it too, if you want. But that ain't no kind of meal for a girl's been workin' hard all day."

Selena let the remark about working hard pass. "I'll have the salad, Mr. Hyde," she said. "With crabmeat and a tall glass of iced tea." She opened a book and began to read.

"Humph," muttered Corey, heading for the kitchen. "Ain't like Selena to be so touchy."

And it wasn't. But lately, Selena herself had to admit that she was quite often what Corey called "touchy" and what she referred to as "cranky." At times, she was even short with Joey.

"You've got spring fever or something," said Joey.

"Spring fever in summer?" asked Selena.

"Don't split hairs," said Joey. "There's something ailing you, and I'm trying to find a polite term for it."

It took Selena a long time before she admitted to herself that she was bored. Not only with the shop and its slackened business, but with herself and her life. Boredom, with a little thread of fear running through and under it. Occasionally she went out to dinner with one of the salesmen who came to the Thrifty Corner, but the word had circulated quickly through their clubby circle. Selena Cross doesn't sleep around. So it was, for the most part, the older, more settled men who asked her out. She saw more of Peter Drake, the young attorney who had defended her at her trial, than she did of any other man. Peter took her dancing and sometimes to the theater, down in Boston. They ate dinner together frequently, either at restaurants at White River or at Selena's house, and most important of all to Selena, Peter and Joey got along well together. Every time Peter took her out, he asked her to marry him, and every time her answer was the same.

"I can't, Peter."

"You're not in love with anyone else, are you, Selena?"

"You know better than that."

"You're not still thinking about Ted Carter, are you?"

"I don't think anything about Ted any more. I don't even dislike him."

"Selena, I'm in love with you."

"I know," she said. "I'm sorry, Peter."

"It's not all that business about Lucas, is it? You're not afraid of me because I'm a man or anything like that?"

"Peter, will you please stop with the two-bit, street corner psychiatry? Lucas wasn't a man, he was an animal. I never thought of him as a man and what I remember of him certainly hasn't turned me into a couch case. Now will you please leave me alone?"

"Selena, what are you waiting for? What do you want?"

"I don't know, I tell you. I don't know what ails me."

"I love you, Selena. I'm not asking you to love me back all at once. Marry me. Maybe with time—"

"I can't, Peter. I wish I could, but I can't."

But all the same, there were times when Peter Drake was a comfort. She could rest her head on his shoulder and give him her troubles to carry for her. If I married him, he'd be good to me. And good to Joey. But at other times, when her boredom was like a prickly sweater, making her itch with impatience and annoyance, she thought, Peter is such a bore. All that love is like too much ice cream. He's tiresome and I wish he'd find himself a nice girl and settle down and leave me alone.

I'm a pig, she thought in self-flagellation. Peter is good and kind and I should either marry him or let him go.

But time went by, and Peter still courted her, and Selena kept on saying No.

Sometimes she would wake in the night, covered with perspiration and feeling the hard, hurtful beating of her heart.

"What's happening to me?" she asked silently, in panic. "Where am I going? Is this all there is to life?"

Often, she caught herself in an attitude of waiting, but she could not think of what it was she was waiting for, nor for whom, nor why.

"There you are," said Corey Hyde, putting a plate down in front of her. "Crabmeat salad. That enough mayonnaise for you?"

"That's fine, Mr. Hyde," said Selena. "Thank you."

"Eat it up," said Corey. "Make you feel better."

At the same moment that Selena dipped her fork into her salad, Seth Buswell stopped his car in front of Hyde's diner.

"Don't know about where you come from," he said to Tim Randlett, "but in Peyton Place it's suppertime. We can't go calling on Allison MacKenzie for another hour or so. Come on. I'll buy you a sandwich."

"Good," said Tim, smiling. "This will be my wild night on the town."

Selena Cross lifted her head when she heard the door to the diner open.

"Well, if this isn't luck!" said Seth. "Now we can eat with you, Selena."

Selena barely saw Seth at all. Her eyes stared into those of the man with him, and she could not look away. Usually, she noticed everything about a person she was seeing for the first time. Her glance took in every detail of coloring, structure and clothing, but with this stranger she saw nothing but eyes. They were a blue-green color, the kind to which Selena had always referred privately as "lucky eyes," for she had noticed the same coloring in photographs of handsome, talented people, the ones upon whom the gods had showered extra gifts, leaving the blue-green eyes behind as the only external sign of their generosity.

"Selena," Seth was saying, "this is Tim Randlett. Tim, Selena Cross."

It was as if Seth had pulled a lever, releasing her, so that she could move again, and speak.

"How do you do, Mr. Randlett?" she said. "Hello, Seth. Please sit down."

"Tim, here, is with the summer theater up at Silver Lake," said Seth. "He's an actor."

"Yes, I know," said Selena. "I've seen you in movies, Mr. Randlett."

Tim laughed. "You must have been a very little girl. That was a long time ago."

"Not so very," said Selena. "My friend, Allison MacKenzie, and I used to go to the movies every Saturday."

"And, speaking of Allison—" began Seth, glancing at his watch, "we'd better eat and—"

"Yes," interrupted Tim Randlett quickly. "If you have to see her, Mr. Buswell, I imagine you'd better run along." He turned to Selena. "May I have dinner with you?" he asked.

Selena closed her book, not remembering to mark her place, and looked up at him.

"Yes," she said. "Yes. I'd like that very much."

As Seth Buswell said to Matthew Swain later that night over a drink, "And that was when I knew that I was *de trop*, as they say."

"As who says?" demanded Matthew, through the beginnings of a small alcoholic glow.

"A bunch of fairies I went to college with," said Seth with Scotch-and-water dignity. "Not that I consorted with them, mind you, but I sometimes overheard their conversations."

"Seth," said Matthew Swain, "you are one of the few remaining members of a species commonly known as bullshit artists. If you ever got anywhere near a fairy, you'd run like hell the other way, worried pissless over your virtue."

"And you, sir, are a vile-tongued old man."

"Maybe vile-tongued and old, but I'd never be so goddamned dumb as to leave Selena with some actor I'd picked up. How do you know what kind of fellow he is?"

Seth swirled ice around in his glass. "Seemed like a decent enough sort," he said.

"What d'you mean by that? Decent enough sort."

"Well, you know. Polite and well spoken."

"On the outside," said Matthew Swain. "How do you know what he's like on the inside?"

"I wasn't with him long enough to know," said Seth, "and even if I had been, and he turned out to be a son-of-a-bitch, there wouldn't have been a thing I could have done. The two of them just looked at each other, and the air between them was enough to give anyone an electric shock."

"You're full of shit and talking like a teen-age poet," roared Matthew. "Things like that don't happen."

Seth Buswell finished his drink and poured himself another.

"Yes, they do, Matt," he said finally. "Yes, they do, I was there, and I saw it happen."

8

In Peyton Place, the black-tarred sidewalks softened in the summer sun and were scarred with U-shaped heel marks that would show forever. Green Meadow Pond was filled with screaming, splashing children, and all day long the cicadas hummed in the trees. But it was a good summer, with rain in proportion to sunlight, so that the northern countryside had an almost tropical lushness. There was a heavy, ripe greenness to everything that stunned the granite-spined farmers, who were too used to either drought or the puny growth caused by no sunshine at all.

"There's somethin' almost indecent about it," said Kenny Stearns aloud, snipping still another red rose from one of his heavily laden bushes. He looked at the thick green of his lawn and saw his apple tree with its burden of swelling fruit so heavy that the branches hung almost to the ground. "Yep," he said. "Almost indecent. Like a whore with big breasts and honey between her legs."

It was easy, that year, to blame the unheard-of, green summer for just about everything. At the Harrington Mills, workers shirked their jobs and gazed out the factory windows while Leslie screamed in impotent rage and blamed the weather. Young girls who had clung to their virginity with leechlike tenacity now surrendered, with little squeals of anguished joy, to the erect demands of their teen-aged lovers. They returned home with their behinds covered with poison ivy, their arms dotted with mosquito bites and their hair full of pine needles.

As Matthew Swain said to Seth Buswell, "If all the maidenheads lost in the woods this summer were laid end to end, they'd reach clear from here to the planet Saturn."

Fathers blamed mothers, mothers blamed boys, boys blamed girls, girls blamed themselves and everybody blamed the weather for everything except the behavior of Selena Cross. For Selena there was no excuse in the eyes of Peyton Place.

"Who is he?"

"Actor feller from over to Silver Lake."

"Come up here from down to New Yawk."

"Usta be in the movin' pitchers."

"Hmph. Think a girl like Selena'd know better. After all, it ain't as if she was born yesterday and didn't know no better."

"Ayeh. There's one girl learned whatcha call the facts of life early. And the hard way."

"Think she'd have a little shame, a girl like that. But no. There she goes, flauntin' herself right in front of the whole town."

For Selena Cross it was a summer of such unbearable sweetness that every moment was almost like pain. There was an ache in not being able to clutch every second that passed, to have to let the hours go, and finally the whole day.

"When I was young," said Selena, "I thought I knew all there was to know about love."

"And what do you know now, my darling?" asked Tim, stroking the soft inside of her arm. "I mean now that you're an old woman of twenty-five."

"I know that I didn't know a thing until now," she said, and turned to rest her forehead gently on his chin.

They were lying side by side on the beach at Silver Lake, talking softly, caressing each other.

"This is agony of the worst sort," said Tim, his lips brushing her ear. "To lie here next to you and be able to touch only small bits and pieces of you. Your ear, your hand, your ankle. It's a form of masochism."

As always, his voice reached deep inside of her, so that her whole body was flushed with excitement.

"Do I turn pink all over when you talk to me like that?" she asked.

"Not really," he teased. "Anyone looking at you would only think that you had a mild case of sunburn."

"I'm not sunburned."

"Selena. If you don't stand up and come with me at once, there's going to be a terrible scene right here on the beach because I'm going to start taking off your bathing suit in exactly three seconds."

Selena sat up. "Come on," she said and led the way to his car.

From the moment Selena had met Tim in Hyde's Diner, she had known the way it would be between them and she had wondered, too, how it would end, for in the beginning there had been no feeling of permanence for her in their relationship. The emotion between them was too ephemeral to be named, too delicate to be used as a rock on which to build.

"Let's walk," Tim had said to her that first night when they had finished dinner.

And she had gone with him at once. Outside, he had taken her hand in his and they had walked through town to Memorial Park.

"There are nights like this on islands in the South Seas," he said.

"Oh?" asked Selena. "Tell me about an island in the South Seas."

"The night is just like this," said Tim. "All black and heavy with stars. You can smell a hundred different flowers all at once and their perfume fills you with a longing and languor such as you've never known before. You lie on a white beach and the ocean is only a whisper at your feet, soft and tractable and not frightening at all. You could reach up and touch the moon if you wanted to and it would be as soft as yellow cotton in your hand."

"How lovely," said Selena softly. "I wish I could go there one day."

Tim looked down at her. "You're there now," he said. "Can't you smell it and feel it?"

"Is it really like this?"

"I imagine so."

"But don't you know?"

"I've never been there, but I'm sure it's just like this."

Selena sat up straight on the bench they shared.

"You mean you've never been there at all? You just made all that up about the flowers and the moon?"

Tim laughed. "Yes," he said. "I made it up."

Selena smiled at him in the dark. "You're just like Allison MacKenzie," she said. "She used to do the same thing to me when we were in school. She'd make up the most fantastic things and have me believing her, then she'd laugh and tell me she had made everything up."

"Then she is far more honest than I," said Tim. "Sometimes I make things up and they become so real that I believe them myself and I never do confess the truth."

They sat for a long time, hands loosely clasped, Selena's head resting easily on his shoulder. He told her about his work in New York and Hollywood and about the way things had been for him once and the way they would be again.

"There is only one bad thing about fame," he said. "Once you have had it you can never do without it again."

"Is that really the only bad thing about it?" asked Selena.

"You bet it is," said Tim. "And don't believe any of the nonsense you read that tells you differently. Don't take the movie queens seriously when they tell you how rough it is to be rich and well known and in demand. They all whine about lack of privacy, but leave them alone for five minutes and they're on the phone to their agents asking where everyone is."

"You too?" asked Selena.

"No," said Tim. "At least I'm honest about that."

"And is that all you're honest about?"

He turned her hand over in his and kissed her palm.

"No," he said. "I'm going to be honest about you."

It was after midnight when they walked to Selena's house.

"Come in and meet my brother Joey," said Selena.

"I'd love to meet your brother Joey," said Tim. "And your mother and father and anyone else who concerns you."

Selena felt her hand stiffen in his. "My mother and father are dead," she said. "There's only Joey. Just Joey and me."

Tim had felt the change in her. "I'm sorry," he said. "But I'd still like to meet Joey. And I have to call a cab."

"A cab?" asked Selena.

"Yes," said Tim. "I have to get back to Silver Lake somehow."

"But how did you get here?"

"With that newspaperman—what's-his-name?"

"Seth Buswell," said Selena. "And I have sad news for you. There are no taxicabs in Peyton Place. I thought you had your own car with you."

"No problem," said Tim, as they walked into Selena's living room. "I'll stay at a hotel."

"Not in Peyton Place," said Selena. "We don't believe in hotels here. They attract tourists."

"Hello," said Tim.

Joey Cross looked at Tim for a long moment. "Hello," he said at last.

"Joey," said Selena. "This is Tim Randlett."

"I know," said Joey.

"Do you?" asked Tim, laughing. "Has my minuscule fame spread so swiftly in Peyton Place?"

"Nope," replied Joey and found himself laughing along with Tim. "Heard you and Selena had met down at Hyde's at suppertime."

"And that," said Selena, going into the kitchen to make coffee, "is the story of Peyton Place. Joey, get some sheets and a blanket out of the linen closet. Tim is staying here for the night."

"Fine," said Joey. "Tomorrow the town will really have something to talk about."

Later, Selena lay still in bed. The house was so quiet that all she could hear was the sound of her own breathing and the beat of her own heart. She could not relax but lay stiffly, every nerve in her body tensely aware of Tim, asleep on the couch in the living room. A sharp resentment went through her.

How can he sleep? she wondered angrily, as annoyed with herself as she was with him.

But a few minutes later she heard a sound. Tim coughed, and then she heard the scrape of his cigarette lighter.

Selena smiled in the dark, and was at last able to sleep.

Within less than a week, Peyton Place talked of little other than Selena Cross and Tim Randlett. Tim was spending every spare minute away from the theater with her, and every day Connie Rossi went to the Thrifty Corner so that Selena could take time off.

"At least it's good for business," Connie told Mike. "People are coming into the store hoping to gossip about Selena."

"When are we going to meet him?" asked Mike.

"Friday," Connie replied. "They're coming to dinner."

"Good," said Allison, coming into the room. "He can tell me all about Hollywood."

"I wonder," said Mike, "which member of our genteel population elected himself to tell Tim Randlett all about Selena Cross."

"I don't know," replied Connie, "but you can bet somebody did."

And, of course, somebody had. It was the policy of the Barn Theater to take in a group of young people every year whom the management called apprentices. For a sizable fee, the apprentices were allowed to paint scenery, act as ushers, look after props and do every other job that was beneath the dignity of actors. One of these was a tall, leggy girl from White River named Helen Dowd, who had sighted Tim Randlett the moment he landed at Silver Lake and had decided to make him her own. When Tim began to make daily trips to Peyton Place, Helen lost no time in telling him, in explicit detail, about Selena.

"Her stepfather," she said. "And she murdered him in cold blood. He was in the Navy and he came home on leave and she killed him with a pair of fire tongs. Then she buried him in a sheep pen."

"Why?" asked Tim, lighting a cigarette and blowing a leisurely smoke ring.

"What do you mean, 'Why'?" asked Helen, enraged at Tim's lack of reaction.

"I mean, why did Selena kill her stepfather?"

"Oh. Well, it came out at the trial that it was incest. At least that's what they called it. But there are plenty of people around who don't believe it. Maybe Lucas Cross was a drunkard, but lots of people don't believe that he'd do anything like that to Selena."

"Anything like what?" asked Tim.

Helen blushed. "Well, you know. Like what I said. Incest."

"Do you believe it?"

Helen was angry. "I don't see that you've got any call to cross-examine me," she said. "After all, I just told you for your own good."

The next day Tim went to the public library at White River and looked at the back copies of the Boston newspapers that had carried the story of Selena's trial. When he had finished, he sat for a long time, smoking and staring at motes of dust caught in a sunbeam that slashed across the library floor. Without knowing that it was happening, Tim's personality and character were changing to meet the demands of the new situation which faced him now.

Sometimes, the personality of an actor is like a blank slate. When he is confronted with a new role, the slate is written upon and the actor becomes what he reads until the part has been played. Then the slate is wiped clean and is ready for still another role.

When Tim Randlett left the library at White River that afternoon he knew that he must go to Selena. He would not tell her what he knew directly, but he would, nevertheless, let her know that he knew. He would be gentle with her, yet masterful, and he would teach her not to be afraid and to trust in him. He would restore her faith in love and in men. As he drove toward Peyton Place, Tim was filled with an almost saintlike feeling of gentleness spiced with the emotion of a virile young man and topped with an overwhelming sense of outrage at the thought of Lucas Cross.

Selena watched him walk toward her and, without knowing what had happened, she knew that he was somehow subtly different.

"Hi," she said, and was annoyed with herself because her voice almost quivered.

"Hello, darling."

He drove away from Peyton Place without a word, and Selena turned to him.

"Where are we going?" she asked.

"My place," he said.

Immediately, her arms were covered with goose flesh and she quivered in the hot July sun.

Inside, Tim's cottage was cool and dim and quiet. From very far away, on the other side of the lake, came the faint shouts of the summer bathers and there was a smell of sunshine and water and pine. Selena turned from where she had been standing in front of the empty fireplace.

"Why did you bring me here?" she asked.

"Because I've never kissed you," said Tim. "And when I do I didn't want it to be in a parked car or in the back room of the Thrifty Corner or on a bench in the park." He walked toward her and stood in front of her without touching her. "I want it to be here where it's quiet and where no one will come barging in, and I think you do, too."

"I want to go home," said Selena in a frightened whisper.

Very gently, he put his hands on the sides of her face.

"Selena," he said. "Look at me." He looked long and deeply into the eyes she raised to him. "Who am I?" he asked. "What's my name?"

"You're Tim," she said, and the color of his eyes was like the ocean. "You're Tim Randlett."

"Yes," he said. "I'm Tim Randlett. I'm Tim and I love you." He put his arms around her then, but still he looked into her eyes. "I'm Tim," he said again. "I'm not Lucas Cross."

"Don't!" cried Selena, and tried to pull away from him.

But he held her tightly against him, and with one hand he rubbed the small of her back and then the nape of her neck.

"I'm not going to hurt you, darling," he said over and over. "Please don't be afraid of me. I love you, darling."

And at last Selena stopped trembling. "Tim," she said. "Tim."

"Yes, darling," he said softly. "Tim."

He kissed her softly with his lips together in dry, unhurried kisses, and all the while he stroked her as if she were a frightened kitten he was trying to calm. He undressed her slowly, almost lazily, and when he put her on the bed it was as if she were that same kitten, quieted now, but who might at any moment, jump up and run away in terror. He made her look at him but did not speak as his hands caressed her thighs and pressed gently against her abdomen. He watched her eyes grow dark and heavy and still he continued to stroke her, and when he kissed her the next time it was Selena who opened her lips, who probed against his teeth with her tongue. Only then did his fingertips seek her breasts, caressing and stroking until she responded to him.

"Open your eyes," he said. "Selena, open your eyes."

He loved her slowly and watched, exultant, as the wildness grew in her eyes, as her mouth opened to cry out. It was as if a dam had burst within her, as if she were fighting a tidal wave of feeling. Until, finally, she let go and gave in to the strength that claimed her, that took everything from her in one shuddering, screaming, ecstatic moment.

9

IT TOOK MIKE ROSSI a week to discover that he did not like Tim Randlett.

"I don't know why," he said in answer to Connie's question. "There's just something about him that rubs me the wrong way. He's like a chameleon."

"He's no such thing," said Connie. "He's a very nice boy and I, for one, am very happy for Selena."

"I agree," said Allison, smiling at Mike.

But, as Mike often said, Connie had an overworked sense of curiosity.

"What do you mean, 'chameleon'?" she demanded.

"He talks to everyone in a different way," said Mike, wishing he'd never brought up the subject. "His manner changes with everyone he meets just as if he were changing color."

"Mike's just jealous," said Connie to Allison. "He's jealous because Tim is young and handsome and sleeping with Selena."

"Mother!" cried Allison, flabbergasted. "How do you know he's doing any such thing?"

"What?" asked Connie, innocently studying her fingernails.

"You know damned well what," said Allison. "Come on. Tell."

Connie shrugged. "It's just a look a woman gets," she said. "And Selena's got it. That slept-with look."

"Honestly, Mother," said Allison.

"Well, it's true," said Connie defensively. "And not only slept with, but slept with damned well."

"All I care about," said Allison, "is Selena being happy. And if sleeping with Tim Randlett makes her happy, I'm all for it."

Mike stood up. "All this sleep talk has made me warm and uncomfortable," he said. "Anybody for a cold beer?"

"You know, Mike," Allison said, raising her voice so that he could hear her in the kitchen, "Peter Drake doesn't like Tim Randlett, either."

"Well, what would you expect?" asked Connie. "Did you think he'd be overjoyed at the appearance of a rival? Peter's been in love with Selena for years."

"He said that Tim's a big phony and I quote," said Allison.

"Maybe he's right," said Mike, coming back into the living room with three brimming glasses of beer. "Not that I'd go so far as calling Randlett a phony. I don't think he means to be phony, but I do think that he's been insincere for so long that he doesn't even realize he's that way."

"Sour grapes," said Connie, licking a little rim of white foam from her top lip.

"You've been in Peyton Place too long," laughed Allison. "You've become a native and now you distrust Tim because he makes a living at something as unorthodox as acting."

"And not only that," said Connie, "but you've become a gossip."

"Ayeh," said Mike in an exaggerated drawl.

But Mike Rossi was not the only one who was worried about Selena's relationship with Tim Randlett. Dr. Matthew Swain had met

Selena on Elm Street and, as he told Seth Buswell later, he almost didn't recognize her. It was as if a light had been turned on inside Selena. She glowed and her smile flashed continually.

"Hello, Matt," she said.

It was the first time in her life that she had called him anything but Doc.

"Well, hello, Selena," said Matt. "My goodness, you look radiant this morning. No need to ask how you are. It's obvious."

"I feel generous, too." Selena laughed. "Come on into Hyde's and I'll treat you to coffee."

Matthew Swain waited until Corey Hyde had served them before he spoke.

"Are you in love with him, Selena?" he asked.

"In love with whom?" she teased.

But Matt did not laugh with her. "With Tim Randlett," he said.

"Yes," she said. "Yes, I am, Matt."

"I thought that summertime actors moved around a lot more than Tim does," said the doctor, lighting his pipe.

"In the first place," said Selena, "Tim is not a 'summer-time actor.' He's a full-fledged, year-around actor. And, yes, actors usually do move around in the summer, but the theater at Silver Lake is conducting an experiment this year in repertory theater and Tim is even getting a chance to do some directing."

"I see," said Matt. "What's he going to be doing this fall?"

"Matt, I told you. Acting isn't a part-time thing with Tim. He'll be acting in the fall in New York."

Matthew Swain took a deep breath. "Are you going with him?" he asked.

Selena looked down into her coffee cup. "I don't know," she said. "He hasn't asked me."

"Will you go if he does ask?"

Selena raised her head and looked the doctor straight in the eyes. "Yes," she said. "And if he doesn't ask me, I'll ask him."

"What about Joey?"

"Joey stays with me, no matter where I go."

"And what does Joey say about all this?"

Selena laughed. "Stop being such a worry wart, Matt," she said. "Joey's crazy about Tim. They get along beautifully together."

"Have you told Peter Drake?" asked Matt.

For a moment, some of the glow left Selena's face.

"No," she said. "But I will."

"He'll take it hard," said Matt.

"Matt, I can't help it," said Selena a little impatiently. "I never meant to hurt Peter, but he's known for a long time that I'm not in love with him and never have been."

"Peter's in love with you," said the doctor.

"Matt, what are you trying to say?" demanded Selena. "For Heaven's sake, spit it out and get it over with."

He looked at her for a long moment. "We've known each other for a long time, Selena," he said at last. "I'm just trying to make sure that you're not going to get hurt. That's all I care about. After all, none of us knows anything about this Tim Randlett, so bear with an old man's concern for a minute."

Selena was suddenly in a raging anger. "No, you don't know anything about him," she cried. "He's not from Peyton Place so therefore he's suspect. Well, how come no one ever suspected a nice Peyton Place resident like Lucas? Tell me that."

"Selena," said Matt, putting out a restraining hand, "I never meant anything like that, I only wondered—"

"I know goddamn well what you were wondering," said Selena furiously. "You're wondering if I'm sleeping with him, aren't you? You and everybody else in Peyton Place. Well, yes I am, Matt. Every single chance I get and even that isn't often enough!"

"Selena," said the doctor calmly, "we've known each other too long. Don't try to shock me."

Selena wilted. "I'm sorry, Doc," she said, reverting to the name she had always used. "I love him. I can't help myself. If he doesn't ask me to marry him, I think I'll die."

Matthew Swain reached out and patted her arm.

"If he doesn't ask you, you send him along to me. It'll be because he's sick."

At the end of the first week in August so many things happened at once that, as Connie Rossi put it, she was hard put to remember which end was up. Mike was offered and accepted a position to teach history at the high school at White River. Allison was invited to go to Hollywood as a "technical adviser" for the making of the motion picture based on *Samuel's Castle,* and Betty Anderson came home. As Selena Cross said to Tim Randlett, "Thank heavens! When they're talking about someone else, they're giving us a rest."

So August passed in a series of heavy, heat-laden days, and the farmers looked with stunned eyes at the earth which seemed ready to explode with its load of fruitfulness. They began to harvest their second crops of hay while in sheds and barns all over northern New England women nailed apple crates together for the outsized crop to come. Potato plants wilted and died as the vegetables below the ground sucked life from them and grew fat with solid, white meat, and everywhere flower gardens struck the eye almost hurtfully with their overloads of bloom and color.

Those grown old resisted hope and promise with a suspicion older than outcroppings of granite.

"'Twon't last," they said. "There'll be the day of reckoning."

But the young stared at the magnificent summer as if each of them had received an overwhelming, unexpected gift. They forgot the summers of drought and the summers of wet cold, and after a while they ridiculously began to assume that all summers to come would be just like this one.

"Well, thank God we won't have to put the house up for sale," said Connie Rossi to her husband. "With White River only nine miles away, you can commute very nicely."

"Before anything," said Mike, "I'd better start reading a few books. It's been a long time since I thought of teaching history to a bunch of kids who don't give a damn about the War of 1812 and are bored glassy-eyed with the Declaration of Independence."

Connie and Allison made several all-day trips to Boston, choosing a new wardrobe for Allison to take to Hollywood, and all of Peyton Place buzzed with the news of Betty Anderson's return and waited to see what Leslie Harrington would do.

No one had the time nor the inclination to think about Selena Cross, and as the end of August drew near no one but Joey and Peter Drake noticed the change in her. The shine of happiness that had marked her and set her apart had faded and her figure grew almost gaunt with an unbecoming thinness. Her eyes were circled with dark shadows and even the electric darkness of her hair seemed faded and lifeless.

"For God's sake, Selena," said Peter Drake. "What's the matter with you? Are you ill?"

"No," she replied shortly. "It's nothing."

And Joey was frightened. He remembered the way Selena had looked all during the months Lucas' body had been decaying under the ground almost at her feet, and she looked the same way now.

"Please," said Joey. "Let's go see Doc Swain."

"It's nothing," Selena insisted. "It's just the heat."

But to Peter Drake, Joey confessed his suspicions.

"It must be Tim Randlett," he said. "He's doing something to her. Something awful, and she won't stop seeing him."

"It can't be Randlett," said Peter. "She claims she loves him."

"I don't care," said Joey, and his voice shook with anger at Tim and worry for Selena. "It must be something he's doing."

"He's asked her to marry him."

"I know it," replied Joey. "And she said yes, but now I don't want her to. In the beginning I thought he was all right. But not now."

Peter Drake closed his eyes for a moment, as if by doing so he could stop the pain that Selena's actions had cost him.

"There's nothing we can do, Joey. There's nothing to do but wait."

10

IT WAS RAINING HARD the way it will only in August, with plump, heavy drops that splattered out on the roads and sidewalks like silver pennies. Betty Anderson held her son, Roddy, tightly by the hand as the train pulled into Peyton Place. The conductor held a black umbrella which he opened when the train stopped and Betty stepped down onto the platform. The conductor reached up one arm to swing Roddy down, but Betty pushed his arm aside.

"I'll do it," she said, and then, as the conductor stepped back, she added more gently, "He doesn't like to be handled by strangers."

"Lots of 'em don't at that age," said the conductor cheerfully. "What is he? About five?"

"He'll be five years old next month," said Betty.

"I'm more than four and a half," said Roddy proudly. "I used to be four and a half, but now I'm more."

The conductor grinned. "Well, then," he said. "You must be strong enough to carry your mother's suitcases."

"No," said Roddy seriously. "I don't have to carry anything but Wendel."

"And is this Wendel?" the conductor asked, extending a hand toward the rather grubby giraffe that the child held.

"Yes," said Roddy. "That's Wendel, and he is very tired from his long trip. When my grandfather gets here, Wendel is going to ride in a car. He likes to ride in cars."

"And do you like to ride in your grandfather's car?" asked the conductor.

"I don't know," said Roddy.

"Come on, darling," said Betty. "It's damp out here. Let's go inside."

"Good-by," said Roddy.

The conductor waved as he boarded the train and Betty and Roddy started toward the station. She did not look back as the train pulled away, but she felt her back stiffen.

I should get right back on, she thought, and keep going, right the hell out of here. I never should have come in the first place. I must have a screw loose or something.

The station hadn't changed any, she noticed. It was still the same shabby structure it had been when she had left Peyton Place five years before.

A little older, she thought, looking at the buildings. A little more weathered and beat up, perhaps, but substantially the same. Like me, I guess.

Roddy was looking up at the high-ceilinged waiting room.

"Is this where my grandfather lives?" he asked.

"No," said Betty. "This is a railroad station where people buy their tickets so that they can ride on the train. Your grandfather lives in a house. A great, big, fine house. The biggest house on Chestnut Street."

"Are we going to sleep there?" asked Roddy, beginning to rub his eyes with the knuckles of one hand. "Wendel is tired."

"I don't know yet," said Betty, and she spoke with an effort, for she had just looked up and seen Leslie Harrington coming toward her. He had Charles Partridge with him.

He must be worried, thought Betty wryly, to bring his lawyer with him. The son-of-a-bitch.

It was Charles who said hello and extended his hand to Betty first. Leslie was staring at Roddy. I knew it, he thought. The boy was the image of his father.

It was true. Roddy had the same dark good looks, the same sturdy body that had been Rodney Harrington's.

"Hello, Betty," said Leslie at last. "Welcome home."

"This isn't home," said Roddy. "This is where we came to visit."

Leslie hesitated, and although he spoke to the child his eyes were on Betty.

"Well, maybe after you visit for a while, you'll like it here so much that you'll want to stay," he said.

Betty looked Leslie straight in the eye.

"Don't count on it, Leslie," she said.

"Are you my grandfather?" asked Roddy.

Leslie felt as if he had been struck a hard blow in the pit of his stomach.

Goddamn old fool, he chided himself. Getting all soggy at the sound of a word.

"Yes," he said, when he could speak. "I am your grandfather."

"Are we going to sleep in your great, big, fine house?" asked Roddy.

Leslie looked at Betty, who stood still and merely looked right back at him. "Yes," he said. "There is a very special room all ready for you at my house."

"Wendel is tired," said Roddy.

Wendel is a very fine-looking giraffe," said Leslie. "And you're right. He does look tired." He looked down at his grandson. "Come on," he said, extending his arms, "I'll carry you and Wendel both right out to my car and we'll hurry home and put him to bed."

"Don't," said Betty quickly, putting a hand on one of Leslie's arms. "Roddy doesn't like to be handled by people he doesn't know."

But Roddy went at once to his grandfather. "It's all right," he said. "Wendel wants to be carried."

"Of course he does," said Leslie as he swung the child up into his arms.

Betty followed Leslie out of the station, and it was only Charles Partridge who noticed the tightening around Betty's jaw.

Same old Betty, thought Charles; and then as he watched Leslie, he thought, And the same old Leslie. Getting exactly what he wants every time. But he'd better not try to put anything over on this girl. She may have let him get away with it once, but she's older and smarter now, and she's still got that stubborn streak.

"You drive, Charlie," said Leslie, as they got into the car. "I have to sit here and hold Wendel."

He'd better not try any tricks on me this time, thought Betty as she slammed the car door. I was dumb once, but I'm not any more. Five years in the city toughens you up real good.

The past few years had not been easy ones for Betty Anderson, but then, she hadn't expected them to be. In the beginning, when she finally knew that Rodney was not going to marry her and that all the money she was going to get from Leslie was two hundred and fifty dollars, she had been almost desperate. Her own family would not help her, she knew. She was on her own and there was nothing to do but make the best of it.

Thank God, I've never been a weeper, thought Betty as she boarded the train for New York. If I were, I'd sure as hell be bawling all over the place now.

She was grateful, too, that her figure still retained its slimness and that she was not plagued with the morning sickness or fainting spells that would have made working an impossibility.

When she got to New York, she found a job before she found a place to stay; then, with her immediate future momentarily secured, she looked for a room. She found one, and although it was a dark, depressing place she was pleased with the rent and, she told herself cheerfully, it wasn't as if she were going to be stuck there forever. Once she got the foolishness of having the baby out of the way and the business of placing it for adoption, she would be free to look for a better job, to look around for a man with money and, finally, to get married. She had not counted on the fact that she might love her child and that, in fact, she might begin to love him even before he was born.

She was working in a restaurant where the tips were fairly good and the customers easily satisfied.

Which, Betty thought ruefully, was a lucky thing for her because she had never been cut out to be a waitress.

129

She was constantly forgetting things, a napkin, glasses of water, filled sugar bowls, but Betty had always had a warm smile and the customers were mostly men. Betty smiled and laughed out loud at herself and twitched her hips, and the men laughed along with her and watched her behind appreciatively and tipped generously.

They asked her for dates, too, but Betty always flashed her left hand with its dime-store wedding band and told them that her husband was six feet tall with shoulders like a brick wall and that he'd kill any man who tried to date her up while he was away in the Army. But she smiled when she said it and she spoke in such a way that every man thought that if things had been different, if she were the kind to run around he would be the one man she would choose.

If I ever get rid of this goddamn bundle, thought Betty savagely, then I'll really cut loose.

But one afternoon, when she was changing from her uniform to her street clothes, she felt a twinge in her belly that left her weak, not with pain but with surprise.

Well, I'll be damned! she thought.

She walked all the way to her room and, as soon as she got there, she undressed and lay down on her bed. She put her hands flat against her abdomen and waited, and then it happened again. She could actually see the movement under her skin.

Well, I'll be damned, she thought again and grinned. Well, I'll be damned. It's alive!

She did not know exactly when the determination to keep her baby had formed in her. Later, when she thought about it, she supposed that it must have been when she felt that first twinge of life within her body. The new thought caused radical changes in her plans and Betty, who had never been one to put things off, sat down at once and began to plan.

Within a week she found an obstetrician who promised to deliver her baby for seventy-five dollars. He reserved a room for her in a hospital and told her exactly what it would cost her to stay there for five days.

"Will you have someone to look after you and the baby when you return home, Mrs. Harrington?" asked the doctor, using the name she had given him.

"Yes," said Betty, hiding the rather wry smile on her lips. "I have a family."

She spent the next months learning everything she could about baby care. She bought diapers and nightgowns and safety pins and decided that she would need neither blankets nor bottles. The baby would sleep in the same bed with her and she would nurse him herself. Now, she gorged herself on the one meal a day she was allowed at the restaurant and she hid cake and bread and cheese in her handbag so that she could eat in her room without using any money.

Instead of taking a drink of water at the restaurant, she drank milk. Water she drank at home. And every cent she could keep from spending went into a bank account to pay for the hospital and to support her during the weeks after the baby was born when she would have to stay with him.

Rodney Harrington, Junior, she thought. That's what I'll name him. He has a right to the name, and he's going to have it. To hell with Peyton Place and everybody in it.

Luckily for her, the owner of the restaurant where she worked was an Italian with six children of his own. His wife had worked right up to the last minute and it hadn't hurt her a bit. So he kept Betty on as she grew larger and larger, cautioning her against lifting heavy trays and to watch out for wet places on the kitchen floor.

"You need something lifted, you call me," he told her. "And don't worry about a thing. It's good for a woman to stay on her feet when she's that way. Makes it easier when her time comes."

The Italian's wife said, "Don't worry about nothin'. Your husband's away, I'll come visit in the hospital. After, I come help you with the baby. Don't worry about nothin'!"

"These days," said the Italian, snapping his fingers, "it's nothin' for a woman to have a baby. Bing, in the hospital. Bing, with the ether. Bing, the baby. All over."

The baby was born at the end of October and things worked out just as Betty had planned. Her delivery was an easy one in spite of Roddy's husky nine and a half pounds, and Betty's breasts overflowed with milk to feed him. From the first, he was a contented baby who never cried except when he was hungry or wet; and, as the weeks went by, he seemed to grow right in front of Betty's eyes. When he was three months old, she knew that it was time for her to go back to work. There were twenty-one dollars and sixty-seven cents left in the bank.

A woman named Agnes Carlisle lived in the room next door to Betty's, and during the time that Betty had lived there, she and Agnes had become good friends. Agnes was a retired schoolteacher, who struggled every month to make ends meet on her pension and was only too glad to look after Roddy every evening for the small sum that Betty could pay.

"He's so good, he won't be any trouble," said Agnes cheerfully. "And even if he were, I wouldn't mind. He's such a beautiful baby."

Betty almost laughed out loud at the sight of the gray, stern-looking woman bending over the bed talking baby talk to Roddy.

"He looks just like his father," said Betty.

The years passed quickly. When Roddy was three, the Italians opened a new restaurant in another part of town and Betty was made manager of the old place. She earned a decent wage now and often thought of moving from her dark, dingy room. But Roddy was as fond of Agnes Carlisle as she was of him, and Agnes was teaching Roddy to read and write so that he'd be ahead of the other children when he started school.

"With our school system the way it is today," said Agnes, "the only child who has a chance is the one who gets outside help. I'll see that Roddy gets that."

So Betty stayed where she was. She dated a variety of men but, as she told Agnes, she wasn't about to get married.

"I like my life the way it is," she said. "Uncomplicated. I've got Roddy and my job and no entanglements. I'm going to keep it that way."

Agnes was the only person in New York who knew that Betty had never been married. Betty never discussed the subject with the men who took her out except when they got serious. Then she would tell them that she had been married and didn't want to make the same mistake again.

It was on the Fourth of July that Agnes saw the advertisement in the personal column of a tabloid newspaper. She, Betty and Roddy had returned from an afternoon in the park and Betty was making iced coffee.

"This is a funny one," said Agnes.

"What?" asked Betty, leaning over Agnes' shoulder.

"This," said Agnes pointing out the advertisement.

"Read it to me," said Betty. "I forgot to put an ice cube in Roddy's milk and as soon as he realizes it he'll start yelling."

"Betty, where are you?" said Agnes.

"What?" asked Betty, turning around, surprised.

"That's what it says here in the paper," replied Agnes. "Betty, where are you? Please contact me as soon as you see this. Urgent. Leslie Harrington, Box 213, Peyton Place *Times*."

Betty sat down on a hassock at Agnes' feet. "Well, I'll be damned," she said softly.

"It's meant for you, isn't it?" Agnes asked.

"Yes," said Betty.

"Is it—" She hesitated and glanced at Roddy who was looking solemnly from Agnes to his mother. She lowered her voice. "Is it Roddy's g-r-a-n-d-f-a-t-h-e-r?" she asked, spelling out the last word.

"Roddy what?" asked Roddy, and then he glanced down at his glass. "Eye-cube! Eye-cube!" he yelled.

Betty took an ice cube from her glass of iced coffee and put it into his glass.

"Yes," she said to Agnes.

"Are you going to write to him?"

"I don't know."

"Are you out of your mind?" asked Agnes. "You told me that he had plenty of money. It's about time he did somebody for R-o-d-d-y."

"Roddy!" cried Roddy triumphantly.

Agnes groaned. "Why did I have to teach him to spell," she said.

"I don't know as I want anything from him," said Betty.

"Don't be a fool," said Agnes. "If he wants to do something for the child, let him. Are you going to be stuck in a hovel like this all your life? And Roddy too? Take what you can get. Don't wind up like me."

Betty looked at Agnes for a long time. She saw herself, grown old, living alone in her dark room. Living on pennies and in fear.

"I'm not going to write," she said. "I'll see how serious he is about wanting to get in touch with me. I'll telephone him. Collect."

She put in the call, smiling gleefully at the thought of Leslie's discomfiture at hearing from her through a nosy, Peyton Place telephone operator.

"What do you want, Leslie?" she asked, as soon as she heard his voice.

Leslie hesitated for only a moment. "I want you to come home," he said.

"Isn't this a little out of character for you, Leslie?"

"I've been trying to find you for years," said Leslie.

"Why?" ask Betty coldly. "There was a time when you couldn't wait to get rid of me."

"Betty," said Leslie, and she was almost shocked at the note of pleading in his voice. "Tell me about the baby."

"Well, he's hardly a baby," replied Betty. "He's going on five."

"A boy," said Leslie, and for a long minute the phone was silent except for his breathing. "A boy. What's his name?"

"Rodney Harrington, Junior," said Betty, and waited for Leslie to protest.

"That's wonderful, Betty," said Leslie, and Betty was so surprised that she took the receiver away from her ear and looked down into the mouthpiece as if she wanted to see Leslie's face. "Please, Betty," he was saying. "Say you'll come."

"I'll have to think it over," said Betty.

"I'll send you a check for the fare," Leslie offered.

"You're damned right you will," said Betty with a humorless little laugh.

"I'll put it in the mail right now," he said. "Just give me your address."

"Nothing doing," said Betty. "The last thing I want is to find you camped on my doorstep. I told you I'd think it over and I will. I'll call you at the end of the week."

"At least give me your telephone number," said Leslie.

"No," said Betty, and hung up abruptly.

The following week was one of hell for Betty. All her life she had hated indecision, and her days were not made any easier by Agnes' almost constant nagging.

"Stop thinking of yourself," said Agnes. "Think of Roddy."

And: "Do you want to spend the rest of your life working in a greasy restaurant?"

And: "I'm not going to be around forever, you know. Who'll look after Roddy then?"

And: "Roddy's one of the most intelligent children I've ever known. Are you going to cheat him out of the advantages he should have?"

And: "What if you should get sick? What would happen to Roddy then?"

"For Christ's sake," yelled Betty, "will you kindly shut up for a minute? I can't think!"

"There's nothing to think about," said Agnes decisively. "Call the old man. Pack your things. And go."

In the end, Betty telephoned Leslie Harrington.

"I can take a week off from my job," she said. "We can come for a visit, but only for five days. We'll have to spend the other two traveling."

"Now will you give me your address so that I can mail you a check?" asked Leslie.

"No," said Betty. "I've thought it over, and I don't think I want to be beholden to you for a damned thing. The only reason I'm going to see you at all is that you're Roddy's grandfather. Every child should have a chance to meet his grandfather. And that's the only reason, believe me."

"Wire me what train you're taking," said Leslie.

"Yes, I will."

The car turned into the wide, graveled driveway in front of the Harrington house.

"Here we are," said Leslie. "Roddy's asleep."

Yes, thought Betty. Here we are, indeed.

11

AUGUST HAD BEEN more than half gone when Selena had become aware of an almost imperceptible change in Tim Randlett. He began to question her about her past, and if she didn't answer him he sulked.

"Listen," he said, "I want you to be my wife. Husbands and wives don't have secrets from one another. If they do it's no kind of marriage."

Selena barely heard his last two sentences.

"What did you say?" she asked in almost unbelieving joy.

"I said that I want you to be my wife and—"

She put restraining fingers across his lips.

"Don't say anything else," she said. "Just say that again."

Tim laughed and took her in his arms.

"Darling," he said, "will you please do me the honor of becoming my wife?"

"Yes," said Selena, "yes, yes, yes. When?"

"In the fall," replied Tim. "After I'm finished here. We'll go to New York and find an apartment and then we'll go to Tiffany's and I'll buy you the biggest diamond in the store with a wedding band to match."

"I love you," said Selena softly. "I'll bet that no one else in the world loves anyone the way I love you."

"You'd lose," said Tim. "Because I love you that way."

Selena believed him in spite of the way he could, on occasion, look at her with a coldness that chilled her with fear.

"Tell me about this Ted Carter," he demanded.

"There's nothing to tell," replied Selena. "We were friends all through school and then one day we weren't friends any more. That's all."

"You're lying, Selena," he said.

She turned to him in disbelief. "I am not," she cried.

"Did you ever sleep with him?"

"Are you out of your mind?" she demanded angrily.

"Don't raise your voice, Selena. And why are you so angry if your conscience is clear?"

"I'm angry because you've not only doubted my word, but because you could even think such a thing about Ted and me."

"Well," said Tim with a sarcasm that hurt her more than any raised voice could have done, "let's face it, darling. I wasn't the first. Not by a long shot."

"You're behaving like a child," said Selena and turned her back to him.

Tim Randlett often behaved like a child. When he was not acting a part, either on or off stage, he reverted to the actions of the spoiled, petulant darling he had once been in Hollywood, and the worst facet of this was that he didn't believe that he was acting childish at all but that he was asserting himself and standing up for his rights. When the few people who had seen him this way accused him of immaturity, Tim either lost his temper completely or exerted himself to correct what he was convinced was a mistaken impression.

136

"I'm not being childish, darling," he said to Selena. "It's just that I love you so, and I want to know every single thing about you."

"Then couldn't you wait until I'm ready to tell you?" she asked.

"Of course, darling," said Tim. "There's no hurry. We have the rest of our lives to talk and find out about each other."

After every such argument, things went well between them for a short time, but then, invariably, Tim would begin again, and what hurt Selena most of all was that he usually chose a time immediately after they had finished making love.

"What did you and Carter do during all the years you were such dear, good friends?" he asked.

"Just what most other kids do," she replied, and prayed silently that he would stop the slightly twisted smile from appearing on the mouth she had just kissed.

"We went to school, and to dances and talked about getting married someday. Just kid stuff."

"Didn't you ever neck?"

"Yes," said Selena.

"Ah. Now the truth begins to emerge. Was he good at it?"

"Tim," she asked quietly, "what does it do for you to hear about such things? Do you get a big bang out of thinking of me kissing someone else?"

"Just answer my question," he ordered.

"I don't know," she said. "Ted was the only boy I ever kissed while I was growing up so I really have no basis for comparison."

"Do you mean to say that in a town like Peyton Place kids don't play kissing games?" he demanded, his eyebrows raised in disbelief.

"Of course they do," she replied wearily.

"And you, of course, being so pure and virginal, refused to participate in these games. Is that what you're trying to tell me?"

Selena jumped up from the bed and pulled a robe around her.

"For God's sake, Tim," she cried, "will you cut it out. You're just like a goddamned peeping Tom."

"Well, did you or didn't you?"

"Did I or didn't I what?"

"Join in the kissing games."

"Of course I did. Every kid does."

137

"Then you lied to me about Carter being the only boy you ever kissed."

"For God's sake," Selena shouted, "how can I remember every boy who was at every party I ever went to."

"If you'd lie about kissing, Heaven only knows what else you'd lie about."

"You're sick!" Selena yelled.

"Don't shout, darling," he said with maddening patience. "And I'm not the one who's sick. People who lie to others and to themselves are the sick ones."

"I don't lie," said Selena evenly. "I never have and I'm not about to start now."

She began to dress, keeping her head averted so that he wouldn't see the tears that she couldn't keep from rolling down her cheeks.

"What are you doing?" he demanded.

"I'm getting dressed," she replied. "I'm going home."

He was at her side at once. He turned her around to face him and kissed the tears away from her face.

"Darling," he said contritely, "I am an absolute heel. I didn't mean to make you cry. Please forgive me."

"Forget it," said Selena. "I just want to go home."

His arms went around her, holding her tightly against him.

"Don't say that," he said and his voice was harsh with fear. "Don't ever say that. If I lost you I couldn't bear it."

"I have to go," said Selena wearily. "I can't take any more arguing, or sarcasm, or your terrible accusations. I'm all punched out, Tim. I just can't stand it any more."

"Please," he begged, and now tears rolled down his cheeks. "Please, darling. Forgive me just this once more. I'll never do it again."

And then, unknowing and uncaring, Selena gave him one last hostage. She threw her arms around his neck and sobbed against his cheek.

"You don't even have to ask me," she said. "Of course, I forgive you. I could never leave you and we both know it. The idea of living without you is something I can't even begin to imagine. I'll never, never leave you."

And again it was better for a while, but now Selena found herself waiting for the quarrels to come. She was constantly tense, watching for the signs that would warn her of the approaching storm. At night she often lay awake, wondering why Tim's constant probing and prying affected her as it did, but the only conclusion she could come to was that she had never been a dweller in the past and that not being so was the only way she had managed to survive at all. She knew, too, that there had been times when she could not remain in complete control of her thinking and then she would have terrible nightmares about her mother, Nellie, in which she saw her mother hanging, dead, a corpse with a black face and congested eyes that moved on the end of a silken cord with every breath Selena drew. At other times she dreamed of running while a gigantic all-powerful Lucas chased her and then she would scream in her sleep until Joey came into her room and shook her awake.

"Time," Matthew Swain had said. "It may be a cliché, but it's true that it heals all wounds."

It happened the way the doctor had said it would. As the years passed, Selena's bad dreams recurred less and less frequently until at last they ceased altogether and the only time she gave in to fear was once every year on the day of the first snow. Until she had fallen in love with Tim Randlett. Now the nightmares were back, the fear, the sleepless nights. For Selena knew that soon now, Tim would get around to asking her about Lucas and Nellie and the trial and that she would have to dredge up the buried ugliness and show it to him in detail.

I won't think about it, she told herself as she tossed in her bed. I won't talk about it, and if Tim wants to get ugly about it, I'll leave him.

But she knew she would not leave him, no matter what he asked of her, and the sleepless nights grew longer and Selena gagged at the sight of food, and her brother Joey said, "What's the matter Selena?" and she had no answer for him.

I'll be calm, she thought. I won't let myself become upset about anything. Tim loves me. He's not cruel.

And that much was true. Tim Randlett did love her, in his fashion, and he was not a cruel man. It was just that now he fancied himself in the role of psychiatrist and had convinced himself that the dark secrets which festered in Selena's mind were like a poison that coursed through her body and that would end up by destroying her and, therefore, him. He saw himself as a great healer and believed that the feeling of accomplishment he got from fitting one small piece of information after another into the puzzle of Selena's background was the joy of a scientist on the brink of discovery, and he never admitted to himself that there was something unlovely and perverse in his excitement.

"I only want what's good for you," he told her.

And Selena believed him because there was nothing else she could do.

They were on the couch in the living room of his cottage one sunny afternoon at the end of August, he sitting up and Selena lying down with her head in his lap. He stroked her hair gently away from her forehead, and Selena had the wonderful floating feeling she always had after they had made love and were quiet and close together. She was on the very edge of sleep when he spoke.

"Tell me about Lucas," he said.

For a moment, Selena was absolutely still; calmness filled her the way it sometimes will when someone has been terribly shocked and thinks, Now the worst has happened, whatever comes after this can't help but be better. But then her heart began to pound and she began to tremble.

"Stop it, Tim," she cried. "I don't want to talk about Lucas or anything connected with him."

"You have to, darling," he said gently. "It's the only way you'll ever get rid of it."

She tried to get up, but he had twisted her long hair around his hand and she was held fast.

"Let go of me," she demanded.

"Darling, don't be afraid," he said softly. "Believe me, I only want what's good for you. You have to talk about it, darling. You can't go the rest of your life with all that hatred bottled up inside you."

"I don't hate Lucas any more," she said. "I stopped hating him the second he died."

"That's not true," said Tim.

This time she pulled away from him with such a wrench that he let go of her hair in surprise. She stood up and faced him, her eyes blazing with anger and pain.

"What the hell do you know about it?" she cried. "You with your insulated childhood and your playacting and your games of

140

psychiatrist and patient. You don't know anything about anything real. All right. I'll tell you about Lucas. Maybe that'll shatter your sickening smugness."

"Don't shout, darling," Tim said in the patient, conciliatory tone that maddened her.

"I'll shout all I want," cried Selena. "You want to hear about Lucas. Well, I'll tell you. He was a pig, a drunk and the worst son-of a-bitch that ever lived. When I was fourteen he knocked me unconscious and tore my clothes off and raped me. And after that, I don't even remember how many times, he'd send my brother Joey out and he'd lock the door and he'd beat me before he got on top of me."

She was standing in front of him, bent forward, with her fists clenched while she screamed. He took her wrists and tried to pull her down next to him on the couch.

"Please, darling," he said, almost frightened at the change in her.

She pulled away from him and kicked his shin when he tried to stand up.

"Sit down," she shouted. "You wanted to hear it and now you'll sit still until I finish. The times when Lucas knocked me out weren't the worst times, you know. It was when I was only stunned and before I could pick myself up off the floor he grabbed me and tied me to the bed and then did it to me. Then I'd be awake and aware of every second and I'd feel him hurting me and smell his sweat and his breath and hear him grunting like a rooting pig. Those were the worst times. What's the matter, Tim? Don't you like the grubby details? My mother knew. I don't know how, but she knew. I'd catch her looking at me and I knew she knew. And Lucas was careful, too. Careful as could be. He'd wait until she was out working before he'd get to me. He was big, Tim. Bigger than you. And most of the time I'd bleed before he got through with me. Lucas didn't bleed though. He got me pregnant and I had an abortion."

Her whole body was shaking now and her breath hurt in her throat.

"I didn't really have to, you know," she said, and her voice was softer now with an almost weird hush. "Have an abortion, I mean. Lucas wasn't my flesh-and-blood father. The baby would probably have been all right. Not an idiot or anything. Lucas used to say that while he was on top of me. That I wasn't his own daughter. It seemed to excite him, as if I were a stranger. No. I didn't really have to have the abortion, but I did. I bled then, too, but not Lucas. Lucas never bled at all until I killed him. And then he bled. Oh, how he bled. Blood gushed from him like a fountain, and I kept on hitting him."

Selena's eyes gleamed and her mouth was like a cut in her white face.

"I killed him," she whispered. "I hit him over the head, and I hit him and hit him and hit him until he was dead, and I enjoyed every minute of it. When I was finished his head was like an egg that had been shattered and I was happy for the first time in years. Lucas was dead, like my mother. Like my baby."

She stopped and stood still, her arms hanging limply at her sides, her dark hair falling over the side of her face.

"Is that what you wanted to hear?" she asked at last, not looking at him.

Tim came to her and she could hear the heavy sound of his breath. He was almost panting and when she did look up she could hardly believe what she saw. His eyes were gleaming and his hands trembled as he reached for her.

"Darling," he whispered hoarsely.

And when he pulled her close to him she could feel his excitement. Too late, she tried to turn and run from him but he held her tightly.

"So you do remember," he said. "You remember how big and strong he was, like a bull. You've never forgotten him."

Selena beat against his chest and tried to bring her knee up, but she could not move.

"A girl always remembers her first lover," he said softly. "Especially if she's been raped."

His hands were hard on her, hurting her through the thin material of her summer dress, and when he kissed her his mouth was heavy and wet and merciless. She twisted and pushed against him and panic was a sickness that threatened to engulf her.

"That's what you've wanted all along," Tim said. "To be raped, the way Lucas raped you. Every time I took you in my stupid, gentle way, you were remembering him and how big and brutal he was. Well, I can be that way too. Like this."

But when he tried to push her down on the floor she managed to break away from him. She ran around the table in front of the fireplace and her hands found the fire tongs as if they had been waiting for her.

"I'll kill you!" she screamed as he started for her. "Don't move, or I'll kill you!"

But Tim was beyond listening or caring. He crept closer to her, and when he was close enough she swung the tongs in a great arc and struck him. If he had not moved at the last second, the tongs would have struck him on the side of the head. But he did move, so that only his shoulder was hit, and he staggered backward and fell over the table and landed against the stone floor in front of the fireplace.

For a moment he was still, and in those few seconds Selena looked down at her hand and saw it clutched around the tongs. She watched in horror as her arm started to raise itself to strike again, and just then Tim groaned and sat up. Selena stared at him and then back at the weapon in her hand.

Almost! screamed a voice inside her head. Almost! I almost killed him!

And she turned and ran out of the cottage. She ran through the woods, dappled green and yellow in the summer sun, and she ran to the highway that led to Peyton Place.

Almost! the voice screamed, and Selena ran until the world blurred in front of her eyes and the sandy shoulder of the road came up to strike her face.

PART THREE

1

In September, Allison left Peyton Place for a week in New York before going on to Hollywood. It meant arriving at the studio two days later than they expected her, but she decided it was more important to have a week with Lewis, an uninterrupted week of being with him and loving him.

Distance does not lend enchantment, she thought, thinking of the weeks of separation, the two months when all she had of Lewis was his letters. Absence had not diminished her love for him, but, sometimes, she was not able to capture the image of his face. She knew that in the first few minutes of meeting him again there would be constraint and hesitation; it would be like meeting a stranger.

She looked out the train window at the familiar landscape. Summer had lingered into September; the blaze of autumn had not yet consumed or even touched the greenness. What a summer it had been! Allison thought. What had begun in beauty and fruitfulness had ended with Selena found wandering, dazed, lost and helpless by the side of a road. Mike had been fired. And Seth Buswell and Matt Swain had made enemies trying to help her.

Peyton Place had been a battlefield. Allison wondered whether she was fleeing in defeat or departing victorious. A little of both, she thought. Mike had a job and she, at least, had not surrendered to the pressures. Her career was in full flower, her success had gone far beyond even her wildest dream.

Allison had never thought of success in terms of money. To her, it had always been a vague, amorphous dream with success consisting, in equal parts, of fame and freedom. Money was the least important part of it. Often she said to herself, I am a rich woman. It was an attempt that always failed. She never believed it, she could not think of herself that way.

Only *old* women are rich, she told herself, trying to push away the thought of herself, Allison MacKenzie, as a rich woman. It was an image she was not willing to face and thought the reason for it was that it interfered with an image she preferred: herself as a writer; as Allison MacKenzie, Author.

She did not want to be a corporate entity, endlessly involved with the investment counselors and tax accountants that Brad had been recommending to her. One of the things she had to do while in New York was to see these people. She had decided that the only way to handle this was to find people she could trust, and turn it all over to them. She did not want to be bothered with it. To think of money matters took one's mind from the writing of books, and that was her real work.

Perhaps David was right. He may have been motivated by all the wrong reasons, but perhaps what he said was correct. The writer's only function is to write. From now on, she determined, that's the way it's going to be. No more interviews, no more salesmanship.

The conductor punched her ticket and made a few remarks about the kind of summer it had been. I've practically become a commuter, Allison thought, between Peyton Place and New York. She looked around her at the faded green plush seats, most of them empty. She felt almost proprietary about this train.

She had an imaginary conversation with Lewis in which she said, "We should all take more train rides, Lewis. It's one of the few places left where we can commune with ourselves and ask the deep questions and make judgments of ourselves and others. It's too dangerous to think of anything but the traffic when you're in a car; and planes are too fast."

Allison put her head back on the seat and closed her eyes, gave herself up to delicious thoughts of her reunion with Lewis. Love's hungers, she thought, are as real as any other kind.

She smiled, thinking what Constance would say if she knew that Allison had become involved with a married man. Constance, remembering her own past history, would think it was a family curse, a seed she had transmitted to Allison, and she would feel guilty and responsible.

That is the difference between our generations, Allison thought. Her mother had felt guilty, had felt a sense of sin at being the mistress of a married man. Allison did not. She accepted it; it was an arrangement; it was the best thing that life had thus far offered her.

Allison sat up, startled by her thoughts. *Thus far?* Was she admitting to herself that what she had with Lewis was just a temporary thing, to be superseded by something better, more permanent? She pushed the thought aside, denied the possibility of it. I am not a gypsy, she told herself, not a wanderer. I have found what I want, Lewis is what I want, and I'm going to hold onto it.

At Boston she changed trains. Walking through the station, she smiled to herself. The world-weary traveler, that's what I am. Such a short time ago, this trip from Peyton Place to New York had been an exciting, new experience, a dream come true. But already it was something she could do with her eyes closed. Is that the way it's going to be with everything? she wondered. Is that what life is?

From Grand Central Station she went directly to the residential hotel where she had reserved an apartment. Driving up Park Avenue, her luggage all around her, she tried to keep from her face the smug smile that tugged at her lips. Oh, give in to it, she told herself. Relax that tight New England conscience of yours. After all, no one gave you this, it wasn't handed to you on a silver platter. You earned it with your own two hands. Now enjoy it.

Her apartment was on the twentieth floor. Following the boy who carried the luggage, bowed in by the manager, she entered a grand living room all white and gold. The manager bustled after her, opened the long windows that led to the terrace, showed her the bedroom which was only a little smaller than the living room, and led her to the butler's pantry where she could, if she wished, do her own cooking.

When she was alone, she looked at herself in the long mirror, as if to assure herself that it was really she, Allison MacKenzie, in this place. Then she went to the phone and called Lewis.

"I am here," she said. "Come to dinner."

"Must I wait till then?" he asked. "I could sneak out the back door. I think it still opens, though I haven't used it since 1936 when the bill collectors used to sit and wait for me in the reception room."

"Oh, how I wish I had been around then, darling."

"I wish it too. You would have charmed them right out of the place, the bills forgotten in their hands. Listen, darling, I know I'm being terribly undisciplined and all my authors are going to start writing me angry letters, but I'm leaving right now and I'll be there in fifteen minutes."

"Oh yes, darling, come at once," she said. And hung up before she could add, "We have no time to waste." The thought had come unbidden, from nowhere.

She undressed quickly. She wanted to shower and dress and be ready for him. She planned on ordering dinner and having it served on the terrace, with candles on the table and a bucket of champagne, able to see all of New York yet remaining unseen. That their life together was secret made it all the more delicious, she thought.

But when he knocked on the door she was not ready and had to pull on a terrycloth robe, the ends of her hair wet, her face washed clean of make-up.

"Don't look at me, Lewis. I'm not ready to be seen."

He laughed. "That's like telling a thirsty man to stay away from the water."

He put his hand on her arm and drew her toward him. When they kissed, Allison went limp in his arms and cried, "Oh, Lewis, how I've missed you!"

"If it was anything like the way I missed you, then I understand full well what you've gone through."

Allison drew away from him and said, "Oh, Lewis, I wanted to be dressed when you arrived, and made up, and looking my best. And now look at me."

"I am," Lewis said.

"I wanted to order dinner and have the table on the terrace, with crystal and candles and champagne."

"We'll have it later," Lewis said, smiling his quiet smile.

When he kissed her again, his hand was inside her robe, cupping her breast; and then, arms around each other, hurrying, they moved toward the bedroom. Allison's knees felt weak and her thighs trembled.

"Oh, hold me, darling," she cried. "Don't ever let me go."

"Never," he said, and the word echoed in his head.

Never, she thought, repeating the word to herself. Lovers are mad, they use crazy, impossible words. What's worse, they believe them.

She buried her face in Lewis' breast in order to shut out the sight of him, of his gray hairs that were the sign of age. She could feel his heart beating against her mouth. *Never* will last only as long as that, she thought, and began to cry.

"What is it, love? What is it?" Lewis asked. "Why are you crying?" He stroked her hair and her back, calming her as a father does a child.

"It's nothing, Lewis. It's nothing." And she took his head between her hands and consumed him with kisses, as if she wanted to make up for all the years that she had not known him, all the years she had not even been born, by the intensity of her love.

Allison was assailed by the thought that there was no time to lose; and that because of the disparity in ages, she must cram into a short space all the love and experience that the years had denied them. She caressed him with her hands and her mouth, and under her hands felt the quiver of his pleasure. She assaulted him with love, with a passionate fury; and when he was ready for her, he turned on her savagely and threw her down, covered her with his hard body, and held her arms pinned to the bed so that she could not move. Like a sea's retaining wall she lay and allowed herself to be buffeted, and felt the tidal pull that, at the end, seemed to draw her soul out of her body. Only then did he let go of her and she drew his throbbing body down to hers.

This is the only truth there is, she thought, this expression of love. The rest is acting out a part.

Her body ached with the knowledge of him. They lay side by side, resting, and Allison watched day slowly dimming and the room receding into darkness. The days were shorter now. Summer was ending graciously, with days of sweet, soft winds, but winter's advance was making itself tentatively felt. Remembering that soon she would leave for California, Allison thought, I am going to follow summer west; I'll have a few extra weeks of it.

149

At the thought of leaving, she turned to Lewis and kissed him. "How are you feeling, darling?" she asked.

"There's a possibility I may recover," he said. "I believe there are some grounds for hope. If I take good care of myself, I might be able to walk out of here under my own power—sometime around ten-thirty tomorrow morning."

Allison laughed. "You'd better summon up all your strength right now, Lewis, because I suspect my reputation will suffer if the waiter walks in and finds you like this."

Lewis sat up. "What waiter?"

"The waiter who is going to bring our dinner." She reached for the phone. "I am about to order dinner, Lewis. Have you any special requests?"

"Yes, I have," Lewis said, jumping out of bed and running to the bathroom. "Wait till I'm dressed."

An hour later, when the manager, headwaiter and waiter arrived—the waiter pushing a cart containing their dinner under covered dishes—Allison and Lewis were sitting, all prim and proper, on the terrace's white wrought-iron chairs.

The headwaiter opened the champagne, the waiter served their food without rattling a single dish and the manager stood anxiously by; he was the kind of man, Allison thought, who seemed always to be fearing the worst. After the waiter had placed before them the bowls of cold vichyssoise, set in larger crystal bowls filled with cracked ice, Allison said, "I will serve the rest myself."

The waiter and the headwaiter bowed themselves off the terrace; the manager took one last worried look, as if he half expected the terrace to fall off the side of the building. Assuring himself it would last a few days more, he wished them *bon appetit* and followed his waiters from the room.

Allison said, "He gives me the feeling that he's terribly sorry New England doesn't have a king and a flag. I think he'd like to fly the flag to announce that I am here."

Lewis was still smiling at the sight of the three men backing out of the room. "New York is full of apparitions," he said. "It's become the final resting place of the ghosts of half of Europe. Those three men, for example, died in Budapest in 1935. New York is the Paradise their souls migrated to."

"The chef's ghost has done well by us tonight," Allison said.

After the cold soup, there was filet mignon with sauce Béarnaise, artichokes vinaigrette and a small salad pungent with herbs. They finished the champagne with tiny wild strawberries that tasted of sun and summer fields.

Standing at the parapet with their coffee cups, they looked at New York, winking and flashing around them. That is what it's all for, Allison thought, not knowing quite what the words meant. Moments like this make the agony of success worth while. But immediately she asked herself, Is it true? Does this make up for the lies and the estrangement of friends?

She thought of David. It pained her to think of him, in his lonely room, only a few minutes away, bent over his work. Perhaps she had misjudged him. Perhaps his integrity was real and his anger with her was genuine, not envy of her success but outrage that success was what she wanted. He believed in her talent. She decided she would phone him, invite him and Stephanie to dinner the next night.

Below, Central Park looked wilted and tired after its three months' struggle for survival against the city summer.

Lewis said, "We should ask the Parks Commissioner to send Central Park away for the summer. It's too old and careworn to spend any more summers in the city."

"I'll draw up a petition in the morning," Allison said. "We'll call it the Fund for Sending Central Park to the Catskills. School children will send in nickels and dimes. Our slogan will be: Central Park Needs Fresh Air."

Lewis put his coffee cup on the top of the parapet and, leaning forward, kissed her mouth gently.

"And I need you," he said. "It's as simple as that. You're my sun and air."

Lewis stayed till after midnight. They talked of their love and, like newlyweds, came back again and again to their plans for being together, to Allison's taking an apartment in New York when she got back from Hollywood. She would be back in October, go to Peyton Place to see Mike and Constance, and then come to New York and they would take up their life together.

"It's pretty rare, you know," Lewis said. "I mean, an arrangement like ours. It's pretty rare when it works. Very few of them last, I'm afraid."

"Why do you tell me that?" Allison asked.

"Because we have to face up to all the dangers, all the pitfalls of our situation if we are to succeed."

"I know what you are thinking, Lewis—that I will become dissatisfied, that I will want more. That I will begin to nag you and demand you get a divorce so we can get married. Darling, don't you think I've thought of all that? I've considered everything. *You* are what I want. *This* is what I want."

"I pray it will always be like this, Allison. And I hope I will never become selfish. I have thought about it a great deal, too, while you were in Peyton Place. I hope I will never make demands on you. . . ."

"And I hope you will, darling."

"—I don't mean lover's demands. I'm talking about the demands of—well, of a selfish partner, demands that have nothing to do with love but only with self."

Lewis swirled the brandy around in his glass; for a moment, it caught the light and glowed with a deep flame, then died and subsided.

"I guess that what I mean, Allison, is this: when my age becomes burdensome to you, don't keep me around out of pity. Not even if I beg you to."

"Oh, darling, darling," Allison cried, and clasped Lewis in her arms. "Don't think of such things. Don't. You are not old. You aren't."

Lewis smiled for a moment. "I'm not now. In fact, I haven't felt this young for twenty years. I suppose I am like most people—fearful of old age. I'd only admit it to you, darling. I have the crazy notion that someday I'll wake up and see my face in the mirror and have to tell myself, You are old, Lewis, you are old. Men are vain and they can fool themselves for a long time; but I imagine the day comes when even the vainest man has to give in to the truth because his bones will no longer permit him to lie."

"I don't want to talk about it, Lewis. Please don't let's talk about it. We're living in the present, here and now. Let's leave the future to the ladies who write the horoscope columns. I'll just take life day by day; and that means you'll have to take it that way, too, because you are going to be with me. Every day."

Lewis left after midnight, and Allison, tired from the day that had begun early in Peyton Place and ended late in New York, went to bed.

She opened the windows wide to the cool night air; the traffic noises were diminished by distance, a stillness seemed to rise from the quiet, deserted park. It enveloped her, she drifted, she slept.

In the morning she had breakfast brought to her on the terrace. It was only eight o'clock. Country girl, she said to herself, making fun of herself for not having fallen into the New York way of sleeping late and then breakfasting on black coffee. She ate a country girl's breakfast of fried eggs, bacon, fruit and coffee with cream.

She was glad she had wakened early. Allison hated to hurry the first meal of the day, loved to linger over the breakfast cigarettes that tasted better than any other. She watched the city wake up. Standing at the parapet, she saw the water truck's white spray; it left the surface of the street a little darker, if not much cleaner.

Beginning at eight-thirty, more and more men and women left apartment buildings and were swallowed up by the omnivorous subway entrance at the corner. Allison smiled, amused to observe that as the hour approached closer to nine, the men and women walked ever more quickly.

At ten, dressed in a tweed suit with a jacket cut like an elegant cardigan, Allison stepped into a waiting taxi, the door closed behind by the hotel doorman.

The driver said, "You know something, lady? Doormen at good hotels are the only people who know how to close taxi doors. They don't slam 'em but they always get it closed on the first try. My taxis would last a lot longer if people knew how to close the doors."

Allison spent the morning in paneled offices, putting into the hands of lawyers and investment men her now considerable earnings. She nodded as they explained things to her; but, no matter how closely she tried to listen, her mind drifted on to other things. But she knew they were honest and capable men; it did not matter that she didn't understand. Perhaps it was better, she thought; at least, I won't be an interfering amateur. Things like this are better left to the pros.

She went shopping in the afternoon and bought the kind of clothes and lingerie she had only looked at before. She ordered suits and dresses that bore the labels that meant money. The floor managers invariably recognized her; charge accounts were immediately arranged.

"I can give you a check," Allison offered.

She laughed to herself at the thought that, now that she had money, she didn't need it.

She had only to give her address and it was sent; her name was the only currency she needed.

When she got back to her apartment, the boxes were unpacked and the contents hung in the closets by the maid. Allison kicked off her shoes and dropped down on the sofa. I'll never get used to this, she thought.

The phone rang. It was Stephanie. A television producer had just called. "It's a small part, Allison, but I have to take it. And rehearsals start tonight, I'm afraid. It's seven hours in a drafty theater for me. I'd much rather be having dinner with you."

Stephanie was in a hurry. She'd call tomorrow, she said, and they'd make a date for lunch.

I adore Stephanie, Allison thought. She's practically the only one to whom my success hasn't made a bit of difference. Some people seemed to feel that there was just so much success around and that if their friends won any part of it, that left less for them. It was an attitude Allison could not understand.

I could understand it, she thought, if I had just picked a winning number in the sweepstakes, or a rich uncle in Australia had died and left me everything he owned which included half of Australia. But I *worked* for everything I have. Nobody gave it to me. She remembered the bitter, vicious letters she had received, hundreds of them, from people who thought that her success made their success less possible of achieving.

She sighed, stirred herself to a sitting position and phoned Lewis. She told him about her day and that only David would be coming to dinner because Stephanie had got a part. "Won't you change your mind and come, darling?"

"I'll phone you at midnight. Perhaps if you're not too tired then, I'll come over. Have a pleasant evening with David, darling. He can give you a lot of information about Hollywood, you know. He was there for a while. I don't know how helpful it'll be, though. He has a pretty jaundiced view of it. But we'll talk about that later."

After she had spoken to Lewis, she called Room Service and ordered dinner for two, to be served at eight o'clock.

154

Before David arrived, she drew a bath and sprinkled it with lavender scent. In the bottle, the drops were amber, but in the bath water they turned to a smoky purple. She was enclosed by the fragrance.

When David came, he found her wearing a simple black dress, its severity relieved only by the rich velvet piping around the cuffs. Her hair was pulled back.

She looked older, he thought, and more beautiful than ever before.

"I was surprised when you called this morning, Allison. And terribly pleased, of course. I want to thank you for ending this ridiculous situation. It was all my fault. That day we met in the coffeehouse— well, to put it bluntly, Allison—I was jealous. I gave myself all sorts of other reasons for what I was feeling, but it was plain, old-fashioned jealousy and nothing else. Forgive me, Allison."

"There's nothing to forgive, David. Let's have a drink and a long evening of talk. We'll drown it all in talk."

After dinner, over coffee on the terrace, the talk turned to Allison's coming trip to Hollywood. By that time, all constraint between them had been dissipated by the good food and the wine that had been chilled to just the right temperature. The hovering Hungarian ghosts had done their job well; and, at ten o'clock, they evaporated, taking their food cart with them, leaving David and Allison with their coffee and brandy.

"You'll hate it out there," David said. "Hollywood is filled with haberdashers who made good, and men who call themselves writers though they've never had an original thought in their lives."

"Nevertheless, I'm going," said Allison. "Brad has already told them so."

"Just what are you supposed to be going there for?" asked David.

"I'm to be technical adviser for the film. I'm going to give the script writer a few pointers and talk with the costume and set designers. Things like that."

"Allison," said David earnestly, "they're making a fool out of you. They don't need you to tell them anything. All they want is to make use of you, to exploit your publicity value for their own ends. They'll make you feel important, invite you to a few parties, flatter the hell out of you so that you can come back East and tell everyone who'll listen what a swell bunch of people they are out on the coast."

155

Allison laughed. "Well, if that's all they want, they're certainly willing to pay a good price for it. Twenty-five hundred a week plus all my expenses."

David shrugged. "You won't like it, Allison. I'm sure you won't."

"Maybe not, David, but I've got to find out for myself. I want every experience that's offered me—or just about."

"I'm only thinking of you," David said. "Wait until they start ripping your book to pieces. You'll feel differently then. You won't be able to stand it. Nobody could."

"I don't have your sensitive, artistic soul," said Allison. "As far as I'm concerned, all I want for *Samuel's Castle* is another forty weeks on the lists. And after what they paid me for the picture rights, they can do anything they damn well please with it."

"I just don't want you to be hurt," said David quietly, and Allison was suddenly ashamed.

"I know it, David," she said contritely. "But I have to find out for myself."

"Let me hear from you," said David.

"Yes," said Allison. "I'll phone you. With the studio paying my hotel bills, I'll be able to do it with a clear conscience."

David smiled. "You've changed a lot, Allison. But basically you're still the little girl from Peyton Place, still keeping your conscience clear. I don't think you could change that part of you if you submitted to surgery."

2

THE HOTEL WAS A HUGE, ten-tiered semicircle made of white stone and glass and it sat in the middle of vast, manicured lawns that were dotted with symmetrical, evenly spaced flower beds.

Allison stood on the terrace outside her ninth-floor suite and thought, I wonder if anything ever gets dirty in Beverly Hills. It was ten o'clock in the morning and everything below, beyond and behind her sparkled as if the world had just been removed from a tissue-filled gift box.

In the room behind her, the telephone rang, and she stepped through the floor-to-ceiling glass doors and went to answer it. The room itself was like a theatrical set, all modern furniture, white rugs and abstract paintings. The furniture was upholstered in a deep royal purple and the linen drapes over the sliding glass doors matched exactly.

"Hello," said Allison into the white telephone receiver.

"Are you ready?" asked Bradley Holmes.

"As much as I'll ever be," said Allison. "I've been standing here admiring my surroundings and I can't quite figure out whether I'm living inside a frosted wedding cake or a purple Easter basket."

Brad laughed. "Wait until you see the studio," he said. "That'll really give you something to think about."

"I can't wait," said Allison. "Are you on your way down?

"Right there," replied Brad and hung up.

A few minutes later there was a knock at her door and he came into her room.

"This is indeed very plush," said Brad, looking around. "The denizens of Glitterville have done right well by you. Naturally, my room is not anywhere near this fancy, but then, I'm paying for mine."

Allison put on her hat and a fresh pair of white gloves.

"You don't like Hollywood much, do you?" she asked.

"Nobody from New York likes Hollywood," replied Brad, as they walked down the hall toward the elevators. "Of course, half the time it's a pose. New Yorkers who'd give their eyes to be called to Hollywood are the ones who scream the loudest about prostitution and lack of artistry in the films. No, I don't like Hollywood, but I keep my mouth shut about it. They keep a great deal of money out here and I enjoy getting my share of it."

"David hated it out here," said Allison.

"Yes, he did," replied Brad. "But, on the other hand, David is never going to get rich. It all comes down to what a person wants from life."

A Cadillac limousine pulled up in front of the main entrance of the hotel and a uniformed chauffeur got out to hold the back door of the car open for Allison and Brad.

"You see," said Brad, "the little niceties, such as being driven about in a car like this, cost money. If one wants things like this, one must sacrifice something. David was never willing to give an inch. I was out here with him a few years ago. He was impossible. Miracle Pictures had paid him a very decent price for his third book in spite of the fact that the hard-cover edition never went over three thousand copies. They wanted David to help on the script. Well, we came out here, David and I, and let me tell you, I never want to spend another such two weeks. David was unbending, unyielding and absolutely deaf to all suggestions made by the producer, the director and the other writers. We were supposed to be here for eight weeks, but at the end of two David went out and got drunk and took a plane to New York. Believe me, it wasn't easy explaining that to the studio. But in the end, they decided that they were better off without him."

"He thought I shouldn't come out here," said Allison.

"I can imagine," said Brad. "Listen, darling, I don't know why you bother with people like David. You're a success now. You don't need these somber, social worker types."

"But David is a great writer," said Allison. "Not just good, not just successful, but *great*. And you know it."

"I know it," admitted Brad, "but I also know that if David relaxed a little and listened to me a little more, his books would do a lot better on the market."

"David hasn't a commercially minded cell in his body," said Allison.

"One of the privileges of the chosen few," said Brad as they rode past the gates.

Allison sat up and smoothed her gloves nervously. As always, when facing a new situation, she was wishing fervently that she had stayed safely at home. The car pulled up in front of a white stone house that looked as if it might belong in a New York suburb. On the front lawn there was a black lettered sign in a wrought-iron frame that read ARTHUR TISHMAN.

"For Heaven's sake," said Allison, "is this Mr. Tishman's office?"

"Yes," said Brad. "Fancy, isn't it?"

"A man with a wife and three children could move in here and live very comfortably," said Allison.

In what would have been the foyer of the bungalow, had it been used as a home, were a desk and two filing cabinets, but these had been so artfully arranged and camouflaged that they did not seem at all out of place amidst the brocaded sofas and oil paintings. Behind the desk sat one of the most beautiful women Allison had ever seen. She was small but with an exquisitely molded figure and her hair was like a gold cap. She wore a severe black dress and silver bracelets on both arms, and her shoes were tiny scraps of black leather.

"I'm so glad, Miss MacKenzie," she said, rising to greet Allison. "My name is Gloria Muir and I'm Mr. Tishman's secretary."

"How do you do?" said Allison.

Miss Muir had an English accent, thought Allison, that would have made Laurence Olivier proud of her.

"And how are you, Mr. Holmes?" asked Miss Muir. "It's nice to see you again."

"It's wonderful to be in California again," said Brad.

You liar, thought Allison.

"Mr. Tishman is expecting you," said Miss Muir. "Please come with me."

Mr. Tishman was tall and heavy and looked rather like a young Sidney Greenstreet. He wore dark trousers and one of the most brazen sport shirts Allison had ever seen.

"Brad!" he exclaimed, coming around the vast desk in front of him. "How nice to see you again. It's been much too long."

The two men shook hands and before Brad could introduce Allison, Tishman turned to her.

"And this is the little lady who has caused all the commotion," he said, smiling and extending his hand. "Miss MacKenzie, I can't tell you what an honor this is."

"How do you do, Mr. Tishman. It's very nice to be here," said Allison, feeling a little as if she were at the Mad Hatter's tea party.

Mr. Tishman took her arm. "And this is Conrad Blanding, our director," he said, "and Joel Parkingson, our script writer."

Conrad Blanding wore dark-rimmed glasses and smiled with all his teeth, but Joel Parkingson did not smile at all. He bowed stiffly and sat down, his eyes fixed broodingly on the sheaf of yellow paper in his hand.

"Would you like a drink?" asked Arthur Tishman. "Coffee?"

"Coffee, please," said Allison and sat down on a leather-upholstered chair.

The walls of Mr. Tishman's office were paneled in walnut and across one wall there was a colorful poster in a frame.

"It's one of Lautrec's best, don't you think, Miss MacKenzie?" asked Mr. Blanding.

Allison started. "Oh," she said. "Yes. Yes, indeed."

In a few minutes, Miss Muir came in carrying a silver tray on which rested a complete silver service.

"Shall I pour?" she asked.

"Yes, if you please, Miss Muir," said Mr. Tishman.

A quiet little ceremony followed during which all the men stood silently while Miss Muir filled their cups from the silver pot.

"Now, then, Miss MacKenzie," said Mr. Tishman, leaning back comfortably in his chair. "By the way, may I call you Allison?"

"Please do," Allison replied.

"Good. Puts things on a friendly, warm basis. I'm Arthur, and," he waved a vague hand in the direction of the writer and director, "they're Joel and Conrad. Well, Allison, we've all been very busy on your book and already have a script of sorts."

Allison glanced at Joel Parkingson, but the writer did not look up. He just sat and looked sadder than ever.

"I'd like to see the script," said Allison.

"Certainly," said Arthur Tishman. "We want you to take a copy along with you when you leave. Read it tonight and tomorrow we'll get together again and discuss things. But please don't think that what we have now is what I call a good, working script. It isn't. Joel here has just been putting down ideas. We've got a long way to go yet, but I do think, and Conrad agrees, that Joel has given us a good base to start working on. Our final script will follow the same lines as the one we have now, but I'm sure that, as a writer yourself, you understand the long, slow process of finishing and polishing."

At first, Arthur Tishman gave the impression of a man who is accustomed to command, and Allison was a little frightened of him. But she soon realized that her presence, meeting her, had made him nervous. As a result, he did not converse but made speeches; it was as if he had it all written down, and then read the lines badly, like an amateur actor.

Allison was familiar with the Tishman legend. He had come up the hard way; everything he had he had made himself. She felt a feeling of kinship with him.

"Now, that's enough business for today," said Arthur Tishman. "We have a busy week plotted for you, my dear. Later today, you have

160

a meeting with Harold Jenks, our publicity man. The papers have been on his neck ever since they heard you were coming. Then, tomorrow morning, we've made a date for you with one of our best photographers, and tomorrow afternoon we want you to go on a tour of the studio. Sort of to get the feeling of the way we work here. Then tomorrow night, there is to be a dinner party for you at my home. Everyone connected with the picture will be there, and a lot of other important people, too. We're all looking forward to it."

"But I had planned—" began Allison.

Brad stood up. "Wonderful, Arthur," he said. "As usual, you've done everything that has to be done very efficiently."

"It's the way we have to work," Arthur said. "Efficiency prevents ulcers. That's my own secret success formula, which I reveal to everyone."

Allison was back in the car sitting next to Brad before it occurred to her that neither Conrad Blanding nor Joel Parkingson had spoken one word to her, once the producer had begun to speak about the script.

"There," said Brad, as the car pulled away. "Painless, wasn't it?"

"Yes," agreed Allison, "but we didn't accomplish much."

"Wait," said Brad. "You'll have plenty to do when things get rolling."

The car stopped in front of a stone building that looked like a post office in a medium-sized city. Brad helped Allison out and led the way to Harold Jenks's office.

Harold Jenks was short and potbellied with dark curly hair and a beaked nose that would have gladdened the heart of a Nazi cartoonist. "Howarya?" he asked, not rising from behind his desk as Brad introduced Allison.

"Fine, thank you," said Allison.

"Sit down, sit down," said Jenks, indicating a chair. "Just get in?"

"No," said Allison. "We arrived last night."

"Met Tishman?"

"Yes. Earlier this afternoon. Before we came here."

"You're cute," said Jenks. "Clean-cut and all that. Should be able to do something with that." He looked Allison over thoroughly, then he pressed a key on the box that sat on his desk. "Send Joe Borden in here," he said. A man came into the room, but Jenks did not introduce him to Allison. He merely waved in her direction. "Allison MacKenzie," he said, as if she were merchandise on a store counter.

"Writes books. We've got to get something ready for the papers. Take her out and show her around a little. Get a line on her and give me something before she leaves."

Allison felt now, not only like merchandise on a counter, but merchandise that had been rejected by a prospective customer.

"Better get a few pictures," said Jenks, glancing at his watch. "Can't have the papers doing it on their own. Go over to Photography with her now."

"But Mr. Tishman said that I'm supposed to do that tomorrow morning," said Allison. "I can't be photographed today. My hair's a mess and I'm all wrinkled and my gloves are soiled."

Jenks laughed. "We've got people who get paid to worry about details like that," he said. "Go on. Go with Borden. He'll take care of everything."

"But I don't like to have my picture taken," said Allison. "It's bad enough in the morning, but—"

Jenks put his hands, palms down, on his desk with a gesture of infinite patience.

"Look," he said, "sitting in the same chair you're sitting in now I've had all the big names in the business. Monroe, Turner, Hayworth. All of 'em. I know what I'm doing. Just don't give me a hard time and I'll do a good job for you."

And he will too, Allison thought, finally impressed with his professionalism. He was the kind of man, met all too rarely, who knew his job, every part of it, better than anyone else. Like Tishman, Jenks was quite clearly not a man who held his job because he was somebody's brother-in-law. In Hollywood, the day of the brother-in-law ended with the birth of television. They're probably all working at the TV studios now, Allison thought.

Allison was combed, made up and photographed. Then she was recombed and rephotographed. The photographer looked at her as if she were something under a microscope and mumbled things to himself, and by the time it was over Allison was almost in tears.

"I wish I'd never come!" she cried as the car drove back toward the hotel. "David was right."

"There, there," Brad consoled. "You're just tired, Allison. You'll feel better after a drink and a good dinner."

At nine-thirty that evening, Allison finished the last of her dessert and looked gratefully at Brad.

"You were right," she said. "I have been acting like a child. Just pet me and feed me and I'm all smiles again. Disgusting, isn't it?"

Brad laughed. "You're wonderful," he said. "With just the right amount of temperament to make you exciting."

"The only thing that excites me now is the thought of a good, hot bath and a nice, soft bed," said Allison.

"Are you going to read the script?" asked Brad.

"While I'm soaking in the tub," replied Allison.

"I'll call you at nine-thirty in the morning," said Brad as they left the dining room. "We'll have breakfast together."

Ten minutes later, Allison drew a tub of very hot water, perfumed it lavishly with bath oil and prepared to soak, relax and read. An hour later, when she had finished the script, she was far from relaxed. Joel Parkingson had left out of his script what Allison considered some of the best parts of her novel; instead, there were pages and pages of inane dialogue and hollow characterization.

I mustn't care, thought Allison, tears streaming down her face. I *won't* care. They bought it and now it's theirs to do with as they see fit. I'm not entitled to care.

But she did care, and with the caring went the only defense that she had been able to build against a word suddenly too much aware of her. She had constructed her wall of indifference carefully, in the very beginning, for she had known that she would need something to hide behind.

"In a little while," Lewis had warned her, "say when *Samuel's Castle* gets close to the hundred thousand mark, it is going to become fashionable to pan the hell out of it."

"But I don't understand," Allison replied. "The first reviews were good. Not raves, exactly, but good."

"That was in the beginning," said Lewis. "But there are a lot of phony people in the world. They are the ones who 'discover' people, places and things and can't bear to keep their mouths shut about how clever they've been. But the minute that the great unwashed public begins to share their enthusiasm, whatever has been discovered is no longer palatable to the discoverers. Then they backtrack."

Lewis imitated the voice of one of them. They always sounded like victims of some terrible fatigue. "Capri used to be *the* place to go, my dear. But lately it's simply too full of the most undesirable types."

Allison laughed. "And is that what they will say about *Samuel's Castle?*" she asked. "That it used to be a good book but now it's become so dreadfully common?"

Lewis' face wrinkled in disgust. "I've listened to them at a thousand cocktail parties," he said. "And believe me you can't fight them. They are the opinion makers and they have got themselves into positions of power."

"I'm not their sort," Allison had said. "They won't waste their valuable time on me."

"They may," Lewis said. "And if they do, it can hurt."

"Don't worry about it, Lewis," said Allison.

But it began to happen as he had said it would. The first indication that Allison had of it was when a reviewer who had written a favorable review of her book wrote an article in the same magazine when the movie rights were sold.

"Century Films have bought the rights to the sexy silly, *Samuel's Castle.* All we can say is that Hollywood must be more hard up for material than usual."

Allison was stunned. She began to overhear conversations at parties and in theater lobbies.

"No, I haven't read *Samuel's Castle,*" she heard one woman, who had referred to the book on her television program as "exciting," telling her companion, "I glanced through it, but, my dear, what a bore!"

The head of a television network, who had tried to buy the rights to the book for a ninety-minute spectacular and had been turned down by Bradley Holmes, gave an interview to a national magazine in which he said, "I dread to think what a number of good books have been ignored while *Samuel's Castle* has clung to the top of the best-seller list."

It was only with Lewis that Allison could let down the barriers a little, and even with him she was careful not to reveal how much she was hurt. For the most part, she did her weeping alone.

"The public loves to create a hero," Lewis had said. "Sometimes I think they do it for the sheer joy of knocking him down from the highest peak. Like a child who builds a house of blocks and then destroys it with one vicious kick."

"I don't care," Allison had cried with forced gaiety. "It's wonderful to be famous while it lasts. And I don't really care that much what anyone says about the book. I don't really care at all."

Allison wept without sound into the pillow on her bed.

I don't care, she cried. Century bought it. I took their money. It's theirs, and I don't care what they do with it.

3

AT NINE-THIRTY the next morning, when Bradley Holmes joined her for breakfast, Allison MacKenzie looked as if she had never shed a tear in her life.

"Did you read the script?" asked Brad, sipping his coffee.

"Yes."

"How did it strike you?"

"As the biggest piece of foolishness one man could possibly get down on paper," said Allison. "If he worked really hard at it, that is."

"Well, it's not the end of the world," said Brad. "Arthur told you that it was only their first effort."

"He also said that the basis they have now will remain the same," said Allison angrily. "If that's so, they're going to be laughed out of every theater in America."

"Come now," said Brad. "It can't be that bad."

Allison shrugged. "See for yourself," she said.

"No time," said Brad, glancing at his watch. "We have to get started for the studio."

"I'd just as soon get started for the airport if you don't mind," said Allison. "The sooner we leave here the better."

"You sound like David Noyes," said Brad. "Come on, Allison, cheer up."

She found it impossible to do so. All the way out to the studio, she sat in the back of the limousine in a little world of her own. It was a world of rancor. She hated Hollywood, Tishman, the writer, the director. All she could think of was that Tishman had bought her book because he admired it and thought it would make a great film; but he had bought it only to change it. She thought of the flat, platitudinous lines of dialogue and shuddered. The film would be called *Samuel's Castle*, her name would be listed on the credits; but it had nothing to do with her.

And yet, it would. She knew that in Tishman's Hollywood world, as in the Broadway world, no matter how remote was your connection with a flop—even if you were only the author of the book and had nothing to do with the adaptation—you were still considered to be partly responsible for it.

Having read Tishman's script, she had no doubt that the film would be a flop, that it would be laughed off the screen, that audiences would be so bored by it they'd leave their popcorn behind and flee the theater.

When she and Brad entered Tishman's studio, he was at his desk going through a loose-leaf folder containing the costume designer's preliminary sketches. On the margins of each sheet he wrote comments in red ink. Allison noted that he had the calligraphic handwriting that always reminded her of monastic orders, of dedicated men working alone. So much for handwriting analysis, she thought; Tishman was no monk, and Hollywood was a million miles from the nearest monastery.

Arthur Tishman looked closely at Allison from under his heavy, hooded eyelids. He swung his chair around and, in a sudden movement, stood up.

"Brad," he said, "why don't you go over to Publicity and look over what Jenks has prepared. I'd like to take Allison and show her around the lot."

"Of course, Arthur," Brad said. "That's a very good idea."

Allison looked at Brad and thought, You've missed your calling; you'd have made a perfect Yes man.

When Brad had gone, Arthur turned to Allison. He moved toward the door and she found herself following him.

"Do you mind walking?" he said.

"I like walking," Allison told him.

"I like it, too. But it takes too long," he said.

Then he was silent. Allison walked along beside him, thinking, What kind of man is this? He has the handwriting of a monk, dresses like a man from Mars—today he wore a sport shirt on which palm

166

trees swayed across his chest, casting their shadows on beautiful Wai-kiki Beach which stretched across his stomach—believes walking is too slow, and thinks he can make a great movie out of this incredibly dull and unimaginative script.

After five minutes of walking, the ordinary world of ordinary buildings was behind them. Allison felt like Alice; the world had gone topsy-turvy. Next door to a crumbling southern mansion was the façade of the palace at Versailles; and when they left those behind, they walked down the main street of a small town that Hollywood, by using it so often, had made the American people (and half the world) believe to be typical. Six cowboys wearing green eye shadow, their lips rouged, loped past them, their horses' hoofs clattering on the asphalt road.

When they left the typical small town Allison saw, on her right, an artificial lake. A rowboat with three wet actors was being tossed about by high waves. From a tower, a voice called, "Okay. Turn off the storm." The wind machines stopped; the storm ended; the actors stepped out of the boat into the knee-deep water and waded ashore.

"When you see that on the screen," Arthur said, "you will be certain it was filmed on the open seas. And if the director is good and the producer is imaginative and the actors right, you will believe in the plight of that shipwrecked trio."

They came to a western town. There was the dusty main street, the sheriff's office, the saloon, the general store, the wood sidewalks. Allison expected at any moment to see Gary Cooper, tall and lean, cautiously move out of the sheriff's office.

Arthur pushed open the swinging doors of the saloon and they went inside. Sunlight filtered through cracks in the roof; the long mirror behind the bar returned their images. Seeing herself, Allison had the feeling she was out of place and out of time, an interloper in the American past.

She sat down at one of the tables. Arthur leaned against the bar.

"You've seen this saloon in a hundred movies. Each time it looked a little different. A few minor changes, a change of lighting, a change of faces, and it becomes a new place. All you need are creative film makers with a new way of looking at things, and the most familiar object or place can be made to look strange to you."

He crossed the room and sat down next to her.

"I want to tell you, Allison, that I know how you feel about the script. You think we've ruined your book and you say to yourself, I don't care that they've ruined my book but they haven't even made a good script out of the ruins. It's all dull, flat and unimaginative."

Allison opened her mouth to speak, but Arthur went on.

"A lot of skills go into the making of a film, Allison. But after twenty years in this place I've come to the conclusion that the most valuable skill of all is the ability to read a script. To read it, see it and hear it. All at once. And then to be able to judge; will this script make a good movie, or just another mediocre movie."

He stood up and began to pace restlessly around the tables, then stopped with his back to the swinging doors.

"It's difficult to explain all this, Allison. You read our script like a novelist. You can't. You've got to read it like a sound camera. A sound camera with an imaginative human brain. Listen, Allison. You've heard the expression, 'the magic of the theater'?"

Allison nodded.

"When idiots use that expression, they mean the 'glamour' of the theater, its aura, its spectacular appeal. But when theater workers talk about 'magic,' they mean something altogether different. To them, 'magic' is the odd, mysterious, inexplicable thing that happens between a director and his actors. The magical thing is that those lines you consider to be dull and innocuous suddenly become meaningful, and reveal qualities you never suspected were there. You make a great mistake to expect that a film script must be literary. In a sense, it must *never* be literary. It has got to have *extra-literary* qualities."

He came and sat down across the table from her.

"What you are looking for is a script that reads like a novel. What I am looking for, always, is a script that reads like a movie. Allison, I'm an old pro. I know what I'm talking about. If I didn't, I'd have been thrown off this lot years ago. Are you going to take my word for it?"

Allison did not answer. All she could think of was her mutilated novel. She walked to the window and looked out. She saw, walking down the dusty street, a group of white-robed, barefooted men. One of them was leading a white donkey. They were on their way to the lot where a Biblical movie was being made.

It was one of the strangest sights she had ever seen, these early Christians walking through a town of the American West. It was all wrong, yet out here it made sense. She realized suddenly that these people could do anything, that on the outskirts of Los Angeles they could, if they wanted to, create New York or a planetary city of the future. They had worked their magic on her since she was a little girl. Why did she suddenly begin to doubt them now?

She turned and smiled at Arthur. "I think I've been suffering from Novelist's Disease. It's what other people call arrogance. We work alone so much that we begin to think we are the only creative people in the world. And, what's worse, that we don't need anyone else."

"Only hacks don't take pride in their work," Arthur said.

He took her arm and they began to walk back toward the administration buildings. At the open door of the sound stage, two ladies in waiting at the court of the Empress Eugénie, wearing ball gowns and powdered wigs, were talking about their favorite rock-and-roll singer. For the first time, Allison began to feel the excitement of Hollywood's creativity and, listening to Arthur, began to have some understanding of the technical aspect of film work.

"We expect to wind up with a great film, Allison," Arthur told her as he helped her into the car. "Not just a good film, but a great one. Tomorrow we'll have an office ready for you. I want to hear all the ideas you've got."

The driver picked up Brad outside Jenks's office. Brad got into the car and handed Allison a large manila envelope. "Your photos," he said, smiling.

She opened the envelope and took them out. She hardly recognized herself. It was her own face, but somehow it had been invested with mystery, with glamour and with a kind of beauty she had never seen in any mirror. She smiled to herself and thought, The magic is even working on me.

She said to Brad, "That lens looked at me with lover's eyes."

She quickly stuffed the photographs back into the envelope. For some reason, it embarrassed her to look at them; it was as if she had been caught in a fraudulent act.

By her second week in Hollywood, Allison had had to throw out the window every preconception she had brought along with her. It was true that there were more swimming pools in Beverly Hills than in any other town in the world, the houses and grounds were the most fanciful copies of Spanish castles and English manor houses, and without doubt Hollywood attracted to itself the most beautiful women—and even beautiful men—from every part of the world.

But the overriding fact about Hollywood, what made the trappings unimportant, was the work of making movies. She never anywhere saw people work with such energy, with such furious drive. It carried over into their private lives; there was the same kind of driving energy in their love affairs and their marriages and in the way they relaxed.

Making movies was for Hollywood what making automobiles was to Detroit. From the window of her office she could see a large area of the studio lot, the trucks and motorized freight wagons that plied endlessly up and down the studio streets, carrying scenery and costumes. Hundreds of men moved about, each performing an assigned task, hundreds of extras and a handful of highly paid actors and directors committed themselves and their reputations to film.

Allison sat at her desk and spent the first week reading the script. She read it now with new eyes, eyes that had been opened and made more knowledgeable because Tishman had shared with her some of the knowledge that only years of working in films can give.

Parts of the script that, on first reading, had seemed to her arbitrary and capricious, she now saw as reasonable changes.

They had changed the time scheme of her novel. She had thought them stupid for doing so. But now, she understood the reason for making a scene she had set in summer take place in winter. The coldness, the bleak landscape, the white and black of snow and bare trees, all this would heighten the mood and give the sequence precisely the emotional overtones it needed.

She met with the set designer and the costume department and gave her opinions on their work. She found only minor errors, the kind of thing no one would notice except the experts who looked for such mistakes.

She left the studio at five every day and returned to her hotel. It was not the studio but the hotel that was the Hollywood of every small-town girl's imagining. In the lobby and around the pool sat the beautiful girls who were not waiting to be discovered but working very hard at it. And there were the rich widows, elderly women who spent hours each day in beauty salons, and who were always accompanied by handsome young men.

Allison was soon able to spot an agent by the way he walked, and could tell at a glance whether a man was an unemployed writer or a director waiting for an assignment. In a very short time she had learned all the gossip and knew, as the waitresses in the dining room knew, why the famous star was *really* getting her divorce, and who the other man *really* was.

Lewis called Allison every evening. They spoke for five or ten minutes and hurried to say all they wanted to say to each other, spoke of their love and their plans and what each had done that day. Until the day finally came when Allison was able to say, "Oh, Lewis, tomorrow is the last day, and I can come back to you!" She had her reservation for six o'clock the next evening, she would be in New York, with Lewis, in the morning.

The night before she left, Arthur Tishman gave a party for her. He wanted her to meet Rita Moore, especially, knowing she was a favorite of Allison's.

Brad had returned to New York at the end of the first week. Allison rode alone in the back seat of the studio limousine, her elbow on the arm rest, smoking a cigarette. She smiled. I'm acting as calmly, she thought, as if I've done this sort of thing all my life.

She wore a simple, sheathlike black gown; her hair was drawn back; a small diamond clip was her only ornament. It was the only jewelry she had bought herself, thus far, with her new money. She always referred to it, to herself, as new money. She had seen the clip one day in the window of a Beverly Hills jeweler and walked in and bought it. She knew that whatever might come in the future, this clip would always be her favorite, because it was the first and because it had been bought with money made from her first success. As the car drove up the graveled drive to Arthur Tishman's house, she touched the clip; it gave her assurance.

Tishman's house was one of the great old houses. It was not California modern; it looked like one of the houses in an old Long Island suburb. It was an extravagant relic, a dinosaur from the ice age of Doug and Mary; it was a proud reminder of Hollywood's regal past.

Architecturally, it was part Spanish, part Tudor; yet this did not, somehow, result in a hodgepodge. As is so often the case with early twentieth-century American houses, the architect's vulgarity had, over the years, become charming. It was a place, Allison decided, that she would enjoy living in. It had not the look of post-war houses; she thought them mean and inhospitable with their functional little rooms and uncomfortably low ceilings.

The car came to a stop at a graceful flight of stone steps with low risers and a carved balustrade. Arthur came down the steps and helped her out of the car.

In five minutes she had had two drinks, was holding her third and had been introduced to twenty people. She remembered the names of none except those actors she recognized. There was one she had had a crush on when she was fourteen. He had sallow skin, thinning hair and an obscene little belly. On the screen he still looked as handsome as ever.

She had quickly gulped down her first two drinks in an attempt to get over the nervousness she felt at being with these people. But all she succeeded in doing was to make herself a little lightheaded. She looked around for Rita Moore but did not see her.

Conversation swirled around her. She put down her drink and stepped out the open doors to the terrace. She took a deep breath of air. I must clear my head, she thought. She walked to the end of the terrace, her heels making a satisfying noise on the terra-cotta tiles. The brightly lighted living room gave way to a dark wing of the house.

In one room an amber light glowed and Allison, peering through the french doors, saw it was the library. She tried the door. It opened, and she entered. It was a high-ceilinged room, vaulted, with a deep stone fireplace. The walls were lined with books, beautifully bound.

They even look as if they've been read, Allison thought.

She took a step toward the books when a head popped up, peered for an instant over the top of the leather sofa and disappeared. But that moment was enough for Allison to recognize Rita Moore's famous face.

"Are you real or are you the ghost of Norma Talmadge?" Rita Moore asked from behind the sofa.

"I'm real enough," Allison said. She walked around the sofa and looked down at Rita Moore. She smiled at Rita and said, "I'm glad to see you have a body and aren't just a voice."

"I *used* to have a body," Rita said, looking down at it. "Christ, did I have a body! When I see myself in old movies on the telly, it breaks my ever-beating heart."

"You're still the greatest, Miss Moore."

Rita's mouth curved in a mirthless smile. "Thanks a whole lot. You could have it for one small farthing if I could have your youth."

She reached for the cut-glass brandy decanter on the small table, but could not quite reach it. Allison picked it up and tilted some of the liquid into Rita's glass.

She drank it down like medicine, like something she had to take because it was good for her. She grimaced and said, "Christ, I'm tired! I'm just plain body tired, and I'm most of all tired of parties like this. When I come to a place like this, the first thing I do is look for the exits. After twenty years in this town I've learned the library is the best place to be alone in. Most of us out here are afraid of books. Reading a book is a sign that we've been alone for a few hours. And out here, to be alone is a phrase that strikes a fear unknown since the black plague swept across Europe."

She filled her brandy glass again. Her soft, silver-blond hair caught the light and shimmered like a jewel. She had high cheekbones that made a diagonal of shadow in her cheeks, like smudges made by her thumbs. Her eyes were sea green and her dress was a deep green embroidered in gold. It clung to her body like a second skin, and where her breasts swelled out of the top her flesh was like heavy cream.

"You must be Allison MacKenzie," she said. "You must be, because I've never seen you before and because you are the only one here who looks bright enough to have written a novel. Especially a novel as good as *Samuel's Castle*."

"Thank you," Allison said.

"Please don't say thank you, dear. It reminds me of my second husband. My second husband was the kind of man who was always saying thank you. He was humble—in an arrogant sort of way."

Allison smiled, but not because she felt like smiling; she smiled because she had the feeling she was expected to.

"My second husband seduced me with Brahms and Scotch," said Rita at last. "The poor bastard."

"Why do you say that?" asked Allison.

"Because that was all he knew how to do," replied Rita. "Seduce women to a sad violin and the tinkle of ice cubes. He was good at it though, I'll say that for him."

"How many husbands have you had?" asked Allison.

Rita laughed. "Don't you ever read the fan magazines?" she asked.

Allison smiled and shook her head. "Not any more," she said. "But I used to. When we were in high school, Selena Cross and I used to buy every issue of *Photoplay* and *Silver Screen*. Then we'd cut out the pictures and make scrapbooks. I wonder if kids still do that."

"In Hollywood, we hope so," said Rita. "Anyway, it's four."

"Four what?"

"Husbands," said Rita. "Isn't that what you asked me?"

"Four!" said Allison. "Good Lord!"

"Well, at least I married the men I fell in love with," said Rita with a little pout. "I know plenty of women who will jump into bed with just anybody. At least I always kept it legal."

"I don't think I'll ever get married," said Allison.

Rita poured more liquor into her glass. "Why not?" she asked. "What have you got against marriage?"

"I want everything to stay just the way it is right now," said Allison, an unaccustomed toughness in her voice.

Rita glanced at her sharply, then said, "Well, aren't you a smug little punk kid."

Allison's head snapped up in surprise. "What do you mean by that?" she asked.

"Just what I said," replied Rita belligerently. "You think you know it all, don't you?"

"For Heaven's sake," objected Allison. "What in the world did I say?"

"You love having things the way they are now," said Rita. "You love being a success, being way up on top where very few people ever get. You love all that lovely money that rolls in day after day, and you love the idea that it's yours, all yours."

"And what's wrong with that?" demanded Allison. "You're in the same position yourself. Don't tell me that you hate being successful."

Rita looked down into her glass and thought for a moment.

"I don't know," she said. "I don't know whether I hate it or love it or just don't care any more."

Allison laughed. "I know a fellow in New York. His name is Paul Morris and he's quite well known in his field so you've probably heard of him."

"I've heard of him," said Rita.

"Well, Paul told me once that successful people who complain about being successful are nothing more than lousy poseurs. If they didn't glory in it, they'd run and bury themselves where no one had ever heard of them."

Rita gave a short, humorless laugh as she poured herself another drink.

"I'll tell you about success," she said. "And believe me, I can tell you a helluva lot more about it than your friend Paul Morris. He never made it except as somebody else's shadow." She leaned back and sipped at her drink. "I think that you have to decide when you're very young that you want success more than anything else in the world," she said.

"Well, I certainly didn't," said Allison angrily.

Rita looked at her. "Don't kid me, love," she said. "I know about you, Allison. I've heard enough. I can figure you out like you were my twin sister. When you were a kid you didn't think you were good looking. You were the odd one who couldn't fit into the group, and you resented everyone who did belong. Without even knowing it you began to think in terms of 'I'll show them all,' and you did."

"All you need is a framed diploma and a couch and you could go into business," said Allison, and she poured a glass of brandy for herself.

"Don't get wise with me, sweetie," said Rita. "I've been there, and I know. Where the hell do you think I sprang from? Well, I'll tell you. From a lousy shack in the backwoods of Georgia. My old man was a sharecropper and my mother was worn out and tired before she even married him. Her father had been a sharecropper, too, and all she ever knew was work, work and more work. And kids and filth and no money and a constant hole in your belly from being hungry. I never had pair of shoes on my feet until I was fourteen, and even then they were discards, but my mother sent me to school anyway."

She paused and drank deeply and refilled the glass. "I don't know what sets anybody else off," she said. "But I know what it was with me. We had a teacher at school who was a real old bag. She didn't have any more business teaching than I'd have, but with her shape and face I guess she couldn't do anything else. She reminded me of a wrinkled-up old prune, but she taught us geography. One day she was telling us about Paris, and she got a kind of look on her face that made her almost good looking for a minute. She showed us pictures, too. The most beautiful pictures I'd ever seen in my life, and she told us about the trip in a ship that got you there."

She leaned her head back and looked up at the ceiling, as if to look back into the past more comfortably. "Right then and there I made up my mind that I was going to Paris, but I was still a kid and too dumb to keep my mouth shut about it. I told her and she laughed at me. She told me that sharecroppers' kids never got out of Georgia, let alone make trips to Europe. But I knew better. I was going to Paris. And I did, too. Five years ago. With four trunks and sixteen suitcases and two maids and a poodle. I stood under the Arc de Triomphe and thought of that old bitch back in Georgia and thumbed my nose at her. I'd made it and I'd come first class all the way. I was with my third husband then. Jay Keating. You've heard of him, I suppose."

"Yes," said Allison. "I've heard of him. He's an English actor."

"English my foot," said Rita. "He was born in South Dakota. He was a pansy on top of everything else."

"A what?" asked Allison.

"Pansy," said Rita. "A real fruit. I caught him in my stateroom with the ship's purser on the trip home. But you never would have read that in any fan magazine. We called it incompatibility and I went to Reno for a divorce. Heigh-ho, and so much for number three." She raised her glass. "Here's to success. It's what you tell yourself you have when it dawns on you that you haven't got anything else."

"It doesn't have to be like that," said Allison. "I've heard of plenty of people who are successful and happily married besides."

"Maybe," said Rita. "If the man is as successful as the woman. It doesn't work if the woman is the big name. Not once in a million times! It didn't work with me, and I guess I knew it wouldn't right from the beginning. I was married when I first began to be somebody.

My first husband. Alan. A real, sweet kid. He worked for the Los Angeles Telephone Company and I married him because I kidded myself
into believing I really loved him. What I was was hungry. And lonely.
So Alan fed me and kept me company. When I was around. But I was
going to make it and make it big and I didn't want a husband around
who was going to make the road up any rockier than it was to begin
with. I had a shape back then, too, and I wasn't particular who I
showed it to as long as there was something in it for me. Alan didn't
like the pictures he saw of me wearing a little more than a G-string
and two sequins, but not much more. He crabbed when I went out
with my agent and he couldn't understand that I had to be seen in the
right places. He wanted me home and I wanted out. So that was the
end of that."

Rita smiled her mirthless smile. "I felt rotten that time. I cried for
almost the whole six weeks I had to stay in Nevada, but my agent,
Charlie Bloom, told me what the score was. Charlie said that I could
either have a diamond necklace around my neck or a husband. Naturally, I chose the diamonds. Do you know Charlie?"

"No," said Allison.

"He's the biggest agent in Hollywood," said Rita. "Charlie has all
the big names in his stable now, but when he started out with me he
was nobody. Just a smart, sharp little guy who knew all the answers
and had more nerve than a brass monkey. Charlie dressed me in a
tight sweater and an even tighter skirt and he taught me how to walk
with a sexy jounce and how to pinch my nipples so that they'd show
under the sweater. He changed my name, too. From Alice Johnson to
Rita Moore. And there was a time when a man could get fired at Century if he slipped and called me Alice. Alice Johnson was a name
without class. It took Hollywood ten years to find out that I could do
more than stick my chest out and wiggle my backside. That's when I
became An Actress. Anyway, three years ago I married John Gres-
ham. John was a real smoothie. He played the piano and told me I
had eyes that he could drown in and that my body was like a flame.
So what the hell. I married him."

"Just because he was a good talker?" asked Allison.

Rita shrugged. "No. He pressured me into it."

"Oh, come now," Allison objected. "Women don't allow themselves to be pressured into a marriage they don't want."

"What the hell do you know about it?" demanded Rita. "John was an artist, let me tell you. He knew what he was doing. The son-of-a-bitch used to make love to me for hours before we were married. He'd stroke and kiss and handle me until I thought I'd go out of my mind, but he never finished anything. He'd tell me he wanted to wait until after we were married because I was so pure and he didn't want to dishonor me by taking me without a ceremony. So I married him."

She stopped to light a cigarette. Allison could not take her eyes from her. "He was good in bed, I'll say that for him. And for a while it was great. We'd spend all day in bed. John was an expert. He knew every trick in the book and when I thought I couldn't do anything else, he'd come up with something new. But there came a day when I had to go back to work and that left John without a job. Still, he was nice to come home to. I'd walk in the door and he'd undress me and make me a drink and play with me while I drank it, and it was fun. I guess he got bored after a while, though, because last year he stopped playing with me and began to play with my money. He got away with over fifty thousand before I put a stop to it. As usual, I put the stop to it all by going to Nevada."

She turned her green eyes, searching and sad, to Allison. "So now you can go back to New York and tell your friend Paul what success is really like. You go along for years kidding yourself that if you're successful you can have everything you want, but all the time you know that the only way you can make it is alone."

Rita fixed herself another drink, and when she had done so she held the glass up to the light and squinted through the dark fluid.

"Alone," she said. "I guess that's the saddest word in the world. You stay at a hotel and order your own coffee in the morning and you hire a masseuse to rub your back and at night your bed is as big as Texas and as cold as Alaska. But you're successful." She swallowed her drink and looked at Allison. "Don't forget that, Allison. You're a success! You're a goddamned big success! And just see what it'll get you. Just you bloody well see!"

When Allison entered her hotel room, much later that night, its expensive splendor suddenly seemed tasteless and repellent. She threw her purse across the room. It struck the wall above her dressing table and fell with a crash among the bottles of perfume and jars of cream. Allison wanted to break every window and rip to shreds the royal purple curtains. She wanted to do something so wild and destructive that it would shake her back into sanity, into a realization of her true self which she now felt was lost.

She had success, more than she had ever dreamed of. But never in her life had she been so fearful of the future, so frightened of the present, as she was now.

She sank down into a chair and cried bitterly. What is to become of me? she asked herself. Will I, ten years from now, be another Rita Moore, working on my fourth divorce or my fifth husband? Oh, Lewis, Lewis, take care of me. Never let me go.

PART FOUR

1

ALLISON RETURNED TO PEYTON PLACE in late October, having spent a week in New York with Lewis. She had had to tell Constance that the stopover in New York was necessary for business reasons. As the train pulled into Peyton Place, she thought, Lewis has become a guilty secret. She did not want to have secrets from her mother, but she knew that Constance would be worried and terribly upset to learn that she was involved with a married man. She wanted desperately to be able to sit down with Constance and discuss it with her, but she knew that for Constance's sake she could not.

Peyton Place lay sheltered under the dome of October's bright blue sky. The tattered brown leaves that hung on the bare branches of trees were winter's flags, Allison thought, the sign of his coming. The air was not cold, but there was a wintry feel to it. On Armistice Day the first snow would fall, and by Thanksgiving the town would be in winter's grip.

She was hardly off the train before Mike and Constance threw their arms around her, welcoming her home. Tears sprang to her eyes; she felt guilty, felt she had betrayed them by staying with Lewis for a week. Constance carried her off to the waiting car while Mike followed, carrying her suitcases.

Constance and Allison sat in the back seat, and Constance held her hand and looked into her face as if to see if those weeks in Hollywood had changed or altered her in some way. Mike took a look at them in the rear-view mirror and laughed.

"Be careful, Allison," he said, "any minute now she's going to whip out a microscope and put you under it."

"You go to hell, Mike," said Constance, and smiled at him in the mirror.

Mike went on. "She was certain you had 'gone Hollywood' and that you'd come back with platinum-blond hair and at least three Mexican divorces."

Allison turned to Constance. "I was working too hard to become tainted," Allison said.

"Tell me all about Rita Moore," Mike demanded.

"That's all *he's* interested in," Constance said. "That old man of mine has hot pants for Rita Moore. Every time I open the bedroom door I expect to find that he's got pin-ups of her over our bed."

"I may be old but I'm not a fool," Mike said. "I know what side my bread is buttered on."

"Mike!" Allison said. "Honestly, I never heard people talk like you two, not even in Hollywood."

Mike and Constance roared with laughter. Constance squeezed Allison's hand. "I'm so glad to have you home, baby," she said.

The car drew up to the house. Allison looked at it with loving eyes. If only Lewis could see it, she thought, if only he were here with me now.

They went into the kitchen. It was, Allison thought, the warmest, kindest room she had ever seen anywhere.

"I'll unpack later," she said. "Right now I want a cup of Mother's coffee."

Mike said, "I'll carry your luggage upstairs, and then I've got to drive downtown and pick up some things for your mother." He bent down and kissed the top of her head. "Welcome home, Allison," he said.

Why is it always such a relief to me when I come back? wondered Allison. Peyton Place is small-town America at its worst. Narrow, provincial, gossipy. Yet, I never feel really safe anywhere else, nor contented. And why is it that I love the winter best? Is it because I can stay safe and warm in my mother's house while the storm rages outside?

Allison yawned and stretched and turned away from the bleak, wintry view outside the kitchen window.

"Tired, darling?" asked Constance, setting down a coffeepot and two cups on the table.

"No," said Allison. "Just lazy. I was wondering why I always feel better when I'm in Peyton Place than when I'm anywhere else." She shrugged. "I guess it must be immaturity. But I love to snuggle down into the cocoon of this house while life raises hell outside my protective shell. How's that? Deep and psychological, huh?"

Connie laughed. "I don't know much about psychology. I only know that I'm happy when you are, and wretched when you're not. Maybe I have an apron string complex or something."

Allison squeezed her mother's shoulder and picked up a coffee cup.

Constance said, "I didn't think you'd want to see anybody today, so I invited Selena and Joey and Peter Drake for dinner tomorrow night."

"Oh? I didn't know that Peter was still on the scene."

"Very much so," said Connie. "Selena never told me what happened between her and Tim Randlett, but when it was over, there was Peter, ready and willing to pick up the pieces."

"I wish Selena would get married," remarked Allison. "Either that or leave town. She's in a dreadful rut here. What is there in Peyton Place for a girl with her looks and intelligence? Nothing."

Connie smiled. "Maybe she feels the same way about Peyton Place as you do," she said. "Perhaps there is a degree of security here for her that she's afraid would be missing everywhere else."

"What security?" asked Allison. "She not only has to look after herself, but Joey, too. And all she has to depend on is her job at the store."

"And Peter Drake," Connie added.

"Perhaps it's just as well that it ended with Tim the way it did. I guess Mike was right about him all along."

Connie shrugged. "I don't know. I always liked Tim well enough. At any rate, he was Selena's last chance to get out of her rut. I don't imagine that she'll be too eager to fall in love with another stranger." Connie paused and looked searchingly at Allison. "And, speaking of love," she said at last, "what about David Noyes?"

Allison looked down into her empty coffee cup. "I don't know," she said.

She longed to tell Constance it was not David she cared about but Lewis Jackman. David, however, provided a perfect smoke screen, so she went on discussing him with Constance.

"He's in love with you, you know."

"It's not David that I don't know about," said Allison. "I'm not sure of myself."

Connie sighed. "I guess every mother wants to see her daughter safely and happily married," she said. "And I'm no different."

"David has been everywhere and has done just about everything," said Allison. "He's been on a safari in Africa and skiing in Switzerland and he's even had himself put in prison so that he could write a book about it. I've never been anywhere or done anything. David would be perfectly willing to get married, buy a house right here in Peyton Place and settle down to writing his books."

"But you've just been telling me that you're never happier than when you're right here," objected Connie.

"I am," agreed Allison. "But it's a selfish sort of thing. I want to be able to come home anytime I want to. But I want to be able to leave, too. At any time for any place. I wouldn't be able to do that if I were married to David. He has this thing where he always wants to shield me from everything."

"What's wrong with that?" asked Connie. "You'd be much worse off if you got stuck with a man who didn't give a damn what happened to you."

Allison sighed. "I know it," she said. "But I can't live through David's experience, either." She stopped and grinned at her mother. "You know what's the matter with me?" she asked. "I want everything. Every experience, every sight and smell and taste and feeling. But I don't want anything to hurt me." She stood up and went to the window. "So you see how impossible it is," she said. "Nobody can have both, can they?"

Connie refilled the cups. She thought, Allison has grown a lot in the past year, but in many ways she's still a romantic little girl. "I can see why you want to wait," she said. "But I do wish that David were coming for the holiday."

"He's working on a book," said Allison. "And when David is working, all the furies of hell couldn't tear him away from his typewriter. Perhaps he'll be up for Christmas. Stevie is coming for Thanksgiving, though. And if it's all right with you, Mother, I'd like to ask my publisher to come too," she added hurriedly.

Constance turned and looked at Allison. "You mean Lewis Jackman?"

"Yes," said Allison. "I'd like him to see Peyton Place."

"Well, of course, dear. You know you can invite anyone you like."

Constance paused to light a cigarette and glanced at Allison over the wavering flame of the match. "He's married, isn't he?"

"Lewis Jackman? Yes, he is. And he's in his forties, too."

"Well," Constance said, "that doesn't matter. Some men are younger at that age than others are when they're twenty."

Allison laughed. "Where did you learn all that, Mother?"

Constance said, "Darling, there are some things you learn just by living and keeping your eyes open. You don't have to personally experience all sorts of men to know that there are some who are born old and there are others who are still young when they're sixty."

"Well," Allison said, "all this has got nothing to do with Lewis Jackman. He's just my publisher and a very charming man. It doesn't matter to me whether he's eighty, married, or unmarried."

Constance said, "What about his wife? Will she be coming, too?"

"I don't think so," Allison said, looking down into her cup. "From what I hear, she's quite sick. She doesn't see anyone but her psychiatrist."

"Oh, I see," Constance said. "Too bad."

Surreptitiously she watched Allison's face. She wondered why talking about Lewis Jackman had made her so nervous, and why Allison did not look at her when she spoke of Jackman's wife. There were a hundred questions Constance wanted to ask her daughter, and it was only with a conscious effort that she kept her mouth shut. You must not pry, she warned herself. When Allison is ready to tell you about this, she will tell you.

Constance was certain something was going on. A young girl's infatuation with an older man, she thought, can sometimes be a very strong thing. She wondered if the fact that Allison had never known her own father might not have something to do with it. Perhaps Lewis Jackman was providing Allison with the father image she had always lacked.

Mike returned. He burst into the kitchen carrying two large bags of groceries. Then he sat down at the table with them, held up the empty cup and said to Constance, "Reward me. I have been a good boy."

Constance filled his cup. "There," she said. "Is that reward enough for you?"

"Ask me later," Mike told her in a stage whisper.

Allison laughed. "Sometimes I feel like you two are my children," she said.

She asked Mike how he was enjoying his teaching job in White River.

He made a face. "If my wife could support me in the manner to which I've grown accustomed, I'd give up that job with just one minute's notice."

Connie put her arm around his shoulders. "You should have swallowed your pride and your honor when the school board here told you they were sorry and wanted you back," she said.

"What's this?" Allison cried.

"It happened just after you left," Constance explained. "Mike's being fired became such a scandal in educational circles that even Roberta got scared. Also, the new principal turned out to be an absolute dud."

"They came to me, Roberta and poor old Charlie, with their hats in their hands—and, let me tell you, Roberta looks better with it in her hands than on her head—and offered me my old job," Mike said.

"Mike told them he wouldn't take the job back until they agreed to a few demands he had to make."

"It'll do them good to stew in their own juice for a year," said Mike. "Besides, they'll need that long to make up their minds to give me everything I asked for."

"Everything like what?" asked Allison.

"Like tenure and a thousand dollar a year raise every year for the next five years." replied Mike.

"Charlie Partridge is all for it," said Connie. "But he can't convince Marion. Roberta is on the fence."

"Well see," Mike said.

"Yes, but when?" asked Allison.

"In March," replied Mike. "When the new contracts come out."

"Thank God it'll be in March," said Allison. "In April the group from Hollywood will be here, and I don't imagine that they'll do anything to improve our public relations with Peyton Place."

"They're really coming then?" asked Connie.

"Yes," replied Allison. "God help us all."

"I heard that it was quite a session when the advance guard met with the selectmen," said Mike. "Tishman's representative was a man named Blanding . . ." Mike went on.

"Conrad Blanding," said Allison. "He's the director."

"Well, Blanding told old Tom Perkins that all the studio wanted to do was use the town for a few weeks, and in return they'd leave approximately a hundred thousand dollars of their money behind. But old Tom wasn't impressed."

"He wouldn't be," Connie said. "He's New England through and through. What's good enough for his grandfather is good enough for his grandchildren. I wish some of these people would get over the idea that progress is sinful. I'm surprised Tom Perkins hasn't organized hatchet parties to smash up every TV set in Peyton Place."

"Stop interrupting with your seditious talk," Mike said. "If you're not careful, I'll have you run out of town on a rail." He returned to Allison and continued his account.

"Perkins told Blanding that Peyton Place had managed to get along very well without outside money for a good many years and that as far as he was concerned we could all stagger along for another century or two without any help from Hollywood."

"I warned Arthur Tishman," said Allison. "But he took one look at photographs of the castle and made up his mind. And when Arthur makes up his mind, *nothing* can shake it."

"Well, it'll give the town something new to talk about," Mike said. "Maybe they'll give Marion Partridge a job as an extra—"

"She could play one of the witches," Connie said. "She wouldn't even need make-up."

"—and she'll forget about me and my job," Mike finished, a look of exaggerated patience on his face while he waited through Constance's interruption.

"Nitwit," she said. "You can help me with dinner while Allison goes up and unpacks. And there's time for a nap, darling, if you're feeling tired," she said to Allison.

"Perhaps I will lie down for an hour," Allison said, and went up to her room.

Her room was the same, exactly as she had remembered it, exactly as she had imagined it during those lonely nights in the expensive hotels in New York and California. It was a simple room, still full of reminders of her girlhood.

Her luggage, which Mike had stacked neatly at the foot of her bed, seemed a violation of the simple spirit of the room. The luggage was new, it was full of new things. It had nothing to do with the Allison MacKenzie whose room this was, with the Allison MacKenzie who had gone to movies with Selena, taken walks with Norman and dreamed childhood's peculiar dreams.

The luggage seemed to Allison a dreadful reminder of how much her life had changed. She lay down on her bed and thought, I live in two worlds now, I am a completely divided person. There is the world of Peyton Place, and I will never be so much at home anywhere else. And there is the outside world of New York and Hollywood in which I play a role, as surely as any actress does.

Except with Lewis. That is the one genuine aspect of the other world.

When her plane had landed at La Guardia, Lewis was waiting for her. All the way back to the city they held hands and just stared at each other, as if their eyes could never get enough of the sight of each other.

At the apartment hotel where she had reserved her suite of rooms, the manager awaited her in the lobby and welcomed her back. Bellboys ran to get her luggage from the car. And when they were finally alone, a small bottle of champagne cooling in a silver bucket, she then had to phone Constance.

It was only after this was done that Lewis finally took her in his arms. It was as if they waited till all the petty little details were out of the way, and they would not have to be interrupted by anyone or for anything, that they turned to each other.

"My God, darling!" Lewis said. "How I've missed you!"

"Oh, I know, I know," Allison said.

"I couldn't sleep nights for missing you. Talking to you on the phone, and you so many miles away, was a torture. And yet I had to phone you. It was better than nothing."

"We'll have a week together now, darling, and after Thanksgiving I'll be back for good and all. But I have to spend some time with Constance and Mike. And I want to be with them for a while, Lewis. I need it. These last few weeks have been exhausting."

Lewis opened the bottle of champagne. "Well start building you up with this," he said. "It's full of vitamins, as you know."

She smiled at him and looked around the high-ceilinged, beautifully proportioned room. It had come to seem almost like her second home, not because of its grandeur but because of the hours she had shared here with Lewis. The terrace doors were closed against the cold; the chairs and table had been taken away from the terrace. It looked bleak and deserted.

She picked up an empty glass and Lewis filled it for her. They toasted each other wordlessly, with their eyes alone. Allison felt the cold liquid explode against the roof of her mouth and send bubbles of warmth coursing through her veins.

When Allison had finished her second glass she broke away from Lewis' arms, and, picking up the champagne bottle, went into the bedroom. Lewis undressed her and when she was standing naked before him he raised his glass to her beauty and drank. In bed together, they finished the bottle, their thighs touching under the blankets and Lewis' arm around her shoulders.

"Shall I order another bottle sent up, darling?" Allison asked.

"Do you think we need it?"

Allison smiled. "I don't think we needed the first one. But it was very nice."

She dropped her empty glass on the rug as Lewis touched her breast and stroked the smooth soft flesh.

"Oh, Lewis, darling, darling," she whispered.

But he paid no attention to her urgency and caressed her with his hands and bit her ear lobes until she cried out. She felt she would suffocate and she threw off the blankets. Words of love came from her mouth in a fierce whisper. She closed her eyes and when he pushed her over she felt the whole world was turning with her. She put her arms around him and drew him to her.

There has never been anything like this, she thought, never, never, never. She rose upward on a curving wave until all thought was driven out of her and only love filled her, tirelessly, until she was replete with love and helpless in his arms and her face glistened with tears of joy.

2

ON THE DAY AFTER Allison returned to Peyton Place, Peter Drake backed his car out of his garage and drove toward the Cross house to pick up Selena and Joey. Peter rolled up his window against the cold wind that stripped the last leaves from the tortured trees.

Elm Street was deserted. The only moving thing that Peter could see was a torn sheet of newspaper that blew against a curbstone in front of the bank. Peter thought he had never seen a lonelier sight in his life.

Connie's house will be warm and cheerful and good smelling, thought Peter. Maybe Selena will be able to relax today.

He did not give voice, even silently, to his other hope.

Maybe today Selena will be over Tim Randlett for good. Maybe today she'll decide that she wants to marry me after all.

Peter Drake was what Peyton Place described as a "well-set-up" man. He was moderately tall, with good shoulders and square hands. His hair was dark brown and his eyes matched it almost exactly. As an attorney in Peyton Place, Peter was not quite as well set up as he looked. Into his office came the people whom Charles Partridge was too busy to see. The ones with rather insignificant problems and the ones with no money. The only way that Peter managed to make a living was by traveling to the surrounding towns and taking the cases of the people there; but he clung stubbornly to Peyton Place.

Peter had never meant for it to happen that way. When he had undertaken the job of defending Selena Cross at her trial for the murder of Lucas, he had planned to make this his last case in northern New England. But when it was over, he had lingered. The job with a law firm in Connecticut that had been waiting for him was soon filled by someone else, and when, a few weeks later, he was offered another job with a firm in Massachusetts, he turned it down.

I'm out of my mind, he told himself often and angrily during the years that followed.

But he was in love with Selena and believed that, in time, she would come to love him.

In the beginning, he had waited while she recovered from the dreadful experience of Lucas Cross. Then he had waited for her to forget the defection of Ted Carter. Now he was waiting for her to stop remembering Tim Randlett.

"I'm stuck," he had once confessed to Constance Rossi. "I love her and I always will and there's not a damned thing I can do about it. And don't think I haven't tried, because I have. I've *almost* taken jobs away from here. I've *almost* become involved with other girls. I've *almost* convinced myself that I could get over her. Almost. But I've never made it."

"Have you ever told any of this to Selena?" asked Connie.

"Many times," said Peter. "And every time she tells me that I'd be better off without her. That she's no good for me." He shrugged helplessly. "It never does any good," he said. "I still wait and hope."

Peter stopped his car in front of Selena's house and made his way up the walk to the front door.

"Come in, Counselor!" cried Selena, flinging the door open for him. "Welcome!"

She was holding a glass in her hand, and Peter knew it was not her first drink of the day.

"Hail, the conquering hero comes, Joey," called Selena. "Fix him a drink. Well, don't just stand there, Peter. Come in."

Behind her back, Joey looked at Peter and hunched his shoulders as he poured liquor into a glass.

"Here, Joey," said Selena. "Freshen mine, will you? I have to finish dressing."

"You look wonderful, Selena," said Peter.

For a moment, she looked completely sober. "Don't lie, Peter," she said. "I look like a hag and I know it."

She turned and went quickly into her room and closed the door behind her.

"When did it start, Joey?" asked Peter.

Joey handed him a glass. "I guess she never really sobered up from last night," he said. "She didn't eat any supper. I found her sitting there, with the lights out and a glass in her hand."

It had started at the end of August, Peter remembered. And since then, Selena had not once gone to bed sober.

"Don't worry too much about it," Connie had told Peter. "Women have different ways of getting over unfortunate love affairs. Selena is hiding right now. Trying to pretend nothing is wrong. Give her a little time. She's a sensible girl. She'll snap out of it."

But the weeks went by and Selena did not snap out of it. She started drinking in the morning to clear her head, she told Joey, and Peter had caught her drinking in the back room of the Thrifty Corner.

"For Christ's sake, Selena," he had said. "What do you suppose Connie would say about this?"

Selena whirled on him. "Mind your own damned business," she said. "If Connie Rossi has any objections to the way I run her store, let her tell me herself."

"You're acting like a fool," said Peter angrily.

"Perhaps that's because I am one and always have been," said Selena.

"Drinking never solved anybody's problems," said Peter.

"Maybe not," said Selena, "but it does bring a measure of forgetfulness."

In desperation, Peter had gone to Matthew Swain.

"Believe me, Peter," said the doctor, "if I knew anything, I'd tell you and ethics be damned. But I don't know a bit more than you do. A couple of tourists, folks from Ohio, found her lying on the side of the highway, and since this was the closest town they brought her here to the hospital. She had fainted on the road. Her face was banged up some, where she hit the gravel, and she was suffering from too much sun, but outside of that there wasn't anything the matter with her. The next day I tried to find out what the hell had happened, but she wouldn't say a word. That actor fellow, Randlett, came over to the hospital to see her, but when I told her he was waiting she just turned her face to the wall and told me she didn't want to see him. He didn't believe it at first, but he finally went away. Joey told me that he went to the house after I sent her home, but Selena called Buck McCracken and told him that there was a man ringing her doorbell and that the sheriff should get rid of him. Then I heard that the summer theater was closing up. Right around Labor Day, that was, and I went up to Silver Lake to see this Randlett. He shut up like a clam when I started questioning him. Wouldn't tell me a thing. The next thing I knew, the whole kit and kaboodle of them had gone off to

New York. And good riddance, I say. Selena was getting along fine before Randlett hove into view."

"She's drinking," Peter told him. "Too much. Every day and every night."

Matthew Swain sighed. "I'll talk to her," he promised.

But it did no good.

"Doc, don't worry about me," Selena said. "Just go back to Chestnut Street and forget that you ever heard of me."

Matthew felt his stomach tighten. He remembered the night, a long time ago, when he had tried to interfere when Lucas had been drunk and beating his wife. A very young Selena had looked up at him.

"Go on home, Doc," she had said. "Go back to Chestnut Street. Nobody sent for you."

"Selena, I only want to help you," said Matthew.

Selena poured another drink. "Doc, there are some people who are born crippled, aren't there? I mean, with only one leg or one arm or no eyes?"

"Yes," said the doctor.

"Well, then," said Selena, "why is it unreasonable to suppose that other people are born with something wrong and twisted inside?"

"What do you mean?" asked Matthew.

Selena smiled. "I mean something evil, like a desire to commit murder, for instance."

"Selena, all that was a long, long time ago. You only did what you had to do to protect yourself. Anyone would have done the same. Forget all that. Put it behind you."

Selena squinted at the remaining liquor in her glass.

"Go home, Doc," she said wearily. "Go home. Nobody sent for you."

Matthew Swain stood up to leave, but he paused at her front door.

"That stuff never solved anything for anybody," he said.

Selena giggled. "That's what Peter always says," she said. "And I always agree with him. I only point out to him that, while it may not solve anything, it blunts the edges a little. Good-by, Doc."

Selena came out of her room. "I'm ready," she said gaily. "Let's go. Will you get my coat, Joey, while I finish my drink?"

"Sure," said Joey.

"Maybe we'd better bring a bottle of our own in case Mike Rossi has been forgetful," said Selena. "There's nothing worse than a party that runs out of liquor."

"I'm sure that Mike has a well-stocked bar," said Peter.

"Oh dear," said Selena. "Look who's getting all stuffy."

"Selena, I'm not getting stuffy," said Peter.

"Well, I don't care if you are," she said. "Go ahead and get stuffy if you want to. I won't stop you."

The afternoon seemed interminable to Peter. Selena was like a toy that had been wound too tightly and would soon snap and break into a mass of pieces and twisted wire. She pecked at her dinner but her glass was filled to the brim.

In the kitchen, Allison said softly to Connie, "Why didn't you tell me about Selena?"

"I thought it would pass," said Connie.

"How long has she been drinking like this?"

"Ever since Tim Randlett left town."

"Good God."

"Yes," said Connie. "Let's just hope that she gets over it soon."

"Has anyone tried talking to her?"

"We all have. It doesn't help."

"What does Peter say?"

"He's waiting for her to stop, the same as the rest of us. What else can he do?"

"Hey, you two!" said Selena from the kitchen doorway. "What's all the whispering about?"

"You," said Allison and turned to her with a smile. "We were wondering how much longer you're going to keep poor Peter hanging fire."

Selena sat down on a kitchen chair. "Let's have a drink, shall we? Just the three of us."

"Sure," said Connie. "Let me take the coffee in for the men and I'll be right back. Allison, get some ice, will you, dear? There's a bottle of bourbon in the cabinet behind you."

"Yes," said Selena, when she had the fresh drink in her hand, "poor, poor Peter. He loves me, you know. You know that, Allison, don't you?"

"Yes, I do," said Allison. "He has for a long time."

Selena began to cry. "Poor Peter. Poor, poor Peter."

"Don't cry, darling," said Connie. "Everything's going to be all right."

"Nothing is all right," cried Selena, her voice rising. "Nothing is all right at all, and it's never going to be!"

"Sh-h," warned Connie. "You don't want the men to hear you."

Selena calmed down. "No," she said. "No, I don't want them to hear me."

Then she put her head down on her arms and sobbed as if her heart would break. Allison went to her at once and put her arm across Selena's bent shoulders. She and Connie looked at each other and both of them knew that there was nothing to be done.

Later that same evening, Joey went to meet some friends with whom he was going to the movies, and Peter Drake drove Selena home. The wind was stronger now; he felt it tugging at the car and tightened his grip on the wheel.

"Make me a fire, Peter," said Selena, when they went into her living room. "A big, beautiful, bright fire to chase the dark out of all the corners." She dropped her coat carelessly over the back of a chair. "I'll make us a drink," she said.

Peter almost said, Don't you think you've had enough? But he stopped himself and began to build the fire.

"No, I haven't had enough," said Selena into the silence. "There isn't enough in the whole, wide world."

Now the fire was burning brightly and Peter sat down. He reached for the glass that Selena extended to him.

"I can't lick you," he told her, "so I might just as well join you."

"Don't you ever stop playing the heavy?" asked Selena. "Any time you don't feel like joining me you don't have to. Just put on your coat. You know where the door is."

"Don't try to pick a fight with me, Selena," said Peter. "I won't let you."

"Who wants to fight?" asked Selena. "I've had a bellyful of fights. Enough fights to last me a lifetime."

"Do you want to talk?" asked Peter.

Selena smiled humorlessly at him. "You remind me of someone I used to know," she said. "Always prying. Always poking his nose in where it wasn't wanted." She gulped thirstily at her drink. "Tell me about it, Selena," she mimicked. "What's troubling you, Selena? Tell me, Selena. You'll feel better for it." She refilled her glass. "I'm sick of talking," she said.

"I wasn't trying to pry," said Peter.

"Yes, you were!" she said angrily. "Everybody in the world is a goddamned prying busybody. Well, what do you want from me, Peter? Do you want to know if I've slept with him? Yes, I did. Are you wondering if I loved him? Yes, I did." Her voice rose until she was almost screaming. "Are you wondering if I've forgotten him? No, I haven't."

Peter watched her, appalled, as the tears streamed down her face and her voice rose higher and higher.

"Are you wondering why I left him?" she cried. "Are you wondering what went sour, and why and how?"

In that moment, the front door blew open. Apparently, Peter had not closed it securely when they had come in, and now the wind took it and sent it smashing back against the wall with a crash.

Selena jumped to her feet, her drink spilling all over the front of her and the glass smashing at her feet.

In one motion, she had turned and her fingers had closed around the fire tongs on the hearth.

"Don't!" she screamed. "Don't come a step nearer! I'll kill you!"

Peter grabbed her from behind, and for a long moment Selena stared at the empty black square at the door, that door which on a night like this had once framed the dark bulk of Lucas Cross.

"There's nobobdy there, darling," said Peter. "Nobody."

The tongs fell from Selena's nerveless fingers and she began to sob. Peter turned her to him and pressed her face against his shoulder.

"I tried to kill him," she cried. "He was just like Lucas and he came at me and I tried to kill him."

Peter held her very tightly against him while she sobbed.

"He wanted to tear my clothes off," she wept. "He said I wanted to be raped and he was just like Lucas and I picked up the fire tongs and wanted to kill him."

"It's all right, darling," soothed Peter. "Don't cry any more. It's all right."

"What's wrong with me, Peter?" Selena cried. "Why did it happen? What do I do that makes men like that?"

Peter kissed her soft hair. "It's not you, darling. You've just had bad luck, that's all. It's not you."

Selena's whole body trembled. "I drank and drank," she said, gasping for breath, "and it didn't do any good. I couldn't forget that I tried to kill him."

Peter gave her a gentle shake. "But you didn't, darling. It's over now. You didn't."

He led her gently to the sofa and held her cradled in his arms.

"Peter, I'm so scared. There's something wrong with me. I know there's something wrong with me," she sobbed.

"There's nothing wrong with you, darling," said Peter. He began to mop gently at her face with his handkerchief. "There's nothing wrong. Come on, now. Stop crying."

Huge, dry sobs shook her as she put her head against his shoulder.

"You react to violence with violence," said Peter. "Some people do, you know." He tipped her head up and looked down at her. "I'll have to remember that," he smiled, "whenever I get the mistaken idea that I can get rough around you."

"You're so good, Peter," she said, and a sigh went through her whole body as she relaxed against him. "I don't deserve anyone like you."

Peter smiled against her hair. "You deserve the best of everything," he said. He began to stroke her.

This is what I need, Selena thought, this is what I've always needed, Peter's gentle strength. It will protect me from all harm.

His hand continued to stroke her hair and back. It was as if his fingers were drawing out of her all the pain of the past and the agony of memory.

"When we get married," Peter whispered, "it will be the true beginning of our lives. You'll see, Selena—what's happened up till now has nothing to do with us. We were other people then. And it all took place in another world."

He had a profound understanding of Selena's needs. She wanted to be able to shuck off the past as cleanly as a farmer rips the corn from the stalk. With Peter, she wanted to be newborn and washed clean of the taint of the past. Her arms moved around him and held him tightly. She lifted her head and he bent to kiss her tear-stained face.

This will be the first time, Selena thought, this will be the first time.

She drew Peter down with her until they were lying side by side on the sofa; she moved and adjusted her body to the length of his. Hesitantly, his hand caressed her thigh, moved up until it gently touched her breast. Her lips parted, he kissed her; she moaned softly when he pushed up her sweater. She clasped her hands behind his head and held him.

"Oh, Selena, darling," he whispered, and she heard the breathlessness in his voice.

He began to undress her. Selena felt faint, felt as if the world were slipping away from her. She covered her face with her hands, and in the darkness under her hands the world held still.

"Oh," she said, "oh, I want you." And she raised her hands to him as if imploring him and drew him to her.

3

WITH THE COMING OF AUTUMN and its electric air, Roberta Carter always felt brisk. It was as if she were sweeping up the sloth and indecision of the past year along with the dried, fallen leaves of her front yard trees. She rubbed her hands together mentally and thought, Now that all the summer nonsense is over with, let's get down to business. Roberta looked around her now spotless living room and should have felt completely satisfied with her housewifely accomplishment, but her pleasure was tainted. Even though Ted and Jennifer had returned to Cambridge early in September, Roberta could still feel the presence of that horrible girl in her house.

I've got to get rid of her, thought Roberta, and refused to feel futile.

She had been trying to get rid of Jennifer for over a year now, and nothing had worked. Ted turned a deaf ear to any remarks about his wife, and Harmon, who had been so diabolically clever when Roberta's problem had been old Doc Quimby, was next to useless where Jennifer was concerned.

"She seems to be a nice enough sort," said Harmon.

"So was Dr. Quimby," snapped Roberta, "but you managed to see that he didn't remain on our scene too long."

"That was something else entirely," replied Harmon.

Dr. Quimby, who had been the only physician in Peyton Place until Matthew Swain came home to practice, had been old and rich when Roberta had started to work for him as a combination house-keeper, secretary and companion. Roberta and Harmon, the children of mill hands, were engaged to be married, but, with the money Harmon earned as one of Leslie Harrington's bookkeepers, marriage was impossible. Until Harmon Carter came up with his plan.

It was a clever, simple plan which, if it worked, would set Roberta and Harmon up for life. Roberta had not needed much persuasion to put Harmon's idea to work. She married Dr. Quimby and he rewrote his will in her favor, and then she and Harmon settled back and waited for the old man to die. They didn't have long to wait. Peyton Place made life intolerable for Dr. Quimby. The town rocked with laughter, and people who had always gone to him with their ailments now assumed that he had turned senile and refused to consult him.

Roberta and Harmon cuckolded him openly, and in the end the old man put his revolver into his mouth and blew his head off. Within a year, Roberta and Harmon were married and had begun the long fight to become accepted by Peyton Place. With time and new-found respectability they had won to a degree. Of course, there were those who remembered and talked, but with every passing year the story grew less and less interesting and there were always new people in new situations to be gossiped about.

It helped a great deal, too, when Roberta and Harmon's son, Ted, turned out to be such a nice guy. So the scandal died and was almost buried, and people forgot. But Roberta Carter did not forget. She remembered very vividly how she had fought to become someone who was looked up to in town as a good wife and mother and an asset to the community. Now there was Jennifer, who threatened to turn Roberta's son from the paths of righteousness with her insane, abnormal sexuality.

I've got to get rid of her, thought Roberta.

But during the past year she had thought up and discarded hundreds of plans. Nothing worked. Ted was as much a prisoner in his marriage to Jennifer as he would have been in a maximum security cell at Alcatraz. Jennifer was crazy and she would make Ted crazy, and in the eyes of most of Peyton Place it was a far greater crime to be insane than it was to be a thief or a rapist.

I've got to get rid of her, thought Roberta.

But it was not until the end of summer that Roberta decided on a course of action that she had previously discarded as foolhardy and dangerous. Roberta burned leaves and vacuumed her rugs and began to plan her strategy.

Jennifer would be back in Peyton Place for the Thanksgiving holidays. I've got to kill her, she thought, and I have to do it well enough so that no one ever suspects a thing.

Roberta Carter began to read murder mysteries, but she did not borrow these from the Peyton Place public library nor did she buy them at the local bookstore. She traveled eighty miles to a city to shop, and she bought paper-backed novels in a large drugstore where she was not known, and she read secretly, behind the locked door of her bathroom.

During the day, when Harmon was at work, she wrote down the plot of each novel and listed the clues that had finally landed each murderer in the nets of the police. In this way, she discarded murder by shooting, stabbing, strangling and poison; and since Jennifer was not the type to commit suicide, Roberta realized that her daughter-in-law's death would have to be made to look like an accident.

Although Jennifer drove a car, Roberta could never hope to tamper with an automobile to the extent of causing a fatal accident. Household mishaps were out, too, for whenever Jennifer visited in Peyton Place or Roberta went to Cambridge, Harmon was always around, or Ted, or both of them. No. It had to be something that happened when Roberta was not with Jennifer and when Ted, also, was away from his wife so that no breath of suspicion fell on him.

Roberta closed the cover of still another murder mystery and sighed deeply. It wasn't going to be easy, but then, she hadn't expected that it would be. In the meantime, there was plenty to do. She must begin to fabricate a fiction of her relationship with Jennifer. Peyton Place must be impressed with Roberta's magnanimity. When it was over and Jennifer was dead, people had to be able to say, "What a pity. And that this should happen to Roberta Carter, of all people. Why, she is the soul of goodness and she and Jennifer were so close."

Roberta was, as she had always been, clever about sounding out people and when, within two weeks after the reopening of school in September, she discovered that the town was more than displeased with the man who now acted as headmaster of the Peyton Place school, she began to agitate for the return of Mike Rossi to his rightful position. Behind the back of her best friend, Marion Partridge, she let Charles know that when the school board considered the contracts for the next year she, Roberta, would be behind Charles one thousand per cent in his campaign to rehire Mike.

"The whole thing has given this town a terrible black eye," she confided in Charles. "I mean, firing Mike just because of Allison's book. I was never really for it in the first place."

And Charles Partridge, the town pacifist, forgot that Roberta had been one of Mike's sworn enemies and accepted her new attitude gratefully.

"It'll take a while for people to get over the way we acted about Mike," said Roberta. "We've managed to make ourselves a laughing-stock in educational circles. But it's nothing that can't be patched up."

"And the sooner the better," amended Charles Partridge.

Roberta began to make frequent visits to the Thrifty Corner where she not only made purchases, but became very friendly with Connie and Selena.

"I'm so very glad for you and Peter," said Roberta to Selena. "He's certainly a lucky man."

"I wonder what ails her," said Selena when Roberta had gone. "I've never known her to be so sweet. It's almost sickening."

But Connie, the incurable optimist, said, "Perhaps she's mellowing. After all, Roberta's no teen-ager any more. She's getting on."

"I still don't believe that the leopard changes its spots," said Selena.

But, as the weeks went by, even Selena had to admit that Roberta Carter had changed. In October, Mike Rossi was offered, and accepted, on terms he had made clear to the school board, his old job as principal of the Peyton Place school. The whole town with a few die-hard exceptions, had been overwhelmingly on Mike's side of the fence. One of the exceptions was Marion Partridge, and in the interests of, as she put it, doing the right thing, Roberta Carter broke with her lifelong friend.

To various women in town Roberta said, "I'm sorry that Marion feels as she does, but I wanted to do what was best for the school."

The women carried the word into their homes and practically everyone agreed that Roberta Carter was the soul of unselfishness. They sympathized with Roberta, too, for Roberta let it be known that what she wanted more than anything was a grandchild, but Jennifer, so far, had not conceived.

"It's a shame," said the women of Peyton Place. "It isn't as if Ted and Jennifer had to worry about money or anything. Heaven knows Roberta and Harmon are more than generous."

Then Roberta let it be known that her son, Ted, wanted to come back to Peyton Place to practice law when he graduated from Harvard, and if there had been any doubt at all in the minds of the town, it was now assuaged. Peyton Place loved a local boy who went away and obtained the best education money could buy and then returned home to put what he had learned to use.

"Ted always had a good head on his shoulders," said the town. "A good boy, Ted. And a smart one."

"Old Charlie Partridge ain't gonna last forever. We'll need somebody like young Carter to take over when Charlie goes."

Roberta counted heavily on the quality in her son that kept him from hurting anyone if he could possibly refrain from doing so. When anyone in Peyton Place mentioned Ted's eventual local practice, rather than answering flatly that he had no intention whatsoever of coming home to set up an office, Ted merely smiled and said modestly, "I've got to get through school first, and that's not going to be easy for a dull fellow like me."

By the end of the summer, Roberta knew that the time had come to act. Jennifer's parents had begun to talk of a trip to Europe for "the children," and Ted was obviously enthused at the prospect.

I've got to find a way, Roberta thought, with the beginning of panic.

Day after day she stayed in her house with her murder mysteries and her notebook. She worked out all the drawbacks to her plan, the risks, the clues she must not leave behind; and she planned a meticulous timetable of the day when it would happen. At last, she locked her notebook away in her desk and breathed a sigh of relief.

Now it was over except for the actual act. She had found a way to get rid of Jennifer that was simple, safe and foolproof. She sat at the desk for a moment, her hands clenched into tight, avenging fists, her mouth compressed into a thin determined line. In her head, Jennifer's terrible words still echoed, the horrible things she had told Ted on their last night in Peyton Place.

She had been listening to them through the air vent, lying in her own sweat on the cot in the storage room. She had heard them make love, had heard Jennifer torture Ted and tease him into doing all sorts of perverse and evil things. She had writhed in anguish for poor Ted.

Then she had heard Jennifer's salacious whisper.

Ted said, "You're insatiable, darling."

"More," Jennifer said. "I want more. Oh, goddamn men, anyway!"

Ted laughed. "We're badly designed," he said. "You'll have to wait for next year's models."

Roberta heard the bed creak as Jennifer sat up and rested her back against the headboard.

"I think I'll get myself a seventeen-year-old boy," Jennifer said.

Ted laughed. To him, talk like this was part of Jennifer's smartness and sophistication. In Ted's eyes, being born to money and high social position gave her the right to say things like this.

But Roberta was so shocked that her body went numb. She could not bear the thought that her Ted would be a cuckolded husband, laughed at and pitied by his friends. She thought of Doc Quimby. For a moment, she believed in divine retribution and that her sins were being visited upon Ted.

Jennifer's cool voice went on. "Or maybe I'll get myself two or three young boys. Yes, that would be even better."

"Where do you buy young boys these days?" Ted asked.

"Oh, you can pick them up cheap anywhere," Jennifer told him, a ring of authority in her voice. "There's that sweet curly-haired boy who delivers the groceries. I can tell by the way he looks at me that he wouldn't have to be bought. It's dull being alone in the apartment all day, Ted. Wouldn't it be nice if I whiled away an hour or two with him in the morning?"

Ted did not answer.

"It would be, Ted. It would be very nice. The idea of corrupting an innocent boy is the most exciting thing in the world. And then, in the afternoon, I could have a daily arrangement with that handsome young Italian who runs the elevator. He goes off duty at two o'clock. How would you like to have a man in uniform come every afternoon to service me?"

Ted laughed, but it was a forced, uncomfortable laugh.

"Teen-age boys are so full of energy," she said. "They have to be taught how to use that energy, of course. I read in Kinsey, Ted, that they can do it four or five times in an hour. And some of them can do it more than that. Isn't that marvelous, Ted?"

She did not wait for him to answer. "I don't think I'll wait for the new models, Ted. I think I'll just buy a couple of those untried, young boys. You wouldn't mind, would you, Ted?"

"Oh, go to sleep, Jennifer," Ted said.

"No, Ted, you wouldn't mind at all. Oh, maybe you'd mind because it would hurt your male pride, whatever that is. But you wouldn't do anything about it, would you, Ted? Not you. As long as you can get your name on the door, as long as you can have success, you'll put up with anything. And I mean *any*thing, Ted."

"Go to sleep, Jennifer. You're talking like a child," Ted said.

They were silent then. After a while, they fell asleep. Everyone in Peyton Place was asleep except Roberta Carter. She lay on the cot with her hands pressed tight against her mouth, her eyes staring at the dark ceiling.

I must kill her, she thought. I must kill her. She wasn't just talking. She's going to do these things. Maybe she's already started doing them. I must kill her.

4

THE MEN OF CHESTNUT STREET gathered at the home of Seth Buswell for their usual Friday night poker game. Seth put a bottle of liquor on the sideboard and filled four glasses with ice while Leslie Harrington began to shuffle the cards for the first hand.

"Another winter is here," said Matthew Swain as he sat down.

"Yep," said Seth. "Ephraim Tuttle's got his stove set up and his bolts of material put away."

"Where did the year go?" said Charles Partridge. "Seems as though it was only a few weeks ago that we were sitting here talking about Allison MacKenzie's book, and that was last April."

"That's because we're getting old," said Matthew. "Time goes by quick as a wink for us nowadays. But I can remember how it used to drag by when I was a youngster."

"You ain't got that good a memory to remember that far back, Matt," said Leslie Harrington.

"Neither have you, Grandpa," said Matt. "Although I must say, you've looked better this past year than I've ever seen you look."

"I've got to keep healthy to keep up with that grandson of mine," said Leslie. "He's a holy terror."

"How's Betty?" asked Seth.

"Fine," said Leslie. "I think she's finally made up her mind to stay right here in Peyton Place."

"Good," said Matthew and Seth almost simultaneously.

Charles Partridge did not say anything. Except for Leslie himself, Charles was the only man in town who knew what torture Leslie had suffered at the hands of Betty Anderson.

"Five pretty little black spades," said Seth Buswell gleefully and raked up the coins from the center of the table.

Spades, thought Charles Partridge. That's what Betty Anderson paid Leslie back in. In spades.

Rodney Harrington, Junior, had been no problem, Charles remembered. The boy had taken to his grandfather as if he had known him all his life, and Leslie, of course, was overwhelmed with love. Little Roddy was the image of his father, and the lines of age and worry erased themselves from Leslie's face every time he looked at his grandson. His friends were not the only ones in Peyton Place to notice how much better Leslie looked. Betty Anderson noticed it, too, and she smiled a tight little smile at the man who had never been her father-in-law. She had been in Peyton Place for two weeks, just long enough for Leslie to begin to hope that she would stay forever, when she started packing to leave.

"I have a job to get back to," she told Leslie when he protested.

"You don't have to work," said Leslie. "There's more than enough money right here."

Betty turned on him. "Listen, Leslie, I got along fine without your money when I was pregnant, when Roddy was born and ever since. We don't need you."

Leslie humbled himself. "I know," he said. "I need you."

"That's just too bad," said Betty. "You should have needed us when you threw me out of your office with a lousy two hundred and fifty bucks and a load in my belly."

"Betty," pleaded Leslie. "I'll make it up to you. I swear I will."

"We don't need you," said Betty and went on with her packing.

In the end, she promised that she would stay another week and Leslie breathed again. But at the end of the week, she started packing again.

"For Christ's sake, Charlie," said Leslie in desperation. "Do something."

"What do you want me to do?" asked Charles Partridge. "You have no legal claim on that child."

"Goddamn it, he's my grandson!"

"Betty and Rodney were never married," said Charles. "And you can't prove that Betty's been an unfit mother. There's nothing you can do except hope that she'll change her mind and stay on voluntarily."

"Well, talk to her, then," demanded Leslie. "Make her see that it's best for the child if he stays here. I don't give a damn what she does as long as she leaves Roddy with me."

"She'll never leave him," said Charles. "If you want the child, you'd better make up your mind to want the mother, too. But I'll talk to her."

"What's in it for me?" asked Betty Anderson when Charles went to see her.

"You could be very comfortable here," said Charles. "You could live in this house and you wouldn't have to work and you and Roddy could be well taken care of."

"I can take care of myself," said Betty. "I always have. And of Roddy, too. I don't mind working for a living. And as far as this house goes, it gives me the creeps. It's like a goddamn museum."

"I'm sure that Leslie would be willing to let you do the house over," said Charles, worried lest he bite off more than he could chew. "I can't see what objection he'd have to that."

"I don't want to do Leslie's house over," said Betty. "I want a house of my own."

Charles's jaw sagged. "But Leslie wants you to live in the house with him. You and little Roddy."

Betty shrugged. "In the words of little Roddy's father, that's tough titty," she said.

"Will you stay until Christmas?" asked Charles.

"Nope."

"Until the end of the month?"

"Nope."

Charles went to Leslie and told him what Betty wanted if she were to remain in Peyton Place.

"A house!" roared Leslie. "What the hell's the matter with my house? It's big enough for an army!"

Charles spread his hands in a gesture of defeat. "I can't help that, Leslie. That's what she wants."

"She can go right straight to hell," yelled Leslie.

But the next day, Betty began to pack again, and Leslie ran to Charles.

"Get her a house," he said wearily. "Any one she wants."

So Betty Anderson became the owner of a cottage at the end of Laurel Street.

"It'll be a nice place to spend my vacations," she told Charles.

"What do you mean, vacations?" asked Charles. "Don't you plan to live here?"

"On what?" asked Betty. "Does Leslie think I'm as rich as he is and can afford to sit on my backside all day long without working?"

"Leslie is perfectly willing to provide for the boy," Charles objected. "You could find work here to take care of your own needs."

"Where?" jeered Betty. "In the Mills? Like my old man? No thanks."

"But we thought—" began Charles.

"I don't give a damn what you thought," said Betty angrily. "I'm not going to take a two-bit job in the Mills working for Leslie Harrington. If I have to work to support myself, I can do that a lot better in New York. And that's where I'm going just as soon as I can get packed."

In the end, Leslie Harrington settled a sum of twenty-five thousand dollars on Betty Anderson and deposited another ten thousand in an account for his grandson. In addition, he agreed to give Betty a household allowance of one hundred dollars a week and buy her a new car every year.

"In writing," said Betty Anderson.

So Charles Partridge drew up the papers and Leslie Harrington signed them.

"One more thing," said Betty before she signed. "There's a friend of mine in New York who used to look after Roddy for me. I want her to come up here to live with me and help with the house and with Roddy. Leslie'd have to pay her fifty a week."

So Agnes Carlisle came to live in Peyton Place with Betty Anderson, and Leslie Harrington agreed to pay her wages. In return for what he gave, Leslie was to be allowed unlimited visiting privileges and the right to keep his grandson with him for a full day, one day a week. In the event of Betty's marriage, she was to keep all monies settled on her and Roddy, but her weekly allowance was to stop and Leslie was to be allowed the same privileges.

Betty Anderson leaned back comfortably in her new living room and Agnes brought her a drink. The two women took their shoes off and sipped their martinis.

"Now I've got it made," said Betty. "Who wants to get married?"

"Didn't I tell you?" asked Agnes smugly. "I told you to get in touch with him, didn't I?"

"Yes, you did," agreed Betty. "And you never made a wiser suggestion in your life."

"For Christ's sake, Charlie," said Leslie Harrington crossly, "are you playing cards or not? We've been waiting for you to tell us whether you can open or not."

Charles Partridge looked at his cards. "I pass," he said.

"One card," said Leslie to Seth, who was dealing.

Old Leslie, trying to fill an inside straight, thought Charles. He'll probably hit, too. He usually gets what he wants. Even if there's a price on it.

At eleven o'clock, Leslie Harrington and Charles Partridge said good night to Matthew Swain and Seth Buswell.

"Let's walk a little," said Leslie when the two men were outside.

"Where to?" asked Charles. "It's late and I'm tired."

"I just want to walk past Betty's house," said Leslie. "I like to make sure everything's all right before I go to sleep at night."

"Do you go down there every night?" asked Charles.

Leslie nodded. "You never can tell," he said. "I might catch that little bitch in a compromising situation someday."

"Leslie!" cried Charles in horror.

"Oh, cut it out," said Leslie. "You've known me too many years to be shocked at anything I say. Come on."

The two men walked slowly down Chestnut Street and turned into Laurel.

Betty Anderson's house was dark and still. Leslie stopped and looked at it, stared at it as if his eyes could see right through the walls—and right into the bitter, unforgiving heart of Betty Anderson, his grandson's mother. It was not only little Roddy's love that made Leslie appear younger these days; it was also the smell of battle. He was locked with Betty in a clash of wills. Nothing made him feel younger than a good fight.

He looked at the house and thought, You've won the first battle, Betty, but the war isn't over yet. Before I die, little Roddy will be living in the big house with me.

5

THE TRAIN PLUNGED HEADLONG into the long space that separated Lewis Jackman from Allison MacKenzie, and Lewis sat in the club car, impatient with his drink and with the way the hands on his watch moved as slowly as if they had been trapped in molasses. The wheels of the train, too, seemed to move forward in slow motion, and Lewis watched water condense on the outside of his glass and looked again at his watch.

Sitting next to him in the observation car was Stephanie. Allison had introduced them during the week she spent in New York after returning from Hollywood. They left Grand Central together and had been traveling together for eight hours. And that's about as many words as we've exchanged, Stephanie thought, eight. If I didn't know better, I'd have to conclude that Lewis Jackman was a man on his way to a heavy date.

"Hello, there!" said a feminine voice behind him, and, even before he turned, Lewis was resentful at anyone who would break into his thoughts.

"Hi," Stephanie said, disinterestedly.

"I remember you," the girl said. "You're Stephanie. Allison's friend."

"Yes."

The girl would not be put off with coolness. "I'm Jennifer Carter," she said. "My husband will be here in a minute. May we sit with you?"

Stephanie wanted very badly to say No, but instead, she said, "Of course." She introduced Jennifer to Lewis.

"Here's Ted now!" said Jennifer, and turned to her husband. "Darling, you remember Stephanie, don't you? Allison introduced her to us last Christmas."

"Sure," said Ted and extended his hand. "How are you?"

"Are you going up to Peyton Place to visit Allison, too, Mr. Jackman?" asked Jennifer.

"Yes, I am," replied Lewis.

The girl's eyes were bright with a shrewdness that reminded Lewis of a snake, and although she was very beautiful there was something about her that was too finely drawn. Her cheekbones were too prominent and her chin had an aggressive tilt to it and her eyes darted everywhere so that they not only seemed to miss nothing but to probe beneath the surface of everything they saw.

"Allison must be a very important writer to drag a busy publisher like you so far away from civilization," said Jennifer, and her eyes fastened on his with a demand for an answer.

"She is," said Lewis. And the simple unemphatic way in which he said it gave his words a great deal of authority.

Jennifer laughed. "It's so hard to think of little Allison MacKenzie of Peyton Place as an important writer, as someone to be taken seriously."

"Jennifer!" said Ted. "Don't say things like that."

"Don't be ridiculous, darling," said Jennifer. "I can't help it if that's what I thought, can I?"

Ted looked away uncomfortably. "Let's order," he said.

"Good idea," replied Jennifer. "I want a Scotch and water, please." She turned again to Lewis. "How long have you had this high opinion of Allison?" she asked, with the same persistence that had characterized her previous questions.

Lewis wanted to stand up and tell her that it was none of her business, but he didn't.

"A long time," he said, and his voice did not encourage further interrogation.

"Since before she got famous and began to make pots of money?" asked Jennifer.

"Yes," said Lewis. "Even before that." He looked at Stephanie and stood up. "I think we ought to be getting back to our seats, Stephanie." He nodded to Jennifer and Ted and said, "If you'll excuse us."

Jennifer laughed as he turned to walk away. "That's what people always say when they don't want to talk to you any more."

"Jennifer!" said Ted.

"Oh, stop saying 'Jennifer' like that," she said crossly. "You sound like a broken record." She sipped at her drink. "Allison isn't getting much of a prize in him," she said. "He's as close-mouthed as you are."

"Perhaps he resented your prying," said Ted with more spirit than he usually showed in front of Jennifer.

"I don't pry," she said. "I'm just interested in people."

"Anyway," Ted said, "he's her publisher, not her lover."

"That's what you think," Jennifer said.

"What makes you think otherwise?" Ted asked.

"Stop cross-examining me, Mr. District Attorney. I just know it in my bones, that's all. Big New York publishers don't come all the way to Peyton Place just to look at a manuscript."

"You're just plain nosy," said Ted and leaned back in his chair. "Plain nosy."

It was true. Jennifer was one of those people who cannot visit anywhere without peeking into the bathroom medicine cabinet and checking the pile of towels in the linen closet. Whenever the opportunity presented itself, she pawed through other people's desks and dresser drawers, and it gave her a deep sense of satisfaction to know that her best unmarried friend kept a supply of preventatives in the drawer of her night table and that another friend received dunning letters from Jordan-Marsh. She knew that her father's dearest friend wore a wide elastic girdle, and every time she saw him she could scarcely keep from laughing right in his face, especially since she also knew that the same man's wife carried on a lively correspondence with a noted French cellist.

Jennifer also knew that her mother-in-law had taken to reading lurid, paper-backed murder mysteries and that her father-in-law collected pornographic picture playing cards. She knew that Roberta and Harmon Carter had seventeen thousand dollars on deposit at the Citizens National Bank and that they carried fifty thousand dollars' worth of insurance, and she knew that when Roberta wanted to be free in the evening she put a sleeping powder in Harmon's after dinner coffee. But best of all was a knowledge so gratifying that Jennifer was hard put to keep it to herself. Jennifer knew that whenever she went to Peyton Place with Ted, Roberta sneaked into the little room next to Ted's and listened to her son and daughter-in-law at night.

"It must be the air up here," Ted said to his wife. "Whenever we're in Peyton Place, you're as horny as a French whore who enjoys her work."

Jennifer almost laughed in his face. "You make me that way," she told him, and thought up new ways to arouse him and make him do unheard-of things to her. It excited her to distraction to know that Roberta was listening to every word and sound. Jennifer squirmed under Ted's hands and she moaned and cried out.

"You're hurting me. You're hurting me. Don't stop, darling. Deeper. Deeper."

And then her muffled scream, and even as she cried out Jennifer thought that she could hear the sound of panting from the other side of the wall.

"Again, darling," cried Jennifer. "Again."

Ted put his hands on his wife's quivering body and said, "Dear God, what makes you like this?"

And, thinking of Roberta who was listening, Jennifer smiled in the dark.

"I love you," she said. "All you have to do is look at me, and I begin to think of us like this."

It would have been a delicious secret to share, thought Jennifer. But Ted would never understand. He'd turn cold and refuse to touch her in his mother's house.

So she had to be content with watching Roberta's face the next morning.

"What's the matter, Mother?" asked Jennifer with a sly, little smile. "Didn't you sleep well?"

"As a matter of fact, I didn't," replied Roberta. "I guess I shouldn't have had that second cup of coffee."

"Well, I slept like a baby," said Harmon.

"I'll bet you did, thought Jennifer, thinking of the sleeping powders that Roberta kept locked in her dressing table.

Roberta kept her secrets locked up, but she wasn't very smart about it. She kept a ring with the keys to everything in the house under her pillow. It hadn't taken Jennifer long to find her hiding places.

As the train hurried toward Peyton Place, Jennifer smiled into her drink and wondered what was new at her in-laws. She hadn't been to the Carters' since August, and there was bound to be a whole new crop of secrets by now.

Jennifer began to complain of a headache right after the train pulled out of Concord, and by the time she and Ted reached the Carter house in Peyton Place she had convinced her husband that all she wanted was to go to bed with some aspirin and a cup of hot tea.

"What a shame," said Roberta sympathetically. "And we were all going to the church supper tonight."

"I won't hear of the rest of you missing it," said Jennifer. "The three of you run along."

"Of course not," said Ted. "I don't want to leave you when you aren't feeling well."

"Don't be silly," replied Jennifer. "And please don't be stubborn, darling. If you don't go along with Mother and Dad, I'll feel like a heel and I'll have to force myself to join you. Please don't make me do that."

At last Ted capitulated and he, Roberta and Harmon left. Jennifer waited until she could no longer hear the sound of the car, then she got quietly out of bed and went to Roberta's room. She picked through Harmon's drawers without discovering anything new and when Roberta's dressing table yielded nothing but a new supply of sleeping powders, Jennifer was petulantly annoyed. Her fingers groped under Roberta's pillow and she straightened up in shocked surprise. The key ring was not there.

Jennifer's annoyance fled on the wings of excitement, and she began to search the room. Jennifer was very good at discovering hiding places, and for that reason she discarded the more obvious nooks

213

and crannies that Roberta might have selected. Her fingers moved expertly through the pockets of all the garments in Roberta's closet, but with no success. She examined the bathroom minutely and when she had finished there she stood for a moment in the upstairs hall, concentrating with all her mind on what Roberta must have been thinking when she hid her keys.

In another moment, Jennifer went directly to the linen closet off the bathroom. Her fingers closed around a box of soap flakes which Roberta kept for washing stockings and nylon underwear, and in another moment her probing hand touched the key ring. She lifted it carefully out of the box of soap flakes, cupping her hand under it so that she would leave no telltale trail of soap on the shelf, and she laughed out loud.

She unlocked the cedar chest in the front hall, but there was nothing there but winter blankets, a bottle of brandy and sixty-eight dollars in two-dollar bills. Jennifer left everything as she had found it and slammed down the cover of the chest. So her mother-in-law nipped at imported brandy on the sly and saved two-dollar bills. How dull, thought Jennifer in disappointment.

She went downstairs and unlocked the desk in the living room. There was the usual collection of bills and canceled checks and unanswered letters. Jennifer examined everything without interest and glanced at her watch. The family would be back in less than half an hour. She unlocked the bottom drawer of the desk, expecting to be disappointed again, but she felt her interest quicken as her eyes fell on a loose-leaf notebook that hadn't been there on her last visit.

She picked it up and began to leaf through it, and her face paled as she read. Roberta had mapped out a plan for murder. A plan so simple and stupid that it might just work for those very reasons. Jennifer's heart pumped hard and fast as she read, and it was not until she heard a car stop outside that she raised her head. They were back.

In a flash, Jennifer locked the desk and ran upstairs. She buried the key ring deep in the box of soap flakes and ran to her room. Before she got back into bed, she looked out the window and was just in time to see Roberta coming up the walk. You sly old bitch, she thought. You jealous old bitch. What a surprise you have in store for you!

Lying in bed, listening to Ted's footsteps coming up the stairs, Jennifer thought, This is going to be a memorable Thanksgiving Day.

Roberta had scheduled her murder for tomorrow.

6

ALLISON, MIKE AND CONSTANCE sat up late with their guests on the night before Thanksgiving Day. Stephanie lay sprawled on the rug in front of the fireplace, Lewis sat in the armchair. Allison could tell that Mike liked Lewis very much. They had all begun the evening by talking about politics and literature, but now the night was coming to an end with gossip about Jennifer.

Stephanie described her behavior on the train, and added, "I know the type. New York is full of them. Glossy, teasing little bitches, all golden promise on the outside and empty as a tin cup on the inside."

Lewis smiled, amused by Stephanie's colorful language. He said, "I've known a few Jennifers. And they've all run pretty much to type. They have the feeling that they can say anything or do anything, and Daddy's money will always be there to protect them. I hope you ladies won't jump on me, but I must say that no man I've ever met—and in my business I've met some pretty egocentric ones—has ever been as arrogant as these women are."

"Why is that?" Mike asked, like the good teacher he was.

"I think there's a very simple explanation," Lewis said. "Men are always a bit worried that if they are too arrogant, someone will haul off and punch them in the nose. But women don't have that worry."

"You can say anything you like about Jennifer Carter," Constance said. "I won't jump on you. She's a queer one. I've never seen a girl so drawn and tense. And, at the same time, there's a nerveless quality about her. I have the feeling she could do the most monstrous thing, and not turn a hair."

Mike stood up. "If I refill everybody's glass, will you all promise to change the subject? I don't think Jennifer Carter is the best choice for an end of the night conversation. I think I'd have pleasanter dreams if we told stories about vampire bats."

"I promise," Stephanie said, and held up her glass.

Not long after that they all went upstairs to their rooms. Allison shared her room with Stephanie, and Lewis slept in the guest room next to it. It tormented her, lying in bed with the knowledge that Lewis was just the other side of the thin wall.

As if reading her thoughts, Stephanie murmured, "Your friend Lewis is a beautiful man." She sighed. "I've come to the conclusion that all beautiful men are married."

"You'll find someone someday who is both beautiful and unmarried," Allison told her.

"I suppose," Stephanie said. "But meanwhile, back at the ranch, things are very lonely. I'm a girl who's good and tired of the single state, Allison. If I didn't have an exaggerated sense of my own worth, I'd accept the first producer who asked for my hand. Not that it's my hand they ask for."

Allison laughed. "You needn't worry. Eventually you're going to meet a man who sees right through you, right through your hard beautiful shell to the soft warm heart beneath. And that will be the end of him and the end of you."

"That's the first and probably the last time I'll ever feel complimented at being called a fraud," Stephanie laughed.

"Oh, I didn't mean that you're a fraud, and you know it. But you've built up defenses, we all have. God knows, after my experience since the book's been published, I wouldn't dream of accusing you of being fraudulent. It would be a case of the pot calling the kettle black."

"Why do you say that, Allison?" Stephanie raised herself up on her elbow and looked at her.

Allison replied, "Lewis says nearly all writers feel this way. They feel like confidence men who have pulled off a fast one on the public. When your novel is successful, when a million people are reading it, when everyone is talking about it, you can't believe that all this is the result of your talent. So you begin to think you've tricked them all and that you're a walking fraud."

"Do you still feel that way?"

"I don't know, Stevie. I really don't know. With one or two important exceptions, I feel my whole life is unreal and fraudulent now. I need to get back to work, to start writing my new book."

"Why don't you? This is the most perfect place for work."

"It's not easy. Sometimes I think it's because life is too exciting. I don't want to seal myself up and cut myself off from it. I have the feeling I'll miss something, something important."

She turned to Stephanie. "I've developed such a large appetite for life, Stevie. Success makes living so delicious that you don't want to miss a moment of it. I guess that's why the Hollywood people are so frightened of being alone. Even for an hour. I guess they figure that they've given so much for success that it would be a sin not to enjoy every minute of it to the full."

"Do you know what you want yet, Allison?"

"Yes," Allison said. "Everything."

Stephanie was silent then, and after a little while Allison could hear her regular breathing and knew she was asleep. She thought of Lewis, so near and so unreachable. She wondered if she dared sneak into his room. I can't, she answered herself, not in Constance's house. Finally, she fell asleep, exhausted by her thoughts.

It seemed only minutes later that she opened her eyes to the brightness of day and heard, remotely, as if from miles away, the sounds of Constance in the kitchen preparing the Thanksgiving dinner. She dressed quickly and hurried down to help her mother.

Mike was at the kitchen table with Constance; they were drinking coffee and talking in soft voices. Allison thought she heard Lewis' name mentioned.

Constance saw Allison standing at the door and said, "What are you doing up so early?"

"I wanted to help you with the dinner," Allison said.

Mike said, "We have the perfect job for you. It calls for intelligence and requires that the applicant be a person of responsibility."

"I don't think she's old enough for it yet," Constance said, playing along with Mike.

"I think we ought to give her a chance," Mike said.

He said to Allison, "Have you got grit and determination? Do you want to make something of yourself? If not, do not apply for this job."

Allison smiled at them. "You crazy fools," she said. "All right. I've got grit and determination. I want to get ahead. Now, what's the job?"

Mike pointed to the stove. "You see that little window in the oven?"

Allison nodded.

"Your job," Mike said, "is to draw a chair over to the oven, sit down on that chair and watch the turkey through the little window. We wouldn't want it to get away, would we?"

"I think the job is too big for her," said Connie. "After all, she's had very little experience as a turkey-watcher."

"I could rise to the challenge," Allison told them, speaking with mock fervor. "Please. This job could be the making of me."

"It's a lifetime career," Mike said. "Don't rush your decision. Here." He pulled out a chair. "Sit down, have a cup of coffee and think it over."

"We'll keep the job open while you're making up your mind," Constance said.

"Fools," Allison told them, shaking with laughter.

"Slacker," Mike said. "Coming down when the work's all done and offering your services."

"Why didn't you wake me?" Allison said.

"Because," said Constance, "we are the kind of parents who like to make sacrifices for our children and then tell them about it."

"Yes, we get our kicks that way," said Mike.

Allison got up and kissed them both.

"What was that for?" asked Mike.

"That," said Allison, "was for *not* being that kind of parent."

Thanksgiving Day at the MacKenzie house began with laughter and continued with laughter, through dinner and after it. Allison had never seen Lewis so happy, his face suffused with the joy of living and the happiness of being with people whom he liked. He sat next to Allison at dinner and, in the midst of laughter, squeezed her hand under the table. It was quick and almost painfully hard, and it expressed his joy and his gratitude to her for having brought him this.

He had once told Allison that until he had met her he had given up all hope of happiness. There were times that Thanksgiving Day when the look of love on his face was so naked that Allison thought Constance and everyone else was bound to notice it.

Dinner lasted two hours. It was late afternoon when they finished. Allison had wanted to take Lewis walking. She wanted to show him Road's End and the view of the town, wanted to share all her secrets and memories with him.

"I wanted to take Lewis up to Road's End," she said to Mike and Constance, "but I'm afraid it's going to be dark soon." She turned to Lewis. "We won't have time, I'm afraid."

"Nonsense," Mike said. "Take the car. You can be there in ten minutes and back again before nightfall."

"Wonderful idea," said Allison. And wondered why she hadn't thought of it. The car would give them more privacy, too. It would be the only chance they'd have for being alone together before Lewis left in the morning.

At the door, with the alpaca hood of her old coat over her head, she called back to Constance and Stephanie, "Now wait for me. Don't start on the dishes till I get back."

"Slacker!" Mike called after her.

When Allison and Lewis had left, Mike admitted that he was stuffed to the ears and needed nothing so much as a nap. He got up and walked to the stairs where he turned and smiled at Constance and said, "Now listen, darling. I want you to promise me that you won't start doing the dishes till I get up."

Constance wadded her napkin and threw it at him. From the top of the stairs, he called down, "Missed."

"He's a wonderful man," Stephanie said.

"Yes, he is," said Connie, "but don't tell him I said so."

Constance and Stephanie began to clear the table and carry the dishes into the kitchen. Steve was wearing a pair of tight, leopard-spotted slacks and she looked more like a contented well-fed cat than anything else. As they washed the dishes they began to gossip. Steve began it by asking about Selena.

"She's going to marry Peter Drake," Connie said.

"Really?" asked Steve, delighted.

"Yes," said Connie. "In June, after Joey graduates from high school."

"I'm so glad," said Steve. "She's such a doll and she's had such a helluva time."

"Worse than you think," said Connie. "Did you ever run into an actor in New York named Tim Randlett?"

"Him?" yelled Steve. "Jesus, yes. He's one of the biggest pains I've ever met."

"Well, he was up here this past summer and made a big play for Selena. For a while, she thought that she was in love with him."

"Oh, no," moaned Steve. "Listen, I'll tell you about that guy. He's the biggest phony in the business."

"What do you mean?" asked Connie, remembering Mike's words about Tim Randlett.

"Oh, you know. The big star bit. He never got over the fact that because he could cry convincingly and made a pot of money in Hollywood he was a star. He still thinks he's the greatest. Honest, like he was Olivier or something. I worked with him on a TV program once. Believe me, he's strictly from squaresville. Thinks he's irresistible because of his profile. You know what he does? He *acts* twenty-four hours a day. I'll bet he even poses in the shower. He chose to see me as the small-town girl gone wrong in the big city and gave me a big pitch about how he could save me from all the emptiness and false glitter. You know. A real creep. Selena is well rid of him. I've watched him with girls when he's been acting the father, the priest, the vile seducer, the big brother. The whole bit. Tell me, what did he play for Selena?"

"I don't know," said Connie thoughtfully. "But it must have been something dreadful. I thought she was going to die from it."

"It must have been his season for villains," said Steve. "That phony!"

"Well, it's over now, thank God. Now that Selena is going to marry Peter Drake, I'll have only you and Allison to worry about."

"I'm waiting for a rich producer," said Steve. "So I'll probably die an old maid. All producers are married. Sometimes I think their mothers marry them off when they're thirteen."

After they had finished the dishes they took the coffeepot and cups into the living room and sat before the fire. They sat quietly, resting, watching the beautiful and strange shapes the fire made, enjoying the peace and silence of the house.

7

AT ROAD'S END, Allison and Lewis sat in the front seat of the car and looked at Peyton Place, diminished and toylike below them. The houses seemed to have absorbed from the wintry sky its dead grayness. They looked like tombstones, Allison thought, and shivered.

Lewis drew her closer to him.

"I don't know why," he said, "but it makes me rather sad to look at Peyton Place from here. It seems so forlorn."

"It's that time of year," Allison said. "I feel it too. It's the melancholy of autumn. Even though we know that every season is a new beginning, autumn always seems like an ending. So many things die."

Lewis took her face in his hands and looked at it for a long time; then, very gently, he kissed her eyelids and her lips.

"I love you, Lewis," Allison said.

"I hope it lasts forever, Allison."

"I know that our love will, Lewis. I wish that we could, too."

He laughed. "Autumn doesn't just make you melancholy, Allison. It makes you downright morbid."

"I know. I'm sure that once I get back to work it will be all right again. When I'm working, I forget what day it is, what season it is, what year."

"I hope you won't forget me," Lewis said.

"Not even if I tried, darling," Allison said. She pushed open his overcoat and pressed her body against his.

"Necking in a car," she said. "I feel like a schoolgirl. Not that I ever did this when I *was* a schoolgirl."

She looked around her at the bleakness of Road's End's landscape while Lewis' hands caressed her body. "I don't think I ever had even a crush on a boy," she said, thinking aloud more than talking. "My daydreams kept me so busy, I guess, that I didn't have time for boys. This is where everything began, Lewis, here at Road's End. Sometimes I think there would never have been a *Samuel's Castle* if there hadn't been a Road's End."

She smiled dreamily in the cocoon of warmth they had created in the small enclosed space of Mike's car. Lewis' hands roved freely over her body. She put her mouth against his ear and with her tongue traced its outline. His hands gripped her tightly for a moment; then he relaxed and said, "Tell me more."

"Once a boy named Norman kissed me here," she said.

"I am insanely jealous," Lewis said, and Allison felt his warm breath on her throat as he laughed.

"If it hadn't been for Road's End," she said, "there'd have been no novel, no New York and no Lewis Jackman."

"Impossible," Lewis said. "Unthinkable. I refuse to consider such an impossibility. If you hadn't existed, I would have invented you." He bent and kissed her sweater where the tips of her breasts pressed.

She held his head, rested her own on the top of the seat, her eyes closed. Lewis' hand moved gently and slowly, her head turned, her eyes half opened.

"Talk to me," he said.

She thought, All of Peyton Place can look up here and see this car, but they can't see us.

"Talk to me," Lewis repeated.

"I can't," she whispered. "Oh, Lewis, I can't."

She drew his head to her and kissed him, her tongue seeking his. He bit her and she groaned at the sweetness of the pain. When he had brought her to the very peak of pleasure, she pushed him away.

Her lips were dry and her voice trembled. "I want all of you." She did not hear her own voice crying out or the fierce words of love she uttered. She was enfolded in darkness, and her voice, hoarse and savage, was unrecognizable to her own ears.

When she opened her eyes, she found herself lying in Lewis' arms. Night had fallen and a sparse winter moon gave a watery light. The shadows of the trees were black on the hillside and black on the road.

"My God," Allison said, her voice low and unbelieving. "I thought we had had everything."

Lewis smiled and said nothing.

"I didn't think it could ever be better than what we already had," Allison said. She put her face to Lewis' chest and felt his heart beating against her lips. "Will it keep on like this, Lewis?" she asked, in a small, frightened voice. "Getting better and better, I mean. Will it? I hope it doesn't. I'm afraid I'd die if anything like this happened too often."

Lewis stroked her hair. Smiling, he said, "I don't think there's any cause for alarm, darling. Human beings are so oddly constructed that they get used to pleasure just as quickly as they get to misery."

"I'm glad I found you, Lewis." She tightened her arms around him. "You'll always take care of me, won't you?"

"Always," Lewis promised.

"And in a few weeks I'll be back in New York, darling," Allison said, "and then I will be there always to take care of you. I'm going to take a year's lease on that gorgeous white and gold room, and I'm going to work all day and make love all night."

She sat up and lit a cigarette.

"Lewis," she said, "do you think that little manager will mind your coming to my apartment every night?"

Lewis laughed. "You are, at one and the same time, the most sophisticated and the most naïve woman I've ever met. The answer is: Yes, the manager will mind; and no, he won't say anything."

"Why won't he say anything?" Allison wanted to know.

"Because you are paying such a high rent that it's profitable for him not to mind. That's why," Lewis said. "As long as we're not noisy and don't disturb the other tenants, you'll never hear a word of complaint from him. The manager of that kind of hotel, the very expensive kind, is a professional not-minder. One of the first lessons he had to learn at school was how to avert his eyes gracefully."

Allison laughed. "He also took a course in How to Walk Backwards. For the final examination, he had to walk backwards through a crowded room, bowing all the way, and never bumping into anything."

"And he did postgraduate work in finger-snapping," Lewis added. "When he snaps his fingers at those Hungarian ghosts, it goes off like a pistol shot."

"If it can't be heard across a hotel lobby, it just isn't good enough," Allison said. "Flabby-fingered managers don't grow up to be Conrad Hilton."

They laughed at themselves; everything seemed delightful. Not even the bleak New England landscape seemed depressing any more, and Peyton Place glowed like a jewel in the valley below. Allison imagined she could tell which house was hers, and imagined Mike and Constance and Steve around the fire. She wondered if they were talking about Lewis and her.

"What are you thinking about?" Lewis asked.

"I was just wondering if they are talking about us."

"If we don't get back soon," Lewis said, "they most certainly will be."

"Oh, I know," Allison said, groaning. "But I hate to leave here. It's so private, darling. It's the last chance to be alone with you until after the New Year." She kissed him lightly. "But I see that now that you've had your way with me all you're interested in doing is getting back to civilization."

223

"That's the way we men are," Lewis said. "I plan to tire of you in a week or two and cast you aside like a worn-out rag."

Allison started the car. "You'll have to wait for a snowy night," she said. "It wouldn't be fair to turn me out in nice weather."

They began the long, curving descent to Peyton Place. Lewis turned on the radio and was bent forward, looking for music, when Allison became aware that something was wrong. She had tried to slow for the wide curve, but the brakes did not seem to respond; the car only swerved oddly. She made the curve and, taking her foot off the brake, found the car handled better. She sighed with relief.

"There," Lewis said. He sat back to enjoy the symphonic music he had found on a Boston station.

Allison touched the accelerator very softly with her toe; she wanted to increase the speed just a little for the upgrade. The car shot forward at a much greater speed than she had expected. What in the world's going on! she said to herself. Again she applied the brakes, and again the car swerved. She released the brakes and then, by the feel of the car, she knew what had gone wrong. The accelerator had stuck!

They were on the downgrade then and the car was going at sixty miles an hour. Allison tapped the accelerator with her toe, she gave it a sharp rap, thinking that would release it. But it remained stuck, only now it was in farther than it had been before and the speed of the car and her helplessness made her feel sick. She gripped the wheel tightly and watched with agonized eyes as the curve drew closer and closer.

As Lewis said, "Don't you think you'd better—" she slammed her foot on the brake, pushed it down to the floor boards and held it there. She smelled the brake linings beginning to burn.

"What's happening, Lewis?" she screamed, overcome with horror.

She saw his hand moving with terrible slowness toward the steering wheel. And then they went off the road and the car turned over and over.

She closed her eyes. She thought, Oh God, how many more times will it go over before it stops?

She sat in the kitchen with Mike and Constance; they were drinking coffee and laughing at one of Mike's jokes. I will never leave them, she thought, they are so good, so good.

Allison. Allison, Constance said. Allison. Allison. *Allison, darling!*

Allison opened her eyes. Gaunt trees swayed and bent above her, the moon caught in the branches like a bird in a trap. She pulled herself up and looked wildly about her.

The car, she said, the car. I must find Lewis.

She felt the pain stab in her chest; it made her weak and she fell to her knees.

Lewis, she called, Lewis. I'm coming, darling. I'm going to take care of you.

She raised her head and saw the car. She began to crawl toward it.

8

JENNIFER STARED AT ROBERTA over the big Thanksgiving turkey. That cold-blooded bitch, she thought savagely. Nobody had better ever say anything about my being nosy again. If I weren't, there's a damned good chance that, by tomorrow night at this time, I'd be dead.

Roberta poured coffee and smiled and talked about who had been at the Congregational Church.

"And did you have a good nap, dear?" she asked.

Jennifer, giving a headache for an excuse, had stayed behind to take a nap while the rest of the family went to the Thanksgiving services.

"I couldn't sleep," replied Jennifer. "So I decided to read."

She waited to see if Roberta would react to that, but her mother-in-law remained as calm as ever.

After they were finished with dinner, Harmon and Ted went to the home of one of Harmon's friends, where they played chess and drank beer until nightfall. Roberta and Jennifer were alone in the house.

"I think I'll take a nap," said Jennifer. "Those enormous dinners of yours always make me sleepy."

"Go ahead, dear," said Roberta. "I have some letters to write."

I'll bet, thought Jennifer acidly.

She went upstairs and, when Roberta peeked into the room a half hour later, Jennifer seemed to be fast asleep. Roberta closed the door quietly and went to the linen closet in the hall.

Thank God for well-oiled hinges, thought Jennifer as she opened her bedroom door.

Through the narrow opening she watched Roberta pick up the box of soap flakes and dig for her key ring. Then she watched her tiptoe quietly down the carpeted stairs. Jennifer went to her dresser and took out the notebook, and then, just as quietly as Roberta had done, she followed her down the stairs. From the doorway to the living room she watched Roberta unlock her desk and reach into the bottom drawer. She watched her stiffen in surprise and yank the drawer wide open and paw frantically through it. When Roberta turned, Jennifer was standing very still in the doorway with the notebook in her outstretched hand.

"Is this what you were looking for?" she asked sweetly.

Roberta jumped up, her face so white that for a moment Jennifer thought that the older woman would faint.

"How did you get that?" Roberta whispered in horror.

"By unlocking your desk drawer, Mother dear," said Jennifer. "Tell me," she asked, and her lips curved in a contemptuous smile, "did you really think you could get away with it?"

"Give me that notebook!" cried Roberta.

"Not yet, Mother dear," said Jennifer with maddening calm. "You know, I wondered why you'd taken to reading murder mysteries. I'd always thought you were a real, dyed in the wool Book-of-the-Month type. But I really never guessed that you'd think up anything as dumb as this. You don't have to tell me why, either, because I know that, too."

"I don't know what you're talking about," Roberta gasped.

"Oh, yes you do," said Jennifer. She advanced slowly toward Roberta and the little smile never left her face. "You're jealous of me," she said softly. "Every time Ted and I go to bed, you're huddled in the little room next door to us and you listen to your son make love to me and you're so jealous you can't stand it."

Roberta staggered back toward the desk as if she had been struck.

"You're jealous," said Jennifer. "So jealous you can't stand it. You wish it was you in bed with Ted."

"You're crazy!" said Roberta and was sure that she had screamed, but her voice was nothing but a harsh whisper.

226

Jennifer burst out laughing. "*I'm* crazy!" she said. "Here. Listen to this, and we'll see who's crazy." She flipped the notebook open and began to read. "One-thirty: Jennifer goes upstairs for a nap. Two-thirty: I wake her with a cup of coffee in which sleeping powder has been dissolved. Three o'clock: I suggest a visit to the Page girls. Three-thirty: Jennifer and I get into car in garage and I start car while wearing gloves. I tell her I've forgotten my glasses and leave her there while I re-enter house. Car is still running. Four o'clock: Jennifer has fallen asleep and I move her into driver's seat and go back into house. Five-thirty: Ted and Harmon return home to find me sound asleep in bed. They discover Jennifer dead in car." Jennifer closed the book with a snap. "I never would have known what hit me, would I?" she asked.

Roberta had sunk down into the chair in front of the desk.

"You're evil," she was saying, over and over, "you're a bad, evil girl."

"At least I never planned to kill you," retorted Jennifer. "And now, do you know what I'm going to do?"

Roberta looked at her stupidly.

Jennifer smiled. "I'm going upstairs to get my coat, then I'm going to take this notebook, get into your car and go directly to the sheriff." She started to walk out of the room and Roberta jumped up to follow her, just as Jennifer had known she would.

Jennifer ran upstairs with Roberta behind her, and when she reached the top she waited until her mother-in-law was standing beside her.

"Did you really think you could get away with it?" asked Jennifer tauntingly, holding out the notebook so that Roberta could almost reach it.

Roberta leaned forward to grab the notebook, and in that second, Jennifer dropped the book to the floor, put her hands against Roberta's shoulders and pushed with all her strength. Roberta fell forward with a scream and Jennifer coolly noted that her head hit the wall twice as she fell. It seemed to take her forever to reach the bottom.

Jennifer stood still at the top of the stairs, and the only sound was the echo of Roberta's startled cry and the quiet of Jennifer's breathing. Jennifer went quietly down the stairs and stepped over Roberta's body. She bent and felt for a pulse, but she knew from the angle of

Roberta's head that her mother-in-law's neck was broken and that she was dead.

Jennifer went back upstairs and burned the pages of the notebook in the bathroom sink, then she flushed the ashes down the drain. Her heart had never altered its steady beating, for she had known that she could not fail. If Roberta had not been killed by the fall, but only injured, Jennifer would still have been safe because she had the notebook with its terrible story and Roberta would never be able to tell that she had been pushed.

Jennifer smiled as the last of the ashes flowed smoothly down the drain. She went to her bedroom and took off her shoes, stockings and panty girdle, just as she did every Sunday afternoon when she got ready for a nap. The bed was already rumpled from when she had used it while waiting for Roberta to look in on her.

Wearing only her slip, Jennifer walked down the stairs and stepped over Roberta's body without so much as a glance. She went to the telephone and paused a minute before she picked it up. When she did, she had held her breath long enough to make her voice a gasping breath. She gave the number of Harmon's friend and when he answered she was screaming for Ted.

"An accident!" she screamed. "Your mother. Come quickly!"

Roberta Carter was buried three days later, and everyone in Peyton Place sympathized with the bereaved family.

"What a shame," said the town. "She was the soul of goodness, Roberta was."

"And how terrible for Jennifer. She and Roberta were so close. Roberta told me herself how much she thought of Ted's wife."

"I know it. Why, Roberta just lived for the time when Jennifer would have her first baby."

"It's terrible. You don't often see a mother and daughter-in-law as close as Jennifer and Roberta were."

The following Friday, Ted and Jennifer boarded the train for Boston. As Harmon said, Ted couldn't stay forever, he had his career to think of. Jennifer wore a wide-brimmed black hat with a veil that hid her little smile. Ted helped her up the steps and onto the train. Inwardly, he shuddered when he touched her. In his heart he harbored a terrible suspicion. He would spend the rest of his life—the rest of his eminently successful life—in dark wonder.

9

ALLISON KNEW THAT LEWIS was dead. Even in the dark depths of her drugged sleep she knew it. When they had brought her broken body into the receiving room at the hospital she had been calling for Lewis, and had continued to call for him until Matt Swain arrived and injected a sedative.

Now, a week later, Constance and Mike sat by her bedside. Allison was still under sedation. Constance stared at her bruised face with tears in her eyes. According to Matt Swain's medical report, Allison had four broken ribs and a crushed collarbone and had suffered a fairly severe concussion. But Constance knew that the tortured, anguished look on Allison's face, the sudden starts, the way she turned her head, was not the result of her physical injuries. Allison was the captive of the terrible, haunting dreams of her drugged sleep.

Constance and Mike came and sat at her bedside every afternoon and evening. Matt let them come only during the regular hospital visiting hours. If he had permitted, Constance would have been there twenty-four hours a day.

"She's young. She'll heal quickly enough," Matt told Constance.

"It's not her broken bones I'm thinking about," Constance said.

"And what makes you think *I* am, Connie?" Matt blustered. "How much of a goddamn fool do you take me for?"

"I'm sorry, Matt," Connie said.

"Damn well should be," he said, and stormed off down the hospital corridor, his white coat flying out around him.

Stephanie stayed with them through the first week and then had to go to New York, promising to come back as soon as Constance or Allison needed her. When Constance said good-by to her, they both cried; and Mike stood by, a helpless look on his face, saying, "Everything's going to be all right, everything's going to be all right."

It was on the second day after the accident that Mike came home with the police report, the results of what had been uncovered by the State Police's examination of the car.

"The accelerator stuck," Mike said. "Allison hasn't had enough experience as a driver to know that you just stick the toe of your shoe under it and push it up. I suspect she stepped down on it, thinking that would release it. But, of course, it didn't."

Constance sat listening quietly, with her hands in her lap. "Judging by the tire marks on the road," Mike went on, "the police think she then tried to stop the car by applying the brakes. It went out of control. She was probably doing eighty to ninety miles an hour by that time."

"Oh God," said Connie.

"They know where the car went off the road, but they can only guess how many times it rolled over. Four or five times, they think, until the trees stopped it."

The car was completely demolished, unsalvageable; and Lewis' body had been found inside. Allison had been thrown clear, she had fallen on the grassy bank and had slid and rolled to the bottom. A car full of teen-agers had come upon the scene minutes after it happened. They had found Allison trying to pull open the buckled door of the car, trying to get to Lewis.

She knew he was dead. She threw her head from side to side on the pillow, trying to shake the horror of her dreams. Horrible as anything else was the feeling of helplessness that came over her as the car begin to careen along the road, its tires screaming. There was nothing she could do, nothing.

"Lewis," she had cried, "Lewis, what is happening?"

She remembered his hand moving slowly toward the steering wheel, to help her control the car. And then they began to turn over. That was all she remembered, but, hour after hour, the dream of those hideous moments pursued her. And deep in her unconscious brain, at the very center of her being, was the knowledge that Lewis was dead.

Early in the morning of her second week in the hospital, that time of day when the nurses begin to turn off lights, Allison woke and found Matt Swain watching her.

"Good morning, Allison," he said. And he spoke to her as gently as he had ever spoken to anyone in his life.

Allison began to cry, weakly; the tears welled up and spilled over and ran down her face. "Tell me, Matt," she said, her voice a cracked whisper. "Tell me."

"You know," he said.

"Tell me!"

"He is dead, Allison," Matt said.

Matt took her hand. She pulled it away. "I don't want to hear any of your consoling words, Doctor," she said. "Words aren't going to help me." Her voice was flat and dead. She closed her eyes.

"Allison," Matt said, "Allison, whether you help me or not, I am going to make you well. Make no mistake about that."

Constance brought books and magazines, and returned the next day to find them untouched. And, in the same way, the food trays brought in by the nurses were returned to the kitchen.

Matt Swain came in and stood by the foot of the bed, stood silently until Allison looked up and met his eyes. Then he said, "If what you're trying to do is commit suicide, Allison, there are simpler and less painful ways of doing it."

He waited for Allison to speak. She closed her eyes and turned her head away.

He made his voice sound rough and brutal; even he was shocked by the sound of it. "In this hospital, I'm the boss. What I say goes. When you get home, when I discharge you from this place, you can do what you like with yourself. It'll be no affair of mine. But you're not leaving here until I say so."

He put his hands behind his back and leaned forward, the stethoscope like a black noose around his neck, his white coat billowing open like a tent.

"You have your choice, Allison. You'll eat what is brought to you, what I have prescribed for you, the nourishment that will bring you back to health; or I will have your hands tied to the bed and stick needles into you and feed you intravenously. It's up to you."

He signaled the nurse who was waiting at the door with a tray of food. She rustled into the room, set down the tray and cranked up the bed. Unwillingly but inexorably, Allison was raised to a sitting position. Matt went to the window and opened the curtains, flooding the room with light. The nurse put the tray on the bed table and pushed it up to Allison.

Allison sat and looked at it, as if it were something dangerous and full of menace.

Matt said to himself, Well, if this doesn't work, I don't know what the hell I'm going to do. Aloud, he said, "This news is going to make your mother very happy, Allison."

231

Allison did not look at him. She picked up the spoon and slowly began to eat the broth.

Matt Swain walked out of the room. In the corridor he leaned against a wall and wiped his forehead. If you hadn't been a doctor, you'd have made a damn good actor, he said, congratulating himself.

In December, Mike came in the new car the insurance company had bought him and took Allison home. She was shaky on her feet but, with Mike's arm supporting her, she walked to the car. When Mike opened the door she began to cry; she turned her head into Mike's shoulder and sobbed: "Oh, Mike, I can't, I can't!"

Mike spoke soothing, meaningless words into her ear, like a mother crooning to a baby, and gently eased her into the car. He ran around the other side and slid under the wheel. Then, driving very slowly, he took her home.

Constance had made up the sofa in the living room with blankets and pillows; a fire burned cheerily. Allison looked around her, as if she had never seen this house before and was wary of it.

If only she would tell me, Constance thought, looking at her daughter, her heart breaking for Allison. If I only dared to tell her that I know.

And Allison, lying on the sofa, with Constance and Mike fussing around her, was filled with bitter thoughts. She felt that her body had betrayed her by getting well again. And that she was betraying Lewis by being alive when he was dead.

David and Stephanie wrote to her, Brad Holmes and Arthur Tishman sent messages and flowers. But she wrote to no one. She read a great deal. Constance wrote to David and Brad, and they kept a steady stream of all the new novels coming into the house. During the day she prowled around the house, walking from room to room, always returning to the sofa. The sofa had become for her the protected place.

Like Road's End when I was a girl, she thought. Road's End. It had truly been road's end for Lewis.

And sometimes she thought: Now you are free. Now you can have all the experience of life that you wanted. You can go anywhere, see everything, do anything. You are free.

And when this thought came she pushed it quickly away, repelled by it. It is like dancing on Lewis' grave, she thought, and hated herself for having such thoughts.

Two weeks before Christmas, Constance asked Allison if she'd like to have David and Stephanie up for the holidays.

Allison shook her head. "I don't want to see anyone yet," she said.

At night, Constance and Mike lay in their bed and listened to the sounds of Allison, prowling about the house, drinking coffee in the kitchen. When they came down in the morning, every morning, there was a coffee cup in the sink and a pile of books on the table. Allison only slept when she took a sleeping pill.

When Constance went to Matt Swain, all he could say was, "I have faith in Allison. We'll just have to be patient, Connie, and bear up and see her through this bad time."

Connie nodded.

Matt said, "Connie, you can just tell me to mind my own damned business if you want to, but was there something between Allison and Lewis Jackman?"

"Mind your own damned business, Matt," Connie said, and smiled for the first time in weeks.

Looking back on it, Connie thought it was probably Matt who had broken the ice and started things moving again. She walked home with a livelier step, and when she opened the door she was struck by the stagnant odor of the house. It smells like a place where life has come to a standstill, she thought. It's wrong, it's all wrong. I must do something.

As she passed the living room she saw Allison lying on the sofa, staring at the ceiling, her eyes full of nothingness. Connie went into the kitchen and began to heat the coffee.

She went to the living-room door and said to Allison, "I'm heating the coffee. Would you like a cup?"

"I don't care."

"Well, have one then, darling. I like company."

She filled the cups and brought them in and set them on the coffee table next to Allison's sofa. Allison sat up and Constance sat down beside her.

"It's cold out," Connie said. "And I think it's going to snow. I'll be glad when this year is over and Mike will be able to stop commuting to White River. It's only nine miles, but when winter comes I begin to worry."

Allison did not say anything.

233

Connie sipped her coffee. "Mmm, that tastes good. I needed something hot. Would you like some cookies?"

"No, thank you, Mother."

Connie looked up then and saw the first snowflakes flatten themselves against the windowpane. Allison followed her glance, saw the snow and got up. She went to the window and looked out.

Allison had lost weight. Her face had lost the last of its youthful flesh. Looking at her, Connie thought, You're a woman now, Allison. She followed Allison to the window. They stood side by side and looked out at the snow falling from the dense, low, late afternoon sky.

"Why is snow always exciting?" Allison asked, hardly realizing she was speaking aloud.

"Maybe it's because it reminds us of childhood," Connie said, "of the days when the world was our oyster and life was a beautiful dream without end."

"It has ended for me," Allison said, and, throwing her arms around her mother, she began to cry. Constance held her close and stroked her hair.

"Cry, baby," she said, "cry." She held her daughter in her arms and thought, She's crying the last of her youth way. Perhaps after the shock of being born, Constance thought, there comes the shock of realizing one is adult, of accepting age and its responsibilities and surrendering to the idea of death.

"Oh, Mother," Allison sobbed. "I loved him. I loved him."

Then Constance led her to the sofa and held her hand. They looked at the fire, and Allison spoke at last and told Connie all about herself and Lewis.

When she was finished, Constance kissed her and dried her tears. Then she said, "Now you must live for him, Allison. And don't think you're the first woman who ever had to make that decision. You haven't a child to live for, as I had. But you have your talent. You must start working again, darling."

"I'm going to try, Mother. I'm going to try."

And in the days that followed she did try. As the snow fell and drifted around the house, she sat for hours before her typewriter, staring at the blank, white paper. But what little she wrote she scratched out. It's so hard to get back into it, she thought. Usually she ended up by drawing pictures on her note pad.

"But at least," Connie said to Mike, "at least she's trying. And she's talking more."

Mike was home all day now, for Christmas vacation had begun; his determinedly cheerful presence was good for Allison. They spent hours sitting at the kitchen table talking about Allison's work, and her inability to get her second novel started.

"Maybe I've got second novel fever," Allison said.

"Could be," Mike granted. "But I think writing is like any other job. When you've been away from it for a long time, it takes a while to get back into the swing of it. You're not so different from the lumberman who has had a three months' layoff. He has to get his muscles toned up again, and you've got to get your mind and temper toned up."

"Sometimes I think I'm written out and don't have anything more to say."

Mike laughed. "If you never moved out of Peyton Place, you'd have enough material to keep you going for two lifetimes."

On Christmas Day, surrounded by the debris and litter of gift wrappings, they were having dinner when there was a sharp rapping on the door.

Mike raised his eyebrows and stood up. Constance said, "Now who can that be?"

"Probably some kids out for tricks or treats," Mike said. Bending down quickly, he kissed Constance and said, "And a Happy Halloween to you, my dear."

"Oh, if I only had something to throw," Connie said, as he walked to the front door. The rapping continued and Mike shouted, "I'm coming, I'm coming."

There was a silence after the door had been opened. Then they heard Mike say, "You are either Rita Moore or the loveliest apparition I've ever seen."

Allison jumped to her feet as she heard Rita's clear, ringing laugh.

"It can't be anyone else," said Allison to her mother's inquiring look.

Rita swept into the room. She was wearing a black greatcoat lined with fur, its high, wide collar framing her beautiful face that glowed with the cold.

"Well, I'm glad to see you on your feet," she said to Allison. "I heard in New York that you were doing the Elizabeth Barrett Browning bit." And before Allison could answer, Rita turned to

Mike and handed him the wicker hamper she was carrying. "Here, Mr. MacKenzie, it's full of champagne and I don't think it will have to be cooled. The taxi I took from White River was refrigerated."

"Taxi!" Allison said. "How did you get anyone to drive you over here on Christmas Day?"

"Not only drive me over, darling. But he's going to wait at some crony's house and then drive me back in time to catch the Boston train. And it cost me only twenty-five dollars, one autograph and my best smile."

Mike stood next to her with the hamper of champagne in his hands. "You should have phoned, Miss Moore. I'd have been glad to come over for you."

"Oh, Mr. MacKenzie," Rita said, "you are nice."

"He's like that all the time. A regular boy scout," Constance said.

"You've gathered, Rita, that these are my parents," Allison said. "Mike and Constance Rossi."

"Rossi," said Rita. She turned to Mike. "And I've been calling you MacKenzie. I am sorry."

"Oh, that's all right," Mike said. "Of course, I'd have killed anyone else." Mike took the hamper into the kitchen.

Rita joined them at the table.

"Now," Allison said, "what in the world are you doing here of all places?"

"Well, I was in New York and I heard about your smashup and I just decided I wanted to have a good old-fashioned white Christmas dinner and so I came. Besides, I've been curious about the background of your story."

"How does it look to you?"

"It looks awfully like New England," said Rita. "Is it supposed to? I mean, when anything is so like I expect it to be, I'm sure it must be a fake."

Mike came in with the champagne and four glasses. "By the time we've finished this bottle, Miss Moore," he said, "I'm going to be able to tell you just how much I adore you. Right here in front of my wife I shall tell you."

"That's the best way," Rita said. "It's no good having secrets from your wife."

"That's the way I figure it too," Mike said.

"And after the second bottle," Connie said, "you can take off your shirt and show our guest your tattoo. You know, dear—the one with the beard that says 'Rita and Mike Forever.'"

"You mustn't be edgy, dear," said Mike to Connie. "I plan on going off with Miss Moore for only a year or two. But I am definitely coming back to you."

"That's what I call devotion," Connie said. And she was thinking, I could kiss you, Rita Moore. Because Allison was laughing. She was alive again, and it was because of Rita, walking into the house so unexpectedly, and bringing with her the bracing air of the outside world.

It was the world that Allison had been trying to hide from, that she had been unwilling and afraid to face. It had brought her a success that frightened her, and a love that had ended in tragedy.

When they had finished the second bottle, Connie said to Rita, "I know this will break your heart, but I'm going to take Mike away now. I think you'll want to spend some time alone with Allison."

"I suspect I'm being taken off to the kitchen to be put to work." He headed toward the kitchen door, saying, "The next sound you hear will be the sound of breaking china."

"They're nice," Rita said. "You've had more luck than most of us, Allison."

Allison made a gesture with her hand, as if to say, That's what you think, and she smiled a bitter smile.

"Full of self-pity, aren't you, kid? You smashed up and your man got killed, and now you're hurt because the whole world didn't crumple up and die with you. And if you stay here much longer, it'll go right on without you, for good and all."

"I'm trying to get back to work again, Rita. It just won't come."

Allison's hand was on the table. Rita reached across and tapped it with her long tapering finger. "It will come," she said, emphasizing each word with a finger tap. "It will come because it must. This is the final lesson, Allison. That is what success means for people like us— that when everything else is gone, friends and lovers and husbands, we have got our work. It's the only constant thing in our lives. And when we betray our talent, then we might as well give up and return to the original chaos."

She emptied the champagne bottle into their two glasses.

"I've got to get back to White River. My lovesick taximan is probably frozen to death by now. And besides, my husband is waiting for me at the White River Hotel."

"Are you married again, Rita?"

"I've been married for two weeks, child. If you weren't snowbound in the Rockies, you'd have heard about it."

"Are you happy?"

"Well," Rita said. "I don't know what's happy any more. I tell you, love, we're cozy together. We understand each other. And it's a nice change. I mean, Jim isn't a fairy and he isn't a gigolo. He's really the first husband I've had in years who works for a living. Some morning I'm almost tempted to get up and pack his little lunch pail for him."

"I'm glad you came, Rita. You've helped me a lot," Allison said.

"Now how did I do that?" Rita asked.

"By reminding me," Allison said, "that the world isn't full of mobsters waiting to cut me down. And by showing me that work will exorcise all the ghosts that haunt me."

"Here's to Love and Work," Rita said, raising her glass.

"I'll drink to that," Allison said.

The taxi horn sounded, a loud blast that shattered the silence of the snow. Mike and Constance came out of the kitchen. Mike helped Rita into her coat. She kissed Allison good-by. "There are a lot of people working for you, love. Don't ever forget that."

Allison went to the window and watched Rita walk down the snow-filled walk to the waiting taxi. She felt the cold through the glass and leaned her head against it.

I won't forget, Allison said. And I won't disappoint you.

She stood at the window and watched till Rita's taxi was out of sight, then she went to the kitchen door and looked in on Mike and her mother.

"I'll be up in my room, working, if you want me for anything," Allison said.

Constance smiled. "I think we'll manage, dear."

They watched her walk up the stairs to her rooms. Constance sighed her relief, and as Mike took her in his arms, she said, "Happy New Year, darling. I have the feeling it's going to be a great year."